BREATHLESS

ROLYNN NEVELS

Fulton Books, Inc.
Meadville, PA

Published by Fulton Books 2021

ISBN 978-1-64952-490-4 (paperback)
ISBN 978-1-63710-430-9 (hardcover)
ISBN 978-1-64952-491-1 (digital)

Printed in the United States of America

To my mom who encouraged me to write.

PRONUNCIATION INDEX

Secret Seven/Crypto-Hept

- Crypto-Hept (crip-toe h-ept)
- Pneumodegyns (new-mow-de-gins)
- Aquagynitive (aqua-gin-e-tive)
- Herbative (her-ba-tive)
- Formicon (form-e-con)
- Anglevi (ang-la-v)
- Ignises (ig-knee-sis)
- Geoangi (g-o-anne-g)

Special Powered Beings/Things

- Gyniatric (gin-e-at-trick)
- Nátàl Mater (nah-towl mate-er)
- Miesgyn (me-es-gin)

Scourgers

- Scourgers (score-gers)
- Caligo (ka-lee-go)
- Alienum Hominem (a-lee-noom) (om-knee-am)
- Arbor Cortice—(r-bore court-is)
- Bellua (bell-u-ah)
- Multumcarne (mult-um-car-neigh)

PRONUNCIATION INDEX

Characters

- Kaura (car-ruh)
- Laiya (lay-uh)
- Mr. Kowalski (co-wall-ski)
- Vivienne (viv-ē-in)
- Octavion (oct-tay-v-un)
- Annora (ă-nor-ra)
- Brees (breeze)
- Cormac (core-mick)
- Beetly (beat-lee)
- Saraphine (sara-ph-een)

Prologue

If someone told me eleven days ago that I would be trapped in a coffin-sized metal box with no way out, I would think that was insane. Yet here I was, locked away and forgotten. I just needed to stay focused and breathe…breathe, it's all right. They would get me out soon.

The sound of low grunts and raspy cries from the vile creatures carrying the box was the only ambience keeping me company in the dark. The box jilted in an upward motion several times before landing on something hard. The lack of light and air made it hard for me to focus. I pushed on the top of the box to try and make it move but with little results. Then the panic set in, and I realized I was in more trouble than I could handle. I came to the conclusion that no one would rescue me in time. The Scourgers would find me in here and gouge me before I even had a chance to fight back.

Okay, breathe. Just breathe. I could not think like that. They would find me, and I would make it. Just take deep breaths. Okay, breathe…breathe…bre—

First Day Back

"Dad, I can't be late," I yelled from the top of our spiral staircase, my backpack placed on my shoulder. As I moved past the bronze oval hallway mirror, I stopped and stared into it. Today, I was a senior. I looked into the mirror to see if I had changed, and then I glanced at my ninth-grade yearbook photo hanging on the wall. I glanced back into the mirror. Nope. I looked the same as I did during my freshman year. Staring at myself in the mirror made me wonder why my features seemed to stand still.

"I know, Jewels," my dad replied, disturbing my thoughts. "I'm just trying to find my glasses. You don't want me driving without them, do you? I mean, I can, but odds are I'll hit every mailbox and trash can on the way to school."

A loud sigh escaped my body as I shook my head. My curly black hair fell in front of my eyes as I stumbled down the staircase.

"I wouldn't want to die when I'm so close to graduating from high school. So please find those glasses," I said, raising my hands in a pleading gesture.

As he saw me, he gave me that smirk I knew so well. It was then that I noticed his glasses, sitting patiently in his front shirt pocket.

"Seriously, Dad, your glasses are in your pocket."

He looked down and smiled. "Well, would you look at that." I stared at my dad. He was getting older. Little specks of gray were protruding throughout his hair. I smiled.

As I walked toward the door, I mumbled, "Someone's getting old."

"I am not," he exclaimed in a demanding tone. "I'm just making sure you're keeping a sharp eye. After all, they say people with green eyes are the rarest."

I opened the front door and walked out while shouting, "Sure, old man."

My dad followed me out the door. The usual drive to school would only take ten minutes, but because of the heavy traffic, it was longer. It seemed like everybody decided to arrive at the same time. Late. Even the buses were running behind schedule. Cars were bumper to bumper and unforgiving to pedestrians. Students darted between cars trying to catch a break in the smothering traffic. It was easy to locate the freshmen among all the acclimated students because they appeared hopeful and carried bright smiles across their faces. Give it a week, and they would be like the rest of us. Tired.

"Don't forget, I pick you up at five."

I nodded and said, "Okay."

When we finally made it to the carpool lane, I said, "Goodbye." Someone behind us laid on their horn.

My dad yelled at the rearview mirror, "Ah, hold on a sec." He then smiled in my direction as the light from the sun hit his face, making him look older than before. "See you later, kiddo."

"Bye, Dad."

I hastily exited the car and took a glance around the front entrance. Being back made me feel sick and at ease all at the same time. Avington High was made mostly of bulletproof glass with a few structure points of evened white cemented walls. It was my second home for the past three years.

The idea of graduating felt strange. I hadn't given a thought as to what I wanted to do. Most of my career choices wouldn't be considered practical, and the practical ones bored me to no end. So I was left contemplating my next move into seniority.

I spotted Kaura dragging her feet toward the front entrance. Kaura and I met in kindergarten and immediately were inseparable. What I liked about her the most was her uniqueness. Her clothes always had vibrant colors that expressed passion and warmth, but her style was never complete without a bow or a ribbon. She once told me she owed her spunk to her Columbian roots.

"Hey, Kaura, what's up?" I was ecstatic to see her.

She turned around and gave me a strained smile. My excitement faded.

"¡ No Bueno! I'm panicking! My summer reading assignment was an essay that had to be seven pages long. I also had to read *A Brave New World* for a comprehensive test that our teacher scheduled for today."

I studied, Kaura, the straight-A student who would be valedictorian. She worked the hardest among our crew and was always on top, but she never could resist the urge to pressure herself until she would implode.

"Kaura, you got this. Just relax and breathe."

She gave a half-smile, indicating that she was still uneasy about the situation.

"*Sí chica*, I can do this." She was trying to convince herself more than me but failed miserably. I could see right through her fake smile. One thing about her was the fact that she was horrible at restraining her facial expressions. If she found anything distasteful, you would know about it.

In the distance, I located Sarah having a conversation with a student I didn't recognize. He must be new. I waved her over. She smiled at me but turned her attention back to their conversation, so I walked toward the entrance with Kaura trailing next to me.

I first met Sarah when I was in seventh grade. She was a new student and was placed in my geography class. I sat in the back of the class, out of sight of my peers and, more importantly, my teacher. There were several empty seats, but for some reason, Sarah came straight toward me and introduced herself. She was a spunky girl with brown hair, dark brown eyes, and a gorgeous smile. I have never met anyone as bold as she was. Days later, I found myself being bullied for a disturbing rumor about my absent mother. Sarah found me in the stairwell crying and sat with me. Sarah told me not to let them intimidate me no matter what they say. Even so, doubts crept through the cracks of my fragile mind. What the girls had said about me, I too have wondered. My dad never mentions her, and the more I pry, the more annoyed he gets. I always wondered where she went? More importantly, I wanted to know her identity and the reason why she left me? The next day, the girls were no longer bullying me.

The ringleader returned to school with a black eye and never crossed my path again.

Kaura and I reached the front entrance. The crowd of students thickened, and in the distance, I saw a familiar body advancing toward us. Keith approached us as we walked through the front doors. Keith and I were friends last year when Sarah introduced us. He had just moved to town, and Sarah was his science fair partner. They spent a lot of time together, so she thought I should meet him too.

"What's up, girls?" was his usual greeting.

I turned to him. "Don't ask Kaura. She's already stressed out, and it's the first day back."

Keith gave a small shrug and shook his head. "Kaura, if you want to make it through high school with a full head of hair, try to stay calm. You're not helping yourself by stressing over things you can't control."

Kaura gave Keith a sarcastic glare of gratitude and charged to her locker. Even when she was mad, her walk still had a rhythmic dance to it.

"Dude, seriously? You know how she can be. We have to keep her sane." I snapped.

Keith twiddled with his shirt and finally decided to place his hands in his pocket. "Hey, I'm just saying we can't keep coddling her like that. We're not going to be around all the time to save her." He walked away from me, but not before he gave me the "You know I'm right" dumb look. He was wrong. Dead wrong.

I walked after Kaura and found my locker one over from hers.

"Kaura, you okay?" I asked, as I turned the dial to the padlock to open my locker.

"Yeah, I'll be fine." Kaura already had her locker open and placed her binders neatly inside. She seemed calm. Maybe she considered Keith's advice?

"Hey, Kaura and Jewels, how's your schedule looking?" It was Laiya who was always dressed to impress. She never went to school or anywhere for that matter without makeup on. Of course, she didn't need to wear any, but she loved to play with it. She wanted to create a web series about makeup, but she never found the time. The reason she never had time was because she was constantly building minia-ture robots in her basement like some mad scientist. She named each one of her creations after a famous warrior from her Japanese culture.

It turned out I had a class with each of them. History was the only class that we would all take together, which was fine by me, as long as I knew at least one person in my classes. The first warning bell sounded through the speakers, and we said our goodbyes.

My first class was math with Laiya. Ms. Kimble used corky say-ings to teach us how to remember the steps. I struggled to stay focused in her class. The clock taunted me as the minutes slowly passed on. Ms. Kimble's high-pitched voice was too loud for the morning start.

Finally, the bell sounded for our departure to the next class. I grabbed all my belongings and stood. Suddenly, a wave of energy pushed my body, sending me back into my chair. My head felt light, and I lost my breath. My chest tightened, and the lack of oxygen made my head pound. The classroom around me closed in and turned into a blurry and suffocating space. I attempted to find my footing, but it was no use. Whatever was happening forced me to remain seated for the pain to relieve.

Then the warning bell blared through my ears. I had to make it to my next class. I wobbled to my feet and painfully walked through the hallway. I bumped into several people, repeatedly apologizing. One of them mumbled something, but it was inaudible. My head felt as though I was underwater. The pressure was relentless. As quickly as the episode came, it went. My vision returned, and the nausea left. I found this to be extremely weird. Was I having an anxiety or a heart attack?

The thought of a heart attack was replaced by the persisted pound in my chest, but I tried to ignore it. I took several deep breaths and slowly released them. I made it to art class and attempted to focus on the purple rockfoil that I was painting. My eyesight shifted the location of my painting as I brought my paintbrush down. My mishap caused me to draw a line right through my flower. I closed my eyes tightly and counted to ten. Then it was gone. I knew this wasn't normal and that something felt wrong.

The walk to history class was rough, but I finally made it. All my friends were sitting in the back with an open seat waiting for me. "Hey guys, how's everyone's day going so far?" I spoke with little energy. I hope they didn't notice. There was a jumble of answers, but basically, they said their day was good. I found it hard to focus on what they were saying. Their voices sounded shallow and cluttered. I felt as though I was watching an episode of *Peanuts*. Their bright and happy faces mixed into one and created a giant slow-moving blob.

"The test is not till next Wednesday, and I racked my brain over it," Kaura said with a loud huff. The others laughed, and I gave her a soft pat on the back. Other kids piled in as the bell sounded, and our teacher, Mr. Kowalski, came in the door with a languid walk.

"Good afternoon, students. My name is Mr. Kowalski, so if you are in the wrong class, please leave now. Other than that, welcome to American history." When he spoke, it was with a slow slur and a soft voice. You had to lean in to hear him.

The class drifted on. My headache returned, and I lost focus. My area established itself as a whirl of discomfort. I couldn't see two inches in front of me. Mr. Kowalski's voice echoed in my brain. Between his irritating voice and the throbbing coming from my headache, I had enough, so I imagined him slowly losing his breath. To be honest, I don't know where the idea came from, but what else was there to do? I had to make it stop. I focused on his throat and visualized it closing. I felt like I was in a trance, and the room was smaller and darker. Nothing could be heard or seen, and I somehow enjoyed this feeling. I felt my body drift off into space. It was a peaceful state. I had never felt more like myself and in control. Something flickered in and out that appeared some yards away from me. My space no longer felt secure. The figure was in human form. I tried walking toward the object, but then I heard a sharp scream, and my sight returned.

Gradually, appearing before my eyes was Mr. Kowalski on the floor gasping for air. He was turning purple and blue, and his lips had no color. I was scared and thought about stopping the strangulation. That's when his hands dropped from his throat, and he sat upright. A small girl hit the emergency intercom button by the door and spoke to the front office. Two minutes later, Dr. Neal, our principal, came charging in the room and assisted Mr. Kowalski to his feet. Every student was standing up front surrounding Mr. Kowalski while I was still seated. A loud ring buzzed throughout the classroom. Dr. Neal instructed us to go to lunch. Everyone slowly walked out of the class, clumped into small groups whispering about what just happened. As I walked by Mr. Kowalski, I could not help but feel responsible for what had taken place. Maybe I was going crazy?

I caught up with my friends, and they were talking about Mr. Kowalski's incident. Keith was speaking, "Can you believe that? It's like he was choking on air."

Laiya commented next. "I know. I can't believe this." She was shaking her head.

"Maybe he choked on his spit, since he slurs so much," snorted Sarah.

Keith gave her a sharp laugh of approval.

"That's not nice, Sarah. He could have died. Did you not see how blue he was?" Kaura asked. She then said, with her back to me, "I also saw how Jewels did not seem to respond when he fell to the floor." They all turned toward me while I pretended to look at the lunch menu.

Keith was the first to speak, "Yeah, Jewels, it was like you were in a trance or something."

I gave a reassuring smile. I'd hope they would forget how horrible a liar I was, "Nah, I just zoned out because he was so boring. That, by far, was the most interesting thing he did all class period." Keith gave me a questionable look while Sarah laughed at my comment.

Laiya asked, "Are you sure you're okay?" She was staring at me with such intensity that I glanced at my feet to answer her.

"Yes, I'm fine. Let's get something to eat and find a table." That had to be the end of it. If I didn't know what was happening, how could I explain the situation to another person?

We sat at a round table by a wall entirely made of bulletproof glass. The sun was setting behind thick marshmallow clouds, and the wind was blowing vigorously. I didn't hear any news about a storm coming this way. Even so, I stared at the wind thinking about how calm it looked. To others, it was going too fast and would mess up their hair, but to me, it was the perfect scenery to gaze at or to draw a painting.

"What do you think, Jewels? Do you want to come?"

"Go where?" I stared at Keith, confused.

Keith looked at me with slight annoyance. But then he straightened and spoke, "To my parents' cookout. It's their twentieth anniversary, so they want to do something big with friends and family. With that said, I get to invite my friends. Do you want to come?"

They all stared at me. "Sure, but I would have to ask my dad to make sure. You know how he is."

"¡Chévere!" Kaura said with excitement. She did a small dance in her seat.

"What?" Laiya asked.

"It means cool," Keith answered for Kaura like it was nothing.

"Oh…well, yes. Let's party!" She snickered. The others joined, but I was still thinking about Mr. Kowalski. The situation was becoming a plague in my mind, and I was determined to keep the thought away from me. One thing was becoming clear to me that I was no longer myself anymore. I was becoming something inconsistent, different, and *different* was never a word I used to describe myself in recent years.

After lunch, we ventured back to our class. When the bell chimed for the class to begin, Mr. Kowalski was not present. Instead, our principal entered the classroom.

"Students, we asked that Mr. Kowalski take a short break and go to the hospital to be checked out. As soon as he is cleared by his doctors, he will return. For now, your instructor will be Mr. Reyes."

Then, as quickly as he entered, Dr. Neal withdrew himself from the classroom.

The Lady in Red

Even though I didn't feel up to it, I stayed after school to work on my art project since my dad would not be able to pick me up till five. I sat closest to the window to look at something other than these cream-colored walls. Before I knew it, I noticed that the sun was setting. I glanced at the clock, and the time was almost five. I decided it would be best if I wait at the front entrance. My dad would be here soon, and the weather was worsening. I didn't want to be caught in the rain. There was a clear difference between loving the rainfall and being in it. I was on the former side.

I made it to the front entrance. The only person to keep me company was the secretary, and she was busy ignoring me as she signed off on papers stacked high, surrounding her petite body. When I looked out the glass door, I noticed the storm was getting closer. The sky erupted a solemn cry of white slashes. The lightning sparked right in front of the school and caught the attention of the secretary.

"Oh my, well, that was a close one. Do you think it could have taken the power out?" Her voice shivered, as if she was suddenly cold. She seemed younger, like a scared child as she spoke. She stared at me, peering into my eyes for an answer that I didn't have.

I took a beat, "No, the school is pretty strong," I lied. She smiled at me, pleased at my decision to lie. I felt better knowing I made her day, even if it was a white lie. The secretary returned to her task, and I faced forward, searching for my dad, through the thick, heavy rain.

That's when I noticed a guy standing outside in the rain. He was the one who had been chatting with Sarah earlier. That's also when I noticed he was staring at me. I immediately turned away and felt the blood rushing to my face. Getting caught starring at someone, accident or not, was still off-putting. I peeked a second time, but he was not there. Maybe he decided to walk away from my view. Perhaps he was never there at all? I could be seeing another hallucination like earlier. Still, he was clear enough to me that I could reach out and touch him. Then...

"You're Jewels, right?"

I jumped and searched for the voice that spoke. It came from behind me, and he was staring at me with a sickening smirk.

"How do you know my name?" I squeaked.

From my peripheral vision, I could see the petite woman's interest now piqued. She too hadn't seen this newcomer surface.

"I have a class with Sarah, and she invited me to sit with you guys at lunch. She pointed you out and told me your name. I didn't mean to scare you. Just thought I'd make another friend."

His response seemed to be genuine, but his posture and smug face told another story. He was tall and broad. Too perfect to be true. Everything about him seemed right, but he also seemed unfinished. His eyes were waiting for an answer behind his black hair.

"Why didn't you sit with us then?" I asked him bluntly.

He just stared at me. He enjoyed taking his time like this was a game and I had missed out when the referee went over the rules. Then he answered, "Because I had to go see the guidance counselor. I'll probably sit with you guys tomorrow—if you will have me, of course."

I felt the redness coming back and turned away to look at the sky. I saw my dad's car pull up and started to leave him standing there. Instead, I stopped in my tracks. "I never got your name."

He smiled. "Ray. Ray Starling."

I thought about that name and how it sounded too fake and perfect to be someone's name. Then again, it fit him with his hazel eyes.

"Well, Ray Starling, if Kaura wants you to sit with us, then that's fine." I threw the words at him as I turned away from him. "My ride is here. See ya later."

"Have a nice night." I heard as I quickly walked away from him. His words had an odd and eerie ring to them. It made me uneasy and sick to my stomach. I rushed to the car and hopped in. The rain came down harder, and the fog set in. Dad's warm face and smile put me at ease, but not enough.

"Hey, kiddo, how was school?"

I kept my head down as I responded, "Fine, nothing really happened."

"Really?" My dad said with disbelief in his voice. "Because I heard one of your teachers nearly died today."

I turned toward him in shock. "How did you learn about that so fast?"

My dad faced the road and said, "We need to talk."

That was the last time we spoke until we reached our driveway. Once we were home, we then saw that a red Mustang was waiting for us.

My dad looked confused. "Not now!" He quickly grabbed his umbrella and exited the car and ran to the front door to open it. I soon followed him, letting the rain hit my head and shoulders.

We reached the porch, and a very tall woman stood at the door. I wanted to know who she was and how she knew my dad. So many questions went through my mind, and before I could ask, he invited her inside. She stepped into our foyer and took off her raincoat. Our mysterious visitor loved the color red for obvious reasons; her heels, lipstick, and nails were red. She wore a black dress with a red belt. She handed the coat to my dad while simultaneously looking me up and down. When she stopped at my face, she smiled. "My name is Vivienne Marks. I'm a friend of your father's." Her pearly white smile never left her face.

I could see her face now, and she was beyond beautiful. Vivienne's jawline was slick with a pointed chin. Her eyes were light honey marble with a hint of yellow. Those eyes stared at me intensely. Vivienne's brunette hair covered the top of her shoulders with a bang to the left side of her face. She was still smiling at me.

I gave a loud snort and mumbled under my breath, "He never mentioned you."

Vivienne's smile fell into a straight line. My dad turned, giving me a disapproving look.

"Jewels, please go to your room."

I gave my dad a fake smile. "Sure, Dad."

I rushed upstairs to change out of my wet clothes. I decided to go with my favorite tee, *Jurassic Park*. I couldn't stay up here forever. I was hungry. As I cautiously walked downstairs, I could hear them whispering, my dad's voice slightly an octave higher than hers.

I walked into the family room, where they were sitting on the couch. "I'm going to make dinner."

My dad was caught off guard. "Thanks, kiddo."

"Well, now, isn't that special," Vivienne chimed in.

I gave her a smug look with a small strained smile and walked into the kitchen without saying another word. I don't know why she rubbed me the wrong way, but I made up my mind that I didn't like her. Maybe it's the fact that she came unannounced. I don't take too well to surprises. They had a way of changing things forever, and forever was a long time.

Whatever the case may be, she was in our home for a reason, and I didn't think it was a good one. I looked through the refrigerator for something to make for dinner. I decided to go with Italian. I grabbed the pasta and the Alfredo sauce. I grabbed a large pot from the bottom cabinet and filled it with water. I turned on the stove and placed the pot over the fire. Little droplets of water sizzled on the outside of the pot.

I could hear my dad apologizing to Vivienne, and her reply was mute. They drowned out while I was cooking. I even tried to walk closer to the living room where they were, but they stopped speaking as soon as they saw me. I found that oddly weird.

"Dinner's almost ready," I yelled while leaning into the living room.

My father smiled in response. Vivienne nodded and then turned to my father. I could tell they wanted me to leave, so I pushed them further.

"What are you talking about?"

Vivienne just looked at me with a straight face while my dad said, "Work."

"One of your clients is having problems?" I continued to investigate.

"Something like that." My dad was short with me.

I shrugged my shoulders and turned around to walk into the kitchen. It was all the secrecy that disturbed me. I could not help but feel that they were talking about me and not about work. My dad and I had no secrets. Or so I thought.

After I finished setting the table, they both walked into the dining room. Vivienne was ahead of my dad. She stood and admired my table spread. "Wow, this is wonderful, Jewels." She seemed impressed. I decided to use the elegant and overly grand table cloth since we had a guest. It had a white and yellow lace trim that contained large circles that intertwined with one another. At the center of the table cloth was a floral pattern of daisies. The border was covered with smaller daisies.

"I made Caesar salad with Alfredo pasta and Italian bread. For your choice of drink, we have water, iced tea, or Sprite." I pointed to each item as I spoke. My dad gave a loud clap that broke the air and seemed louder than usual. I gave a bow and shouted, "Thank you. I will *not* be here all week." They both laughed, and Vivienne's laugh was just as weird as my dad's. Sharp and annoying, almost like a hiccup.

The room was filled with nothing but cold air as we sat eating until Vivienne spoke first. "So, Jewels, your father was telling me about an incident that took place at your school today. Have you heard anything else about it?" she casually asserted. She moved the food around her plate, never taking a bite, only pushing it to seem as though her plate was being emptied.

My mind was racing. I wanted to know who this strange woman was asking questions that were clearly none of her business.

I quickly answered her, though, because I didn't want to make my dad more upset. "Yeah, today was a crazy day." She glanced at me, clearly desiring more information. So I added, "I heard he was headed to the hospital. After dinner, I'll call my friends to see if they heard something else." I paused and looked at my dad. "Speaking of which, Keith invited the crew to his parents' house for their anniversary party. Can I go?"

Dad looked at me, asking, "Oh, really? You've never been to his house before. When is it?"

I wanted to make this line of questioning as easy to get through as possible, so I just casually said, "It's this Saturday at noon."

He hesitated before speaking. My dad was taking his time. I could tell his wheels were turning, probably wondering why Keith, a *boy*, wanted me over. To be fair, I would not be alone. So there was no need to be a cop about it. He has always been too protective.

With a slow slur, he breathed, "Sure." Finally! I could see Keith's house. It was a long time coming.

"Thank you." I sighed and leaned back in my chair after taking a bite of Alfredo. But it stuck to the roof of my mouth like glue.

Then as suddenly as that interaction ended, the lady in red decided to make her move. "I'm sorry to interrupt, but we need to tell her, Warren."

I looked at them both, and they were staring back at me with concerned faces. My dad placed his fork on his plate. I could tell that his appetite was gone. Mine had left long ago.

"Tell me what?" I asked in a shallow voice, barely hearing myself.

"Just listen to what she has to say, kiddo," my dad added.

"What I'm about to tell you may come as a shock. So please, if you need some time to digest what we are going to tell you, I understand," Vivienne said with sensitivity.

I was frightened. Somehow, I could tell this conversation was going to be surrounded by Mr. Kowalski's incident. My stomach tightened, and I felt lightheaded. I tried to focus on my dad's face. I tried to imagine the lady in red was gone…gone…just gone.

"Dad, what's going on?" I leaned forward in my seat. Their attempt to safeguard me was no longer of help. I rather, they just tell me what I already suspected.

Vivienne's answer startled me. "You are a part of something bigger than this world."

This entire conversation took on a spooky edge. Despite the fear, I asked, "What? What do you mean bigger?"

She was patient. "I mean, you come from a bloodline of fighters and protectors."

"So are we secret spies or something?" I asked with curiosity and excitement in my voice. Who would have thought I could be a spy? Not me, that's for sure.

Vivienne laughed, "No, dear, you are a part of a civilization that protects humans."

"Oh my gosh, are we aliens? I can't believe this...we're aliens. How? Why?" The excitement from being a potential spy quickly dissolved into a feeling of foreboding.

"Kiddo, take a breather—you are not an alien. Just a modified human being," Dad said, trying to ease the shock of this revelation.

"So is our civilization from Earth?" I asked him.

Vivienne answered instead, "Yes. It's only a percentage of us who have developed faster than other humans. The ones that are modified can be found in our haven. If the world knew about us, we would be feared and considered a threat."

"So why am I involved with this?" My posture was sunken, and my energy was depleted. Today's events had taken a toll on my mind and body. I could feel the last bits of my sanity leaving my body and escaping far away from this crazy fest.

Vivienne's voice amplified as her excitement grew. "Well, you are one of the seven protectors. Each protector is given a gift that will help protect the Queen from the evils that face us and the world. By keeping the Queen protected, you are keeping humanity intact. Am I going too fast?"

The Queen? Who was the Queen, and the Queen of what?

My head was spinning a mile a minute. I wanted them to stop talking so I could think, but I wanted them to finish too. I could not believe I was not human or at least one like my friends. Why didn't my dad tell me about this before?

"Okay, so I'm human but not human. I have a gift, and it's powerful enough to protect the whole world. There is a secret place in the world where...what are we called?"

"Refashion." Vivienne smiled at the thought.

"Okay, there is a secret place in the world where Refashions are held. I am a part of the special Seven that protect the Queen from evil. Did I miss anything?"

Vivienne's grin never left her face, "Well, there is a lot more, but I understand if you need time."

I briskly jumped from the table and paced the floor. What was happening to my life? Everything was normal until today. Between the incident at school, the strange new kid, and Vivienne's visit, my life has made a turn for the worse.

From the corner of my eye, I could see my dad staring at me, just waiting for me to explode. Whatever Vivienne and my dad had to say seemed important; I needed to hear the rest.

"No, I'm fine. Please continue," I said, knowing I was far from "fine."

"You may have noticed that you frequently have dreams about the earth's elements or that you spend most of your time drawing nature. It's because you are connected to the earth, and with that, you were given the ability to control air."

I felt my face stiffen and become numb and cold. My heart pounded, and I was sure they could hear the constant thunder coming from my chest. Maybe it was me who hurt Mr. Kowalski. Part of me was certain, but I could dream, right?

"Today, in class, was that me?" The sound of my voice seemed foreign.

Vivienne trailed on, "Yes, a person who is meant to protect the Queen will reveal their powers when the world needs them most. Today was your first time." She was practically enjoying herself. I chalked it up to being able to enlighten someone about a secret civilization and not my discomfort. Even so, her smiling face made me feel debilitated.

"But how could you possibly know I was the one?"

"As a civilization, we are connected. But the Queen is the only one connected to the Seven." Vivienne laughed.

I asked her, "How *did* you find me?" My face moved from shock to skepticism.

"She's much like you in ways, gifted. Because of her gifts, she felt your fear, power, and excitement. The image that flowed from your mind through hers allowed her to locate you here in Colorado."

"Woah!" That's all I could say. My mind wanted to ask a million and one questions. But the more she talked, the more I was exhausted. I should choose my question more carefully.

"How is Earth in danger?" My head was pounding. I felt my feet become paralyzed.

"Our enemies are called Scourgers. We have been at war with them for centuries until our previous Seven destroyed their leader and put an end to their terror." She paused and looked sullen. "So we thought. You may know of the Black Death. The Scourgers started it. What about the measles that hit from 1955 to 2005? Or leprosy? All of those illnesses were the effects of the evil that tried to destroy our Queen and the world. There are many more diseases that the Scourgers are responsible for, but each time, we have defeated them. To make sure the antidote to the virus or disease gets in the hands of the scientists, we established our people into the CDC. Scientists take the credit while we do the heavy lifting. Just works that way." Vivienne shrugged.

Her body language read frustration as she talked about the Scourgers. "A couple of years back, we got word that the Scourger King was still alive. We tried to investigate, but we were unable to locate him. Our Seven actively pursued him but never got the chance to come in contact with him. He was underground until recently when the Scourgers were spotted in Europe. Their increased presence has alerted us that their king is up to something. That's why your gift has manifested along with the others. But I know you and the others can defeat him…this time."

Her last words were forced. "Every day that the Seven are separated, the King gets stronger. We believe he has created another virus and is causing more harm."

I looked at the woman who was telling me all of this and asked, "You're telling me that all vaccines were made by you guys—I mean, us—and that all diseases and viruses are caused by the Scourgers whom we are supposed to protect humans from?"

Patiently she answered, "Not all of the viruses are made by them. Humanity always finds a way to make themselves sick. We do, however, lead the scientists in the correct direction when making antidotes."

Now the lower part of my body was stiff and callous. I didn't know if I could hold on much longer.

"How did you get your people into the CDC?" I asked her, trying to distract myself from the sudden sharp pain traveling up my limbs.

"It's quite simple. They just had to grow up *normal.*"

Vivienne seemed to spit at the word *normal.* I grew up normal, and I turned out fine. Unless that's not what she meant by the word?

"They established themselves all over the world. Helping the humans and keeping an eye out for Scourgers. We…" Vivienne's voice trailed off, and she looked at me. I was suddenly aware that I could no longer feel my body. I had been standing this entire time, and my knees were weak. I grabbed ahold of the chair to catch myself. My dad jumped from his seat and ran to catch me. Yet it was too late; I hit the floor hard…out cold.

Reality Hits Hard

I awoke on my bed, still in my clothes from yesterday. I was a little dizzy and lightheaded. Bits of yesterday flooded to the surface, and I could hear Vivienne's voice repeating the phrase, "You are modified." Maybe, everything was a dream. A horrible dream, and I wasn't a part of some secret society that protected the earth. I mean, advanced humans that have powers and protect a magical queen get real. A soft knock on the door took me from my thoughts.

"Are you up, kiddo?" Dad asked.

"Yeah, dad, come in." Just to make sure I wasn't dreaming, I needed to ask my dad about last night. I slowly sat upright in my bed. "Did a lady by the name of Vivienne Marks come over last night to tell me that I would be protecting the earth, by any chance?" My dad looked at me with a sweet smile that confirmed my doubt. Defeated, I crashed back in my bed. I was in the middle of a battle that has been going on for centuries. If they couldn't stop them, then what chance did I have?

"Kiddo, I know you are thinking about the effects this may have on your life. But you will be able to continue to go to school and train on the down low for the anticipated battle up ahead. Vivienne and I discussed your arrangements, and I think it's best if you remain here. She will teach you how to focus on your powers so you can control them. You don't have to be afraid of your gift," my dad said, trying to be optimistic.

I still felt light-headed, and my stomach was in a knot. I couldn't verbalize any words because my mouth was too dry, so I nodded in response. "Well then, if you don't want to be late for school, I suggest you get a move on," he said as he kissed me on the forehead and walked out of the room. How was he able to act so normal about this? His only child was responsible for the safety of the entire world.

I looked around my room, and everything merged into focus. All the scenery drawings I placed on my walls—all the pastel-colored

27

beaches, dark green forests, and bright, raging fires—made sense. I was attempting to draw home or at least connect with it.

Wait, did he say I was going to be late? I looked at the clock, and I had exactly thirty minutes to get out of here if I wanted to get to school on time. Life just officially got worse.

Twenty-Five Minutes Later

I arrived at school with five minutes to spare. I rushed to my classroom as the final bell chimed. Ms. Kimble gave me a warning instead of a penalty since it was the second day of school. I found my seat next to Laiya, and she gave me a raised eyebrow look. "Are you okay? You look like death itself."

I shrugged my shoulders and faced forward without a word. The entire day, I secluded myself. I tried to join my friends' conversations, but I was too wrapped up with what happened to me last night. *I could not believe I was different. I could not believe I had been living a lie.*

The one thing I did pay attention to was the fact that Ray didn't sit with us. I asked Kaura if she had seen him in class today. She smirked at me and said, "Lover boy's out sick." I rolled my eyes and went back into my thoughts. Mr. Kowalski was not back from the hospital yet; the rumor was that he had a crushed trachea. I was responsible for his injury. I ruined his life. Or at least a portion of it. The others were laughing about how he choked on spit and was injured. I didn't find that funny. In fact, I wished I was anywhere but sitting in class today.

My dad had to work late again, but I couldn't bring myself to stay in this cold and large building one more second. So I called and told him I would get a ride from Kaura.

"So you've been quiet all day. What's going on in that *mente preciosa* of yours?" Kaura asked as she turned her head slightly, keeping an eye on the road.

I stayed quiet for a minute or so, trying to decide if I should tell her or not. I mean, it wouldn't hurt to have a friend that could understand me. She could even come with me for training days.

Then again, she might think I was a freak and shame me for life. "Nothing," I said. "I just have cramps, that's all."

She tilted her head sideways and hit me on the shoulder. She laughed when I looked at her. "What's really going on?" She tilted her head further. Her concern for my mental state grew. Occasionally, she glanced at the road.

"I will tell you when we get to my house to make sure you don't kill us while you're driving."

Her face screamed confusion. "Okay, if you say so." She finally kept her face straight.

My comment made her aware that she was driving *and* prying.

I had a total of ten minutes to think about how I was going to tell her that I was a modified human being who was destined to save the Earth. I could break it to her slowly, bit by bit, but she might think I need to go to a psych ward, or I could tell her fast and to the point. Rip it off like a bandage. That way, she couldn't process the information. Somehow, ten minutes turned into five because we were at my house already. I hesitated and stayed glued to my seat.

Kaura turned to me and said, "All right, we are at your house, spill." I thought of a million reasons why I should *not* tell her.

Instead I offered, "Uh…let's go inside first." I dreaded telling her.

"Fine, but you will tell me either way." She exhaled and opened her car. I followed suit, only slower.

Every step I took felt like I was stepping in quicksand. Kaura grabbed my shoulders, pushing me toward the door.

"Open it," she ordered.

I slowly found my house key and turned the lock. Kaura impatiently pushed the door open while grabbing my arm and pulling me inside. "Whatever has you acting like this must be important. You have to tell me." She faced me in the foyer.

"Okay, let's sit down on the couch first." I motioned to my living room. Kaura was impatient, but kind, saying, "Fine, but no more stalling. The wait is too much."

We sat on my brown-cushioned couch, which usually felt comforting and soft. But all I felt was fear and coldness. Here goes nothing, or should I say everything?

"You know how Mr. Kowalski started to choke in class?" Kaura shook her head in agreement, motioning for me to continue. "Well, I caused it." I squinted my eyes enough not to see her reaction.

Instead, she burst out with laughter and spoke at the same time, "Are you for real, Jewels? I don't think human beings can do such a thing. Muchacha, I thought you or your dad was sick." I opened my eyes. Kaura was staring at me, the concern she had in the car no longer carried on her face.

"That's just it, Kaura, I am not a human." I remembered what Vivienne said and corrected myself. "Well, I am, but just modified. I'm a part of an advanced civilization that protects the earth." She stopped laughing.

"Now, Jewels, that was a good joke, but you need to stop, okay? You don't have powers, nor are you a part of a secret civilization."

A straight face replaced her laughter. She truly believed I was making this up. I expected her not to believe me, but it still hurt.

"I can prove it," I said petulantly. My grumpiness showed through my posture as I leaned further away from my friend.

"Go ahead." She crossed her arms and leaned back on the couch.

I stood from the couch. Then I focused on the air in the room and imagined it evaporating into nothing. My surrounding was now dark, and the room fell silent. The only noise I heard was from the ringing in my ear. The space between me and earth seemed to close, and I felt at peace.

"Jewels, stop. You stop right this instant."

I slowly came back to reality. Kaura was lying flat on her back on the floor. My dad was kneeling next to her. "Why would you do this? You should not be using your powers."

I was in shock for two reasons. One, it didn't feel like I was choking Kaura for a long time. Or at all. Secondly, I was not expecting my dad home for a couple of hours.

"I'm... I'm sorry Kaura, I didn't mean to—"

My dad cut me off. "Do you realize what could have happened? Don't ever use your gift without the proper training! Do you understand?"

"Yes. I'm so sorry, Kaura," was all I could find the words to say.

Oddly enough, she still could speak. "It's okay, Jewels. I believe you now. You have to tell me everything."

Kaura was left with a swollen pink and red handprint around her throat. It was as if I had physically choked her. I bent down and hugged her, "I will, but first you need to get checked out." She tried to shake her head but made a wince.

"No, I'm fine. You only took my breath away, no big deal."

Her voice was raspy. I gave a sharp laugh and watched my friend as my dad helped her sit on the sofa. I sat next to her, and she looked at me with amazement.

"*Dios mío*, I can't believe you're not human. What are your people called? Is Jewels even your real name?"

"Okay, slow down. You—" I was suddenly interrupted, again. There was a sharp knock on the door, and then the doorbell rang.

"Jewels, go get the door, I will get some ice for your throat, Kaura." He was still disappointed with me. His voice bellowed too loud for the room.

"Thank you, Mr. Stellar," Kaura managed to say.

I walked away to retrieve the door. To my surprise, it was Vivienne. As I suspected, she was wearing red and a lot of it. This time, it was a red jumpsuit with nude-colored hills. Her lips were also red. Around her neck was a red and nude-colored necklace. Her bracelet had a large ruby in the center; she wore a golden chain to keep it all together.

What was she doing here? I silently wondered. Yet I offered a pleasant, fake smile. She did the same as she asked, "How are you feeling, Jewels?"

"Fine, besides the fact that I and six others have to save the world." My voice heightened to give false excitement.

"Ah, well, splendid," she replied on cue. I don't think she got my sarcasm.

She walked into the house and saw my friend on the couch with an ice pack on her neck.

"Jewels, what did you do?"

I already felt guilty, but Vivienne made me feel even worse. I couldn't explain in words the look she gave me. Somehow, she knew it was my fault, and she let me know she figured it out.

"Well, I thought it would be nice to have a friend who could help me through everything. So I told her about me. Surprise."

I stretched my hands in the air and shook them back and forth. Which didn't help at all. She gave me a stern glare and glanced in my dad's direction, who didn't come to my defense and said, "Don't look at me. I just found out."

Vivienne walked over to Kaura and sat next to her. "Are you okay?"

Kaura tried to shake her head but made another wince. Vivienne gently placed her hands around Kaura's throat. As Vivienne's hands moved about Kaura's throat, it healed. Kaura's face relaxed from the soothing relief. The redness and swelling went down as the pink handprint faded away. Then Vivienne let her go. "How's that?"

"A lot better. Thank you." Kaura seemed to be her old self again. She was smiling and carried a brightness to her. At the same time, Kaura and I shouted, "What are you?"

Vivienne gave a small smile and said, "I'm from a small section of our civilization called Gyniatric. We can heal others and ourselves." I sat and lamented how Vivienne now seemed like a heroine.

"Wow, that is amazing," squeaked Kaura with enthusiasm.

"Yes, it is. Jewels, your kind is called Pneumodegyn. Meaning 'air breather.' Pneumodegyns can control the air. Make it foggy, windy, or translucent. What Kaura and Mr. Kowalski have experienced is on the darker spectrum of the gift. However, with help, you can master it and place people in a deep sleep rather than a coffin." Now she had jokes on top of everything else.

I rolled my eyes then asked, "So how would I protect the Queen and the world exactly?"

Vivienne explained, "You and the other six will come together with the unique gifts bestowed onto by the Queen and defeat the Scourgers."

"Okay, I believe you've said that about a million times. How will we defeat them exactly?" She was elusive, and I didn't have time for that.

"Well, first you have to meet the other six and train with them. Then we develop an effective plan to diminish the Scourgers for the last time," Vivienne said this as if it were the most natural thing in the world to do. I could get behind training, but what she was instructing me to do didn't align with what my dad said.

"I'm training at my house, right? My dad mentioned you said it was okay." I looked from Vivienne to my dad. They seemed to have a mini stare down; she was confused. Did my dad neglect the truth?

I didn't want to think about all the things that would change, especially between my dad and me, so I asked, "Why now? I haven't heard about an outbreak." I still could not believe this. If our gifts were awake, then there had to be a virus or disease, and I had heard nothing that would cause seven people to go into hyperdrive.

Kaura spoke, "Actually, there is a virus out now. They are calling it Klemers. So far, it has hit Germany, France, Spain, and Portugal, and it's spreading fast." I just sat amazed.

"How did you hear about this, Kaura?" asked my dad.

She answered proudly and rapped her finger through her hair, "I have family in South America, and they were telling me about it."

Vivienne turned toward Kaura, "Have you spoken with them lately?"

Looking a bit puzzled, she answered, "Yes, they are fine. They said if it gets worse, they will stay with us for a while."

"Well, I'm glad to hear that they are okay." Vivienne's voice was genuine.

My dad stood and looked at his watch. "Well, it's almost six o'clock. Would you ladies like to stay for dinner?"

Kaura stood as well. "Actually, I should get home. I haven't wrapped Keith's parents' anniversary gift yet, and I still need to find my outfit for tomorrow. I'm stuck between my white and navy blue polka-dotted bow or the red-and-white striped bow."

"Always red, my dear," said Vivienne. We all exchanged a genuine laugh. For a split second, my reality was normal. I was normal.

I walked Kaura to the door. When we stepped out of earshot, I turned to Kaura and said, "You're not going to tell the others, are you?"

She gave me a small smile. "Of course not. But when you decide to tell them, I'll be there with you for support."

I gave her another hug. "Thanks, you're the best sister-friend a girl could want."

She gave a small burst of laughter. "I know I'm the best, and you still have to tell me everything."

"As soon as I know everything, you will too."

Kaura gave me another smile and then walked to her car. I watched Kaura back out of my driveway. I walked into my house and shut the door lightly. I couldn't believe I told her and she was okay with it. Now I had to deal with my dad. Maybe the worst thing was that I was grounded for a day, since I had to save the world and all.

Behind the Mist

Well, I was grounded for life. Thankfully, Vivienne convinced my dad to let me go to Keith's party. She said it wouldn't be fair to me, seeing how it would be my last time to have fun before I started training. Truth be told, I just wanted to see his house. None of the crew had ever stepped a foot into his home. Whenever one of us mentioned hanging out at his place, he came up with lame excuses why we couldn't. Sarah once said that he lived in a dump. Of course, Kaura said Sarah was rude, and then they got into an argument.

My dad and I pulled up to his house. It turned out, he lived in Cherry Hills Village, which was an elegant gated community. His home was three stories with dark-brown wood panels place on a hill. The land had to be around four acres. The front double doors were a rich deep brown with golden doorknobs shaped like a diamond, and there were several small bushes neatly shaved in the front yard. The walkway was made of stone and embedded in the grass were small lights evenly spread along the grass and stretched from the sidewalk toward the front door. There were a lot of cars parked along the street and cul-de-sac. He invited everyone he knew, which seemed to be the entire grade. When he said a small gathering, I wasn't expecting this. I should have dressed more for the occasion. I was in a pink ruffled blouse and dark blue jeans, almost black. I wanted to change, but I was already here.

I jumped out of the car. "Thanks, Dad. You can pick me up at five."

He agreed, saying, "All right, have fun and be safe."

I turned around and gave him a wave goodbye.

I faced the house and noticed Laiya walking to the front door. She was wearing a beautiful yellow sundress with heels. "Hey, girl, love that dress." I smiled.

Laiya turned around and greeted me with a smile. "Hey, you," she said. "Are you feeling any better? I was worried yesterday. You didn't seem like yourself."

I assured her, "Yeah, thanks. Yesterday just wasn't my day."

Laiya looked more concerned than relieved. I decided to change the subject. "Can you believe we're at Keith's house?"

Giddy with anticipation, she said, "I know right! This is going to be interesting." It wasn't that hard to steer her away. She's like me in ways. We both hate to dwell on things that make us anxious.

We walked into the house, and one of Laiya's classmates called her over. In the distance, I saw a table stacked high with gifts. I walked through the thick crowd of people and set my small gift on the table. I turned around and looked for Laiya, but she was swallowed by the crowd. Then someone spoke. "Hi there, you must be Keith's friend?" I turned to the voice, and it was a middle-aged woman. I know it's rude to say, but she looked off somehow.

I awkwardly smiled. "Yes, my name is Jewels."

The woman's face stretched into an oversized grin. "How wonderful." Then her smile dropped, and she walked away. Weird. I left the table to try and find Laiya. Laiya was still in the huddle of teens chatting. I tapped on her shoulder and mouthed, "We need to talk." She nodded and excused herself from the group.

"What's going on, Jewels?" Laiya asked after we made it to a corner of the house.

"Nothing too serious. I just had a run-in with someone weird." I shrugged.

"Oh, okay. Well, are you okay?"

"Yeah, just don't leave me," I said.

She laughed in response.

We searched for what seemed like an hour to find our friends. It would have been shorter, but Keith's family kept pulling us into different conversations. I zoned out for most of the conversation. Each relative asked the typical question you asked a senior, "What college are you going to?" It was exhausting when I had to tell them, "I don't know yet" and receive questionable glares. I'm sorry, I couldn't plan my life out at the age of seventeen.

36

Keith's weirdest relative was his grandfather. That man was everything your parents warned you about. He lacked personal space and decency.

While Laiya was talking to Grandpa Ben, I looked for Sarah and Kaura. I found them talking to Keith and his parents. I turned back to Laiya and said, "Come on, Laiya, we have to greet the host."

She got the hint and jumped up from the couch, "Of course, it was nice to...have a good day, Grandpa Ben." Then we rushed over to Kaura and Sarah.

Keith's mother, Mrs. Wood, was the first to speak to us. "Hello, girls, how are you all?" She seemed like the perfect mom portrayed on an old TV show. She was poised, pleasant, and pretty. Laiya and I looked at each other; it seemed like we both had the same thought.

"Fine, except Grandpa Ben is too comfortable with his hands," Laiya blurted out.

Sarah gave a small laugh, while Kaura looked concerned. Keith just shook his head. Mrs. Wood looked shocked and turned to Mr. Wood. "I think you should have a conversation with your father." Then she turned to us, and her smile was back.

"I am truly sorry about that," Mr. Wood said as he walked off to address his father.

Laiya was the first to speak. "Happy anniversary, Mrs. Wood."

Still a bit embarrassed, she said, "Thank you. Keith has told me so much about you all."

"Really?" Sarah asked.

"Yes, you sound surprised." Keith's mom looked at Sarah and then at her son.

Sarah proceeded to explain her statement. "It's just that he never—"

Keith then interjected, "Mom, Aunt Maggie is waving you over."

Still a little confused, she walked away, saying, "Oh, thanks, son. We must pick up later, girls."

Keith said, giving Sarah a rile stare, "What's with the 'really' remark?"

Sarah countered, "Well, it's true we weren't allowed to come over, and I wanted to find out why."

Keith was clearly irritated now. "I told you already, my parents like to go on trips to find new artwork, and they don't allow me to have guests over when they are not home."

Sarah would not let up. "Ah, that sounds like bull to me."

Just then, a voice pulled my attention away. "Hi, you're Jewels, right?" I turned and found a small, slender girl about the age of ten. She wore a pink and orange dress with long yellow socks that stopped at her knees. She also had a black and white cat walking between her legs.

"I am. Who are you?"

"Alice, but we don't have time for formalities. I need you to come with me."

"Excuse me?" I was in shock; this child had spunk. "I don't think I'm going anywhere with you."

"We don't have time, come on." Alice left through the crowd and down the back hall.

"Jewels, are you okay?" It was Kaura. She had a concerned mother's look on her face.

"Yeah, I don't know what she wants," I said.

Kaura looked confused. "Who?"

"The little girl, that was just here. Maybe you didn't see her because you all were fighting?" I added.

"Sure," Sarah said with skepticism.

"I'm not making this up, guys." I snapped.

As if she heard me talking about her, Alice walked right behind Keith and Sarah. The cat was with her too. She waved me over, urgency on her face.

I nearly jumped into the air, "Right there. Look!"

They all turned to where I was pointing, but none of them seemed to show any acknowledgment that they saw her. I said, "You see, I told you."

Keith, now frustrated, snapped, "What are you talking about? I don't see anything, Jewels."

Laiya turned from the direction I was pointing at and said, "Me neither." Sarah backed up, almost stepping on the cat.

"Are you sure you're okay?" Kaura grabbed my arm.

"Excuse me for a second?" I said.

I grabbed Alice's arm and walked away from my friends. They each carried different expressions on their face. I was sure I looked insane to them, but if I was right, then Alice was not who I thought she was. I finally found a closet and thrust the door open. Alice and I squeezed into the tight space. I found the light switch and looked her dead in the face.

"Can others see you?" I looked down at her. My arms crossed over my chest.

"Nope." She kept her expression the same as before. Annoyed.

"Explain yourself." I figured she was a part of my other world.

"I was trying to, but you wouldn't listen, and now we're wasting time." She showed frustration as she crossed her arms.

"Well, spit it out already," I snapped.

"Okay, my name is ALICE, but it's short for 'Analyzing Lucrative Intelligence Central Engine.'" She was impressed with herself.

"So you're a robot." I got to the point.

"No, I'm more than that. I'm an expensive computer—an android." She crossed her arms and turned her nose toward the ceiling.

"I didn't mean to offend you. But why would you make me look stupid in front of everyone?" I finally dropped my arms to the side.

"Technically, it was only four people. Let's just be honest, the probability of you telling them about me and everything else that is going on with you is a ninety-five percent chance."

"Well, you're right. I was planning on telling them." I looked her over; she was too real to be an android. How they managed to do that, I could only imagine.

"We have to leave." She was serious again.

"What's wrong?" My voice was quiet.

Suddenly a loud thump broke the air, and the house shook. The clothes dropped from their hangers and piled on our heads. ALICE grabbed ahold of me. Out of fear or to protect me, I couldn't tell.

The house stood still. Outside the closet, the guests were quiet. Then the sound of glass breaking and thuds took over. Screams echoed through the hall all the way to our hiding space. The house vibrated again, and ALICE looked at me. "We need to go."

She opened the door and rushed out with my arm in her hand. The house was in a frenzy, as people ran to the front and back doors. Others were covering their mouths because of a purple-grayish smoke that was spilling in from the windows and upstairs. The smoke was moving with a purpose; it was heading straight for ALICE and me.

"We need to leave now," she instructed.

She was pulling my arm so hard I lost all feeling in it. We turned in the opposite direction and ran to the other end of the house. We made it to the kitchen, but there was smoke already building, so ALICE pulled me further down the hall.

"Let's go through here," she commanded as she pulled me through an office room and opened a window. "Come on, hurry up."

I put one leg through the window and brought my head through next. I was finally out when the smoke burst through the doors and consumed the room. ALICE squeezed out of the window into my arms, and we fell on the ground. We made it to the front of the house, and it looked horrible. The smoke didn't seem to expand like it usually would. It stayed in the house and circled around it. The street was crowded with people yelling, crying, and the few that were curious.

"We need to leave now," ALICE ordered.

I countered, "I understand, but I need to check on my friends."

ALICE said to me sternly, "There's no time. If they sent Miesgyn, then they are not far behind. We need to leave now."

I screamed, "No, please! I need to check on my friends."

ALICE stood still and hissed, "Why are humans so stubborn?" I was very irritated by her comment, but she let me go, and I didn't want her to change her mind, so I kept my mouth shut.

I found Kaura and Laiya together. They were sitting on the curve, holding each other's hands. Kaura was comforting Laiya.

"It's not your fault. He's going to be fine," Kaura said.

Laiya scowled at Kaura and gave an angry reply, "How do you know that?" She sobbed even more. Kaura abruptly stood and met me halfway.

"What happened?" I asked.

Kaura gave a loud exhale. "Keith, was helping Laiya get away from the mist when it started to circle around them. He pushed her out of the way, but he didn't make it."

"What? What do you mean, he didn't make it?" I asked.

Laiya looked at me, disturbed. "The mist swallowed him," she said.

I felt a tiny crack form in my brain. A part of me knew how he could be taken, but I still had to ask, "How is that possible?"

ALICE approached me and sternly said, "We need to go!"

I shouted, "I know!"

Kaura puzzled over who I was speaking to asked, "You know what Jewels?"

I just shook my head and said, "Oh, nothing, Kaura, I just... I-I need to go." It made no sense to explain ALICE to them since they could not see her anyway.

Laiya said, "At a time like this, are you kidding me?"

The only thing that I could say was, "I'll explain everything later, I promise." I ran after ALICE. She rushed to a familiar red Mustang. It was Vivienne's. I got in the front seat, and we drove off.

Vivienne asked, "Are you all right, Jewels?"

I was in shock. The crack in my brain was increasing in length. My stomach started to ache, "I guess, thanks for the ride."

"Oh, by the way, I'm fine too. Thanks for asking," ALICE said sarcastically. Who would have guessed they allowed that kind of behavior in programming? Then again, she did deceive me earlier.

Vivienne looked in the rearview mirror. "Glad to hear it, ALICE." Vivienne then turned to me. "I will take you home, Jewels, but only to get a few things. Then we need to get out of town."

Leaving didn't seem all that bad, but I would like it if my dad tagged along. "Does my dad know what's happening?" Vivienne paused and caught her breath. I knew what would come next would be bad news.

"Your dad is missing. I went to your house earlier, but he wasn't there. I had ALICE to retrieve you while I looked around town for him," Vivienne said with little emotion. She was trying to keep me calm, but guess what? *It didn't work*!

I wanted to scream, shout, and punch someone all at the same time. Why couldn't anything be simple anymore? First, Keith was taken, now my dad. I didn't want to think about what else could happen. I took my phone from my pocket and dialed for my dad. The ringing wouldn't stop. When it did, I only received my dad's voice mail.

My body felt hot, and a film of salty water trickled down from my forehead and arms. I felt too much at once, and it was about to come out, just not in the way I expected. Vivienne seemed to catch on and pulled the car over.

As soon as I opened the door and stepped out of the car, my body got rid of the anger and disbelief I had as I threw up. I entered the vehicle, and ALICE gave me a napkin to wipe my mouth. Vivienne dug in her purse and pulled out a stick of mint gum and handed it to me. I sat in the car, quiet. The silent hum of Vivienne's car rolling off the gravel and on the street was the only noise as we drove away.

After a while, I spoke. "Sorry about the smell," I said. My brain worked hard to function the rest of my body. Everything slowed down to a millisecond. I thought I waited an eternity for one of them to respond.

Vivienne feeling sorry for me, said, "It's all right. I can hardly smell it."

"I can't even smell," ALICE said sarcastically. "So it's all good."

I gave a small laugh that turned into a cough. "You know, you're really something, ALICE."

"I know." I couldn't see her smile, but I felt it.

Long Day's Journey

We reached my home, and my dad's car was parked in its usual spot. I suddenly felt horrible at the sight of his car. Our car. I tried to take a deep breath, but my chest ached, and a sharp pain vibrated from my stomach to the tip of my neck. I grabbed the door handle and thrust Vivienne's car door open. Out of nowhere, it rained with a ferocity that made the water sting as it hit my shoulders. Quickly, I ran to the front door, the others followed. What I encountered was odd. The door was partly open. ALICE stood in front of me to protect me. After she took point, we walked in. I could already tell that she was going to be a great little friend. We walked in with caution. Searching for a sign of life. But the house was just like I left it. Nothing was missing, except my dad. I wished there was some sort of sign as to where my dad went, but nothing. Only the sound of the TV.

"Grab your things. We leave in five," Vivienne said as she walked toward the kitchen.

I grabbed my backpack that was by the door and ran upstairs. I passed the photos on the wall of me, happy, and thought, *If only she knew what would happen to her.*

Packing seemed foreign. I'd lived in Colorado since I was little, and now, I was embarking on a journey where the unknown was my new life. I just hoped my life didn't change drastically, where I could no longer recognize the girl I was.

Vivienne yelled, "Jewels, you need to hurry up."

I rolled my eyes and picked up my school bag from the bed, which I filled with anything I could grab my hands on. I paused when I came across my old T-shirt that read, 'Orange you glad you visited Florida?' It was the first time my dad had to leave me for a business strip. I stayed with Kaura for the whole week. To this day, Kaura would ever so often mention how big of a brat I was when he left.

I lost focus. "I'm coming," I yelled as I ran down the stairs.

ALICE and Vivienne were watching Breaking News in the family room. One of the news reporters was talking about Keith's house. The reporter said that the CDC placed the family and others who were at the party in quarantine until they could determine if the gas was harmful. The reporter also stated that they never witnessed something so horrific before. Well duh. I mean, it's not every day purple smoke decides to appear out of thin air.

I asked Vivienne, "Is the gas harmful?" The only thought I had was that I had left my friends there.

She answered, "Not that particular gas. The purple gas hides the Scourgers so that they can take victims. Other colors are far more deadly. For instance, if you see red gas, stay away. It reacts to human breath. Once activated, the red smoke makes the air toxic." Vivienne looked at the clock on the wall. The time read 4:00 p.m. "We should head out."

I asked, "So my friends will be okay?"

Vivienne reassured me, saying, "Yes, don't worry."

We were heading to the door when it suddenly burst open. ALICE jumped in front of me and bent down into an attack mode. Vivienne pulled a 9mm Glock from her purse and pointed the gun at the intruder, intending to hit her mark and, no doubt, kill it. "Woah, don't shoot!" It was Sarah with raised hands. She was drenched from the rain and carried a small black bag with red and blue flowers on it.

I stepped in front of Sarah to shield her from Vivienne's gun. My hands were raised just like Sarah's when I spoke in a high-pitched voice. "It's all right, Vivienne and ALICE, this is Sarah. She's one of my best friends."

Vivienne said, "You're late, Sarah." She stowed her Glock back in her purse.

Then Sarah said, "Sorry, it was hard getting away from the CDC and police. They blocked off the neighborhood."

I instantly was confused. My hands dropped to my sides as I pondered over this new encounter. What did Vivienne mean when she said Sarah was late? How did they know each other, and why was I just finding this out? I didn't think my body and mind could take any more surprises. But here it was, and Sarah was at the center of it all. I turned around and faced my friend.

"Sarah, what's going on? How do you know Vivienne?"

She tried to brush me off, "I'll tell you everything, but we need to go right now." No way. I was tired of the games and half-truths.

I stood my ground. "No, you are going to tell me now."

She let out a loud huff. "If you want to know so badly, then you're just going to have to follow me to the car."

She walked out the door, Vivienne not far behind. Vivienne's voice was raised as she talked to Sarah. ALICE and I were the only ones left in the house. The sound of the rain hitting the roof, keeping us company. ALICE stared at me while I stared at the spot that my friend was just standing in. *Once I stepped outside of these four walls, my life would not be mine anymore. I would become one of the Seven destined to save the world.*

"Are you ready?" She asked. I could feel her eyes on me.

I finally looked at ALICE. "Nope, but let's go."

I took my first step from my house, and the rain hit my face and shoulders as it landed. I made no effort to shield myself. I let the rain consume me, piercing my eyes. Through the shower, I struggled to find focus, just like my mind struggled to understand reality. I sat in the back seat of the car with ALICE, away from Sarah. Sarah occasionally turned around to look at me, but I gave her no recognition. I knew it seemed stupid to be mad at one of my best friends, but she had been living a lie for five years. I even knew it was for the right reasons, but it still felt like a betrayal. I was also stubborn, so she was going to have to do a lot more than just look at me to gain forgiveness.

"Are you going to tell me what's going on, or are you going to keep staring at me?" I asked my so-called friend.

By now, we had been driving for hours, and the streets looked unfamiliar to me. I glanced at a few signs that may have been familiar, but who knows? My mind could just be trying to hold on to what sanity I had left.

Finally, Sarah answered. She faced forward. Her eyes fixed on the blue truck ahead of us. "Jewels, I never intended to deceive you.

My father was a Refashion that protected the last Secret Seven. But he died in combat. I wanted to do good like him. So they assigned me to protect you at a very young age." Sarah faced me. She seemed younger, more vulnerable. That's not the Sarah I knew.

She took a short pause; then she drilled on to hide the hurt in her voice and eyes. "I can't imagine all the hurt and pain you feel right now, but I want you to understand that all the times we shared together were real. I never faked being your friend. You are truly a special person, and I am proud to have been of service to you."

I just stared at her. Nothing came to mind of what to say but, "Dang, why did you have to say an amazing speech about our friendship. Now I can't hold a grudge against you. But let me guess, you already knew that?"

She gave me a nice-sized smirk. "Yes, I did. Are we okay?"

I returned her smile. "Yeah, we're cool."

"Good," said ALICE "I'm glad you guys made up, because this car ride couldn't get any more boring and awkward."

Everyone gave a gentle laugh; even Vivienne let out her sharp hiccup.

I was finally able to get one of the questions I had off my chest. "Sarah, can you see ALICE?"

Sarah answered, "Only if she wants me to. You two are connected just like the other six are connected to theirs. That's why you can see her all the time." Sarah faced forward again. She didn't want me to see her wipe the tears that never fell from her eyes. I felt horrible. I made her revisit a place she tried to forget for so long. As an effort to take her mind off it, I asked, "So when you can't see her, you see a cat?"

"Only if she wants us to see that. She can make people see whatever she wants," Sarah said with a little excitement. She was herself again; I saw it in her hazel eyes.

Vivienne butted in, "Girls, we are going to need to make a pit stop soon. If you guys want some snacks better do it while I'm filling up."

"Snacks sound delicious." ALICE perked up.

I said to her, "I thought you couldn't eat ALICE?"

She laughed, and so did the others. I missed out on the joke. "I can, and it's how I keep my energy up. I eat all the time." ALICE smiled.

I countered, "Well, you don't' look like it."

"I know right, great engineering," ALICE said with a proud smile.

"Indeed," said Vivienne. "It cost a lot too."

We finally reached Wyoming, and it was late by the time Vienne pulled off the freeway to a Conoco gas station. We pulled up, and there was only one car parked at the gas station. The vehicle was a green four-door directly in front of the station. A black truck pulled in after us and parked on the side of the building. After Vivienne parked at the pump, Sarah, ALICE, and I got out of the car to go fuel up on food and drinks. Vivienne stayed to pump the gas in her car. She asked, "Will one of you bring me back a vanilla latte and a Snickers?"

ALICE immediately said, "Yup, putting it on the list."

Vivienne smiled, "Thanks, ALICE."

Her little legs could move at an incredible speed. I said, "ALICE, would you slow down? We have plenty of time to select what we want."

She said, "It looks like I'm walking fast because you are walking way too slow."

I rolled my eyes and realized she was going to do what she wanted. ALICE walked ahead of us, so I grabbed Sarah's arm. She turned to me. "What's going on?"

I still loved Sarah, and I wanted her to know it. "Hey, I'm sorry about your dad. I remember you telling me he was gone, but I didn't know it was from fighting the biggest war of the century." Her eyes filled with tears as she said what her heart didn't mean, "It's all right—it happened when I was young. I don't remember him really." A sudden crackle and pop filled our ears as lightning struck a tree behind the gas station. Smoke rose from the shredded tree, and a small spark ignited. Then the rain pour emerged with intensity. The fire was quickly contained in the rain. Sarah and I turned from the tree and glanced at each other. My smile dropped from my face.

I watched as a figure dressed in all black came up behind Sarah and hit her with a purple spark to the head. She went down before I had a chance to move my arms to catch her. My body couldn't move or cry for help. I just stood there as I watched my friend's body go limp and hit the hard pavement.

The figure held a cold and hard object to my stomach and ushered me to move. Out of amazement, my feet moved one after the other until I was next to the black truck. My head felt heavy, and my eyes were blurry from the tears that filled them. "Get in the car, Jewels." I knew that voice. It was familiar and yet so hard to place. Why couldn't I figure it out? Maybe it has something to do with the gun pointed at my back. His voice was soft and yet demanding. Ray Starling. It must be. I turned around, and sure enough, it was him. He carried the same smile on his face. The one he had when I first met him. The one that appeared false.

He ordered, "Jewels, I need you to get into my car."

I finally could muffle up a word. I do mean a single word. "No!"

He gave a deep belly laugh, one that did not seem to fit him at all. "Are you serious? No, that's all you can say?"

"Well, I can say more, but I don't speak with profanity." I crossed my arms and looked him in the eyes. I wished Vivienne or ALICE would come now.

"Get in!" he shouted.

I had all I could take at this point. "You know, I'm really tired of people telling me what to do." I shouted back.

He reached for one of my crossed arms. I took a step back to get away from his grasp. At the same time, a loud ring echoed through the night sky. I covered my ears and shut my eyes as the ringing continued to bellow. When I opened my eyes, I saw Ray with a gunshot wound to the stomach. He did not drop to the ground or show any inclination that he had been shot. Instead, he healed himself with white sparks, which radiated over his body as he turned around and pointed the gun at Vivienne.

She ran for cover as he emptied his magazine. I saw my opportunity and ran to Sarah, who was still on the ground with a purple glow escaping from her body. I didn't see her getting up anytime soon, so

I grabbed her arms and pulled her toward Vivienne's car. I looked back, and Vivienne was stuck behind the small green four-door car as Ray rained bullets down on Vivienne. When he finally stopped, I thought he was going to run to his car, but his hands exhaled a white glow that glided right toward Vivienne. As if on cue, ALICE jumped in front of the blast and shielded Vivienne from it.

ALICE's body turned bright yellow as she shielded Vivienne from death. Every inch of her radiated like the sun. Her body seemed to suck up the white fire, and when Ray was finished, she turned his white blast back to him. He jumped out of the way but didn't make it far. ALICE hit him. The explosion could be heard for miles. So could the sirens that were headed toward us. Ray hobbled to his truck. His car made a loud screech as it burnt rubber and left smoke.

ALICE helped Vivienne up from the ground, and they both ran to her car. To my surprise, ALICE picked Sarah up and placed her drenched body in the back seat and held her. I jumped in the front seat. Vivienne seemed flustered. No one talked in the car, but we all wanted to say something. Well, except Sarah, who was knocked out. I hoped that she was not seriously injured.

I glanced through the rear window and noticed law enforcement arriving at the gas station. The whole ride, I was worried about getting pulled over. What seemed like forever was only fifteen minutes before we found a hotel. Vivienne told us to stay put as she went inside to get us a room.

So as not to attract any unwanted attention, Vivienne came out and told us to go through the side door. Our room was spacious, with two beds and a couch. There also was a separate section that had the bathroom, closet, fridge, and microwave. ALICE set Sarah down on one of the beds. Vivienne walked over and started her healing process. Like before, she moved her hands over Sarah in a circular motion.

She looked at me. "Whatever that guy did to Sarah penetrated deep within her body."

I corrected her, "His name is Ray. Ray Starling."

Vivienne said, "Whatever his name is, he messed with Sarah. She is fighting hard to stay away from his power. He cast a shadow over her mind that hinders her in a world of chaos and pain."

I asked through my tears, "Can you help her?"

Vivienne's voice was comforting. "I'm trying. I must first heal each section of her mind. But she has to keep fighting while I heal her."

I grabbed Sarah's hand and kneeled next to her. "Come on, Sarah, I know you can fight this. You always told me never to give up. Now I'm telling you. If anyone can beat this, it's you." But she didn't wake up. She just laid there as I stared at her. ALICE tried to busy herself by moving our bags into the room. Then she moved them next to the beds. She finally decided to place them on the couch, and she sat there, just staring as if she were frozen.

A New Awakening

I don't remember falling asleep, but somehow, I woke up in the bed next to Sarah. I turned toward her, and she was staring up at the ceiling. She was awake, alive!

I hugged her, "Sarah, are you okay?"

She quietly answered, "Honestly, I don't know. I feel like something happened to me, but I can't remember anything after seeing stars."

I told her, "A lot happened after you got knocked out."

"Really?" She couldn't recall what happened.

"Yeah, Ray—"

Vivienne cut me off. "She needs to rest some more. She took a nasty hit when she fell."

Sarah looked at me and asked, "So you're telling me that after I was knocked out, you didn't try to catch me?"

I gave a strained smile. "Sorry, I couldn't move. Besides, I didn't realize what was happening until after you fell."

She rolled over on her side, "I'm going back to bed."

Vivienne spoke once more, "Good, we leave at twelve. We need to get on the road."

As soon as Sarah turned over, she was back asleep. I whispered to Vivienne, "Where are we going?"

She replied, "To a safe house in North Dakota. From there, we go to Manitoba, Canada. Then we take a plane to Nunavut, Canada." That's a strange name for a town.

I asked her, "Nunavut, Canada. Is that where we're from?"

She responded, "Not really, our people live there because other areas were unsafe for us."

I pressed forward for answers. "So Nunavut is a sanctuary?"

Vivienne exclaimed, "Exactly. It was inhabited in 1999 by humans, but we've lived there way longer."

I asked her, "Isn't it cold there?"

She agreed. "Very, that's why we created a place underground."
I frowned. "You what?"

She assured me. "Don't worry, it's safe."

"No, being above ground is safe. Where there is air and space to move. Living underground is just asking to die," I remarked.

With all the technology they possessed, they couldn't create a secret hideout in the jungle, with an invisible shield?

Suddenly, ALICE entered with four plates full of breakfast food. I was famished, "Ah, thank you. It's like you read my mind." I smiled.

She looked confused then smirked, "Oh, did you think this food was for you, silly child."

Now I was confused, and my stomach groaned from the excitement of having food. She had to be kidding. "Are you for real?"

Jokingly, she said, "Of course not. Here's your plate." She then handed another plate to Vivienne, who was surfing the Internet for who knows what.

"You can pass me my food too." We all jumped at the sound of Sarah's voice. She just shrugged her shoulders. "What? I can't sleep well if I smell food."

She's telling the truth. Sarah's a light sleeper and wakes at the mention of food. When I first slept over her house, her mom made pancakes, and she didn't bother telling me. In fact, Sarah would have left me sleeping if it wasn't for the fact that she forgot I was sleeping on the floor. She stepped on my head, and I yelped in pain. Her response, "Oh, sorry. I didn't see you there. Mom made breakfast if you want to come down." I was purely stunned by her then and still am now.

We would have eaten in silence except ALICE entertained us with a story about a guest who had a *live* monkey on his shoulder downstairs in the dining room. She kept stressing the living part. As if monkeys are not living creatures. The story ended with the monkey drinking from the orange juice dispenser and snacking on the pancakes. She said, "That's why we are eating apple juice and waffles for breakfast." I couldn't hold in my snickers any longer. She was an amazing person. Even if androids didn't classify as human beings.

After breakfast, we got ready for the drive to North Dakota. I mentioned to Vivienne the option of taking a plane to Canada, but she said driving closer to the destination was safer than taking a flight straight there. Too many things could go wrong. I reminded her of our run-in with Ray, and she replied with, "Imagine if we were on a plane with him." Out in the car, ALICE was packing our bags in the trunk. Vivienne was putting our destination in the GPS. Sarah and I were sitting on the sidewalk, waiting to leave. Sarah finally asked me, "So what happened?"

I hesitated but told her, "You won't believe it. Or maybe you will. Anyway, Ray is the one who knocked you out."

Sarah acted like she didn't believe me, "Really? He seemed odd, but I wouldn't have taken him for a bad guy." How naïve could she be? I saw the truth from day one.

"He also healed himself when Vivienne shot him in the stomach," I informed her. "His skin created white sparks while he was moving, and they healed him. The bullet wound didn't seem to affect him at all," I said out of breath.

Sarah laughed. "Let's see him heal himself from a gunshot wound to the head." She finally seemed to realize Ray was no angel.

I laughed with her. "Oh, no, you didn't. Savage, girl."

The car started, and that was our cue to get in. We drove off and headed for the interstate once again. Wyoming was pretty to look at. Their close-knit towns felt warm and cozy. Occasionally, we passed farmland filled with cows and horses. Other times, we saw tractors on the road.

The trip would take a total of twelve hours and forty-one minutes, and that's without traffic and detours. I'm *so* pumped. ALICE, of course, tried to distract us with facts and jokes, but it became old quickly. We were all in an agreement to mute her voice box. She didn't like that. She decided to go into sleep mode instead. Even better.

We were now five and a half hours into the trip. We had reached South Dakota and still had seven hours and fifteen minutes to go. I was tired and felt the need to scream again. I missed my dad but couldn't show it. I was sure Sarah missed her mom, but she was not making a big deal about it. And I was sure Vivienne was tired of driving, but I didn't hear one complaint from her. As for ALICE, she was back on board, but there was less chatter from her. I felt like the quicker we got to our destination, the quicker I could get my life back.

"Anyone hungry?" asked Vivienne.

"I thought we established that I'm always hungry," ALICE said.

The car was filled with laughter once more. We kept up a conversation for another thirty minutes until we found an exit that had lots of food stops. We decided on DQ Grill and Chill Restaurant. Our waiter was a down-to-earth girl named Stacey. She was short with mocha skin and had a dream of becoming a famous screenwriter. I had promised to watch out for her films one day. Stacey recommended the milkshakes and fries, which I ended up loving.

Then we were back on the road, trying to finish the last seven hours. By the time we made it to Bismarck, North Dakota, it was almost one in the morning. I was beat. Thankfully, Vivienne had a nice house here, so we crashed at her place. It was on Sorrento Circle and had four bedrooms and three baths. I couldn't tell much from the outside since its dark. Apparently, it's a decent-sized house.

We all were given our separate beds, which I enjoyed. "Good night, everyone. Get some much-needed rest. We have a big day ahead of us." Everyone said good night to Vivienne. When ALICE and Sarah were out of earshot, I turned around. "Hey, Vivienne. You did some great driving these past two days. You also kicked some serious butt back there." She turned to look at me. "Thanks, Jewels. It means a lot."

The Next Day

The smell of biscuits broke the morning air. I walked out of my room into the hallway and got a good look at Vivienne's second home. It was grand with tall ceilings and light gray colored walls. She had wood flooring that was tan in color. The hallway opened to the kitchen, where there was a marbled island with white chairs and cabinets to match. What seemed weird to me was that I found no red anywhere. In fact, there were no personal items displayed anywhere.

The living room/family room was boring as well. It connected to the kitchen, and she had a white-colored carpet with white leather couches. They had purple striped throw pillows on them.

Vivienne greeted me with a warm smile. "Good morning, Jewels. How did you sleep?"

"I slept great. You know, I pictured you with a red house." I joked.

She gave a slight hiccup. "Yeah, this is not my cup of tea. It's nice, but not my home."

This was puzzling. "So this house, you don't own?"

She said, "Nope, it's a safe house until we make it to Canada."

A sharp yawn came from the hallway as Sarah stepped out. She stretched while speaking. "I haven't slept that good since we left."

I smiled. "I can tell, you're usually up before me."

She looked confused. "Where's ALICE?"

"I'm glad you asked. I went out to search the area to make sure everything is okay," ALICE said as she came through the back door.

"That's very helpful. Did you see anything unusual?" Vivienne asked.

ALICE answered, "Matter of fact, I did. The mailman didn't get chased by any dogs. They always get chased in the movies."

Sarah laughed, "Oh, ALICE. You know everything, but still know little."

She cared little about that remark. "Anyways, let's eat. I'm starving," ALICE boasted.

"ALICE, you're always hungry," Sarah snapped. Sarah and I exchanged a glance as our devious grins stretched from ear to ear.

"I called a cab, and he should be here at twelve to take us to Bismarck Municipal Airport," Vivienne informed us. She clearly missed the fun.

"Wait, are we riding in a private plane?" I asked.

"Yes, only the best for our Crypto-hept," Vivienne said, smiling.

"Our what?" I asked her.

"Secret Seven," she explained. Yup, that totally makes sense.

After breakfast, I walked back into my room and looked out the window. Two lark bunting birds were sitting in a nest high up in a dead tree. Their coats were jet black with just enough white showing on their wings. Funny enough, they were looking to create a life with their eggs, but they chose a dead tree as their home.

I heard a soft knock come from the other side of my door. "Come in."

Sarah asked as she entered, "Hey, how are you feeling?"

I muttered, "Okay, I guess, just drained."

She said, "Ah, me too. I know we haven't been able to talk about your powers lately."

I tried to sound indifferent. "If I'm honest, I almost forgot about that."

Sarah was taken aback. "How could you forget that you have powers? That's like forgetting how to breathe. No pun intended."

"What would I do without you?" I said through my chuckle.

She said, "I ask myself the same thing. We probably should get dressed. Since the cab will be here soon."

I smiled at her. "Yeah, you're right. See you soon."

She walked out as quietly as she came in. Once again, it was just the birds and me. They had a lot to say, unlike me. I felt the need to talk more, but what could I say without being a nuisance. I was sure the other six are strong and can handle what has been giving to them. I was just thrown into this. I was expected to defeat a darkness that didn't seem to die. Regardless, I would give my all. I just had to find my dad and Keith. Then I could defeat the Scourger King once and for all.

The ride to the airport was a short one. We boarded the Challenger 604. When Vivienne said only the best, she meant it. The Challenger 604 was a luxurious plane made to fit nine to sixteen passengers. Our jet transferred six seats into sleeping arrangements. There was an oversized couch on one side of the jet. Two flight attendants, two pilots, and two masseuses were on board. If that wasn't enough, there were TVs placed at every station and three small bedrooms. The inside had brown marble installed throughout, and the seats were creamed leather. I was going to love the next four hours. I had never been on a plane before, so this was the best first experience ever. When we flew over the Hudson Bay, I promise, I saw a large fishing boat sailing through that looked the size of my nail.

I felt at peace up in the air, where everything else seemed small. I should have flown before because this was an exhilarating feeling. Even ALICE felt at home. I think it had something to do with the all you can eat menu. As usual, she ate three times as much as any of us. Sarah and Vivienne spent their flight time getting deep tissue massages.

After Vivienne finished with her massage, I asked her a few questions that were on my mind.

"Vivienne?" I called.

"Yes?" She was seated in one of the chairs. Her eyes were closed.

"How are you guys able to afford all of this: the plane, the car, the house, and the hotels?" I asked.

She answered through closed eyes, "We make our own money." One of her eyes opened, and she was watching my reaction.

"What?" That's all I could say.

"I'm messing with you." She finally sat up and looked at me. "We have private investors. We help them invent new creams for cures, and in turn, they provide us with resources to sustain us."

I was interested in this. "Wow, do the people of Nunavut help too?"

She nodded. "Yes, they help shield us from visitors."

I took her zealous attitude as an opportunity to ask more questions. "I have another question."

Vivienne was patient. "Okay."

I pressed on, "Do our pilots know about us?"

She responded with a smile. Her smile proved that I wasn't in the loop. "Yes. This is our plane."

I wanted to know more. "Who are they?"

She explained, "The pilots are Jerad and Thomas. They've had several jobs over the years. Working closely with the Queen. The massage therapists are Kristy and Hester. Our air hostess is Amanda."

"Okay. That's nice to know. I'm not complaining about all the nice treatment. I just wanted to make sure you didn't rob banks for a living."

Sarah snorted at my comment.

"Ladies, we are now entering our final approach. Please prepare for landing." One of the pilots said over the intercom.

I buckled my seatbelt. The hostess, Amanda, came by and collected our drinks and any plates that we had. We were landing in Kimmirut, a tiny community in the Qikiqtaaluk Region of Nunavut, Canada. Kimmirut was on the shores of Hudson Strait. We finally made it to the Kimmirut Airport.

I liked going up in a plane, but coming down was another story. I didn't like the stomach drop feeling. When the seat belt signs turned off, everyone got up and stretched. Vivienne walked up the aisle, saying, "Guys, I have some heavy snow jackets you might want to wear. It's cold here, especially in August."

Sarah placed the heavy black jacket on, "Thanks, Vivienne."

"Yeah, this has been a great ride," I said as I grabbed a snow jacket from her.

"I'm glad to hear it." Vivienne smiled. When she did, you could see why she was Refashion. She glowed, and it was beautiful.

We stepped off the plane and immediately felt how cold it was. I was from Colorado, but this was a new level of cold.

Vivienne turned back to us on the steps. "I told you it's cold here."

It didn't help that the wind was blowing thirty-nine-degrees Fahrenheit weather, right in our direction. I had to yell to be heard over the wind, "Yes, you did," I said to her.

There was a blue car waiting for us on the tarmac. A young man in his twenties came and took our bags and put them in the trunk. The inside of the car welcomed us with warmth. I asked through freezing lips, "Why does the sanctuary have to be in one of the coldest places on earth? You couldn't have picked Hawaii or the Caribbean?"

Sarah joined in, "For real. We were only outside for five minutes, but I can't feel my butt. Jewels, your face is red, especially your nose. You are officially Rudolf."

I laughed, "Look who's talking, miss tomato."

ALICE decided to chime in. "I don't know why you guys are complaining about the cold?"

I said, "Are you kidding me, ALICE, it's freezing out here."

Sarah teased. "She's joking Jewels, she's a computer, remember? She can't feel anything. Unless we decide to shock her with electricity."

I played along. "That sounds like a good idea."

ALICE trembled slightly. "Jewels, don't even think about it."

Sarah and I looked at each other then at ALICE. We were rubbing our gloved hands together, trying to spook her.

Vivienne intervened, "Ladies, please."

Sarah whined, "Sorry, Mom."

I snickered, "Nice one, Sarah."

"Let's just get through this ride without any incidence, yes?" Vivienne's face was redder than everyone's combined. I bet at this very moment she hated the color red.

"How long will it take us to reach our destination?" I felt cooped.

Vivienne said, "About an hour or two. We are going out where the mountains are. There is a hidden passage behind one of them."

"Then it's underground. Oh, I just can't wait," I said through chattered teeth and as much sarcasm I could muster.

Vivienne said, "Jewels trust me; you will be fine."

The thought hit me like a lightning bolt. "Vivienne, can we trust our driver?" I whispered.

Vivienne said without hesitation, "Yes. Ladies, this is Ash. He's on the task force. He protects the Queen and the rest of the sanctuary."

Sarah said, "Woah, that's hot."

I shook my head, "Seriously, Sarah?"

She joked, "What? I'm just speaking the truth."

Ash gave a small laugh, indicating he heard her, but he kept his eyes on the road. His eyes were bright yellow, with a hint of orange. His skin was a light caramel, and he had broad shoulders. Another perfect modified human being.

Vivienne asked impatiently, "Can we also get through this ride without anyone hitting on the other?"

Sarah said, "Sure thing, Mom."

When we pulled up to the mountain's entrance, Ash turned around and shouted, "Hold on." I was about to ask why, when the ground shook violently. The car dropped at an alarming speed. A faint scream escaped my small body, one that I soon regretted. I grabbed the door handle to hold on, but it didn't help much. We were going too fast, and my stomach was aching from the immediate drop. I could see Ash smirking at me from the review mirror.

I looked around the car, and Vivienne seemed to be fine; so was ALICE Sarah had her hands in the air to simulate a real roller coaster ride. Was I the only one who felt a certain death? The sun roof's cover was drawn back. I looked up to see if that would help. But when I looked, I didn't see sunlight, I saw darkness and what seemed like stars. We were far down, and I was sweating, and fear took over once more. I tried to fight it, but it was no use. My vision blurred, and I heard ALICE's mumbled voice, "Jewels, you okay?" Then I felt something hard, and I blacked out.

THE GREAT HALL

When I awoke, all the images beforehand rushed to my brain and caused me to feel light-headed once more. I grabbed my head and remembered hitting it on something hard. I tried to focus on one object in the room and found a tree-shaped lamp with moss growing on the trunk. The tree looked very real to me. Not an imitation that you would find in a home goods store. Then I noticed the desk it was placed on. It was made from redwood and had a note neatly folded on it. I grabbed the letter, which was written on a leaf.

> There are fresh clothes at the end of the bed for you. Also, when you finish readying yourself, please ask for directions to the Great Hall.
>
> Thank you,
> Beetly

What an interesting name. I slowly pulled the covers off me and moved my feet off the side of the bed. I took one step off the bed and felt the soft carpet, but it wasn't carpet. I was surprised to find a bed of purple saxifrage put together with vines. It was the most beautiful and softest thing I have ever stepped on. I found the clothes at the end of my bed, which were white pants and a shirt that seemed too big. I walked over to the bathroom and found a washcloth and soap and decided to take a shower. The water was warm but not warm enough. Maybe it had something to do with being underground? Either way, I didn't stay in it long. I quickly dried off and tried on the clothes that were left for me. Like I suspected, they were way too big. I barely took a step before my pants fell to the ground. I looked through the room, trying to locate my bag of clothes.

The room was dome shaped, filled with wonder. The walls were made of clay and dirt but had a sweet smell. Like flowers and honey.

There were several purple saxifrages in vases placed throughout the room. A painting of a storm at sea was hanging on the wall.

I turned once more and found my bag placed on a couch made from wood and flowers. The wood wasn't neat, like from a manufacturer. It was handcrafted. It had bends and twists all through, and the flowers were compacted to make a nice cushion.

I walked over to my bag and pulled out several shirts before I found a pair of white jeans. I slipped them on and decided to go with a white shirt. Since they gave me white to wear. I was almost dressed how they wanted me to be. The only differences were the texture and look of my clothes. I took one last glance in the stand-up mirror and decided I looked fine. My hair was up in a high ponytail, which wet my back from the shower. I wanted to dry it, but I couldn't find a dryer in this compacted space. Then I remembered I had powers and tried to blow dry my hair. I took my hair out of the ponytail, and it sat wet on my shoulders. I pictured the water evaporating and my hair sitting perfectly dry on my shoulders. What came next, I wasn't prepared for. My hair shot to the ceiling as a gust of air dried it with the speed of light. Even my shirt was dry. I was proud of my success until I realized my hair was standing straight up. I yanked on my hair to come down and tried to pull it into a ponytail. My hair was dried, but it looked like a mangy mess. I gave up trying to fix it and decided to go to the Great Hall.

I stepped from the redwood door and poked my head around the corner. I saw no one and decided it was safe to exit. I turned left, and the room opened to a well-lit hallway. The walls were the same red clay as my room. The lights were small fireballs that levitated inside a glass jar hanging from the wall. My mind tried to wrap around the possibility of what I was seeing. I thought I would be used to this kind of stuff, between Vivienne's powers and the purple mist, but it still amazed me.

The hall was concluded by another red-colored wooden door. I pulled on the door, and it opened into another hallway. Except this one was filled with people going in and out of different rooms. I noticed these human beings weren't normal. They looked perfect; they all were different and yet similar in some way. Some were short, and others were tall. Some were thin others carried more weight on them. But they still were perfect. Their faces held a sense of urgency as they bustled through the hall. Only a few stopped to look at me.

I also noticed their outfit choices. Some wore green; others, blue. They also had some in black and gray. A small lady passing by me had on a light orange sheer dress with goddess sandals made from brown vines. She stopped and smiled at me. "Can I help you, dearie?"

I returned her warm smile with a nod. "Yes, I'm looking for the Great Hall. Do you know—"

She cut me off in an instant. "Say no more, I will take you there myself. But first, we need to change your clothes." She looked me up and down with a disapproving smile. I felt the need to explain myself.

"Oh no, I tried on the clothes, but they were too big for me." She walked away, and I struggled to keep up with her.

"That's all right, dearie, I can fix that."

For a small woman, she walked fast. Her feet never seemed to touch the floor. She was graceful in her step and how she carried herself. Without me having to tell her where I lived, she found her way to my quarters. She was about to open my door when I noticed a unique insignia placed at the center of it.

"What does that mean?" I asked her. She stopped midway and glanced in the direction I was pointing. Then she smiled.

"That is your symbol and your symbol alone. It means air." It was beautiful. The symbol was enclosed within a thick circle. Three evenly spaced swirls surrounded a triangle that was cut in two by a line. Looking at the emblem made me feel a part of something greater. Not just the war but my ancestry.

She opened the door further and ushered me to follow. She shut the door closed with a soft knock, unlike what I had done previously. "Now then, show me your outfit." I was suddenly overcome with embarrassment as I looked back at my room. I didn't realize the gust of wind had knocked over the white outfit and the bedsheet. She just gave me a smile and cleaned up.

"Are you just going to stare, dearie?" she asked. I immediately picked up my clothes and stuffed them back in my bag. I found the white outfit lying on the floor in a tangled mess. The small women walked over to me and gently took the clothes from my hand and laid it on the bed.

Sternly she ordered, "Now then, take off your clothes."

I blushed and looked down at my feet. She seemed to catch on but didn't care, "I've seen everything, dearie." She pulled my shirt off and placed the large white shirt over my head. I pulled my arms through the slots and stared at her.

She asked me, "Do you want me to take your pants off too?" I quickly grabbed my waistband and rushed my pants off. She handed me the white pants, and I hopped while putting them on. Her laugh was a shock. I half expected a squeak because she was so small. However, it was a deep growl like an animal's laugh. She smiled at me and turned me a full circle before deciding what to do. "Dearie, you are a small thing."

I smiled. I loved how she called me *dearie*. Every time she said it, it was like honey pouring out of her mouth. Sweet and slick. It made me feel safe and warm. I realized I never got her name or vice versa. So I said, "Hello, my name is Jewels."

She smiled warmly, "Nice to meet you, Jewels. My name is Saraphine. I am from the anima side of the earth."

What was that? "Anima?" I repeated.

She smiled, the same sweet smile. "Yes, meaning spirit. Animal spirit."

I suddenly understood, "Oh, wow. Can you do anything special?"

She smirked. "Yes, I can fix your outfit." I was taken back. I don't know if she was joking or being totally serious. But I didn't want to hurt her feelings because she was the only one who was willing to stop and talk to me.

"Thank you, that would be great." She laughed again, and it was louder than the first time. I jumped back at its power, and she stopped and stared at me. I felt sheepish and lowered my head once more. "It's all right, dearie, I am not going to hurt you." I stared into her milk chocolate eyes and felt as ease. She pulled needles from a small brown sack that she was carrying and pinned my clothes. She worked at an incredible speed. I wanted to know more about her and where I was. But I didn't want to interrupt her. She seemed to be in her own world. It was only a short period before she told me to take the pants off. Saraphine worked on the hem. I think I blinked, and she was telling me to put them back on. I was stunned, and my jaw dropped.

Her laugh broke the silence; this time I didn't jump. I felt like this was an excellent time to ask her questions. "Saraphine, how old are you? If you do not mind my asking."

She smiled at the thought. "I will be fifty soon." I took a double-take and stared at her again. She looked gorgeous, youthful, and full of life. How was this possible?

"How—"

She cut me off yet again.

"Modified human beings can control their genes. Like an immortal jellyfish. We last longer than any human being. Once we hit a certain age, we slow the aging process. We don't even get sick. Did your parents not tell you this?"

At that moment, I remembered that my dad was taken from me and that my mom left me when I was little. All the sadness that was creeping below the surface rushed to the top, and I let out a small cry. Saraphine grabbed ahold of me, and she rocked me back and forth as we sat on the bed.

She softly said, "I'm sorry. I did not mean to make you upset."

I tried to muscle up words, but they came out as a croak. "It's okay." But it wasn't.

She again took charge. "Well then, let me get you dressed. You don't want to be late."

I regained myself and ask the question that had been on my mind since I woke up. "What day is it?"

Saraphine looked at me and said, "August 17."

I shook my head. "I slept through a whole day."

Saraphine recognized the shock on my face and rubbed my back. "It's all right, dearie. One day of sleep is not bad."

I stood and faced Saraphine. "Well, how do I look?" I was done sulking.

She smiled at me. "Wonderful. Now then, let me take you to the Great Hall."

She pulled open the heavy door with ease. I walked through, and she followed. Without turning back, she shut the door, "Pay attention, dearie, you may have to find this place on your own next time." We traveled the same way I went before. The same redwood door that lead to a crowd of Refashion was less crowded now. She then opened the third door on the right. The room was a grand library. All the books were written on green paper and neatly placed between vines. The room used the same red clay and fireballs from the hall. The ceiling was far from reachable, at least forty feet from the ground, and the depth was even greater. To access the different levels, you had to climb stairs made of wood and vines wrapped with pink and white tulip flowers.

She talked as we walked. "This is a short cut, dearie. The interesting thing about the library, we have every book ever written under the sun."

"Wow, that's amazing,"

"This way, dearie."

She brought me through a smaller door. This door led to an open hallway. The hall turned into an open circular area where you could look over the balcony and see the floors below. We were on the top floor. I glanced at the ceiling made of clay. There was no sunshine. Just the hum of the red fireballs dancing in their cages.

We continued to walk until we came to the stairs. They were made up of rock, rubies, and emeralds. I almost didn't want to step on them. But Saraphine glided down like it was an everyday occurrence to walk on expensive and valuable jewels. I stumbled after her. She suddenly stopped, and I bumped into her.

My mishap had no effect or her small body, and I bounced right off, smacking my butt on the stairs. Saraphine turned around and gave a slight snarl of laughter. "Sorry, dearie. I will give you better warning next time." She picked me up with one hand and turned back, giving something else her attention. I looked in her direction, and I found two men in black suits made of rubber and cloth walking a large man down the hall. The man's face was covered with a black bag. He was thrashing and screeching, trying to break free. Saraphine watched me as I looked at the man. "All right, dearie, we need to be moving on." She continued down the steps with urgency.

I hurried after her. I kept looking back. "Who was that?"

She ignored my question with her own. "How was your trip?"

I tried putting the conversation back on what I wanted to know. "Was he a prisoner?"

She was better at averting than I was. "We're here. Now you go in there and make a great first impression. I will see you around." Swiftly as she came into my life, she was gone. I watched as she disappeared and noticed she walked fast, faster than she initially did with me.

I pulled the large door open and crept my head through. Everyone in the room turned to look at me. I pulled the door open all the way and stepped through. The name fit the image. The room was like no other room I had seen so far. The walls were made of glass, and there was a large garden behind the glass. I could see animals of all kinds in there, along with different terrariums to hold their temperatures needed for their survival. The floor of the Great Hall was like the stairs without the rocks, just jewels and rubies. The table was pure mahogany and never seemed to end. The chairs matched to perfection with a flowery cushion for seating. There were four other tables just like it. In the far corner, there was a large water fountain with fish of all kinds. Surrounding the water fountain were round mahogany tables.

The light in this room was brighter than the hall, a clear yellow like the sun. I looked at the end of the table and saw six other modified humans sitting down. There were three girls and three boys placed evenly in the seats. I was late, but none of them seemed to mind. A girl of average height stood up and walked over to me. "Hi, I'm Gwendolyn Sparks. You can sit next to me." She was gorgeous. She was of Latin descent, and she had hazel eyes with a hint of orange in them.

She grabbed my arm and pulled me over to the table. I noticed all our outfits were different. Gwendolyn was wearing a light-brown shirt with dark-brown pants. The texture seemed rough and itchy. They seemed to fit perfectly on her body, though. She even had jewelry on. Her earrings were a gleaming marble brown rock with a necklace to match.

Across from her was a boy. He looked nineteen, but after meeting Saraphine, he could be any age. He was perfect. His skin was dark chocolate, and his jawline was sharp. His eyes were shamrock green with just a hint of gingerbread. He saw me staring and gave a small smirk. "I'm Derek Collister." His voice was like Saraphine's; it invited you in. It was warm and smooth. Derek wore a sleeveless dark-green shirt that showed off his muscles. Unlike Saraphine, he had no problem showing off. The texture of his uniform was different from mine or Gwendolyn's. His were made of leaves and twigs, soft but rough looking.

A girl wearing a bright red outfit was next to Derek. Her attire was a jumpsuit of sheer cloth. Underneath the jumpsuit was a black skintight tank top and shorts. Her jet-black hair popped off the red and her pale skin. "I'm Flair Manser, and I control fire. Hot Stuff next to me controls plants." She was pointing at Derek. He looked back at Flair.

"Now why did you tell her that? I wanted to see if she could guess what we were based on our outfits." He looked at me. "It's quite easy, you know."

Gwendolyn spoke next. "Derek, if you want to make a good impression, I suggest you keep your thoughts to yourself."

Derek winced in response and spoke with sarcasm. "Oh, how you wound me, my dear."

Impatiently another voice spoke. "Anyways, my name is Annora Wilcocks." Annora's outfit was a baby-blue cotton silk shirt with navy-blue shorts that hugged her legs. The only jewelry she had on her was a ring shaped like a dolphin. She was milk chocolate compared to Derek. She was elegant in how she moved. Everything seemed to come naturally.

I took the chance to speak. "Let me guess, you can control water?"

Derek clapped, and Annora nodded her perfect head. "Exactly." She smiled.

Up next was a hefty guy. His body was filled with muscles that bulged when he moved. Even though he seemed hard and mean, his face gave off a softer tone.

"Hey, my name is Octavion Eason." His voice matched his body, deep and slightly ragged. His outfit was a pale orange and seemed flexible to fit his large physique.

"What can you do?" I was at a loss.

He chuckled, "I can shapeshift into different animals." He leaned back in his chair with pride written all over his face.

"Neat, can you show me?" I asked.

Gwendolyn interjected and said, "We are not allowed to use our powers right now."

Last but certainly not least was Quint. He controlled light. He seemed imperfectly perfect. He wasn't quite like the others. More like me. I've been told on separate occasions that I was beautiful, but everyone here made me seem average. The same went for him. He had small areas of freckles on his cheek and arms. Pure ginger. He was beautiful but not perfect. His outfit was like mine, a T-shirt, and pants made from soft cotton that floated on the body like a cloud.

Everyone sitting at the table seemed to fit with each other. I asked, "Have you guys been friends for a long time?"

Gwendolyn spoke for the group. "Yes, we've lived here our whole life. Best friends. Never would have thought to be the Crypto-Hept."

Derek added, "Yeah, except Quint is like you, from the outside." I looked over at Quint. His face never changed. I wanted to ask him where he was from, but he never looked up from the table.

The door whooshed open, and a short man walked into the room. He barely reached the height of the table. Even so, he was perfect. His eyes were green with yellow surrounding the outer ring of his iris. His voice was quick and pleasant. His outfit choice, on the other hand, was out there, compared to what I had seen so far. He was wearing a shimmery brown vest and a green blazer over it. His blazer had two tails extending the coat. Like a cockroach's shell. His capri pants were black silk and showed his white socks.

"Hello, my name is Beetly, and I will be your advisor through-out your training days. I will also be here if you need anything else outside of training. To start off, I would like everyone to stand and follow me." We all stood and walked after him. Of course, I was the last to follow, trying to catch up. I got a chance to look at Quint's walk, which didn't seem as uniformed as everyone else's.

Beetly escorted us to the end of the Great Hall and opened the door that took us to another hallway. We went down two levels. He opened another door, and a tall woman was standing in the center of it. She was wearing a lime-green dress that was embroiled with diamonds and a train that flowed beyond her height. Her shoulders were covered in a lime laced sleeve with small white flowers at the ends. Her hair was long and black. Her hair was braided into several smaller braids looping together to make one large braid. There was a sheer white cape attached to her dress that was laced with flowers at the end. She turned around to greet us. Her skin was pure caramel. Smooth and perfect. Her smile was filled with white teeth. Her voice was even better than her looks.

"Greetings everyone, I am Nàtàl Mater. Or Mother Nature as others may know." She was looking at Quint and me. I looked at Quint, who looked at me, and we had the same look. Stunned! All this time, she was real. I felt bad. I blamed so many things on her. The others seemed used to her presence. They even clapped for her. Her introduction was meant for the two of us.

She nodded for them to be quiet, and the room fell silent. She entered the space with the warmth of ten Saraphines. "I appreciate your sacrifice to protect me, the others, and the humans. I want you to know you are not alone. When the time comes, and it will, I will be there with you." They roared once more. She raised her hand with little effort.

"You will be practicing for the next few days. Their king has grown strong, but I need you to be stronger. The only way to accom-plish what you are destined for is to work together. I look forward to great things." And then she turned gracefully and walked away through a rear door.

"All right, you heard Nàtàl Mater. We will train immediately. Then tonight, we will have a grand feast, specially prepared for our Crypto-Hept." The others cheered loudly, and this time, Quint and I joined in. Beetly seemed happy as well and let us shout for a while before he ushered us to hush. We walked through a different door than Mother Nature. This one took us to the garden. Once through, I could see the Great Hall above us.

The garden was magnificent in its structure. The first section was a rainforest, and beyond that was a desert. Across from the desert looked like the Arctic Circle. Lastly, there was a section that looked like the African plains. "How are you able to keep these sections intact?" I asked Beetly once everyone had gone through the door.

"Simply, Mother Nature. She doesn't even concentrate really. It's like miniature Earth."

"Beautiful," escaped my jaw-dropped mouth.

Gwendolyn approached me and pointed to the ceiling. I looked in the direction of her finger, and there were two Bonobos in the trees eating bugs from a stick. There also were several different birds flying around. Some native to America; others to the Arctic and Africa. I was utterly taken back with the beauty this place held. Nervously I asked, "Will the animals hurt us?" Octavion let out a sharp laugh that sounded more like a snarl.

"Not at all, they are at peace here. You can be too," Beetly said simply.

"Let's train already," cried Flair. The others nodded in agreement.

"All right, all right. First up is Octavion. We will start with the basics, please. A frog," Beetly instructed.

Octavion seemed at home here in the rainforest. He looked at every creature running around and settled on a red-eyed tree frog nestled on a leaf. He appeared to be studying the delicate creature. When he was satisfied, he turned to us and winked.

FORMATION

I couldn't get over the fact that a large man transformed into a tiny creature. His body shrunk into the shape of a frog with ease. There was no sound of bone cracking or wince of pain coming from him. He just glided into the creature. Beetly was pleased with how Octavion performed and told him to transform back. That was more disturbing. The frog or Octavion enlarged before he shifted back into a human. It was a slow process to watch. Beetly told Octavion with more practice, he would be able to change within seconds. Octavion was pleased with his performance and motioned Beetly to turn up the heat.

"You have to master transformation before taking on larger animals. You could get stuck in between. Now that would be a ghastly sight," Beetly joked with a serious face. We didn't know whether to laugh or shudder.

Beetly pointed to Annora next. She stepped forward while Octavion took his spot next to Derek. Octavion and Derek exchanged a quick high five of approval. We all had to move a little into the forest to find the river. She took off her shoes and stepped into the river. Annora made fluid motions with her whole body. The water climbed and caressed around her ankles, then her knees and finally her waist. When she finished her water dance, she stretched her arms outward, and the water dispersed into mist and sprayed all of us.

"Thanks for the cooldown, Annora. It was getting hot," Flair said with irony and just a hint of sarcasm.

"You're welcome." Annora smiled, pleased with herself. She stepped from the river and placed her shoes in her hand.

She looked at Beetly, who also gave her a satisfactory expression. "Well done, Annora. In no time, you will be able to make hurricanes."

Up next was Derek. We went to the center of the rainforest. Around us lay several types of plants, trees, and vines. There were orchids, banana trees, poinsettia plants, cacao trees, and many more.

Derek stretched out his arms wide, and the world around us moved. The vines shifted; the birds and monkeys reacted to the presence of a live jungle. They hopped and flew to a section that wasn't alive. Derek seemed to put a lot of effort into trying to make the large section of the jungle move.

"Try to start off small. It seems you are straining," Beetly told him. Derek scaled it down until he could gain more control. He chose a smaller section, and the jungle moved with little effort. The flowers closest to him danced in the wind. The trees' leaves thrashed in the air, and the vines climbed to great heights. When Derek finished, everyone clapped for him. Annora whistled. Derek gave a bow and stepped from the center of the forest.

It was Gwendolyn's turn. She had a small physique but carried ten times what Octavion could do with his muscles. We traveled to a remote mountain, allowing her to bend the earth to her will. She stomped her foot, and the ground beneath her rose. It reminded me when the car dropped to get down here, and I felt queasy again.

Once she was several feet off the ground, she took another slab of rock from the ground and jumped to the next piece of land. She then commanded several medium-sized stones to circle her. The rocks created a barrier around her, and nothing could get through. She then threw the rocks at the mountain, and a small avalanche came tumbling down. Everyone except Beetly ducked for cover. Before the rocks could hit us, she stopped them in midair. She then pushed them back into the mountain, like it was clay. Gwendolyn slowly made her descent back to Earth. She received a roar of approval from everyone. I gave a loud yell for her. She returned it with a gentle smile and a wave of the hand.

We then made our way to the desert district, and Quint was next. Beetly wanted him to control the light. Make it darker where he was standing. Quint looked determined and motioned for the light to spread away from where he was standing. The light moved away from him but flickered in and out. Then all together, the light went away, and only where he was standing was darkened. Beetly wrote something down and looked up at Quint. "That's decent. More practice is needed. But don't worry, you will catch up in no time." Quint walked back to his spot, and the crowd gave him a clap. The guys gave him a pat on the back and said something to him. He laughed in response and looked over at me. I immediately felt like they were talking about me, so I faced forward.

Flair was next. Her task seemed simple enough. Make fire. She found a nice heated spot and focused her eyes on it. Her eyes turned from her almost black ones to a raging tiger. They flashed red and orange. Her concentration was intense, and eventually, the fire erupted from the ground. She then attempted to expand the fire and succeeded. The fire was larger than her now. Beetly motioned for her to contain the flame. Instead, it kept growing. The fire expanded fast and too close to the rainforest. Beetly turned toward me. "Jewels, take the oxygen away."

I was put on the spot, and it felt cold. Flair looked at me, not with hate like I had imagined but with helplessness. I shook my head as I tried to gain focus. I imaged the air smothering the fire. That the fire was getting smaller and dying. I was slipping into the trance again but not entirely because I heard loud cheers. Then I felt my feet leave the ground. I opened my eyes, and Octavion had picked me up and was chanting, "She breathes fire."

I joined in the cheering. Then it hit me. "I did what?" I abruptly asked.

Octavion and the rest also looked confused. "Don't you know? You sucked the oxygen from the air, right? Well, you took the fire with you too. Fire breather!" Octavion said with too much excitement. I was stunned. Did I really swallow fire? I didn't even feel it. That's amazing. I found Flair's eyes, and she mouthed "Thanks" to me. I nodded in response. Beetly motioned for Octavion to put me down.

When he did, Beetly turned toward Flair. "Not bad. We just need to work on your recall, yes?" She gave a sheepish nod and walked off back to her spot. Annora gave her a reassuring look.

Beetly pointed to me. "You are up, Fire Breather." I didn't find Beetly's type of humor to be amusing.

For my demonstration, he wanted us to head to the Arctic Circle. At the border were different-colored jackets. We each picked our color. Beetly stopped in front of open water with an iceberg resting in the center. He then turned toward me. "Make wind, and if you can, make a storm." I stepped forward, not sure how to make it windy. So far, I had only taken oxygen away and messed my hair up. But I was willing to try. Besides, Nàtàl Mater was counting on us. I needed to make her proud.

I closed my eyes and imagined the wind sleeping but now awake and thrashing through the sky. Yelping for attention. My body drifted, and I was in my dark but warm space. It pulled me deeper into nothing. Unlike the other times, I couldn't see anything. It was too dark.

I felt a distant hand on my shoulder. I decided to come back to reality and open my eyes. It was Gwendolyn, and she was mouthing something. I couldn't hear her over the sound, and then it hit me. The sound was coming from the sky. It was crying with dark skies and thunder.

I focused on Gwendolyn's words and finally understood what she said, "You can stop now." Immediately, I stopped focusing on the sky. Everything slowly turned back to normal. No more rushing wind, and the clouds were no longer darkened. Just peaceful scenery. Beetly looked at me the same way he looked at Flair and Quint.

"You can start it, but you have a hard time not giving in to it. We will fix that, don't you worry," he said with confidence. I believed him.

Gwendolyn and I walked back to our spots and watched Beetly as he scribbled down information. He looked up at us. "Well, you all did as I expected. Now for the fun part. Come together, everyone. We are going to practice a simulated battle. Your objective, keep this crown from the Scourgers. You will take it to the Green Castle." He tossed the large man's crown at Derek. The crown had three horns on it that bent into a dome. There was a red satin cloth where the head would lay. On the outside were diamonds strategically placed to make the crown sparkle from all angles.

"What is the Green Castle?" we all asked in unison.

Beetly answered, "You'll see." Then he suddenly disappeared into the forest but not before he shouted, "Oh, and complete the task within a thirty-minute timeline."

When we turned around, the scenery changed. The sky was a dark purple with black clouds. The sun was no longer in sight. I couldn't even see one arctic animal.

"Well, there goes my power," shrugged Quint.

"I'm sure we can find you a spark," said Flair.

"How about we get from the center of the field and go over a plan?" bellowed Octavion.

"Okay, let's go over that hill right there," said Derek.

Gwendolyn led the way. She was surrounding us with boulders that she picked from the ground. They moved in a circle, over our heads, and around our bodies. Nothing was getting through us without a scratch or two. We finally made it over the snowy hill and saw a cave on the other side and decided to go into it. The cave didn't go deep. More like a roof without any sidewalls.

"All right, if the castle is green, it has to be in the rainforest where it can camouflage," said Gwendolyn.

"That's smart," Annora said, smiling.

"Way too easy," said Derek.

Annora shot back, "It's the easy things that make people second guess themselves. The castle is definitely there."

"Why don't we just have Gwendolyn fly up above on a rock and see overhead?" They all looked at me after I spoke.

Gwendolyn smirked and gave a small comment. "Sure, put all the pressure on me."

Derek was next. "That's not a bad idea. If she doesn't want to do it, have someone else fly on the rock."

Gwendolyn said defensively, "I was joking, Derek." She seemed upset. "Of course, you were." He gave her a look, which only made Gwendolyn angrier. "I don't have to sit around and listen to your smart mouth." She got up and took a large boulder from the ground. She carefully balanced herself, then she was off. Derek just rolled his eyes. We all stepped from the cave's safety to watch Gwendolyn in the sky. For something so heavy, she made the boulder look like it was lighter than a feather. The rock turned in a circle as she surveyed the landscape. Her head was like a tennis match, bobbing back and forth, trying to locate the castle. "Do you see it yet?'" shouted Flair.

Gwendolyn shouted back, "No, not yet. Maybe I need to go higher?"

Suddenly the sky broke into a loud cry and thrashed the air with a bright light. Gwendolyn lost her focus and tumbled back to Earth. She was trying to get control of the rock, but it was halfway down to the ground. She couldn't stretch her powers that far yet. Once she realized she was in trouble, a high-pitched scream yelped from her mouth.

Flair turned to Octavion. "Do you think you could turn into a large bird and catch her?"

Octavion looked slightly defeated. "I haven't had a chance to study any large birds. But I can talk to them. Let's see if they can make a soft landing for her."

"Do it," Flair demanded. She was careful not to let her nervousness show.

Octavion made a soft bird call that quickly turned into a repetitive vibrating hurry. The sounds came from his throat with such urgency that the birds rushed from their hiding spaces.

They were Arctic Terns. They were beautiful creatures, with blackheads and stuffed white bodies. Their beaks had a little orange spot peeking through all the black. Hundreds of them rose to meet Gwendolyn. They came together, flapping as one. Once the last bird was locked into place, they stopped in midair. Gwendolyn's body dropped on top of the birds, making a dent in the bedding. The birds quickly regained themselves after catching her and made a slow descent to the ground. Gwendolyn's feet hit the ground and then her knees. She gasped for air. Octavion rushed over to her and picked her up by the arms.

"You okay?" He was taller than her, so his neck had to bend at a full ninety-degree angle.

Gwendolyn nodded. "Yeah, thanks a lot."

Quint's voice broke the air. "How are we going to find the castle now? We only have twenty minutes' left?"

Gwendolyn smiled, the same sweet smile. "Actually, I saw the castle before I fell."

Annora interrupted, "Where?"

Gwendolyn picked up, "It's definitely in the rainforest. We need to hurry. I also saw Scourgers in the African plains."

I was stunned. "Real ones?"

They all laughed except Quint, who felt the same as I did about the situation. "No, Fire Breather. This is simulated. Although you can really get hurt," roared Octavion.

"Oh, okay." I felt childish. Of course, they weren't real. Nàtàl wouldn't allow those vile things to come into such a sacred place.

Derek interrupted my thoughts and said, "Let's move. We don't have much time."

We all jogged toward the desert except Annora. She walked to the top of the hill. Once she made it to the very top, she spread her arms out wide and slowly gathered water from the snow below her feet. I was amazed at how easy it came to her. "Come on, you two," shouted Derek. I couldn't see the others anymore. They must be halfway to the desert by now. Derek was waiting by the hill made of moss and massive rocks. Annora quickly trotted from the hill with such grace and sprinted toward Derek. I tried to keep up with her, but she was too fast.

Annora caught up with Derek in no time, and they looked back at me as I attempted to sprint. They didn't look at me any particular way. They just stared with blank expressions. When I finally caught up to them, Derek looked at me and smirked. "Thanks for the small break. Not that I need it, of course."

Annora gave Derek a friendly stare but kept her tone serious. "Don't mess with her—she's not used to running so much." She gave me the same friendly expression but used a kinder tone. "Do you need a lift?"

A lift would be great, but I couldn't have them thinking I couldn't handle the load. After all, I was one of the Seven. "No, I'm good."

She shrugged and turned toward the exit. "Okay, but try to keep up." Like that, she was off again.

Derek was a little slower than Annora but still fast. I trotted after them, managing to stay within a couple of feet. Annora's water moved as fluidly as she did. It never left her side or changed shape from the circle she formed initially. Her concentration was unwavering.

We made it to the edge, and sure enough, the others were waiting in the desert with their jackets off. Gwendolyn stepped forward. "What happened?"

Annora spoke frankly. "Nothing. Jewels is just...well, slow." Gwendolyn laughed and looked me dead in the eyes. I felt exposed. Why was I so different?

"All right, listen up, everyone." Derek was taking over the role of leader. Somehow, he fit the job description. "We need to go through these last two territories fast, and with Jewels on the slower side, we need to help her out."

"I can take care of myself, honestly," I snapped. The last thing I wanted them to think was that I was a child needing guidance. Even so, none of them paid any attention to my remark. Derek just carried on with his speech, as if had I never spoken.

"I thought maybe we have Gwendolyn carry her on one of your rocks. That way, she stays with the group." Derek was proud of his decision.

I, on the other hand, was not. I don't need charity. "Guys, I'm okay. I can keep up." I was trying to be more relaxed. They still ignored me. My blood boiled inside my head.

Gwendolyn agreed with Derek. "Sure thing, and I'm up for the challenge."

I had reached my limit; I was not going to let them carry me the whole way. "Listen!" I yelled. They all stopped and stared at me. "I can keep up. I don't need Gwendolyn to carry me."

Derek smiled. "Good. All right, scratch that, Gwen." Then he said, "We will need a diversion. The closer we get to our mark, the harder it will be. Octavion, you and Annora will lead the front. Gwendolyn and Jewels will hold the rear. Quint and I will hold the sides."

Flair asked, "What about me?"

Derek said, "You have the best part—you're the diversion."

Flair looked overjoyed by that announcement. She hopped from our little huddle and swung her arms back and forth, saying, "Let's do this." After Derek finished explaining the plan further, we walked deeper into the desert.

We stayed in one big group until it was time to execute the plan. Getting through the Desert was easier than I thought it would be. No Scourgers in sight. It was sweltering, but thank goodness Annora decided to bring water with her. She distributed the water to us. We didn't take her gift lightly. I drank every drop that she gave me. By the time we made it to the edge of the territory, she was out of water.

"The African plains are off to the side of the rainforest. Keep an eye out. They will be moving in soon," Gwendolyn said through parched lips.

"Everyone, take your formation," barked Derek.

Gwendolyn grabbed my arm, and we traveled to the back of the pack. Annora and Octavion took the front. Derek took the left side and put Quint on the right. Flair walked ahead of us. She was a good fifteen feet in front. Then she stopped and stared at the ground. The ground ignited and sent a spark to the next twig and so on. Then she gripped some of the fire and created one giant fireball. She threw it into the neighboring trees. The sound was louder than any firecracker. More of a bomb. The ground shook, and the trees were falling. Her fire spread with such ferocity. The air smelt of burnt wood.

Suddenly, the trees started to move once more. As they vibrated, a few leaves fell from their branch. This time it wasn't from Flair's fire. They came at us with such speed. Describing a Scourger was not easy. They are solid and yet look like mist. They are black and gray vile beings with the ability to transform. A couple of the Scourgers were humanlike, while others looked more like ghosts in a scary movie. Some crawled on all fours, while others had four of everything. Some even looked like rotting trees. They were genuinely disgusting. They also carried a deathly odor, which turned some of the trees black as soon as they passed by them.

Derek shouted, "That's our cue!"

Flair fell back from her position and caught up with us. She had so much adrenaline pumping through her veins that she spoke in a hurry, "That was amazing. Did you see that four-legged creature? He didn't like the fire very much."

Quint squinted his eyes and shook his head up and down. "You know what, you're right."

I added, "Maybe that's their weakness."

Derek shouted with half belief and half uncertainty, "Possibly."

Quint smirked. "I also noticed the ones who look like ghosts stay in the shadows. Maybe they hate the sun."

Octavion snarled, "Only one way to find out."

Derek looked at Gwendolyn and gave her a nod. She responded with the same nod and turned to me. Gwendolyn pointed to one of her rocks, waiting on the ground. She was giving me one last chance. I shook my head. Not this time. She gave me approval, and she started sprinting. I followed her.

Gwendolyn and I took the back route to the green castle. All the action was happening behind us. I was tempted to turn around, but I lost my speed, and we slowed down. "Try not to look back. We don't have much time left," she said as she picked up her pace again and glided through the rainforest. I decided to peek back, just to see how the others were doing.

The sight was ghastly. I noticed Quint first because he grabbed the sun and cast it into the shadows. The crooked trees, now black with their disease, shined with a black shimmer. The ghost-like creatures scattered for protection but were unable to achieve safety. They vanished into smoldering smoke with a loud high-pitched scream. The sound vibrated through the forest and caught the whole team off guard. Annora pulled them back into the fight by hitting a target with her water. She pushed it into another Scourger, and they both hit the ground forcefully. She held them there until Flair came and roasted their bodies.

I noticed something crawling on all fours toward our direction. It didn't seem real, so I didn't scream. Until the image focused and I saw the large, hairy, black, and gray spotted Scourger. Its front was much larger than its rear. But that never stopped it from running. It was digging up the dirt as it ran toward us. Teeth thrashing in the air as it howled. I tried to get a word out, but nothing came. I was mute. It took one last pounce and bounced in the air. Claws ready to sink into my flesh. I finally spoke. "Uh, Gwendolyn. We have a huge problem." She turned her head but never stopped her feet. Her eyes widened only for a second, then they closed into a sharp crease.

Gwendolyn gathered two of her large boulders and swung them in the Scourger's direction. The first one missed him as he swiftly dodged it. Like Gwendolyn, it never broke its stride. The second boulder was not an easy miss. It hit him across the face; his body smacked against the adjacent tree. Cracking the stump. The Scourger got up again, but Flair came to the rescue. I never saw her coming until she was on top of the Scourger with fire surrounding her.

The creature came toward her with staggering steps. A closer look, and you could see that a large piece of bark had embedded itself into the beast. Black-green blood spilled from the wound. Then Flair gathered a ball of fire and sprung it at the creature, forcing it back into another tree. This time the monster did not get up. Instead, it lay there, squished between two pieces of crushed bark.

"Wow." I was amazed; the way they were fighting made me feel like we had a real chance at saving the world.

Gwendolyn gratefully said, "Thanks, Flair."

Flair grinned. "No problem, Gwen, see you at the finish line."

Gwendolyn said, "We got this."

"I agree," I said. We continued to run.

I could finally see the green castle. Not what I imagined it to be. The castle was green because of all the moss and algae on it. Underneath all the moss was a bronze surface. Other than that, the castle was beautiful. The front entrance was grand. Large marble steps made for giants. The walkway expanded to two mahogany doors with goddesses for handles. There was an inscription on the doors written in what I assume was Latin.

Ex Nihilo Nihil Fit

Gwendolyn saw me looking. "It means nothing comes from nothing. You need to work hard if you want to achieve greatness, and that is exactly what we are going to do. Come on, we need to go."

I agreed with her. "Yeah, time is running out."

The entrance looked much longer up close than far away. Gwen took the lead, running with her peaceful stride. I manage to keep up with her. The stairs wore my legs out. I stopped to take a short breath, but Gwendolyn took me by the arm and pushed me through the doors. The temperature inside was cooler than outside. I took a long deep breath before running further into the castle.

Gwendolyn asked me. "Now where would they keep the crown?"

I could only think of one answer. "Where everyone could see it. In the throne room." Gwendolyn gave me one of the biggest smiles I've seen from her all day. The feeling was warm and approving.

"Let's finish this." She beamed.

I returned the smile. "Yeah, let's do this."

The inside wasn't a typical castle. The castle hallways were long, and the ceilings were high. The walls weren't just stone and wood but rubies, diamonds, and emeralds. The jewels sparkled from the sun emitting through the windows. The floor reflected our image through the polished marble. The ceilings were painted with vibrant colors of earth's elements. These elements were swirling to become one, and at the center was unity and power. Power like no other. I saw this in the ceiling; it was beautiful. I stood in awe, just taking everything in. "This place never ceases to amaze me."

Gwendolyn also shared my amazement. "Beautiful, huh?" She pointed to an open door "I think I found the throne, and look who is sitting in it."

I walked through the door and found Beetly sitting in a king's chair. The chair looked way too big for him with its large armrest and tall neck. He even seemed to sink into the red cushion of the seat.

Proudly he said to us, "Hello, ladies."

"I can't believe it. It seems way too easy," I whispered.

Gwendolyn felt uneasy as well. "I know what you mean."

Beetly stood from the king's chair. "Now if you would give me the crown."

I turned to Gwendolyn. "Something is really wrong." That's when Beetly transformed into something worse than the creatures outside. Beetly grew twenty feet tall and he had to bend inside of the castle. Its face was a mushed mess of meat. The yellow pupil eyes were barely visible under the roles of fat. Its teeth were sharp and crooked, creating a gate of yellow. Its skin was a deep gray that looked tight, almost like it could rip from its brash movements. The muscles on the beast were maximized to the extreme. Three fingers and hoofed feet allowed it to move rapidly. I couldn't see any ears but two deep holes in its place.

"Run!" Gwendolyn mouthed to me. We made a run for it. As we left the room, the creature screamed, one that was loud enough to shatter the windows, and I covered my ears as the screaming continued to shake the castle. Beetly, or what used to be him, burst through the wall with little effort.

She ordered, "We need to go up."

I asked, "Why? Let's just go out the front door."

She screamed, "No, the crown needs to be placed. We don't have time."

I yelled back, "I understand that, but this thing will catch up to us soon." We were yelling at each other because we couldn't hear the other over the creature's loud breathing and shrieking.

Gwendolyn hollered, "Not if I run fast."

I yelled back, "Okay, but how will that help me?"

She didn't say anything. She just took a fallen stone from the creature's destruction and placed it in front of me. "Hop on. I would stop, but I don't want us to be eaten by a mangy mutt," she half-joked. I was still running when I jumped forward, hitting the stone flat on my stomach. I let out a loud groan as the pain surge through my chest. Gwendolyn had little time for sympathy. "Shake it off, Jewels."

I talked through breaths, "I...will...try."

Proudly she said, "That's my girl."

Traveling on the rock made the world one big blur. Gwendolyn was accelerating. I could tell she was pushing herself, and carrying me only made it worse. Gwendolyn kept going through different halls and doors, slowing him down every time he had to break through something.

I don't know why I decided to do what I did. But I knew I had to help. I couldn't stay on her rock every time the going got tough. So I jumped off and stopped. I stopped dead center in the hall. The beast was a few yards behind us. I had a couple of minutes before he was on us.

Gwendolyn finally realized I wasn't on the rock and skid to a stop. She looked angry and tired. "What are you doing? Are you insane? Get on the rock, Jewels."

"No," I simply stated. "I will give you the time you need to find the crown's proper placement."

"You're clearly messed up." She thrust the stone in my direction and motioned for me to get on.

I stood my ground. "You're wasting time, Gwendolyn. Go find it."

She gave me a look of defeat. She turned to run and yelled, "Don't die on the first day, Fire Breather."

I yelled back, "I won't." When she was out of sight and earshot, I mumbled, "I hope not."

Focus

My heart was pumping so fast I could feel the vibration through the floor. I needed to think fast. I only had a minute before he came. I glanced around the room, trying to find something that could help. I only saw four large glass windows evenly placed in the room. One of the windows had a crack, and the wind rushed through the tiny sliver of space. There also was the stone Gwendolyn wanted me to sit on patiently waiting on the ground. I smiled at the sight of the stone. Even though she had left, she was still looking after me.

I needed to think fast. I could feel its giant footsteps coming closer to me. Its muffled breath started to become more transparent. From the back of my mind, the thought came to me, *If only I could fly*. Then it hit me like a lightning bolt. *That's it! I needed to fly. If I could choke someone, dry my hair, and swallow fire, then I could fly. I needed to focus.* I focused on my breathing. My heart slowed its pacing, and my lungs took in more air at less intervals.

I focused on the air around me. I felt the temperature. I felt the humidity on my skin and the smell of fresh grass. I focused on my goal. I needed to stop the creature, giving Gwendolyn more time. I opened my eyes. *I was ready.*

My first attempt ended with my butt on the floor. The second attempt ended with me lying flat on my stomach. But the third attempt was successful. I was ten feet off the ground when the beast came through the wall. It startled me, and I almost lost my concentration. He seemed to take in the scenery and realized that the other girl was not here. This was my chance.

Gathering the wind that was blowing through the broken window, I took control and pushed the stone. It screeched along the floor until it was in the air, headed for his face. Even though he was a fast runner, he couldn't dodge as fast as the smaller creatures. The impact was stronger than I expected, and it took him off guard. Just what I needed. I gathered some more wind and pushed it in his direction. The combination of the stone and wind knocked him on his back.

The castle shook, and the chandeliers shattered. I was glad to be in the air since the impact would have taken me down. I didn't stop there; I took the same stone and smacked him again. This time in the chest. The creature roared from the impact. It tried to get up, but I gave another whack and another. It was screaming a deadly scream. But I didn't stop. I had to make sure Gwendolyn was safe. The final blow carried such force that he did not get up. I almost felt bad. Almost.

I turned around and saw Quint, Annora, Octavion, Derek, and Flair staring at me. The look on their faces made me feel powerful. It was shock, approval, and awe. I came down to the floor and walked over to them, "Hey, guys. What's up?" I said this to them with an air of confidence.

Octavion marveled, "What's up? You just killed a giant. That's what's up."

I joked, "Oh, I hadn't noticed."

Flair gave a shout, and the others clapped. There was a soft hum, and then the creature disappeared. Next was the broken glass and the walls. Then the ceiling and the floor. Finally, we were standing outside in the rainforest. The color was returning to a nice blue sky and white puffy clouds.

"I think Gwen returned the crown," I said.

"I did." Her voice appeared out of nowhere.

We all turned and ran to her, cheering and jumping up and down. Nothing could be better than this. Beetly, the real one, greeted us. "You all performed better than I expected. Quint, good job figuring out their weaknesses. Flair, nice save. Octavion, great use of your animal choices. Derek, great leadership. Annora, great choice with the whirlpool. Gwendolyn, nice effort to protect your team and a great job and a superb finish." Beetly was cut off by Octavion's cheering. Gwendolyn gave a small curtsy.

"Finally, Jewels, your sacrifice was well appreciated. You handled the pressure well," Beetly said, beaming. Everyone roared and clapped. I just looked at my new friends and felt at home. Nothing could change how I felt right now.

"Now it's time for the party. You guys will have time to freshen up. Then it's off to a great night." We all clapped in response. "You are dismissed," Beetly said. Then just like before, he disappeared into the forest.

"Why couldn't he walk with us to the front?" I asked.

"Who knows? He likes to be mysterious," responded Gwen.

We made it to the exit, and I happened to look up and meet the eyes of Nátàl. I was surprised to find out that she was watching the whole time. She gave me a soft smile and exited her observation room. I was a little puzzled. "I didn't know she watched us practice?"

Gwen, also puzzled, said, "Me neither."

When I returned to my room, I found out that the hallway I was assigned to was where all the seven slept. Like my door, they each had a symbol on theirs.

Gwen's room was in the same hall as mine, just a few feet away. Her symbol was intricate. Within the circle was a sizeable upside-down triangle. Inside the triangle was a thick line that held a ring at the very top. The ring was broken up into three halves. At the bottom of the line were two *e*'s facing backward.

Next to Gwen's room was Annora's. Her symbol was simple yet beautiful. Inside the circle was a very large raindrop located to the right. The tail of the raindrop curled into three swirls. Inside the large raindrop was a smaller one. Behind the raindrop were two thick lines and an upside-down triangle.

"What are you staring at?" I was startled by the sound of a soft voice. Annora was standing right next to me. I never realized she was there; her feet were like air.

"I'm admiring the artwork." My eyes were fixed on Flair's door. Inside the circle was a thick and smaller circle that was shifted to one side, leaving more space on the left. Within the circle was a thick bordered triangle that enclosed the fireball.

"Yeah, they're pretty cool. My favorite is Octavion's. The creativity used in his…is just." Annora stopped in the middle of her sentence and pointed. I followed her hands that pointed across the hall to the first door. She was right—his by far was the coolest. Within his bordered circled was a centaur. The creature was standing on its hind legs, and the front horse legs were in the air. The centaur's human arms were crossed over its chest. Underneath the arms were two thick lines, reaching at an angle. Next to the centaur was an olive branch and a crown placed between the branch. What better way to show-case the power of animal transformation than a centaur?

"You're right. That is pretty neat!" I finally looked at Annora. She was smiling.

"Yeah. I'm going to get ready now. You should do the same." She gave me one last smile before she walked down the hall to her room.

I stayed outside to see the last two doors and their designs. Quint's symbol was not of your typical sun. The sun was in the center of the circled border. The rays were small and large triangles that were a few centimeters away from the sun. Three rays were evenly placed between twelve o'clock, three o'clock, six o'clock, and nine o'clock swirls that almost appeared to be a captain's hook. At the head of the circle was an inverted triangle with three lines in it. Next to Quint's room was Derek's. Derek's symbol was a mound of dirt. A plant was taking root inside and growing. Three leaves were sprout-ing. The plant was between six rectangle boxes. Three on each side.

I grabbed my door handle and opened the heavy door. For some reason, it felt heavier than before. I must have used all my arm strength during the fight. I shut the door and let out a much-needed sigh. I turned to find Sarah and ALICE waiting for me. I was relieved to see familiar faces. Some of my energy returning to me. I ran over to them and gave them the biggest hug I could.

"You guys. I'm glad you're here. You wouldn't believe the day I just had." My body was tired, and yet my voice was ecstatic. Sarah smirked. Apparently, she had some dirt too. "You will not believe ours either." I was shocked. Somehow Sarah looked different. I was curious.

"What happened to you?" I sat down on the bed, scooting in close to my friends.

ALICE bluntly answered, "Well, it turns out Sarah was really messed up in the head from our encounter with Ray." Now this came as a shock to me.

"What? I thought Vivienne healed you?" I thought Vivienne's powers were bulletproof. But somehow, this mystery guy keeps slithering his way into places he clearly doesn't belong.

Sarah nodded, "I thought so too. Even Vivienne, but Nátàl Mater said otherwise."

Surprised, I asked, "Wait, did you meet her too?"

Sarah said, "Yeah, she wanted to thank us personally for bringing you here safe. Also, I'm from here. I've met her several times." Sarah playfully nudged me.

"Right, of course. Silly me." My laugh quickly evaporated into the air.

"Anyways, you were saying, Sarah?" ALICE was trying to pull us back into focus.

"Oh yeah, well, Ray's powers traveled into the deeper parts of my brain, allowing him to track us here." Sarah finished her statement like it was no big deal. This was just another walk in the park. I, on the other hand, was shocked.

"Are you kidding me?" The words escaped my mouth with such force that they both moved back an inch.

Sarah shook her head. "Not at all. As a matter of fact, they found him circling the area looking for the entrance. They captured him. But not before he injured five of our men."

Amazed, I said, "Wow, the poor guys. I guess they never had a chance. With his powers and all?"

ALICE chimed in, "They will be all right, though." I pondered over the news and decided to ask Sarah a question that had been weighing on me since Saraphine stopped us in the middle of the stairs. If I was right, and lately my hunches are, then the mystery man was the intruder.

Sarah's voice shook me from my thoughts. "Jewels, what's going on? Did you hear a word I said?"

I hadn't heard her. "No, sorry."

She shook her head and said, "It's all right. What were you thinking about?"

I said softly, "I think I saw Ray on my way to the Great Hall."

Sarah smiled. "I'm not surprised. You could hear him too. After a while, his laugh turned into a deep chuckle. One that traveled through the whole place." So it was him. Now for my question. "Do you know how he has those powers?"

I've never seen Sarah stumped over a question. Not in school and certainly not over social issues, but today she had no answer. Her face was twisted in an expression I wasn't used to. "No, I'm not sure. I can ask Nátàl or Vivienne? They might know."

I frowned. "If you don't mind, I need to know."

"Sure." Sarah's face was back to normal. Bright.

I was exhausted. The high from earlier was wearing off, and I didn't like the feeling. Everything that was wrong with me—my life, my friends, and my family—came flooding back to me. Front and center with a perfect broadcast in my mind. I decided it was time to change the subject. "On a brighter note, I met the rest of the Secret Seven, and they are spectacular."

ALICE took the invite with open arms. "They are spectacular, and I had a chance to meet their ALICE too. By far, I'm the coolest one. You lucked out, Jewels."

A small and weak laugh came from my body. "I sure did."

Sarah was up next. "So what were they like?"

I easily described them in one word: "Perfect."

"Really?" Sarah was not convinced. She believed in no such thing.

I ignored her skepticism. "Yeah, their gifts are amazing, and their friendship is stronger than anything. They welcomed me with open arms." My energy slowly regained after every word I spent talking about them.

"I'm sure they did." I heard Sarah's sarcastic tone. Her tone suggested pity and ignorance.

I looked at Sarah for a moment. "What's that supposed to mean?"

Sarah seemed to catch how she had spoken to me and stepped back. "Nothing. Are you ready for the party? You have to be there in an hour."

She was evasive, and I wasn't ready to let the situation drop. "What did you mean, Sarah?"

She showed frustration. "Jewels, just forget about it. It's nothing. *I* meant nothing."

"ALICE, do you know what she meant?" I looked at her half-joking and half with seriousness.

Puzzled, ALICE responded, "Not a clue. I can't read minds, you know. Whatever she was thinking stayed deep in that hollow skull of hers."

Sarah smacked ALICE on the shoulder. "Watch it." Sarah gave ALICE a scolding glare. "Remember, I can make you go to sleep involuntarily," she added.

ALICE refused to be threatened. "Oh, really? Well, it will be hard if you can't find me." ALICE wittily made herself invisible so that Sarah could not see her. Of course, I could still see her.

Sarah laughed nervously. "Oh, come on, ALICE, you can't be serious? I was only joking." Then under her breath, she said, "A little."

ALICE looked at me. "You need to get dressed."

I said, "Yeah, I know."

Sarah looked confused. "What do you know?"

I stared at her. "ALICE is just telling me to get ready."

Sarah said, "Oh. Well, you do need to."

"Why is she repeating me?" ALICE huffed and crossed her arms.

"I don't know," I snapped.

Sarah again said, "What don't you know?"

"Why you..." I trailed off. I realized this was ridiculous. "You two need to stop this. Either you guys help me get ready or you leave."

"Well, actually..." they said at the same time. Sarah shrugged.

I asked, "Actually, what?"

Sarah offered, "Someone else will be helping you get ready."

"Who?"

I was a little bit terrified. If it were anything like the first time someone helped me get ready, it would be awkward. "Saraphine. You met her earlier today." Immediately, my heart returned to normal rhythm. I would see Saraphine again. After our meeting, I compared everyone and thing to her.

Sarah said with a devious smirk, "I take it you like her."

"Why would you say that?" I said with tenacity. Or at least I tried. My voice chimed an octave higher.

"No reason, just the fact that you are grinning from ear to ear."

I said casually, "Really? I hadn't noticed."

"You totally are. It's kind of cute." She was laughing, so she almost fell off the bed. ALICE leered in her safe spot, just staring at me.

Suddenly there was a soft knock on the door. ALICE walked to the door. She opened it, and there stood Saraphine holding fabric and a large wooden box decorated with studs. I jumped from the bed. "Saraphine, come in, please."

She walked into the room and set the fabric down on the couch. "Thank you." She looked through the room and noticed how neat it was. She seemed pleased. "Now then, for the fun part. Sarah and ALICE, would you kindly exit?"

"How did you know ALICE was in the room?" I asked.

Her reply was prompt. "Well, the door certainly didn't open itself, now did it?"

"No," was all I said. Saraphine was grinning. Hard. She was a few seconds away from her famous laugh.

Sarah stood from the bed and gave me a long hug. Her eyes said, *See you later*, but she never spoke. ALICE came out of stealth mode. I knew this because Sarah grabbed her by the arm and pulled her out of the room.

Once they both left, Saraphine placed the fabric on the bed and looked at me, "Now then, how are you?"

Happy to have a moment alone with her, I smiled, "Great, actually. You won't believe the day I had."

She gave me her sweet honey smile. "No? Try me."

I rambled, "Well, first, the Crypto-Hept are awesome. Second, Mother Nature is real. Third, I kicked Scourger butt."

She said. "Sounds like an eventful day. What did you think of Nátàl?"

I gushed on, "Wonderful. She was beyond what I pictured Mother Nature to be. In fact, I felt bad for her."

Saraphine looked confused. "Why is that?"

I simply stated, "Do you know how many girls complain about how Mother Nature is not fair?"

She just smiled. "Ah, yes. Well, I think you have Eve to thank for that," Saraphine snarled loudly.

Saraphine nodded. "Now then, let's get you dressed."

Saraphine had a way of shutting down conversations. A method you could admire. I finally got a good look at her, and she was wearing an orange dress. The orange was a light tangerine color. The dress hit the floor and flowed from her feet. At the base of the neck was a sheer turtleneck that connected to the heart-shaped base. The material gathered on the sides to create a ruffled look. She looked stunning in it. This time she wore gold goddess sandals. Her face was contoured with the most elegant eyeshadow. She created a colorful smoky eye with burnt yellow, orange, and black.

I looked at my fabric placed on the bed. It was a beautiful color. Or colors. For the most part, it was dark and light purple. But there were spaces in between that were white. Other sections of the fabric had very thin white slashes. The image of lightning.

I asked her, "Is that a thunderstorm on the fabric?"

She grinned, "Indeed, it is." She touched the fabric and spread it, allowing me to see the entire dress.

I smiled. "That's awesome."

"Yes, it is." Saraphine placed the fabric against my skin. It felt soft and homey. She continued, "Nátàl thought you should wear something more unique than a white dress. Besides, you aren't getting married." She playfully added, "Are you?"

I quickly countered, "Oh, gosh, no." She then dismissed me. "Now then, freshen up while I make your dress."

Before leaving, I added, "I can't believe you can make a dress in an hour." She smiled, "Well, believe it, dearie. Now go on."

I stumbled off to the bathroom to freshen up. I noticed the water seemed warmer than before. Refashion was already growing on me. It wasn't until I was in the hot shower that I noticed how tense my muscles were. The heat from the water loosened every ache in my body. When I stepped out, the cold room quickly attacked my freshly opened pores. I rushed to dry and lather my body in lotion.

I walked out of the bathroom and found Saraphine sitting on the bed, moving her hands in a smooth but fast pace. She never looked up. She was focused on her work.

Saraphine took a short break. I was sure she didn't need it. She made conversation with me. "I brought you some perfume. You can choose the one you like best. It's in that box." She pointed to a bedazzled jewelry box on the couch.

"Would I ever?" I paused. "Thank you, that was very thoughtful. I also appreciate you making my dress."

Ever so kindly, she said, "You're welcome. How was the shower?" I walked over to the box and picked out several perfumes. "It was nice. I didn't realize how sore I was." I chose to try the honeysuckle. It reminded me of Gwen.

Saraphine sniffed. "Ah, yes. If we work too hard, eventually, we will crash." She paused for effect. "Hard."

I admitted, "I didn't know that. Can I ask you a question?"

She grabbed the fabric once more and worked. "Of course, dearie."

I said, "During practice, today it didn't seem like the Secret Seven new anything about Scourgers. We were fighting blind."

She waited patiently. "Your question?"

I went on, "Why is that?"

She let out a small sigh. "No one really knows about the Scourgers except Nátàl and our army. Nátàl doesn't believe in evoking fear into us. We live our lives not knowing."

I found this puzzling. "Even the Secret Seven?"

"Yes, the Crypto-Hept remain unknown until their gift is revealed. Therefore, you can't know who it will be."

"That doesn't seem like a safe way to handle the situation."

"It usually works. But this time, two of you were outside of the sanctuary. We lost time to practice with you."

I shook my head. "My dad said I would be practicing back home." That's the first time I mentioned him aloud. It felt weird.

"He wanted you to stay in school. Stay with him. But Nátàl and I felt like it was a bad idea."

"Why couldn't he come with us?" I asked. Saraphine placed the fabric next to me, measuring my height.

"Not certain," she plainly said.

That was my cue to stop asking questions. But how could I not stop? So many thoughts were traveling through my brain. Was Saraphine to be my friend all along? Was it by choice, or was she forced? How come I lived outside of the sanctuary? Why was I different from everyone here? Even Sarah seemed to fit in perfectly. Why couldn't I? Who am I, really?

"I can see that the wheels of your brain are turning. Do not worry about it, dearie. Tonight is a celebration."

"You're right." And she was. But one day, I'll get those answers.

She stood up and said, "Now then, let's put this dress on."

WE ARE CRYPTO-HEPT

The dress was beautiful. I couldn't get over the thunderstorm that was brewing on my dress. My gown was a ruffled heart-shaped top with the bottom a puffed sheer ball gown. The material was slippery and yet durable. The storm was placed perfectly in the center of the dress. The rest was dark purple and black, smothering the lighter purple and white. My shoes were outstanding. They were dark purple, almost like a plum. Throughout the shoes were gray spots that melted into the dark purple.

"I love it." I was twirling in the stand-up mirror. My hair was perfect for once. She pulled it up into a curly Mohawk. My black hair slicked to the side. She then added the same purple flowers in my room to my hair. I was floating in pure joy.

"I'm glad, dearie." She smiled at me through the mirror.

"I'm ready for the party now," I said with confidence.

"I bet you are. Come along, dearie." She grabbed the trail of my dress and helped me through the door.

At the Great Hall entrance, Saraphine and I were told to wait by two guards dressed in black leather. A loud horn was heard from the inside. Then the doors opened, and the guards stepped aside. Saraphine fell back. I turned to look at her, and she motioned for me to keep going. "You're really going to leave me?" I was terrified. My confidence from earlier seeping away.

Saraphine said with certainty, "Dearie, you can do this. You look wonderful."

I tried to return a confident smile but fell short. She pushed me further into the room. I turned to see her one last time, but the doors were closed. The Great Hall looked different from before. I never noticed the other doors placed along the walls that opened to the room.

The other six were in their doorways, just like me. Each one of us looked stunning. All of us were uniquely representing our gift.

As for the Great Hall, it was magnificent. Nothing was left bare in the entire room. The tables were covered with white cloth and scattered flowers. Golden candle holders and flower vases neatly placed along the tables. Inside the vases were black and red roses. For an underground civilization, they had some modern luxuries. They had a strobe light and a DJ. He was playing techno and fast-paced instrumental pieces. I couldn't believe my eyes. The dance floor was crazy.

The dance floor was decorated with crowds of dancing people. Their different colored dresses and suits clashing with each other and the strobe lights in a harmonious way. I laughed to myself after seeing some of them dancing. It was only a few people. Many of them were good dancers.

The music came to a slow stop, and then the lights came on. You could see everyone's face. The girls didn't need makeup, but they had elegant swirls and dots around their eyes. With dark- and bright-colored lips.

From where I was standing, a tall and very slinky guy came up and blew his trumpet. The sound received everyone's attention. Then the grandest door in the room opened, and Nátàl Mater stepped through with grace.

She looked marvelous from head to toe. Her gown was a shimmering blue and turquoise that hugged her torso and spread beyond her legs. The train in the back heightened in length more than the front. The top had a turquoise wrap attached. Her hair was wrapped with curls falling from the side. Her dark hair shimmering with gold glitter. Nátàl stood in the doorway with just enough time to look at her surroundings. When her eyes went from the crowd to the Crypto-Hept, she moved and found her place among a large outstretched table and sat down.

The crowd cheered and shouted, "Nátàl Mater Custos, Medicus et provider." They repeated the chant a few more times before her hand was raised. The crowd fell silent. Then she spoke, honey dripping from every word. "Thank you for the warm welcome. Normally our head chamber man would introduce you to the Crypto-Hept, but I've decided to do it myself."

Nátàl then stood. "The very first and the leader of the Crypto-Hept is Derek the Herbative. Derek has quickly proven to be a helpful resource in the role of a leader. He takes the lead role very seriously. Careful not to overstep his comrades, he allows them to voice their opinions while still keeping the focus on the task at hand." She then raised her voice in a commanding and spirited volume. "Derek is Herbative. He *is* one of our Crypto-Hept."

Derek then took three steps forward before raising his right arm and crossing it over his chest in a fist. His muscles contracted in response. I was not sure, but I thought I heard a few girls yell in response. He then took his place back by the door. The crowd bellowed in response. Their cheers bounced from wall to wall. I was sure the guards could hear us from beyond the doors.

With a slightly raised hand, Nátàl made the crowd's cheering cease. Nátàl spoke. "She has proven to be the right-hand man and well adverse in situations. She's light on her feet yet commands the ground. Her power creates the perfect deception, which she plays well, might I add." Nátàl smiled to herself. "She is none other than Gwendolyn the Geoanagi. She *is* one of our Crypto-Hept." Gwen stepped forward. She raised her arm then crossed it over her chest in a balled fist. She stepped back, and the crowd gave her the same cheer as before. She gave the people the same smile she gave me, warm and welcoming.

As if on cue, the crowd fell silent, and Nátàl introduced the next person. "You could say he's the bronze of the operation if Gwendolyn was not here, of course." Girls giggled, and boys cheered to her joke. "All jokes aside, Octavion's ability to make any situation better will guide our protectors into victory. He is equipped with the ability to make the tiniest of creatures useful. He is a Formicon. He *is* one of our Crypto-Hept."

The crowd cheered as Octavion followed the same pattern. A raised arm crossed over the chest in a fist. Derek, Gwen, and Octavion seemed to eat up the attention. They were in their element. I felt queasy; somehow, I knew I was up next. I looked around the room and saw a few people staring at me, looking at me with interest and slight intimidation. I felt out of place here. But there was nothing I could do about that. For some reason, Quint and I were different. I needed to find out why.

I didn't realize that Nátàl was talking about me until it was too late. She had just finished saying, "She is Pneumodegyn. She *is* one of our Crypto-Hept." The crowd gave me a soft cheer. Almost like they were uncertain with my presence. Then they were silent. I stared out into a thousand faces that seemed to look right through me. Friends turned to each other and whispered only what I could imagine.

The only thing I could do was follow the others before me. I lifted my arm in the same manner and crossed it in front of my chest with a fist. I was not expecting the crowd to give me the response they did. Their cheers were louder than the others. Why I have no clue. Whatever it was, it made me feel warm inside. I felt connected to them. Magical, really—it had only been two days, and yet I felt more at home here than Colorado.

Nátàl raised her arms, and the crowd fell silent. Not before a couple of distant yells were heard. She then raised her voice and spoke with authority. "This young man not only has the brightest of gifts, but he is great on the field. Quickly, he recognized the Scourgers' weaknesses and help gained the Crypto-Hept a significant advantage. He is Quint, and he is known as Anglevi. He *is* one of our Crypto-Hept."

The crowd gave Quint a loud cheer, like mine. Following the motion of the others before him, he crossed his arm over his chest. But something magnificent happened. The light in the room brightened then quickly turned back to yellow. The room dimmed. He crossed his fist over his chest and then took a step back. The Refashions turned to one another and cheered louder than anything I have ever heard. The ground beneath our feet shook. Even the Queen seem to appreciate Quint's surprise.

After a minute or so, she raised her hand. Everyone slowly regained themselves. Nátàl continued, "Flair has proven herself to be a team player. She is strong-minded and determined to protect our way of life. She is Ignisess. She *is* one of our Crypto-Hept."

Before the crowd could applaud, Flair took all the fire from the glass bulbs and candles, making a tornado of fire. She then made it disperse into two waves. They danced in the air effortlessly. Flair seemed to have much better control than earlier. The crowd was eating her show up. Every face was filled with bright red light. We stared at her in awe.

For her final trick, she took all the fire and made a waterfall. Just when it looked like the fire was going to hit us, it froze. She then put all the fire back into their bulbs and candles. We all cheered for her. "I couldn't let you have all the fun, Quint," she said as she turned to him and gave a smirk. He returned her words with a respectable applause and smile. Flair crossed her arm over her chest and took a step back. The crowd didn't need to be shushed by Nátàl. They were waiting patiently for her to introduce Annora. They wanted to see what she could do.

"Last but certainly not least is Annora. She is the essence of life. She is what flows through our bodies. Her gift can cure as simple as dehydration. She is Aquagynitive. She is Crypto-Hept." No one cheered. They all waited to see what she would do. At first, she just stared at the crowd. But then she gave a large smile and nodded her head toward the back of the room. Everyone turned around, and there was a large wall of water covering the back of the room. It looked magnificent.

You could see through it and how the other side seemed to be covered in water. Then the wall of water gushed toward the ceiling and formed into a mushroom and formed a dome. There were even fish swimming in there. They looked peaceful. The water moved toward Annora and stopped right in front of her face. Next, it circled her body with a slow motion, making sure not to disturb the fish. After a while, she returned the water back to the fountain. There was a short pause before we all gave Annora a round of applause. She then crossed her arm in a fist over her chest and stepped back.

Nátàl stood with admiration. "Now. That was a show. I believe we are well cared for. Don't you?" The crowd roared in response to her question. She continued to speak. "I want everyone to enjoy this night. You all deserve it." She then walked away from the stairs and was out of sight. The music resumed, and the lights dimmed. I looked around, and the rest of the Secret Seven were heading to the dance floor.

Quint was the first to speak. "That was awesome, Flair. You really know how to step up your game."

Flair smiled coyly. "Thanks, Quint. You weren't bad yourself. You guys, let's have some fun!"

Annora agreed, "Yeah, we deserve it. After all, after tonight, we will be in nonstop training."

Gwen shook her shoulders. "Don't remind me." The others disappeared in the crowd to dance the night away.

Everyone's outfits were stunning. Gwen's dress was a dark and light gray empire waistline. Her maxi dress curved in and out like rocks on a hill. She had speckles of jewels neatly placed in the crevices of her dress. Her necklace had a morion jewel in the center with small jet-black diamonds, connecting the band around her neck. She was glowing from all the sparkles escaping her body. Gwen's hair was pulled up in a tight bun with few curls on the side of her face. She gave me her famous warm, welcoming smile that I have grown to love.

I admired her. "You look stunning, Gwen."

She twirled around. "Do I? I feel a little bland in this dress."

I shook my head. "Not at all. It's perfect."

She smiled. "Thank you, Jewels. I really appreciate it." Then she stepped back and looked me up and down. "You look wonderful. A true beauty."

"Ah, stop. I don't know about that," I said modestly.

"Yes, you do." A familiar voice spoke.

I turned around to find Quint standing there. He was staring back at me with his maple-brown eyes. I was flushed. "Thank you."

I took a quick glance at his attire and noticed that his yellow wasn't as bright. But it was still present among all the other colors in the room. He was wearing a yellow silk blazer with a red undershirt. The cufflinks of his suit were light topaz. He was wearing yellow slacks with a faint pattern in them. They were swirls that cascaded to the center of his suit, like sunbeams. "You look nice as well," I told him.

He smiled faintly and quickly replied, "Thanks. Funny enough, I'm not a fan of yellow. It makes me look pale."

I pondered over his remark. I don't know how he looked at himself, but what I saw was something different. Maybe everyone was like that? I was going to tell Quint he looked fine, but I saw Flair dancing toward us. She was wearing a scandalous dress that was dark red fading into black. The sides of the dress were cut out into a *V* shape that contained a smaller *V* shape cut inside of it. She had a crisscrossed back that went into a braid connected to the bottom of the dress. With her natural waistline and handkerchief hem, she glided toward us.

Flair stopped dancing in front of us. "Why are you guys not dancing?"

Gwen responded, "We will. You look drop-dead gorgeous."

Flair laughed. "I know."

The song changed to a fast-paced, heart-throbbing beat. Flair recognized the song and grabbed Gwen's arm. "Come on, I love this song." Off they went, and it was just Quint and me. *I shouldn't feel weird, but I do. What should I do now? Do I make a conversation or just go after Gwen?* Oh, how I hate small talk. I never know what to say, and talking about the weather was overrated.

Suck it up. A song only lasts two minutes, and Gwen would be back soon. "So where are you from?" The words stumbled out of my mouth.

Quint turned toward me with a "Why am I making small talk?" face.

He gave a soft snort. "I'm from California. You?"

I smiled, "That's really cool. I always wanted to visit there. I'm from Colorado."

He just shook his head. "Hmm, sounds boring."

I was quick with a reply. "It's not. We have Hockey, Garden of the Gods, Cliff Palace, Balcony House, Steam Boat Ski Resort..." I trailed off. I sounded like I was trying to sell Colorado. I decided to change the focus. I asked, "How is California?"

A bright smile cascaded across his face. "It's amazing, I go surfing all the time. I love being on the sea. It makes me feel at ease." Making sure he didn't lose me, he added, "You know?"

I gave the nod to reassure him. I smiled at him. "I really do. I love drawing scenery. Specifically, nature. It makes me feel alone but also surrounded."

He smiled even brighter. "Exactly! Have you noticed that we love things that are the opposite of our gift? You, nature and me, water."

I agreed, "It's crazy. I feel like the universe did that on purpose. To make sure we all liked each other and what the other has to bring to the table."

Quint added, "That, or they thought it was a sick joke."

Smiling, I said, "Yeah, that sounds about right."

He was laughing too. His laugh came as a shock to me. It was a deep cackle, not a scary one. Just deep. When he finished laughing, he stared at me. "If I may be honest with you?" He waited for my reply.

I told him, "I would prefer if you were."

He then admitted, "None of you are like how I imagined. Everyone is humanlike."

I chuckled, "I know what you mean. When Vivienne first told me about Refashion, I thought we were aliens." His deep laugh surrounded our small space. "Wow, we think alike. I completely freaked out when Martin told me. Even my personal protector was weird." He shook his head and grabbed a soft drink from the bar.

"Right! ALICE made me feel stupid. I met her at a party and she—"

I turned and realized that I was cut off by Gwen. "Don't you two look like you're having fun?"

I was disappointed that the song was over. I wanted to talk to Quint some more. He seemed more like me than the others here.

"Yeah, just getting to know my fellow Crypt. How was your dance?" Quint asked, trying to include the rest in the conversation. I wished he wouldn't.

"Why don't you find out?" Flair said with a giant grin.

As Flair was pulling him into the crowd, he turned around and gave me a look of apology. Then he was gone, swallowed by the sea of moving bodies.

"Dancing with Flair is like dancing with fire. Always moving and jumping. Poor Quint, he doesn't even have a chance," Gwen said after taking a sip of her drink. I turned to face Gwen, who was facing front.

I asked her, "She's that energetic?"

Gwen nodded. "She really is. Two minutes is too long on the dance floor with her."

She looked at me and tilted her head. "You okay?"

I lied and said, "Yes, I'm fine. Just thinking."

"About what?" She seemed genuinely interested. It reminded me of Kaura and how she was like my older sister, mom, and best friend wrapped into one.

I told Gwen, "I'm just thinking about how different I am to the rest of you. If I am truly a Refashion, why do I look more human?"

Gwen thought about my question. "That really is something to think about. To be honest, I never thought of you like that. Maybe you should ask Nátàl."

I nodded. "Yeah, I guess. I just don't want to seem shallow."

Gwen soothed, "Nonsense."

I hugged her. "Thanks, Gwen."

She held me close. "You're truly welcome. Now let's get out there and dance."

I smiled. "Okay."

We made it on the floor and found Derek and Annora at the center. They were probably the cutest non-official couple I have ever seen. Her beauty and delicateness and his handsomeness and leadership made a perfect match.

Annora asked, "Hey, girls. Don't you love a night out?"

"I do. This is probably the highlight of our lives." Gwen bopped to the music.

Annora didn't miss a beat. "Maybe, but we are the chosen ones, you know."

I said, "Right, that never escaped my mind." Both Annora and Gwen were laughing. Derek just smiled, mostly at Annora.

The more I frolicked with them, the more Refashion felt like home. Even so, at the back of my mind was a hammer smashing my reality. That I had a real family, and they were all lost.

The song changed, and a faster tempo filled the room. Everyone in the room plummeted and danced hard. The impact caused the room to shake. The bass was powerful and caused my heart to pound to the beat.

I scanned the crowd and found nothing but happy faces. They all seemed frozen in a state of adolescence, but in actuality, they harbored any age.

"Dance, silly." Gwen was moving on the beat. The disco light hit her golden skin and illuminated her figure. She was having the best time of her life.

"I will. I'm just taking it all in," I said through a distant gaze. My attention was on Flair, who was bouncing to the beat, and Quint, who was struggling to keep up with her. The sight was entertaining. His body wasn't fluid and jabbed whenever he attempted to wiggle a certain way.

"Gwen, look at that!" I pointed at the two of them. She had to witness this once in a lifetime event.

"Oh, no...he's doing it all wrong," she snickered. After catching her breath, she said, "The poor thing."

I agreed with her. "Yeah, it's unfortunate." My eyes moved from their awkward dance and found Octavion, who was dancing with a girl. One who looked familiar.

I walked over to them and found Sarah dancing. She looked amazing. This was the most dressed I'd seen her.

"Wow, Sarah, you look amazing!"

She was surprised to see me and gave me a big hug. She smiled and said, "What? This old thing." We both laughed, and I just stared at her with happiness. She was home, and I could tell she was happy to be back.

Her dress was a navy-blue ball gown with diamonds on the waistline and at the cut of the dress. She had a sapphire necklace, with a bracelet and earrings to match. Her long hair was filled with curls. Some strands had sparkled jewelry in them. Sarah said, "You look amazing too, Jewels."

"Thanks." Octavion made a noise interrupting our small conversation.

Octavion was wearing a burnt-orange suit. It hugged his arms as he moved. He even had an animal bowtie. It made his suit complete. So I flattered him. "Oh, you look nice as well, Octavion."

He put his hand on his chest as to be surprised and said, "Who me? Why thank you." We glanced at each other, and in unison, we laughed. I had to stop because my muscles convulsed, causing a sharp pain in my side.

Sarah said to him, "Wow, you are something special."

He stopped laughing. "No more special than you." Then he winked.

Sarah gave out a sharp insecure laugh and stared at me with big eyes. I decided to excuse myself. "You guys have fun."

"Jewels!" Sarah yelled after me.

I turned to leave, containing my excitement from the two of them. The floor was still filled with people, and I had to wiggle my way back to where Gwen was. Before I could reach her, a large hand grabbed me and spun me into his arms.

"He-hello," I said, confused. He was very tall, with muscles. Not as much as Octavion, of course. I haven't seen one person as big as Octavion.

His chiseled chin moved. "Jewels, right?" His voice was like the others, smooth with honey.

"Yeah, what's your name?" I screamed over the loud music.

"Banter." He twirled me away from him, stopping me before I hit the person in front of me. Then he pulled me back to him. He engulfed me in his arms.

"Nice to meet you," I said. I was too close to him and felt uncomfortable.

"You too." He looked at me and gave me a very convincing smolder.

Then he continued, "Why didn't you show off your powers?"

This was why he stopped me. He wanted to see what I could do.

"I didn't want to," I said plainly. He didn't care for that answer. His shoulders slumped, caring his face into my space.

"Why didn't you?" He repeated.

"I have my reasons," I said with enough force that he would drop the interrogation. He released me from his arms, and I walked away, never looking back or hoping to see him again.

I saw Quint by the refreshment bar, alone. I slowly walked over to the table and grabbed a refreshment. I sipped for a while before asking, "How was your dance with Flair?"

He looked at me and frowned. "Long. I exercise, but dancing with her, I felt out of shape."

Remembering his attempt at dancing made me laugh, "She seemed to really know how to move," I said, gleaming.

"Yes, she does. Anyhow, where did we leave off earlier?" Quint asked. I don't think he wanted to talk about his unfortunate attempt at dancing.

"Oh, uh. I believe we were talking about our personal protectors and how they made fools out of us," I said through a grin.

He snapped his finger. "Yes. You were at a party and..." He trailed off, allowing me to fill in the space.

I told him, "I was at a friend's party, and she popped up talking to me. Everyone around me gave me looks. Apparently, I was talking to a black and white cat." His profound chuckle filled our bubble once again, "That's ruthless. My ALICE showed up while I was on a date."

I mumbled a quiet, "Oh."

I know I shouldn't feel the way I do. We had separate lives before this. If I weren't one of the Seven, then I would have never met him.

I added, "What did she do?" I didn't know if he caught on to my disappointment or not.

He just replied, "She walked up to my table and asked if I knew where the bathroom was. I asked her, isn't that a question for your parents? My mom then asked me who I was talking to."

I was confused. "I'm sorry, your mom?"

He looked at me sheepishly. "Yeah, my mom likes to have dates."

I sounded way too happy. "Oh, that's really sweet."

He simply replied, "Yeah, I guess."

I wanted to know more. "And then what happened?"

He filled me in, "Well, my mom thought I was going crazy and tried to take me to the hospital. I convinced her otherwise. ALICE, however, was still hanging around for the whole day, and I had to pretend not to see her. It wasn't until Martin came that she dropped the act."

"Insane. Do both of your parents know about you?"

"No, my dad left a long time ago. My mom had no clue I was special. What about you?"

I said as little as possible. "My mom left us but, my dad knew about the Refashion. I can't ask him about it, though."

Quint wanted to know more. "Why?"

I gave a soft puff. "He's missing. I don't know what happened."

He reached for my hand. "I'm sorry. I know what it's like to miss your family."

"Yeah, I guess you do."

We talked for hours. We would take turns asking each other questions. Mostly about our old lives. Who were our friends, how well we did in school, what we were interested in. Quint was a great listener; he never seemed bored with the conversation. He respected me enough not to ask too many personal questions. Although I could tell he was curious, just as I was of him. It amazed me how much we were alike.

Before I knew it, the lights came back on, and Nátàl walked back into the room. "Did everyone have a wonderful night?" The crowd clapped and shouted in response. She smiled. "Would the Crypto-Hept please join me up here?"

Quint turned to me. "That would be us."

The crowd split apart to let the Seven through. When we reached Nátàl, she had us take a spot on either side of her. I took my place next to her, and she leaned over. "If you don't mind, I would like to talk to you later." I was surprised. I had a feeling she knew I wanted to talk to her too. "Sure, that would be great, actually." She smiled and straightened up. "Wonderful."

Her smile disappeared as she faced the awaiting eyes. "I have received some horrible news. The disease that has taken over Europe has spread to Africa and South America. Soon it will reach North America. Our schedule has moved up a couple of days."

You could feel the air leave the room and hear a pin drop. No one moved or said anything. They were all in shock. Nátàl continued, "Fear not, these men and women standing next to me will stop them once and for all. The Scourgers have no chance." All those hungry eyes cheered. "I also have some wonderful news." She paused for effect. "Our lab is getting closer to a cure."

Everyone and I do mean everyone cheered hearing that. The other six Crypto-Hept were clapping and smiling. I too was excited. That meant my friends would be okay.

She concluded her speech with, "May God bless this world, and may He keep the Crypto-Hept safe." Then she turned around and was out of the room once again.

Gwen walked over to me. "Well, the night is officially over."

Flair added, "Can you believe it's five o'clock in the morning?"

I was stunned; it didn't feel like it. "Insane." I looked around, and the sea of people started to dwindle down. There were only a couple of lingering people. Some were stuffing their faces with food. Others were getting in last hugs and goodbyes.

"All right, let's head back to our hall," said Derek.

Who am I?

I awoke to a soft knock on the door. Just for a moment, I tried to figure out where I was. The night before was surreal. Everything came rushing back to me in a jumbled scene. I saw flashes of Octavion changing into an animal and Flair, setting a fire in the Great Hall. I also remembered talking to Quint. Our conversation dwelled in the back of my mind, reminding me of my mission today. To find out who I am.

The knock on my door persisted. So I said, "Come in." It was Vivienne. I was happy to see her, "Hi, Vivienne. It's…nice to see you."

She gave a bright red smile. "You as well. I just wanted to say hello. I didn't get a chance yesterday. You looked lovely."

"You saw me?" I was surprised. With the sea of people, it was hard trying to find anybody.

She nodded. "Yes, but only for a second. I was called away."

I sulked, "Oh, that's unfortunate. It would have been nice to see your red dress." Vivienne's sharp hiccup laugh consumed my ears, and I winced a little.

"Sorry, it's too early?" She smiled.

"No, you're fine."

After a short pause, I asked, "Where's ALICE?"

Vivienne hummed. "She's in training. She will be by later to see you. But I'm here as a friendly reminder for you to meet Nátàl Mater at twelve in her office. Hallway C. She would like to talk with you."

I nodded violently, which gave me a headache. "Yes, I remember. Thank you." The loud music from last night left a drumming pulse in my head.

"You're welcome. How are you adjusting?" She looked at me with a caring face, only what I assumed a mother would have. She really cared for me, and I found it was better to give her some slack. I decided this was a good time to lie. "Pretty well, really. I have slightly more control over my gift."

She responded, "So I've heard." She didn't believe me. So much for the slack.

I wanted to change the subject. "What time is it?"

She understood. "Ten. I thought you might want to grab breakfast before you see Nátàl Mater."

"Oh, I'm not hungry just yet. I'm still full from last night." She gave a small nod and seemed to run out of things to say.

She turned and walked toward the door. "Oh, Vivienne?" I stopped her.

She faced me, excited to continue our conversation. "Yes?"

"Do you know what I hit my head on in the car?"

She hiccupped again. "Oh right, the door handle. We were never meant to go that fast, but the lever has been acting strange lately."

"Ah, huh, it's good to know that. Thanks."

"You're welcome. Well, I'll let you get ready."

I smiled and said, "See you around."

She responded, "Definitely."

Then she was out of my room. I quickly jumped out of my bed. I had a mission, and I couldn't wait to find out the truth.

I walked to the bathroom and found another white outfit waiting for me. After taking a shower and getting dressed, I stepped from my room into the hallway. I didn't see any of my friends, so I continued through the heavy double doors. Like before, it was busy. Only this time, when I entered, everyone stopped and stared at me. The silence was maddening. I felt like an animal on display for everyone to see.

Then someone clapped. That clap sparked a fire in everyone else, and then they all were cheering. I smiled when I saw Saraphine and realized that she was the one who started the tremendous welcome. She walked to me, and I gave her a hug.

"Hello, dearie, how was last night?"

I smiled, "It was wonderful! I'm sad that I didn't get to see you. I would have loved to share a dance with you."

She returned my smile. "Indeed, I would have as well. When you win the war, I will share a dance with you. How does that sound?"

I looked at her knowingly. "Great."

I never knew it was possible to miss someone that you recently met, but I did. This place, Refashion, was my home. "Now you need to be on your way to see Nátàl Mater, yes?" She beamed at me.

I tilted my head. "How did you know?"

She gave me a smile that let her animal growl escape. "I know everything I need to know about you. Remember, I take care of you."

Saraphine said softly, "Now then, dearie, let's get you to that meeting."

We passed the second double doors and turned left through the open hallway. Instead of going through the library, like before, she took me through another door that opened to a stairwell. After taking the stairs down two flights, we made a right.

The hallway we entered looked familiar. It then hit me that I was in the same hall I saw Ray in. The same hallway where he looked like a real animal. I knew if I asked Saraphine about his current situation, she would dismiss it. Tell me not to worry. However, I did worry. He wanted to capture me for a reason. But asking Saraphine would only lead me with more questions than answers.

After taking me past a couple of doors, I was standing in front of Nátàl's office. I was suddenly anxious. I wanted to find out about myself. I also wanted to know if there was any news about my father's and Keith's location. But there was no certainty that I would love the answers. A drip of sweat collected on my forehead. I quickly wiped it away. I had to focus.

Saraphine glanced in my direction. She knew I was nervous.

"I'm ready," I lied.

Saraphine gave a soft knock on the door and walked away. Over her shoulder, she said, "I hope she answers all your questions."

Before I could respond to Saraphine, the door opened, and Nátàl was standing there with her honey smile. "Good afternoon, please come in." She took a step back and allowed me access to her office. Like before, her office was dim and warm. She pointed to a soft flower bed couch. I sat down and was reminded of my couch back home. She was the first to speak, "Now I understand you have a lot of concerns. I would like to answer them to the fullest of my ability."

I measured my words. "Yes, I do. I appreciate the time you have taken to address them."

Nátàl patiently asked, "Of course. So what is your first question?"

"Well, why do I seem different? Not to put Quint on blast but—"

Nátàl Mater understood. "Yes, you both are different because you both are not fully Refashion. Your father would have told you one day, but considering there is a one and thousandth chance, you would have been involved with us at all…"

I interrupted her, "Wait…so…if I weren't chosen, then my father wouldn't ever have told me about this place?"

Nátàl looked at me and answered, "That is correct."

"Why? I mean, I love it here. I don't think that's fair. Do you?"

She looked at me and said, "Well, you should hear this from your father."

Whatever she had to tell me, I wanted to know. "Please, I can handle it."

"All right, your mother is the one that was born here. Your father met her twenty years ago. She was on a mission to find the exact location of the Scourgers. We had heard some rumors of a disease outbreak." She paused.

"I'm with you," I replied.

She continued, "Your mother was a part of our protection detail. She was accompanied by four other members, and they traveled to New York. At the same time, your dad was there on vacation. Later, your mother found out that the information they had gathered about New York proved incorrect. So they decided to stay the night and head home early the next morning.

"Your mother ventured away from her team members and collided with your dad. Long story short, your father and mother fell in love. Your father convinced her to stay, and three years later, they were married, and you came into the world."

I breathed.

Well, I still wanted to know. "So if they lived together, why is she not here?"

Nátàl explained further, "She left your father a year after you were born. She wanted to come back here to help. She missed her home. Your father, however, did not want to live underground. They fought over who could keep you. Your father won the argument because he told her if she died, who would take care of you?"

I couldn't say anything. I was in complete shock. I couldn't believe my sweet old dad would fight so dirty. He never seemed capable of doing something like that.

"What happened to my mom?"

Nátàl took a deep inhale and exhale. "She went on another mission years later, and we lost contact. We sent a full team of Guard members to find her trail, but instead, we found a survivor who was badly injured. He told us after they broke into the warehouse, Scourgers attacked, and they were defeated. She was lost in the chaos, assumed dead. I am truly sorry."

I couldn't shed a tear because I didn't remember her. "I'm guessing my mother told my dad about you guys."

Nátàl paused and said, "Correct."

I still probed further. "He wasn't friendly in the whole process, huh?"

She replied, "No, he wasn't, I'm afraid. Believe me, we are looking for him. Any other questions?"

"Yes, how far are you truly with discovering the cure?"

Nátàl explained further, "Honestly, we are far behind. I don't believe invoking fear into the heart of others. But we will find it, I'm certain."

Okay, I could breathe. "I believe you."

Nátàl beamed, "Wonderful."

I added, "My last question. What happens to us after it's all over?"

"Us? Please clarify."

"The Crypto-Hept. What happens to us?"

"Oh, you mean your powers." She moved from her chair in the corner to the couch and sat next to me. "The seven of you will no longer carry the gift that has been bestowed upon you. Just like it came, it will fade away. When the world does not need the powers anymore, they shall disappear."

I wondered what would happen then. "So I would leave?"

Nátàl answered, "Only if you want to."

There was a soft knock on the door. As if she knew who it was, Nátàl spoke, "She is always on time." She graciously stood from the couch and walked to the door. She opened the door, and Saraphine was waiting patiently. They exchanged a few words, but I could not understand them. It sounded like they were speaking Latin. A dead language, or so I thought. The people here have been using it since I've been here.

"Now come then, dearie." Saraphine softly spoke.

I walked over to the door. "Thank you for the answers." A small smile came across my face. I was grateful, but now more questions surfaced in my thoughts.

Nátàl placed her hand on my shoulder. "You're welcome, now run along. You have training."

With that, she stepped back and closed the door. I faced Saraphine with a shocked face. "I thought that was going to be terrifying, but it felt like I was in there for five minutes."

Saraphine corrected me, "Thirty actually. Now come along. We need to move along. You don't want to be the last one to arrive, right?"

"I do not want to be that person," I told her.

She said, "Well then, let's get a move on."

We traveled back the way we came; except when we went to the stairwell, we made a right into the Great Hall. She stopped by the door. "I won't be picking you up. I have some business to attend to. However, I'm certain the others will help you get home." She gave me her last smile and walked away. I called after her. "Oh, wait."

Saraphine turned around. "Did you know my mom?" She smiled the most beautiful smile.

"She was my best friend." Saraphine winked and then turned around down the hall.

Wow. When I get the chance, I have to know more about my mom. I walked into the room and found Gwen and Quint talking. Flair was playing with fire on her fingertips. Derek, Annora, and Octavion had not arrived yet. A large projector on wheels was placed at the end of the table, and seven extensive files were scattered across the table.

"Hey, guys."

"Good afternoon," said Gwen, standing up to greet me with a smile and a hug. "How's it going?"

I didn't want to appear uneasy. "Great. A little tired from last night." As for a distraction, I added, "Gwen, how old are you?"

She responded, "Oh, well, I am only eighteen."

Absentmindedly, I said, "Oh, I expected you to be older."

Flair snorted at my response. I realized what I had said, so I tried to clean up the mistake. "I mean, it's just that Saraphine is almost fifty, and she looks twenty."

Gwen didn't seem bothered at all and explained, "Well, in that case, yeah. Sometimes others stop aging at different ages. She stopped when she was twenty-four."

I took the liberty to ask more questions. "When do you stop aging?"

Gwen responded, "I don't know—whenever my body is ready, I guess."

I said to her, "Interesting." I then turned my attention to Flair. "How old are you?"

She gave me a smirk. "Wouldn't you like to know."

I said, "Yes, I actually would."

At the same time, the rest of the seven came into the room. They were laughing and boasting about last night's dance.

"Well, it's nice of you guys to join us," Flair said, pushing.

"What! We aren't late," Octavion snapped.

"Yeah, we know. Come in, Jewels was just asking us our ages," Gwen said with a lighter tone.

Annora gave a small chuckle. "Oh, this is going to be interesting."

"I just wanted to know. Since you guys don't age as fast as humans do," I said defensively.

Octavion simply said, "Well, I will save you some time. We are all between the ages of eighteen and nineteen."

I was a little disappointed and said, "Oh."

"Yeah, nothing fancy," Flair said. She stopped playing with her fire and blew the flames out.

The door across the hall opened, and Beetly came gliding in with his wobbled walk. "Afternoon everyone, please take a seat. We have lots to do." He turned around and turned on the projector and attached a computer to the system. The lights suddenly dimmed, and we would have been in complete darkness had it not been for the screen.

"Now I understand that you are curious about what you all experienced yesterday? More specifically, what you all fought." Beetly clicked on the slide. A 3D image of a Scourger popped into the center of the table. Specifically, the one that looked like a black cloud. "This is a Scourger. This is also known as Caligo. They can go through anything. Their stench alone can kill a human. But you are more than human, and it just stinks to you." Beetly paused. I found this to be a perfect time for a question. I raised my hand.

"Yes, Jewels?"

"Because of the make of the Caligo, is Quint the only one that can kill them?"

"I'm afraid so, we were trying to create flashlights that were as strong as Quint's powers, but we were unable to recreate that gift ourselves." He then clicked the next slide. A large tree barked Scourger appeared in the middle of the table.

"This one is known as Arbor Cortice. Their tree-like features are just another way of disguising the disease that is lurking beneath. They release the disease through the cracks and leave behind residue that later disintegrates everything." He clicked again. "We call this one Bellua. Its bite is strong and toxic. Stay away. It runs at a great speed, up to fifty miles when it's hungry."

"Oh, great. Just what we need. A rabid dog." Flair scoffed. She received snickers from her comment, but Beetly wasn't amused. He clicked to the next slide. This time a human was over the table. "This particular Scourger is responsible for diseases that are transmitted by contact. They are not among the deadliest in terms of fighting, but the diseases they carry are more potent than the Bellua and Arbor Cortice combined."

"And finally,"—he clicked to the next slide—"this is Multumcarne. They can reach as high as thirteen meters…"

Quint raised his hand. As if Beetly knew what he was about to ask, he said, "That is forty-two feet." Quint dropped his arm.

Beetly continued, "Now these Scourgers are best killed with sheer force to the head, and anything less may feel like a tickle to them." The slide ended, and the light burned bright once again. Beetly turned off the projector and faced us. "Come along." Then he was out of the door. We all exchanged looks.

"He likes being mysterious, huh?" Gwen said in a chilling voice.

"Yup," added Quint.

"Well, let's not keep him waiting," Derek instructed.

After catching up to Beetly, he took us downstairs to a lab. The lab was filled with test tubes and medical equipment. I looked closer and saw red liquid in the tube. What I assumed to be blood.

A clear liquid in another beaker was bubbling on top of a stirring hotplate. Beetly faced us. "This is where we are trying to make the cure. I wanted you all to see how hard they are working. Working to protect humanity."

"What does the virus do to humans? Besides kill them, of course," Flair asked with no certain tone.

Beetly bluntly explained, "The virus destroys their muscle control. They slowly lose control over their body. They forget how to talk, walk, eat, and even breathe. They die soon after. During the process, there is a lot of pain. Their skin turns yellow with splotches of dark purple. They bleed from their eyes—"

Flair gagged and said, "You can stop now."

Beetly stiffened and stood straight. "I thought you wanted to know, Flair?"

She looked disgusted and told him, "I guess not."

Beetly sharply turned and walked deeper into the lab. He stopped in front of a thick glass cage. A cage that had a Scourger in it. Unlike the Scourgers in the woods, this one was docile. It just stared back at us. Never blinking with its black eyes. The skin on its body seemed like it was rotting. Like a decaying body. Derek was the first to speak. "How could you? How could you think that this is safe?"

Annora agreed, "Derek is right. That *thing* could break out at any moment."

Quint tried to rationalize by saying, "They have the creature because that's how they are going to cure everyone."

Derek wasn't having any of it. "You don't know what you're talking about, Quint. That thing shouldn't be here. Neither should that prisoner remain here."

I almost forgot that Ray was captured and taken somewhere and that everyone knew about it.

Gwen soothed, "You need to calm down, Derek."

I noticed that the Scourger seemed to enjoy our argument. It swayed back and forth in its cage. Moving its eyes to the sound of our voices.

"Who are you, Gwen?" Derek yelled back.

"Are you referring to Ray?" I decided to chime in now.

"The beast has a name. Lovely," Derek scolded.

I said, "He's much like you, you know. He doesn't look like the thing in the cage."

Derek snapped, "Jewels, seriously. They are all the same thing."

Beetly raised his hand and shushed us all. "Quint is right. This is how we've always cured the humans. By capturing a Scourger from his leader."

Quint asked, "What is the leader's name?"

I thought that was a good question. "Yeah, Vivienne never told me either," I implied.

Beetly quietly said, "No one knows."

This response was not good enough for Octavion, who asked, "Then how do you know they are called Scourgers?"

Beetly paused. "We gave them that name. They decimate everything they touch. That is what the name comes from."

Flair sarcastically jabbed, "Well then, I say for a high-tech human race, we are not so ahead."

Beetly told us, "We are learning new things every day." He looked from face to face. "Now let's get started with your training."

The scientists entered the room. One of them, a woman, came near the cage and moved it through the wall. The wall swallowed the Scourger and the pen. She gave us a smile and then continued her work at one of the lab tables. Quint and I were the only ones stunned. Gwen gave me a funny look. "What, haven't you ever seen someone walk through a wall before?" I could tell she was being sarcastic, so I decided not to answer.

Stepping from the room, I had an idea, "Why can't you guys just use your blood to cure the humans?" Well, that idea didn't fly with everyone.

"Are you kidding me?" Derek yelled.

"No? You guys are stronger and have healing properties," I insisted.

"Unfortunately, we've tried that before. The humans cannot handle our blood. It makes the disease worst for them. Our blood is too potent." Annora spoke.

"So human blood is on a different frequency?" I asked.

"Exactly! It's like if a person goes to the hospital to get a blood transfusion. Their blood has to match the donor for the transfusion to work properly," Gwen said. Gwen gave me a pat on the back. She also grabbed my arm. A signal that she wanted to talk.

As the rest of them walked down the hall, we slowed down. "What is it, Gwen?" I asked.

"How was your chat with Nátàl Mater?" she pressed.

I mumbled, "It went well, I guess."

That wasn't enough for her. "Go on." She was motioning for me to continue.

"You know, you remind me of my friend back home. She's nosey too."

"Really? She sounds great." Gwen pushed me slightly. "Tell me."

I responded, "Well, I found out why I'm different. It's because I'm half Refashion." Gwen didn't stop me, so I piled right through. "My mother was a warrior here. She met my father in New York. They got married and had me three years later. But she wanted to go home, and he didn't want to leave his. They split up, and I was left with my dad. My mom died in battle years later."

Gwen was amazed at what I had revealed. "Wow, that is a lot to take in. I am really sorry about your mom."

I sniffed. "It's okay. I don't remember her much."

It's true. My father had never mentioned her, either. I have no real memory of her. "But still." Gwen gave me a hug. One that felt warm. I melted in her grasp.

"Thank you, Gwen." She smiled and ushered me forward.

We caught up to the group, and they were waiting for us by the entrance into the multi-world habitats. "It's about time you two. What were you two doing?" Derek said, using his authoritative tone.

"Nothing," Gwen shot back at Derek.

Beetly demanded, "Everyone in."

The entrance looked different than before. It was no longer a rainforest but a volcano. Octavion rhetorically said, "I'm guessing the first one up is Flair."

She stepped forward and added, "It's about time. I love a challenge."

She turned to Beetly, he then spoke. "You are to collect all of the lava and then place it in the ocean. Forming a mountain."

Flair snickered, "Is that all?" She stretched her arms and her legs. Then she jumped up and down. The rest of us gave her cheers and encouragement. She stepped forward to the bottom of the dormant volcano. Instead of raising her arms like she usually does, she closed her eyes. We all gave each other a look of concern because nothing was happening yet.

Beetly was about to speak when the mountain roared and shook. Then red-hot lava came floating from the mouth of the volcano. Flair opened her eyes and watched the lava smoothly float in the air. The ocean was miles away, but she managed to hold her focus and drop it into the sea.

The cold, icy water sizzled against the boiling hot liquid. Slowly a mountain was forming in the water. It started wide then came to a thin, sharp point. With small crevasses here and there. We all gave Flair her well-deserved congratulations. She bowed and walked back to her spot with a smile of confidence. "Gwen." The sound of Beetly's voice broke our cheering, and all attention was on him. "You will take the rock and put it in the rainforest. After which, you will form an object."

She asked, "What kind of object?"

Beetly responded, "Whatever you wish."

She smirked, "My kind of object."

Gwen stared at the immense mountain that was now stuck in the ocean. The mountain made the slightest shift then stood still. She tried again; this time, it shifted more and kept on moving. Moving straight into the air toward the rainforest a couple of miles away.

Seeing a large object float in the sky against the rules of gravity was astonishing. Not one single piece fell from the mountain. Her control was beautiful. When she set the mountain down, it shook the ground. We almost lost our footing.

The sound was loud and echoed within the dome-shaped miniature earth. I stumbled to regain balance and said, "Nice job, Gwen."

She smiled, "Thanks, Jewels. Do you guys want to see what I turned the mountain into?"

She didn't have to ask twice. "Of course!" shouted everyone.

We walked past the empty volcano, deep into the jungle. Once we made it to the rainforest, we were all speechless. Gwen had created a marvelous work of art. She carved all of us in battle with the Scourgers.

"I thought it would be nice if we were remembered like this," Gwen chirped. No one said anything. We just stared at the masterpiece in front of us.

Gwen's statue was on top of a hill crushing twelve Scourgers with a giant boulder. At the bottom of the hill was Flair with fire gushing from her hands at a giant. Some of the fire even surrounded her feet. To the left of the hill was Quint. He had his leg raised kicking a Scourger back. The other Scourger was being blinded by the sun. Across from Quint was Annora. She had eight Scourgers in a hurricane. The hurricane was bigger than the hill and broader. I looked at Annora, and she was smiling with approval.

We walked around to the side of the masterpiece. There was Octavion in mid-transformation. He was shaped into a saber-tooth cat. That animal was extinct, but he made it look so lifelike. Octavion gave a large belt of approval. "That, by far, is the coolest. I'm going to need to try it."

Beetly said, "Now, now, you need to master the skill first."

Next up was Derek, who had captured several Scourgers in a maze of vines and weeds. "You got my good side," smiled Derek.

"You're facing forward, and your whole face is showing," implied Flair.

"Exactly," Derek smirked. The silence was immediately replaced by our snickers. Everyone seemed to be on that hill. Even so, we had a lot of work to do if we wanted to reach that goal.

I was up next, and I was in the air. Well, not really. Gwen had me on a thin piece of rock that was attached to my back, giving the illusion that I was in the air. I was looking down at the ground below me. There was a Scourger also suspended in air lying on his back, as if I blew him away. I wasn't trying to be biased, but I liked mine better. I was amazed at how she got all the details about us sketched into the rock. Even the scene where the battle had taken place looked real. From the grass to the trees, she had made a true masterpiece.

Beetly was overjoyed. "Wonderful job! I don't think a Geoanagi has ever decided to make something so personal!"

Gwen proudly answered, "Thank you, Beetly."

Quint asked, "What do Geoanagis usually make?"

Beetly answered, "Oh, a castle, New York, etc."

"Well, this is personal." Quint grinned. His clap was a sharp burst of energy in the air. Then the rest of us joined in. All sounding as one unit, giving Gwen the praise she deserved.

Gwen gave a small curtsey, saying, "We are going to defeat them. For centuries, our kind has, and we are no exception. I believe in each and every one of you. You guys are my family. We are Crypto-Hept."

Our roars were loud. Octavion and Derek boosted Gwen in the air, and they cheered, "Potest non prohibere nobis."

I asked, "What are they saying, Flair?"

She answered proudly, "Nothing can stop us." She was smiling, more than I usually see her smile.

"Flair, if you don't mind," I said. She looked at me, cross-eyed. But she didn't stop me from talking, so I continued, "Do you guys have a family? You know, like a mother and father?"

She just stared at me and walked away. I didn't know what it was, but she didn't like me very much. I thought we were on good terms since I helped save the forest from the raging fire yesterday.

Annora snuck up next to me with her fluid and relaxed movement and said, "Don't worry, she doesn't like talking about her family. Never has."

"You sure it's not me? I did make her look bad—"

Annora assured me, "Nonsense. You only did what was necessary."

"Maybe, but I can't help but feel responsible."

Annora shook her shoulders. "I can't help you there."

I wouldn't let it rest. "You can help me by answering the earlier question."

She repeated my question, "Do we have a family?"

I insisted, "Yes." I wanted to know everything about my estranged family. She looked at the group, still cheering and chatting. Flair had joined them and was talking to Quint. Occasionally staring back at me as if to taunt me. I thought Refashions were supposed to be nice.

Annora said, "We all are what you call orphans. Our parents died a long time ago. They fought together in the Measles outbreak."

I pressed on, "That was back in 1955?"

"Yes, like we explained to you earlier, we're not that old. We've been friends ever since they were on tour together. We also became a family when they were murdered."

The use of the word seemed harsh, but then again, my mom had been murdered as well. I wanted her to know I knew what it felt like, but honestly, I didn't. I never knew my mother. She was someone I considered who abandoned dad and me. I never would have guessed she was a secret hero. A hero no one will ever know. I decided it was better to keep that to myself.

Beetly urged us forward, saying, "All right, let's get back to business. Up next was Derek. I want you to make the rainforest dance. I know you tried before; however, you could only do a certain amount. I think you can do much better."

Derek stepped forward with outstretched arms. His muscles flexed from an invisible force that was being released from his palms. After a short pause, the first thing to move was the grass. Next was the Orchids and Lilies. Derek moved to a beat only he could hear. The task of making the forest come alive seemed to come at ease as he swiftly made the lobster-claws rise to the sky and groove to the thunderous beat of the walking rubber trees. Next to follow were the cocoa fruit as they clanked together, creating a sound slightly thicker than the sound of a cymbal. Different species of bromeliads in all colors swayed across rocks and trees.

The Liana vines bounced back and forth. Swooping across the sky, catching themselves on the adjacent trees. Shrubs shimmered in their places, the symphony increasing in strength. My favorite part was watching the walking rubber trees. They glided across the earth with their roots transforming into stubbled feet, their roots digging up the dirt and dragging it across the ground. Worms rose to the surface and wiggled their way free, now able to escape the freshly damaged ground. Derek then moved several palm trees reaching 197 feet. They detached from the earth and danced alongside the rubber trees. For stiff trees, they could dance. Their leaves covered all of us and created shade as they bent their trunks. After a few minutes, Derek placed every flower, vine, and tree back into its place, deafening the chorus.

"Well done," Beetly voiced.

"I agree, that was awesome. If only I could dance like that," Quint smirked.

"You are pretty bad at it." Flair smiled at Quint.

"What's next?" I asked, trying to bring focus to the group.

"It's Quint's turn. I want you to make the whole building go dark."

Quint had only made light. Never had he taken it away. This should be interesting. Quint stepped forward, taking on a much serious tone. Like Flair, he didn't use his arms to make the light do what he wanted. His eyes were closed. The sun was still burning bright. Nothing was happening. "Don't focus so hard. Relax. Visualize what you want the light to do." Beetly's voice was restful.

It was like a switch went off, and the area suddenly turned pitch black. The animals howled and screamed, their sight taken from them. "Wonderful." Beetly's voice was still calm.

"Turn the light back on," Octavin sang.

"Not yet." Beetly quickly stopped Quint. "Octavion, I want you to guide us to the Artic. If you all hope to defeat the evil, you must trust one another."

"Well, go ahead. Help us get out of here," Derek's strong voice boomed.

"All right," Octavion trailed off, and then there was silence.

I didn't know how he was going to communicate with us if he was in animal form. As soon as the thought crossed my mind, I heard a pintsized voice in the back of my mind. It was between a half shriek and Octavion's voice mixed together. "Hey, guys. I will talk you through this. Just listen."

Annora yelled, "Woah. This is freaky." She was right. Octavion was able to speak to us telepathically. If that wasn't bizarre enough, he could do it while in animal form too. Refashions were beyond modified; they were aliens of the sort. They had advanced far beyond what the human brain could understand. What *I* could understand.

Derek then asked, "Yeah, Octavion, what happened to your voice?"

I could hear Quint's voice closest to me. "Better yet, how are you able to do this?"

"We are connected, are we not?" Octavion's small voice said.

"We are connected, but who knew we were *this* connected?" Gwen said.

"Octavion, you can proceed," Beetly said. I could hear him shifting in the dark.

"Wait! Out of curiosity, what animal are you?" I could hear the ridicule in Flair's voice.

There was a long beat before Octavion spoke. "A-a possum."

Flair's derision worsened, and she cackled at Octavion. "That's cute."

Annora's voice was filled with annoyance, "Ah, leave him alone, Flair."

Yet Flair persisted, "Whatever. Go ahead, Mr. Possum." I wished Flair could see my eye roll.

Octavion ignored her comments and said, "Everyone grab one another's shoulder. Then we will head out."

I felt a warm hand on my shoulder. "Hey!" I shouted.

"Hey, back." It was Annora. I was leading the rest. No one was guiding me.

"This is kind of weird, huh?" I whispered.

"No, kidding. We are just full of surprises," Annora remarked.

I bobbed my head in response, forgetting she couldn't see me, so I added, "We are. By the way, did you catch what Octavion said?"

"Yeah, I think he said to duck," she whispered back.

I raised my hands in front of me to protect my face. I felt a large bark and moved my head beneath it. "Watch out," I called to her.

She grunted, "Thanks, that was a close one."

A couple of seconds later, Flair yelled, "Ouch!"

Octavion squeaked, "Oh, did I forget to tell you about the tree, Flair? I'm sorry."

"Nice one." Annora shifted her hand on my shoulder, tightening her grip. I tried stretching, a small sign that her grasp was firm. Even so, her hand stayed planted on my shoulder.

Octavion continued to warn us. "Everyone, step over the fallen log. Now, Jewels." I followed his instructions. Never tripping. We had to turn left then right. Occasionally, he told us to pause while animals passed. "We're almost there. Just a mile or so. Jewels, stop." I halted immediately, which cast a domino effect. The force of the others bouncing into me almost toppling me over.

"Watch it. I like these shoes," Gwen hissed.

"Sorry," said Derek.

"I never saw this before." Octavion was confused.

"What is it?" Derek tried to sound in control, but the lack of sight didn't give the illusion that he was.

"We're on the edge of a mountain. I'm trying to figure out the safest route," Octavion simply spoke.

"Can we go around?" Annora's honey breath hit the back of my neck.

"That will take too long." I could hear Octavion's frustration.

"Whatever you decide, we will follow." I wanted to reassure him and let him know that we are all in this together.

"Well, we have to. We are blind after all," Flair insisted.

"Thank you, Captain Obvious," I had enough with her attitude. It was apparent to me that she and I had a predicament, but if she had a problem with me, she should talk to me. She shouldn't take it out on the others. It was becoming old.

Octavion sternly said, "Guys, let's focus. We can go down."

"Straight down?" Heights were on my list of things that I hated.

"You will be fine," Gwen's voice was far behind me.

Octavion said, "Jewels, I will need you to step to your left. I want you to step on the boulder. Once over, take a couple of steps—"

"Can you be more specific? I don't want to step off and fall." I tried to reason with myself to face my fear.

"Okay…take three steps," Octavion calmly said.

I inhaled then let the air out at a steady pace. "Here I go." I stepped to my left. My foot hit a rock, which I assumed was the one I was supposed to step over. I took three baby steps. Each step that ended with the land below my feet, I thanked God. After taking all the steps, I felt Annora behind me again.

"Now, I need you to turn right and walk straight. Till I tell you to stop," Octavion ordered.

"What?" my voice squeaked. I couldn't believe he expected me to walk without any information.

"Trust me." Then he was quiet. I gathered whatever courage I had left and walked straight. What felt like forever was only a minute or so.

"Stop. Make a slight left. Then continue straight. Try not to go fast."

I chuckled. "You don't have to worry about that."

Octavion was doing a great job leading us down the mountain. He even distracted me with random questions. Mostly about my favorite things to do, eat, and watch. One thing I did notice about this haven was that they were missing a television.

"We're almost there," he said. I could feel the chilly wind on my face and arms.

"Can we grab the jackets at the entrance?" I asked. My teeth were locked together.

He said, "Sure. Just a bit further."

Octavion finally then said, "We're here. Everyone reach to your right." I felt the jacket. I placed it on—instantly warmer.

"Much better," I mused.

"Now if the lights could come back on," Gwen said. She was right next to me. I reached out and grabbed her arm. She jumped with a slight yelp escaping. I chuckled under my breath, careful not to let her hear me.

"You may turn on the lights." Beetly's voice came out of nowhere. I jumped from the sound. Karma. "Where did you go?" I asked.

"Nowhere." He was done explaining. "Quint, the light." Soon the light was back on, and we could all see each other. After having no light, I sunburned my eyes. I blinked several times before my eyes adjusted. Slowly, the bodies before me came into focus.

"Well done, Quint. You are doing much better. Octavion, you handled the situation well. Just be fair to all of them. No matter how frustrating someone can be." Beetly looked in Flair's direction. Then turned and faced Annora. "You're up next. I would like you to make an eighteen-and-a-half-meter wave or above."

Annora looked at Beetly in shock. "Do you know how high that is?"

Beetly spoke sternly. "Sixty-one feet. Please, go ahead."

Annora walked to the edge of the ice patch and swayed back and forth, taking in a deep breath. Letting it out, she raised her arms. The ocean moved. A small wave formed. The wave moved closer to land. Becoming more abundant. It was only about twenty feet high. The wave faltered and decreased in size.

"Focus. You have more power than you know," Beetly encouraged.

Annora's body language screamed stress. Her arms lowered. The wave was still growing but slower than before. "You got this," I shouted. The others chimed in. Giving Annora the support she needed. Finally, the wave reached sixty-one feet. It was closer to the shore and blocked our view from the sun. Annora let the wave drop. The wind rushing past us. Annora looked tired. "That wasn't bad," I said, trying to give her hope.

"It's okay. I know." She faced Beetly, already knowing what he would say.

"More practice. You will get it soon," he said.

That wasn't as bad as I thought it would be. Then suddenly, Beetly turned his attention to me, "Jewels, please make a cyclone." I couldn't believe it.

I asked, "Aren't cyclones made by warm water and wind? It's freezing over here." I knew a few things about the weather, and what Beetly was asking me to do was impossible.

"That's outside where no human has control over the air. Make the cyclone," he ordered.

Now how was I supposed to make the ocean warmer? I contemplated. Once the air was warmed, it made moisture, which turned into clouds. When cooled, they form a circular motion, but I had no control over moisture.

"We're waiting," Beetly said, breaking my thinking process.

Think, Jewels, think, I thought. A light bulb went off in my head. I got it. I visualized the air over the sea, making a circular motion. Like a dog chasing its tail. The wind increased in speed. Taking droplets of water with it. The sky up above formed dark gray clouds. They hovered above my cyclone. Lightning struck from nowhere. It came close to hitting me.

I blacked out. The image of the dome was replaced by a familiar dark scenery. I was in my safe place again. The area was dark and warm. I floated in nothing. My body's instincts took over, and I was suddenly fearful. My body shivered. That's when the figure was in front of me. Its outstretched arm, trying to grab me. The head was moving back and forth, mouth wide open. I couldn't hear what it was saying. I leaned into the figure, trying to get any clue as to what it wanted. Still nothing.

I did hear Octavion's voice in the back of my mind. "Come back." I opened my eyes. I had done it again. I had lost control. I looked out to the sea and saw the Cyclone dissolving back into the ocean. "Was it bad?" I waited for the round of responses I would be getting. All unpleasant.

"At least you completed your task," Gwen offered.

Oops. I did something horrible.

"What happened?" I pushed again.

"Nothing, really. We just had a deadly light show," Derek said with caution. I could feel Derek's pity.

I would need to learn some control. "Sorry, guys. I'll do better next time." I was trying to convince myself more than them.

Beetly reassured me, "Don't worry, Jewels. You will have more practice." He then addressed the whole group. "Now for the fun part. Another group challenge."

Octavion belted, "Sweet."

Beetly continued, "For this exercise, you will be working on trust. One of you will be locked away, and the others have to retrieve their member before time runs out."

Flair demanded, "What's the catch?"

Beetly countered with a devious smile, "No powers."

Our confidence disappeared from the room. The air was thick with doubt.

"What? You have to be kidding me." Annora placed her hand on her hip and leaned to one side, "Isn't the whole point of practicing is so we have better control over our powers?"

Beetly scolded, "Yes, but you guys don't trust one another, like you should. Derek, you will be the one captured."

Derek mumbled, "I'm the leader. Shouldn't I be...you know, the leader?"

Beetly said, "That's exactly why they must do this without you. You all will have the same time limit as before. Remember, no powers, everyone." Beetly disappeared right before our eyes. Derek too. That's how Beetly was able to go and come as he pleased. He transported himself anywhere and everywhere at his own will. I wonder what they call his powers?

"What's the most logical place to have someone locked away?" Annora asked our now dazed group.

"We are just going to dismiss the fact that Beetly transported himself?" Octavion asked.

"Yes. Please, some ideas. Anyone. Don't all rush," Annora asked as she searched through our faces.

Flair jumped at the opportunity. "Our last battle was in the rainforest. I don't think they want us to fight in the same area."

I said shortly, "So that leaves us the Arctic Circle, desert, and the African Plains."

Quint insisted, "They won't be in the desert. Too much sun. The Arctic is too cold for them. African plains it is."

Annora asked Quint, "They might be there. If they are, where exactly? The African Plains are slightly open, except for a few trees here and there?" He mulled over her question. Trying to find the right answer.

"Underground," a voice responded. It wasn't Quint who came up with the answer.

Octavion stepped closer to our huddle. "If the Scourgers don't like the sun or cold, then the only safe place for them is underground." Octavion's theory made sense. They are dark creatures that go bump in the night. If they wanted to stay hidden from the world successfully, then they would be underground.

The only problem, I hated going underground. My first encounter coming to Refashion wasn't the nicest. However, this was a challenge, and I couldn't let that stop me. If I could climb down a mountain blind, then I could walk underground.

"Where do you guys think we should start?" Annora asked softly.

Quint said, following in her tone of voice, "They should have an entrance."

Flair further offered, "Yeah, their hideout should be somewhere dark. It will allow the mist Scourgers to have easy access without burning."

Quint added, "Look for multiple trees together, the ones that create a lot of shade."

We were doing great so far. We figured out what terrain they were in and how to find them. All we need to do was save Derek. No big deal. We broke our huddle and departed toward the African plains, keeping the same triangle formation from last time. Everyone was on high alert as we traveled from the different terrains. Making it to the mini African Plains was magnificent. There were zebras and gazelles. I even saw Zazu resting on an Umbrella Thorn. In fact, there were a lot of Umbrella Thorn trees clumped together. It must be.

"Hey guys, I think I found it," I shouted.

Annora came over to me. The rest followed. Our triangle was now a straight line. She said, "I believe you're right. Nice work."

I felt proud. "Thanks. Now how are we going to approach this?"

Octavion shouted, "We go in blazing."

Annora quickly reminded him where we were by hitting him on the arm. "No! We go in with a plan. Um… I think we should have Quint lead."

Quint cleared his throat, "Me? Why?"

Annora explained, "If there is Mist Scourgers in our way, you will be able to kill them. Also, we won't be able to see much."

"Okay," he said with confidence.

"Flair, I think you should be behind Quint. Better yet, to his side. Your fire can kill things a lot faster than my water or Octavion's transformation. And Jewels, air bending," she said my name like an afterthought.

"Fine by me." Flair was ready to go.

"Octavion, you're going to be to the left of Flair. Jewels, you will be in the center. Gwen and I will pick up the rear. Does everyone get it?" Several nods surpassed Annora as she scanned her new followers. "Great. Let's move out."

Octavion quickly stopped the group. "We can't use our powers, remember?"

Annora slowly realized and looked defeated. "Okay then, Quint, we won't need your light." Quint seemed neither happy nor sad, just relieved. We walked toward the clutter of the Umbrella Thorns in our new formation. I tried keeping up with the others. I did better than yesterday. Being in the middle helped me. I didn't want Gwen or Annora catching up to me so, I pushed through the leg pain.

The closer we got to the cluster of trees, the more birds I saw clustered together. There were lilac breasted-rollers, kingfishers, larks, barbets, and hornbills. I remember drawing these same birds for my art project. All of them were making their own music. *Rak-rak, kyow-kow-kow*, and *krrdii*. Finally, mixing together to make one gigantic symphony.

"Be on the lookout," Annora said from the back of the group. Her voice, quiet but present.

"I see the entrance." Quint pointed to a bottomless hole next to the largest Umbrella Thorn. Most of the hole was covered by fallen branches and tall grass.

"Be careful, Quint." He never turned around but nodded to acknowledge Annora's warning. Quint went through and was swallowed by the darkness. We followed after him. We all stayed within arm distance.

I felt claustrophobic. I tried focusing on the others. What they were saying. But it was no use. My mind wanted to drift. "Jewels, are you hanging in there?" My eyes flew open as I tried to figure out who called my name. The others were converting. No one looked my way. The voice came again, this time I recognized that it was from my head. "You got this. Just talk to me." It was Octavion being the savior. An ease fell over me. "Hey Octavion. Thanks." He then looked in my direction with a smile. "No problem," he said inside my head.

I walked over to the group and caught the last bit of their conversation. "We should just keep straight. We are bound to find him."

Annora sniffed, "That might take too long. We only have thirty minutes to find him."

Flair countered, "Well, what do you suggest?"

Annora's patience was running thin. "I don't know. Any other suggestions?" We were silent.

"See, my plan is better." Flair scampered off.

"Let's go," Annora said, sending glares to Flair behind her back. We jogged after Flair. Our formation broken.

"Wait up," Annora called after Flair. Flair slowed down, just enough for us to catch up. "We have to stick together." Annora was furious.

"Okay." Flair seemed to realize the destruction she had caused. "Sorry."

Annora's voice was genuine. "Just keep in mind our task. We are supposed to trust each other."

"Keep moving, we are running out of time." Octavion's voice echoed through the shallow tunnel.

"All right, keep straight," said Annora. We kept straight for a while. I was fearful that we wouldn't make the time. The rusted and black smudged tunnel never seemed to end. We were running out of time and patience.

"Are we there yet?" I could tell Octavion was trying to be funny, but the others didn't appreciate it. They missed the joke.

"I don't know where we are." Poor Gwen, she even seemed frustrated.

"Look!" I shouted. There was a red humming flair coming from underneath a large rock. The rock was three feet deep, a perfect circle. "How are we supposed to move that? We can't use our powers," I snapped. More frustrated with Beetly than anything.

"We are going to have to push it ourselves," Annora stated simply.

"Like that's going to work," commented Flair.

"We have to try," Quint insisted. All of us gathered on one side of the rock and pushed. It would not budge. We stopped for a short break before continuing. Quint and I were panting more than the others. When this was over, I needed to see about a gym. "One more time, guys," I said.

We pushed, Octavion taking most of the load. The rock shifted slightly. There was hope again. We pushed harder, the sound of rock colliding with rock made my ears ring. "Almost there." Octavion's voice was stressed. I looked up at him, and his face didn't look strained, but his veins were bulging. I cringed at the sight. "There," he finally said. We stopped pushing. Octavion's veins relaxed. The light from the other side flowed through, brightening up our faces. I could see everyone better. They all look tired.

"Let's move," Annora said. Once again, going from straight darkness to light, disturbed my eyes. I blinked to regain focus.

There was a pit of fire that was at least six feet deep. The walkway surrounded the entire cavity. Above the fire pit was a cage. The cage was thick barbed wire. "Hey, guys. Nice to see you." Derek was looking down at us. Smirking.

"There you are." Annora beamed. "Let's get you out." She turned to face us. "Now how are we going to get him down?"

Gwen was the first of us to speak. "We could make a rope and throw it up there."

Annora asked, "What material will we use?"

"What if we—" Quint was cut short by the sound of the opposite wall opening. The wall none of us noticed had a door. Six large beasts came through. They were tall like a moose and thick as a pit bull. Their skin was tight and stretched over their muscles. Scales covered the top and sides of the body. The front was larger than the back. I've seen these types of Scourgers before. One of them was chasing Gwen and me during the earlier simulation. What was the name Beetly used? Oh, forget it, it was in Latin. I decided to call these Scourgers, Malfise instead. They stood cemented in the doorway. My heart stopped in its tracks then beat with the rhythm of a drummer during his solo.

"What are they waiting for?" I heard the tremble in Flair's voice. It wasn't noticeable to the others, but I'd felt what she feels now. I've seen that face before. Flair was more human than I thought.

"Gwen, find a way to make a rope," Octavion said through gritted teeth. The six Malfise were still blocking the other entrance. They stared at us, their eyes locked onto ours. It was an intense stare down, each of us jockeying for position.

Gwen had taken off her top and had an orange tank top underneath. "Guys, give me your shirts." She tied the shirts together by the arms. On the final shirt, she placed a rock inside of it and tied it into a knot. "That should work."

"Hurry," Derek yelled softly.

The Malfises charged toward us. Their bulky bodies hitting one another as they tried to be the first to sink their teeth into our flesh. Out of nowhere, swords popped into our hands. They were beautifully crafted, slick, and light in hand. "Now that's what I'm talking about." Octavion was the first to break our line, heading straight for the leading Malfise. Sword raised, he swung at the beast. The sword had no effect on the scaly texture. Octavion stood dumbfounded. The creature took the opportunity to backhand him into the wall.

I heard something crack when he kissed the wall. "Octavion!" Gwen shouted. She ran to his side. His body was limp. Gwen's relieved face told us he was just knocked out.

Quint yelled, "How are we supposed to kill them? The swords don't penetrate the scales."

I answered, "We go for the soft spots. The belly and hind legs. Those areas don't have scales protecting them."

With full energy, Annora said, "Sounds good to me."

Gwen came back to us with Octavion's limp body. She placed him behind a rock. Then she stood on that same rock and tossed the ladder made of shirts. One of the Malfise let out a deep growl. Its growl vibrated the small enclosure. Rocks fell, and the cage swung back and forth. We all took cover. One large rock hit the cage in the right spot, and its latch broke. Now we had a time limit. The other latch couldn't hold Derek for long. "Gwen, I hate to say this, but work faster," I cautioned.

Gwen snapped, "I know." We were all stressed and tired. It was clear that we wouldn't finish this task in time. The demands were too much. We were falling apart. The beast still charged around the corner. Gwen was still trying to give Derek the ladder. It didn't matter, though. The cage fell into the fire, and the room was dark.

The lights came back on. We were outside by the entrance of the dome. "That was a disaster." Beetly was standing before us. Not angry, just disappointed. "Never have I witnessed such hostility from the Seven. Flair, control your anger. Gwen, don't get upset so easily." He then addressed the whole group, "You all will try this simulation again. For now, take a break and eat lunch." He disappeared.

"That could have gone better," Quint said underneath his breath.

"Oh yeah?" Flair tested him.

"Knock it off. You guys could have easily gotten me out of there," Derek yelled over his shoulder as he exited the dome. Flair huffed and stormed out of the room. Octavion was talking to Quint. They rushed off as well.

"I honestly just want to take a nap," I mumbled. I was too tired to eat. The simulation had drained me emotionally.

"Me too. Hey, do you want to have a small sleepover?" Gwen said through a small smile. She was tired too. Saraphine told me they could do a lot, but eventually, they would crash.

Grinning, I responded, "Sure, that's a great idea. Annora, you can tag along too."

She said, "I was already coming." Gwen and Annora laughed at each other. I stood, waiting to leave. They finally stopped and walked toward the exit.

My room felt warm and cozy. The others didn't say much as we laid down on my bed. I drifted into sleep. But it wasn't Rem sleep. The same dark figure from before reappeared. It was farther away than before. The figure wasn't looking at me. I called out to it. My voice sounded foreign. The figure's back was still facing me. I called again. "What do you want?" It abruptly turned toward me. Then flickered. I sat up in my bed. The others were still asleep. I got out of the bed as quietly as possible.

My feet touched the mat of flowers. "Leaving already?" I turned to find Gwen and Annora sitting up in the bed.

"You guys scared me." I frowned.

"Had a nightmare?" Gwen jumped out of bed and came over to me.

"No. I'm fine. I was just thinking about the simulation," I lied. "I'm trying to figure out a way to get Derek out of the cage without using powers."

Annora knew I was lying, "Sure. We'll go along with that."

Gwen asked, "What were you thinking?" I gave her a soft smile.

"I was thinking that we can bring vines from the jungle with us. That way, we can make a proper rope."

Annora was pleased. "That just might work."

"Now that we got that taken care of, can we go back to sleep?"

"Sure." I just wanted to drift off into a dream. A dream of my dad and me, together again.

Making New Enemies

I felt rested and ready to start the challenge. Annora and Gwen told the others of my plan, and they seemed to like it. Beetly took Derek once more and left us to fend for ourselves. "Okay, everyone, gather vines," Octavion took the role of leader. Annora was pleased with the decision.

Octavion instructed us to disembark into the wild and find our fair share of vines. I found a patch of vines lying by a walking palm tree. I grabbed as many as I could.

I slowly walked back to the group, careful not to drop any vines. Once one fell, they all would. It was like laundry day back home. You dropped one sock, and the rest fell right after.

I returned back to our meeting spot, and the others were giving their vines to Flair. "Nice." Flair weaved the vines into a strong crocheted rope. "Almost done." She was moving fast. "There." Flair's thread was finished, and we were ready to go.

Getting to the Scourger's location was easier than before. I found the same cluster of Umbrella trees. "There." I pointed in its direction. The others followed my finger.

"Let's go." Octavion was leading. Annora right next to him. The boulder was not in front of the hole. It was off to the side like we left it. "That was nice of Beetly," Flair commented.

"I'll take it." Annora smiled. We went through the opening. The fire pit was still there. Dang.

Derek was secured in the cage. "Throw the rope!" he yelled. Gwen looped it like a cowgirl and tossed it in his direction. With ease, he seized the rope and fixed it to the cage. Gwen and Octavion tugged on the rope. The cage swiveled in their direction. "Guys, I think we have company." I looked in the direction of Quint's voice. The six Malfises were standing across from us. "Now if the swords would mysteriously appear again, that would be great." He spoke.

Octavion and Gwen were still trying to pull the cage closer to them. Derek was pinned to one side of the cage as it tilted toward the fire. We waited impatiently for the swords to appear into our grasp. As time went by, the Malfises advanced closer to us. Unlike last time, they didn't charge at us. They slowly approached like a lion in the African plains waiting for the right moment to attack its prey. "Got it." I turned back to find Gwen and Octavion finally pulling the cage from the pit. Now all they had to do was open it.

I also made a mistake. I turned away from the Malfises to witness the progress that Gwen and Octavion made. When I looked back, one of the Malfises was right in front of me. "A little warning next time?" I yelled at the others.

"What could we have done? We are a little busy," Flair snapped back. She was telling the truth, though. They were busy with their own Malfise in front of them. The question was, where were the other two?

The beast slapped my body back like a rag doll. I couldn't brace for impact as I hit the jagged rock wall. My skin opened to an outpouring of blood on my left arm. For some strange reason, I was half expecting to see a different color of blood. I've bled plenty of times before, and it was always red. I don't know what I was thinking.

The Malfise was still coming toward me, claws out. I sat up against the wall, using it as a brace. Once my feet hit the ground, the sword decided to appear in my hands. "Really?" I gripped the sword and used my non-dominant hand to cut at the Malfise. Every time my left arm moved, blood dripped onto the sand, making a mound of dark red mud. I tried to block the pain. I felt my body slip into the darkness. I quickly shook it off. I had to focus.

I reached out with the sword and found the meat of the beast. As I dug my blade into its flesh, blood dripped down my arm. It smelled of rotten eggs. The blood ate at my shirt. I watched as the blood tore at the fabric. I panicked and dropped my sword to rip off the sleeve. I was unsuccessful at first. My left arm could no longer support itself. I saw Gwen in the corner of my eye as she ran past me. She slaughtered the beast. I felt the blood eating at my flesh. The pain was enough to take an elephant down. I hollered at the sight of it. It was like acid being poured over me. The others surrounded me as I screamed for them to make it stop. My vision dulled as the pain took over.

"It will. Just hold on," Annora assured as she grabbed my back. She was holding me down, as I thrashed about, trying to will the pain away. The room went completely dark, and then light reappeared. The pain was gone. I looked at my arm and found no sign of the erosion. I was healed.

"Jewels, are you, all right?" Beetly was kneeling next to me. He was genuinely concerned for my well-being.

"Yes. Thank you. Did we pass?" I wanted to know if my pain was worth it. Beetly stood and smiled.

"Yes, you did. Training is now over." Then he was gone in a cloud of smoke.

"Can someone please tell me what happened?" I spoke through shallow breaths.

Gwen grabbed my arm as she pulled me to my feet. "For starters, you tried to kill a Scourger and—"

I cut her off, "Oh no, I remember that part all too well. What happened with you guys?" I corrected.

Quint spoke for the group. "We did what you suggested and went for their Achilles heel, which happened to be its underarm."

I was shocked my plan had actually worked. "Really? Well, if I see a Malfise, I'll just let you handle it." As soon as I said it, I regretted it.

"Malfise? What's that?" Gwen stepped back to look at me. I was met with curious faces.

"I call the dog ones Malfise," I said plainly. I wanted to avoid any more humiliation.

"What do you call the other ones?" asked Flair. I wasn't looking at her, but I could feel her smirk.

"If you all must know." I paused. "Because the names Beetly gave us are too difficult to remember, I named them Mist, Malfise, Treed, Human, and Giant. I'm still working on the names, so…" I looked at their faces, none of them indicating any expression or thought.

"I like Malfise." Octavion smiled in my direction.

Embarrassed, I said, "Thank you."

"Why call it human? They are not human." Derek voiced.

"They aren't, but they looked human. When we first had our battle, they walked like them," I responded.

"Still, would you want to be classified with that thing?" Derek pushed, baiting me even.

"I'm not like them. Besides, I said I was working on the names." I didn't yell, but it was close.

"What about Impostor? For the human." Gwen broke our conversation.

"Sounds good to me," Annora added.

"Or Humanoid?" Octavion added with glee.

"Octavion, that makes them sound like robots." Flair snapped, but not in an aggressive way.

"Okay, Impostor it is." Octavion was content.

"You guys were telling me what happened…" I realized how off-topic we were.

"When the… Malfise attacked, we came together. To have better odds. You were too far from us by then. I ran to you as soon as I could." Gwen informed, trying not to smile while using the word *Malfise*.

"How did you get Derek out?" I asked.

"They pulled the cage away from the fire and broke the lock with a rock." Derek shrugged. The whole task was simple.

"That's all?" I said.

"I'm afraid so. Beetly wants us to meet with him tomorrow. More training." Annora grabbed my arm, examining it.

"It's fine," I said, moving my arm away.

"Okay. Let's get out of here." Annora led the group out.

My body felt sore from yesterday's fight. My arm no longer burned, but the memory still burned in my mind. I tried taking an ice-cold bath to soothe the aches but, more importantly, to distract me from my thoughts. It seemed lately that I was always hiding from my past regressions and fears. Even so, one way or another, they'll eventually surface and cause me grief.

I couldn't stay in the freezing water any longer. The ice stuck to my nerves like glue and sent a piercing pain down my spine. I swiftly maneuvered my way clear of the ice and out of the tub.

I walked into my room and found a folded leaf on my dresser. The note read:

Meet the team in the Jar Room.

Thank you,
Beetly

Another day. Another practice. I just hope there are no more Scourgers involved, maybe something peaceful.

I grabbed my attire and placed it on. Finally, the designer team has figured my body size and the clothes fit. I was sure Saraphine had something to do with it. She was always looking out for me.

I glanced at myself in the stand-up mirror. The sleeves were made of stretchy material, allowing me access to my arms. The leather pants bell-bottomed with three translucent white swirls going up the leg. My legs were showing just a little from the swirls access point. I decided it would be best if I placed my hair in a high ponytail. I had no clue what Beetly planned to do today, and having my hair loose didn't seem like a well thought out plan. Satisfied, I left my room.

The heavy door clanked as I shut it. I looked across the hall and found Annora closing her door. "Good morning, Jewels. How are you feeling?" She was smiling and obviously well-rested, unlike me.

"I feel much better," I lied. "You look very cool." I distracted her with the truth.

She was wearing a teal leather suit like mine; only hers came with a hood. "Thank you. You look great too. I wonder what we are going to do today?"

"Me too. Are we the last ones?"

"Yes. They left early to catch us a table." Annora walked toward the double doors.

"Wait up," I called after her. If it was possible for humans to float, she had mastered the art.

"Sorry." She slowed her walk enough for me to catch up. "I'm glad you are feeling better. The cut on your arm wasn't pretty." I had to laugh at her. She was worried about a two-inch deep cut and not the arm that was melting off. "Don't get me wrong. The acid was bad as well," she corrected herself.

"No, kidding. I never want to experience that again."

We made it to the stairway, and the area was busier than usual. For the first time, I saw kids. They were dressed in school uniforms. A bright-blue shirt with black pants. My jaw dropped. "That's my first time seeing kids here," I blurted loudly. They didn't seem human, more like perfect mannequins.

"Really? We need to show you around more." Annora was laughing at me now. Her laugh was pretty and musical.

"We're here," I stated, trying to get away from her laughter. It would have been fine if she was laughing with me and not at me.

The Great Hall was transformed into a bed and breakfast theme. The tables were covered with white cloth, and jam jars filled with candles were placed on top. Brown hay-like yarn wrapped the rim of the jars. The room was filled with the smell of breakfast. "Where does the line start?" I was hungry since I skipped lunch and dinner yesterday.

"Line?" Annora questioned.

"You know where we pick up our plate?"

"Oh." Annora's face brightened. "Servers bring our food to us. We just have to find the others." She walked deeper into the room and easily found her way around the mounds of people seated at their tables. A couple of them stared at us because of our distinct out-fit choice. It was clear that Refashions only wore earth tone colors, so seeing us was like a pop of color. We found the other five seated at the last table toward the water fountain.

"Good morning, everyone." Annora was the first to greet them. I took a seat next to Sarah.

"Good morning, Annora. Jewels, how are you feeling?" Derek asked. He appeared to be concerned as his body was leaned in. I was shocked. He didn't seem like he cared that much yesterday.

"Fine, thanks." The rest of the group had the same material as Annora and me. The only difference was that they wore their specific color as usual. Annora, Quint, and Flair had hoods. Octavion and Derek had no sleeves. Gwen and I had the same swirls on the sides of our legs.

"What happened to you?" Sarah asked. ALICE was giving me a concerned look.

"Nothing. Just a brutal practice." A waitress dressed in a light-green, almost mint jumpsuit came over to our table. She was young like us. Probably the same age. She wore green eyeshadow, which looked gorgeous against her brown skin. She took our order, and within minutes, our food was placed in front of us. There was fresh-baked biscuits and grits.

Along with waffles, pancakes, and fruit. "You guys don't eat meat?" I said after taking a bite of my waffle.

Octavion's growl bellowed. Again, I was at the center of their laughter. "Uh...no. The whole protect the Earth, and Mother Nature kinda alludes to no harm of animals." Then he bit into his biscuit.

"Oh." I looked down at my plate.

"Sarah, how've you been?" I asked after a sip of my orange juice.

"Great, ALICE and I have been working on some new updates for her. It's not finished yet. I also have been working closely with the Guard," Sarah said proudly.

I interjected, "Oh, you mean Ash." I still remembered the car ride.

Sarah took a bite of her pancake. "I don't know what you're talking about."

ALICE said, "Please, you practically—"

"I wouldn't finish that sentence, ALICE," Sarah joked with her.

"Fine." ALICE tilted her nose in the air. She then turned her attention to me, "But my updates will be cool. You just wait." ALICE smiled. She looked more like a nine-year-old kid than the smartest android on the planet.

"Sounds great, ALICE." I was enthusiastic for her. She was becoming more and more like an annoying little sister that I never had.

"Are you guys always like this?" Quint asked.

"Only when we are together," Sarah replied.

I asked, "Do any of you know what we are doing today?"

"I do," Sarah spoke up.

"Really?" Derek carried skepticism in his voice.

"Yes." Sarah held her ground. "You guys are working with the Guard today. You will be training for combat."

"And to think I thought we would do something relaxing." I leaned back in my chair.

Annora softly patted my shoulder. "Not today."

After breakfast, we went straight to the Jar Room. The walk wasn't supposed to last long, but then again, we are the Crypto-Hept, and many people wanted to have a word with us. Others just wanted to admire our outfits. Finally, we turned onto a hall where there were no Refashions insight.

"Has anybody been in the Jar room before?" Quint asked.

"Nope, only the people of the Guard are allowed." Derek turned to look at Quint.

"I'm guessing you don't know why they call it Jar Room?" I asked.

"You would be correct," Derek said as he stood in front of the door. His muscular body only took up a third of the door. It was black and bolted. A symbol was etched into the door frame in red. It was a large cross inside of a circle and a diamond behind the cross.

The door swiftly opened. Cold air rushed out, hitting our faces. "Gosh, Jewels. We didn't need that!" Octavion screamed.

"Ha. Ha. Ha. Very funny." I mocked Octavion. The inside of the room was spacious and dark. The walls were black with red stripes perfectly stationed in the center and corners of the walls. At the back of the room was a large metal garage door. To the far left was a six-feet-wide, eight-feet-tall cage enclosed in glass. Inside the enclosure were swords, guns, and armor.

"Woah!" Quint whistled at the sight of the stash.

"Nice." Derek approved as well.

"Look." Gwen was pointing to a large rock-climbing set. It started at the ground, but then stretched all around, hitting all the crevices of the room. At the center of the room was a large ring. No ropes.

"This room is huge," Annora's voice echoed.

"The ceiling is high. Just like the Dome," Quint observed. I figured out why it was called Jar Room. The ceiling was high but closed off like the top of a jar. "They even have a weightlifting section." Gwen ran over to it and lifted a fifty-pound weight like it was five pounds.

Suddenly a voice offered, "I'm glad you like the place. Maybe we can arrange something." We all turned to the person who was speaking. It was Ash with six other Guard members. "My name is Ash. I will be training you. You will learn how to fight hand to hand combat, fight with a sword, and to control your powers. Behind me are Zappa, Axel, Beckett, Heather, Lois, Brees, and Cormac. They will be assisting me in training."

Zappa was broad and tall. He had curly brown hair with his tips dipped in bronze. His skin was a soft caramel color. Axel was shorter than Zappa but still tall. He shifted in his stance. His sharp blue eyes reminded me of Flair's. Beckett was the coolest one standing there. She wore black lipstick, and her hair was in a braided ponytail. Her skin was copper, just like Nátàl's. She seemed to smirk at the sight of us. Next to Beckett was Heather. Heather wore red lipstick and was pale. She had black hair. Her stance was firm. Lois looked softer than the rest. Like she just turned eighteen. Her hair was in two braided ponytails. Brees and Cormac were twin brothers in their twenties. The two of them were average height and fit. They each gave sinister glares. I got the feeling they knew something we didn't.

The Guards' outfits were slick. The black leather and rubber stretched over their chest. The collar of their suit had thick red stripes. Their pants matched with one red line going down them. They each carried a holster on their side. Instead of a gun in its place, a blackened steel-edged sword was patiently waiting to be used. The handle was carved with the same symbol as the door. "Our first task is to establish blocking. You will be paired off. Guards, choose your opponent," Ash instructed.

They each stepped from their spot in line and walked up and down, examining us. It was intimidating. When they finally chose, Gwen was with Beckett. Derek was with Cormac. Annora was with Lois. Octavion was with Brees. Flair was with Heather. Quint was with Axel, and I was with Zappa. We each took a spot on the large ring. "Hey, Jewels, right?" Zappa stuck out his hand.

"Yeah." I had to tilt my head all the way back to look at him. "Is Zappa your real name?" I asked after shaking his hand. He stepped forward with his left leg. I stepped back with my right leg.

"Yes. Why does it sound like a nickname?" He smirked.

I said, "It really does."

We repeated the same steps without the arms. His pace increased the more times we completed the routine. He was enjoying himself. He added his arms into the routine. I placed mine in front of my face to block his jab.

He smiled. "When I was born, I had a full set of hair, and it stood up for hours. No matter how much my mom brushed it, it bounced right back."

I stopped in my tracks. "So I was right, in a way."

"I guess." Zappa was picking up his pace. It was hard for me to keep up. The only thing motivating me was the thought of getting hit by a large man in the face. "How old are you?"

Zappa laughed uncontrollably. "I heard you would ask me that." I didn't realize the word got out. This was a small community.

I felt bad now. "I'm…sorry. You don't have to tell me." He was still smiling at me.

"It's okay. I'm fifty-five. But I stopped aging when I was twenty." That's not old at all.

"I'm still trying to understand how you guys barely age. Is there a point where you guys look older?" I finished blocking his jabs. It was my turn to attack him. I played several combinations I had seen on television. A left punch, then right. An uppercut and a side punch.

Zappa ducked. "Yes. But that's not for a long time."

He was easy to talk to. "Can you give me an example?" I was throwing my punches as hard as I could.

"If you're able to block this." His smile turned into a grin. Devious. "What?" I stopped throwing punches.

Zappa grabbed my arm and placed his leg behind my right leg, flipping me on my back. The air was knocked from my lungs. I was on the floor for a good ten seconds before Zappa decided to help me up. "Number one rule. Always expect the unexpected."

I snatched my hand away from him. "You could have just told me that. Now I can't breathe."

"Can't you control that?"

I saw his smirk through my squinted eyes. The pain I experienced yesterday, combined with today, was killing me. "Was that supposed to be a joke?" I glared at him. I couldn't feel anything at this point. I was allowing muscle memory to take over.

"Yeah, sorry about the flip." He seemed sincere.

"Just take it easy," I told him.

"We can't take it easy. The enemy won't take it easy." Ash stood at the end of the ring. Everyone stopped to pay attention to him. "Your first day is the easiest. It only gets harder. Each of my friends is showing you your weaknesses." Ash paused then walked to the center of the ring.

"Quint, you hesitate with your right arm. Annora, you step before you punch. These are just some of the flaws I've noticed. I'm sure they have told each of you something by now."

Beckett kept staring at us. "I think we should have some fun," she said. Her dark lips opened into a crooked smile with white teeth.

Ash also smiled. "I think you're right. Guards, get into position." Zappa and the others moved back and forth. Dancing in a rhythmic motion. They connected with one another and surrounded us. "You need to block the best fighters in the Guard. If one of them can get into your circle, you are out."

"Everyone, stay even," instructed Derek. He was at the head of our circle. Cormac was the first to charge at our barrier. He thought he could get through by going between Gwen and Flair. Big mistake. Gwen tossed him back a few steps. He stumbled in surprise. Cormac and Gwen held eye contact for a few seconds. Cormac nodded approval to Gwen. Beckett charged at Flair. Flair welcomed the challenge. She mocked Beckett as she ran. Beckett was furious and swung her right arm. Flair caught her fist with her left hand. Annora came over and punched Beckett back.

"Good. Use each other." Ash liked the double team. In fact, he was enjoying the whole process. He stood off to the side with a conniving grin on his face. I tried ignoring Ash and focused on the task. Brees and Lois moved in on Quint and me next. They charged for us. Lois gave the first punch. I pushed her arm to the right, crossing her chest. I then took my left fist and punched her side. I stepped back with a massive grin on my face. It was soon replaced with a sour look. Her fist connected with my stomach. I stumbled back but quickly regained my spot in line.

"You punch like a baby." Lois was trying to bait me to leave the circle. "Come on, half-blood. Do your worse." Half-blood? What was that? Did everyone know I was not like them? Was it that obvious? My face hardened. My nose wrinkled.

She still taunted me, "Oh, did I upset the baby?"

"Lois, cool it. She doesn't have control over her powers yet." Ash came next to her. He tried to whisper in her ear, but I still heard him.

"It's okay, Ash, I can handle myself." I was pissed at him too.

"Is that so? Why don't we have a one-on-one, then?" I was trying to take her seriously. It was hard. She was my age.

"Fine by me," I snapped.

"You haven't had much practice. Jewels, I need you to think." Ash was worried. I wasn't. I was irritated.

I said, "I am thinking. Let's go, Lois."

Ash motioned for the others to leave the ring. The spotlight was on Lois and me. We circled one another for a while, slowly inching closer to one another. "Jewels, focus. Watch her closely." Ash was speaking from the sidelines. I watched Lois's steps; she moved toward her target then backed away. Her arms were steady. I decided if I was going to win, I had to make the first move.

I cautiously stepped toward her. Arms raised. My first punch went to her left. She dodged it and jabbed in my direction. My left side was open. I had to think fast. I brought my left arm back. Since she was bending forward to punch me, I placed my right fist below the chin. She caught my fist and picked me up with one hand. She put her other hand around my throat. I dangled in her grasp.

Lois threw me across the mat. My body connected with the floor with a loud thud. I coughed, blood came out of my mouth, dropping onto my white shirt. I wiped my mouth then stood to my feet. I proceeded to jump up and down, trying to get feeling back in my legs.

I advanced toward her, my arms raised in front of me. She threw another punch. I dodged to the left. Lois came at me again. I turned right. She followed my every move. I took two steps toward her. I fake-jabbed to the left, which she proceeded to block. Her body was open on the right. I double-punched her side. I then grabbed her head and pushed it down. Her stomach was now exposed to my knee.

Repeatedly, I punched her stomach with my knee. Lois grabbed my knee and tossed me on my back. She struck my face again. My head pounded from the impact. She was sitting on top of me. I grabbed her throat and squeezed. She reached for my hands, trying to pry them apart. I then tossed both of us on our sides. Lois was making faces at me. Pleading faces. Zappa told me never to let my guard down. Her actions could be a trap to make me stop. I kept going. I felt warm hands on my shoulder as they ripped me from my victory. Lois was on the ground holding her throat. "You could have killed her," Ash screamed. I jerked from my captor's grasp and faced him. "You could have killed her," he repeated.

"No..." I whispered.

"Jewels, you were choking her with your mind," Derek yelled in my direction.

"No. My hands were around her neck," I stated.

"And somehow that makes this all better?" Ash was heated. "Come with me." He grabbed my arm and led me out of the Jar room. I glanced back to find Mr. Kowalski on the floor, gasping for air. I closed my eyes and opened them. Lois was sitting up and surrounded by the others. Gwen gave me a last look before I was dragged from the room.

Moments Later

"I didn't mean... I don't understand what happened. I promise you I had control."

"Control!" yelled Ash.

"Ash, please. Go to the infirmary and check on Lois." Ash reluctantly left the room. The door slammed behind him. I jumped at the sound. I was staring at Nátàl Mater. I felt nine again. It was my first time in the principal's office. I was accused of doing something that I didn't do.

"Nátàl Mater, I don't..."

"Hush now." Nátàl's honey voice melted into my anxiety. "Please sit."

I sat on the same couch as before. But this time, it wasn't a friendly visit. It was my hearing.

"Now explain to me what happened."

I told her what we were doing in the Jar Room and how Lois and I fought. I also explained to her how I specifically remembered grabbing her throat with my hands.

After I finished, I was out of breath. Nátàl Mater was silent for a while.

"Half-blood, huh?" She gave me a saddened look. "I'm sorry about her behavior, however, you need more control. In the west wing, we have a private room where you can practice, so there will be no pressure."

"Don't forget danger," I said under my breath.

"Yes. That is true. However, you can't presume your gift was only meant for destruction, can you?"

I grudgingly admitted as I lowered my head. "No, I suppose not."

Nátàl finally sat down in her chair. "I have a question for you." I raised my head in her direction. "How is it possible that you pictured yourself choking Lois? Have you ever visualized anything similar before?" Nátàl's face was stern yet curious.

"I don't understand it either." I left it at that. I was a terrible liar, and history proved if I kept running my mouth, she would eventually find out the truth, the whole truth.

Her face didn't change. She took a deep breath. "You will go back to practice. You will go to the west wing another time."

I sat looking at my hands, the ones that had caused this situation I found myself in.

I felt that Nátàl Mater wanted to punish me, not help me at all. "You want to send me back into that place?" I was shocked, then my emotion changed to anger. Doesn't she know how *dangerous* I am?

"Jewels, the best revenge is never giving up." Nátàl Mater stood. I took that as a sign to leave. I opened the door and left her. I never glanced back.

THE LION'S DEN

Walking back into that room was a death sentence. I received glares from the Guard. The other members of the Secret Seven were giving me concerned looks as well. The only one not present was Lois. It looked like they just finished going through combination moves. Ash was back from the infirmary, instructing the group. I walked over to Gwen. "How is Lois?"

She looked down as she answered me, "She's okay. Martin is fixing her."

"Martin?" The name sounded familiar, but I couldn't place him.

"Yeah, he's like Vivienne." She spoke in a hurry. She was not entirely avoiding me, but she seemed eager to stop talking to me.

"That's good," I spoke. She stopped listening to me.

My body felt numb. I turned my attention back to the group. Ash looked in my direction. "We are going to take training to the next level. It's time for some target practice." Ash walked toward the garage doors.

"Follow him," Zappa instructed. I swiftly followed. I gave a quick glance at Zappa, but he never acknowledged me. He, too, was angry with me.

Ash placed a combination code into the keypad. Then the garage door opened. The other side was dark and mysterious. After the door cleared, Ash walked through. The other Guard members pushed us through. Now I was placed behind everyone, dubbed the outsider.

Bright fluorescent lights turned on one after the other as we walked through the door into the room. The Jar Room was deceiving. It housed a whole other section of rooms. There were several garage doors evenly spaced throughout the room. Each of them had a specific number, and the first door was labeled J1.

The room was concrete and had several pillars for support. Ash's demanding voice hit the surrounding walls. "Brees and Cormac." They both turned in his direction. "Show them how it's done."

Simultaneously, they walked to the center of the room. Ash pointed to Zappa, who was next to a pad. A shallow beep echoed as Zappa pressed the buttons. His face glowed from the white light of the screen.

Suddenly there was a loud, sharp, repetitive alarm, then dead silence. Then the door, J15, opened. Humans with guns charged from the opening. They were covered in all black with Heckler and Koch 416D Caliber guns in their hands. There were eight fighters. I could hear the clicking from their radio communication. It was apparent that they were searching for someone.

As they walked from the gate and into the room, it magically converted into a hotel. Suddenly there were patterns everywhere, and nothing seemed to match. The hotel we were now in loved checkered designs and red décor. The hallway had red and white diamond-shaped wallpaper.

Everything changed about the men as well. Their outfits were no longer from the twenty-first century. The leader of the group had a black fedora with a red feather on the left side. His suit was tweed gray. His white-collar shirt was covered by a vest and a black tie. To make the outfit stand out, he wore black lace-up oxfords and a FN 1905. His minions wore a mixture of Homburg and Bowler hats. Their suits were black or gray with a plaid herringbone pattern. The youngest of the group had on a tweed newsboy cap, a gray bowtie, and a white shirt. The kid's trousers were gray, matching the bowtie. Each of them carried their own weapon: a Colt 1903, Smith & Wesson .38 Special, and a sawed-off shotgun.

Brees and Cormac were at the end of the hall in one of the rooms. Everyone else watched from the designated viewing area. I felt like I was watching a scene from a 1920s movie. "What are they supposed to do?" Gwen said as she moved closer to the electric field that blocked us from them.

"They are supposed to escape," Heather uttered.

"They can't kill them either," Ash added.

"So how is this target practice?" Flair seemed annoyed.

Heather let go of a large inhale and stepped toward Flair. "Just wait." Heather wanted to say more but glanced in my direction. Then she stepped back. Heather could have beaten Flair up. I sure wasn't going to stop her.

"Be patient," Zappa insisted.

The Mafia was getting closer to Brees and Cormac. They were about to open the door and capture the two, when the brothers clapped their hands. Brees and Cormac were now behind the Mafia. Brees grabbed the youngest member and twisted his body, so the kid was facing him. Brees then placed his hand on the back of his neck and pushed him forward into his knee. The kid went out like a light.

The other seven men turned around and shot at Brees and Cormac. They jumped out of the way onto the walls. Cormac was first to land on the ground. He took the tallest guy's Colt 1903. Then the lights went out. The men shouted.

"Where are they? Find them." The leader barked jumbled orders.

Guns went off as the lights flickered on and off. Sparks of light were tossed all throughout the hallway. For the last time, the lights turned on. Every man was on the ground, moaning in pain as Brees and Cormac stepped over them.

The hallway was a mess. Wood chippings and wallpaper were spread throughout the floor. Large and small holes marked the once decorated walls and ceiling. Cormac and Brees came closer to the field barrier. "Is that all you got?" They asked.

Ash smiled. "Zappa, turn up the heat." Zappa walked over to the pad and made some changes.

The room was transformed into a war zone. The area was clearly deserted. Several buildings were missing parts of their structure, and all the glass was knocked from their windows. This time, Brees and Cormac's outfits were more modern. Tan camouflage with tan hiking boots. "Where are they now?" I asked. The room was silent before I got a reluctant answer from Ash.

"Iraq, fighting with the Americans."

I stayed silent after he answered. In the distance, I heard gun-shots and cannons booming. The force from the cannons shook the grid. I spotted the brothers coming from a corner hunched low.

"Do they even know their target?" Quint asked.

Before one of the Guard could reply, the brothers stepped out in the open, and shots were fired. Cormac raised his M4 Carbine and shot at the adjacent roof. A man fell from the top, landing on his stomach. Brees and Cormac covered each other's six as they walked further out. Moving fast, they made it to the next building. They counted off as they briskly charged through the door quietly. The first room was empty. They briskly walked into the next room. Inside was a group of children. They were American. Brees was the first to speak. "Come with us. We are going to get you out." The four children gathered and followed the twins out of the house.

Waiting for them were four men on a truck with a machine gun attached to it. The men on the truck had their faces covered with different colored scarfs. Their clothes were dirtied from the gust of the wind and lack of care. The man controlling the machine gun immediately discharged his weapon. The repetitive sound of the bullets shattered the air. The loud dropping of the shells on to the truck's floor could be heard ringing through the fire.

Brees and Cormac secured their guns on their back and swooped up the children as they ran for cover. One of the bullets came close to hitting Cormac in the shoulder. The intensity of the situation had no effect on the brothers. They moved with intent and without fear. The truck followed behind with their every step.

They finally made it to the next house. Brees instructed the kids to lay flat on the floor. Bullets came through the broken house, and they pierced the back wall. Cormac fired through one of the widows. He missed. He tried a second time, and the bullet hit its intended mark. The largest man on the left of the machine gun fell to the ground; a pool of blood surrounded his body. The men were angry with the brothers. The man on the right of the machine gun raised his gun and fired. More bullets came into the house. The children screamed. Cormac said something, but it was inaudible with all the gunfire. The children were quiet after a short break. Cormac looked at Brees, and they seemed to understand one another. Simultaneously, they both stood and fired. Both men on top of the truck fell. Their bodies covered the front of the truck. The driver hopped out and ran. Brees shot him in the back.

They gathered the children and filed out of the house. Checking the surrounding area, they moved forward. The group traveled, making several turns. Every so often, they would fire at the enemy. They finally made it to their target. The building read Embassy of the United States of America, Baghdad, Iraq. American soldiers rushed out and gathered the children. They covered them from all angles and then disappeared back inside the Embassy. The room went dark. The simulation was over, and we were back inside the garage.

"Now that's target practice," Octavion stated as he clapped when the twins stepped from the center of the room.

Ash stepped forward. "You all will be working with our simulation. You will become fearless. This demonstration and many others we will do will focus on using close-hand combat and heightening your reflexes *without* the use of your powers."

Beckett nodded, saying, "But they have a long way to go."

Ash stared at Beckett, "Really? What do you mean?"

"Gwen flinched every time one of the men got shot," Heather pointed out.

"Your point is?" Flair bucked at Heather.

"My point, you guys are too soft. You don't have what it takes," Heather continued.

"That's why we are training," added Quint.

Beckett and Heather seemed to flow over his comment as though he wasn't in the room. Ignoring logic.

"We need to toughen them up some more before we send them into the simulator?" Ash was trying to receive clarification.

"Exactly. I mean Jewels can't even—"

"What?" I barked. Beckett stopped in her tracks. The scene of Lois and Mr. Kowalski flowed through my mind. My balled fist relaxed, and in turn, my face softened.

"What do you suggest we practice first?" Derek stepped from the line. He addressed Beckett with inquisitiveness. If she has a problem with us, I was sure she had a solution. That was how these things worked, right? Beckett was quiet for a while.

"You can start by enhancing your combat skill and you need more structure as a team. Lastly, you need to learn control."

The last sentence was meant for me. However, I was determined not to pay any attention to her intended assault because I was strengthened by Mother Natel's definition of revenge.

"Let's continue with combat. This time, we will add swords." Ash brought us back on track.

"Why are we using swords? Why can't we use guns?" Quint questioned Ash as he stared at the enormous gun supply stacked in the corner cage.

Ash stood tall. "Call us old-fashioned, but swords suit our purposes better for training. Especially in a confrontation involving improvised weapons such as pipes, crowbars, or spears, you will discover that understanding fencing techniques will give you a lifesaving advantage. You will learn the concept of timing and distance, which is useful to help you get out of the way to grapple your attacker to the ground and go for the kill. Sword training will help you obtain the will to act when it's vital to do so. You will not lose your nerve to take out the enemy."

"Then why do you have them?" Octavion uttered. He was next to Quint, checking out the 9mm Glock.

"Scourgers are not the only threat we face." Ash never elaborated on his statement. I could only assume he was talking about the people outside. They were the reason we were down here.

Ash hollered, "Beckett, open J3. Crypto-Hept, grab a sword."

Ash pointed at the gate that Beckett just opened. Dozens upon dozens of swords were displayed behind the gate. They were neatly placed on a vertical steel shelf. The swords were all uniformed. They had a black handle with the Guard's red symbol. The blade was made from black steel. I could see my reflection in the sword. After we all picked our sword, Beckett closed the gate.

Across the hall, another gate opened. "You guys will go inside J16 and learn the basics of combat," directed Ash. Derek was the first to walk toward the entrance. We followed soon after.

"Have fun," Zappa sarcastically said as he pressed a button to close the door behind us.

The room had no smell. The air was cold and thin. At the end of the room was a purple light. It expanded the closer it came to us. The room opened, and we were in a large box. It was the size of a theatre room. The purple light soon consumed the walls.

"Good afternoon, and welcome to The Zone. You are here because you are the chosen. You are also here to practice the art of the sword." The female voice came from nowhere in particular, but it was calming. It didn't sound like a robot. Was someone watching us? "I will be testing several key elements. It's your job to work as one and succeed. If you fail, then the training is over, and we must start again," she paused, "Let's begin."

The purple glare was gone. The room expanded into a forest. There were hills in the background, and the dirt beneath our feet shifted. The smell of the room changed. It smelled of wood and salt. To the far right, I saw the shores, and to the left was thick woods. Behind the woods was a mountain that reached past the tallest tree. The sun was relentless with its heat.

"Is this real?" I asked, feeling the pressure of the sun.

"A simulated real," Gwen replied.

She twisted her sword back and forth in her hand. "I'm not sure what we are supposed to do, but we can't stay in the open," she added.

Derek demanded firmly, "Gwen's right. Let's move further south. Move into the trees."

Once inside the safety of the trees, Annora said, "Do you guys see that?" Her arm was outstretched as she pointed to a figure coming straight for us. The speed was unreal. Suddenly, the figure broke into three parts. There were now five people running toward us. Their formation was like a flock of birds heading south. The more they advanced, the better I could see their stature. They were samurais. The armor was magnificent. Jet black and gold trim, with six golden buttons on the chest armor. Their faces were hidden behind a mask and a horned hat. They held their Katana in one hand as they advanced toward us.

"Guys, get ready," Derek spoke with aggression. "Take your formations from our last practice."

"And if we don't remember them?" Octavion's attempt at lightening the mood went unnoticed.

Quickly, Derek reverberated our last positions. Annora and Octavion were in the front. They had the most force. Derek was to the left, and Quint was to the right. Flair was placed in the center. She had a perfect shot of the samurai. Gwen and I took the rear. She was on the left, and I was on the right.

We held our stance as they came toward us. Their feet removed the earth as they charged. The leader gave a foreign command to the others. His voice was rough and stern. Japanese, maybe?

"What did he say?" Quint shouted toward Flair.

"No survivors." She crouched down her arms turned bright orange from the fire, engulfing them.

"Easy Flair, wait till they get a little closer," Derek commanded as he altered his stance. Moving at the same pace, they brushed past trees and bushes. They were closer to us now. Too close.

"Now!" Derek hollered.

Annora and Quint were the first to act. Annora took water from a small stream. She turned it into ice and thrust it at the samurais. Their reflexes were sharp but not that great. Jagged ice edges caught two of the samurai in the chest. They lay in the trees, dead. The other three still moved with determination. Quint blinded them. The effort was noted, but they were wearing masks. They stomped right through. They used the light to their advantage. They jumped in the air, right where it was brightest. We lost track of them. Out of nowhere, they were in the center of our form. Each of them took a victim. Annora, Quint, and Flair were stabbed in the stomach. The room turned bright red. Then a soft hum blared through my ears.

The mysterious voice returned. "You failed. A reminder, you are learning how to use the sword. Please refrain from using your powers on the samurai. Try again."

Like a video game, we were reinstated into the simulation. Annora, Quint, and Flair flickered back into their spaces. Each of them was grasping their stomach.

"What just happened?" Derek said as he marched over to Annora.

"I don't understand?" Annora stated, obviously in shock.

"Are you guys all right?" He asked

"Not really, it felt real?" Quint said when he finally caught his breath.

"I thought simulations weren't supposed to hurt?" I questioned. First, it was me. Now them? I was confused. Since the beginning, Octavion promised that they couldn't hurt us. I scanned our surroundings for the Samurai.

"I don't understand either, but we can't focus on that." Gwen stepped forward. She took a knee next to Flair.

"I think we need a better plan?" I said.

"Like what?" Octavion asked.

"Well, we tried playing offense. I think we need to play defense. We know for a fact that they can beat us. So let's take them by surprise."

Derek was now intrigued. "How do you suggest we do that?" he asked.

I whispered, "Come close." They all huddled next to me. I didn't want Ash to hear the plan, just for the off chance that he could change something. "We need to split them up," I exclaimed.

"Okay, but how?" Octavion asked.

I then revealed the plan. "We spread out. There were five of them. We easily have more numbers. That leaves two of the groups to have two members in them. They might send the strongest to the weakest. I suggest we put Flair by herself." I looked at her. "You can handle them." She nodded and grinned at my compliment but then regained her stoic demeanor. "Derek, you are with Quint. Gwen is with me. Annora and Octavion are by themselves." I could tell my team was getting my drift, understanding my plan. They seemed to brighten in stature. Belief spreading across my team.

"That might work." Annora thought the plan over and asked, "Which group goes where?"

I said, "Annora, you head toward the shore. Gwen and I will head up that mountain. Derek and Quint, you stay in the forest.

Flair, go to the center of the field where it's open. Octavion, stay close to this area."

Derek said as he broke the huddle, "Sounds good to me. We should head out."

"See you at the finish line," Octavion said before he went charging into the forest. Flair turned back to where we first landed in the game. Annora glided toward the shore. Derek and Quint went deeper into the woods, just opposite of Octavion. Gwen and I ascended the mountain.

"I hope it works," I said under my breath.

"It will." Gwen was focused on the task.

"Are you mad?" I asked. She stopped and turned around.

"Why would I be mad?"

I wasn't sure about the reason, so I offered, "Lost of trust?"

She laughed. "Gosh, no. You made a mistake. It happens, no sense worrying about it."

I didn't agree but still said, "I guess, but Ash and the other members of the Guard hate me."

She shook her head. "Not true. *Hate* is a strong word. They dislike you...strongly."

"Thanks, that made me feel a lot better." I rolled my eyes. Of course, she could not see me. Her back was facing me. She climbed the hill; rocks fell after her steps. I jumped out of the way, careful not to go careening off the mountain. We were almost at the top. I could see the peak and the surrounding trees. An eagle was soaring in the sky. The bird occasionally whistled a tune in our direction.

Suddenly, "Stop!"

I paused to the sound of Gwen's urgent shout. At the top of the hill, I saw the leader of the Samurai. I recognized him because he had a different mask from the rest. His mask had a deep frown with thick angry machete eyebrows. He also happened to be the one who had stabbed Flair.

"If he found us, then the others were probably fighting as well. Are you ready, Jewels?" Gwen asked sternly.

"I'm ready," I said with confidence.

Gwen ran toward the Samurai.

Hiding the Truth

Her speed was incredible. I tried staying even with her pace. The combination of heights, rocks, and speed was not in my favor. I slipped twice before making it to the top of the mountain. I regained my stance and trotted forward. Gwen had already arrived at the top. They were fighting. Gwen tried to keep up with his movements. The fact that he was a computer-generated program made him invincible. His sword swiped left. It was going to connect with her side, slicing her. I thought of one thing. I blew her out of the way. She flew to the other end of the mountain. She landed on the ground with a loud crash. Rock pieces made their way into the air.

The voice never said we couldn't use our powers on each other. The samurai now realizing it was two against one and faced me. My sword placed in my left hand, I charged. He came toward me.

Our swords collided. Steel hitting steel. I tried not to focus on the sound that it made. Nothing was worse than the sound of sharp metal gliding together. I tried holding my ground. Gwen was still on the bed of rocks unconscious. The samurai pushed me closer to the edge of the mountain. The wind increased in strength and tried to pull me off the cliff.

Not today, I thought to myself. I pushed harder. The samurai stuck in his tracks. I pushed with more force; his feet slowly dragged backward. Once I was clear from the edge, I thrust my sword back and forward, slashing at the air. Finally, I connected with something. It was the tip of his mask. I pulled at it. The mask lifted. I tossed the mask on the ground. Zappa was staring at me. How was I supposed to kill someone I knew? Better question, how could they kill one of us?

"Are you serious?" I yelled.

He looked puzzled. "What? If you're lost, you pick up that blade and attack me. So come at me."

I didn't appreciate his attempt at mockery.

"Gladly!" I shouted as our blades connected again.

From the corner of my eye, I could see Gwen struggling to stand. After a few attempts, she laid flat on the ground. I didn't think I hit her that hard.

"You're not focusing," he barked.

"Are you sure?"

I struck at his right side. He blocked it easily.

"Nice plan, suggesting that you all split up."

He was trying to distract me.

"Thanks." I was trying to focus. I was also trying to keep him occupied. He liked to brag about being good. So in his case, this made him weaker.

"How could you stab Flair?" I snapped.

"She's fine," he simply said. There was no regret.

"Are the others here?" I asked him.

"Some of them are."

As we talked, I watched Gwen stand. I didn't stare at her directly. I wanted Zappa to be surprised when she stabbed him in the back. She crept her way over to us. Zappa and I were still fighting. He was winning—for now. He slashed at my side. My leather fabric ripped open. My side bled. I grabbed the cut. The pain was horrible, but I had to stay focused.

"One more question," I said through gritted teeth.

"Only one?" He smirked.

"That's all we have time for," I returned the smirk.

"Fire away!" He shot back at me.

"Are you sensitive on your right or left side?" I asked.

"What kind of question is that?" He stopped moving.

I taunted him, "Just answer."

He scoffed, "Neither."

So I looked him in his eyes and said, "Then this shouldn't hurt much."

"What—?"

Gwen forced the blade in him. Zappa arched his back from the sudden pressure. He tried to inhale, but nothing came through. He plopped to his knees and fell face forward. Then his body broke into a million tiny pieces, and he wasn't there anymore.

"Are you okay, Gwen?" I knew she could bounce back from my sudden burst of air but not from killing someone.

"Yeah, I will be fine. Let's get off the mountain."

She passed me without a glance. "Sorry about the sudden jolt," I said to her earnestly. She still didn't look at me.

"It's fine. I needed a nap." Gwen was forcing herself to feel normal. It was painful to watch.

"We're almost at the bottom." I couldn't think of anything else to say. We walked through the forest in silence.

"Gwen, do you think the others need our help?" I asked softly.

"No…maybe… I don't know." She was feeling down.

"Hey, if it makes you feel any better—" I stopped because she finally faced me.

"Go on," she said, and her voice was barely audible.

"Uh…he's still alive." I sounded small. Her laugh was jolting. It vibrated through the air and bounced against the mountain.

"Thank you, Jewels. You are something." Then she jogged deeper into the forest.

I yelled after her, "In a good way, right?" She was back to her old self.

"Sure," she mocked me.

We turned the corner and found Derek and Quint. Derek spoke first. "Did your Samurai turn into a million pieces?"

I answered, "Yes. He was also Zappa."

Quint was shocked. "Woah. We didn't get to see who ours was."

Gwen said, "He put up a fight, though."

Derek seemed tired. He wasn't carrying himself like he usually does. He wasn't acting like the boss. "Someone is not finished. We should find them and help," I said.

"Agreed." Gwen led us out of the forest.

We found Flair. Her arms were covered in scratches. Her red outfit had cuts all over it. The Samurai looked tired as well. He moved slowly. Derek was the first to run toward Flair. The Samurai noticed Flair looking in our direction.

He backed away from Flair. His body was open to both her and Derek. At the same time, Derek and Flair moved toward him. Flair was the first to connect her blade. The samurai pushed her back.

Derek charged with more force. Derek threw a mighty punch. The fighter wasn't expecting that. He staggered back from the force. "It's too hot in this thing." I recognized that voice. She took her mask off. It was Lois.

"I guess she feels better?" My voice held bitterness.

I looked at Quint. He was shaggy. His clothes were no longer clean and had holes here and there. His face was covered with dirt.

"Rough one, huh?" I said.

"Yeah, just a little," he admitted.

I turned my attention back to Flair and Derek. They cornered the enemy. They both engaged, one coming from the north and the other from the south. Lois jumped into the air. Flair's sword almost connected with Derek's chest.

"Sorry," I heard her say.

We all watched as Lois descended back to earth. Derek quickly sliced her arm. Her armor exposed her shoulder. Flair attacked her from the other side. Her blade connected with Lois's chest piece. With Flair's sword stuck in the armor, Lois jumped and twisted her body. Flair holding onto her sword also twirled in mid-air. Lois landed on her feet. Flair landed on her back. Derek took the opportunity to attack Lois from behind. Derek placed his arm on her shoulder. Lois grabbed it and set her left foot back. She then pivoted her weight and sent Derek flying over her. He also landed on his back.

"I think we should help?" Quint said as he raced to the scene. I followed him. Lois turned her attention to us. She glared at me. Her stern face no longer looked eighteen, instead now a woman, a woman who had experienced life and death. I felt her anger as she raised her sword at me. She had no intention of fighting Quint. He was in the way. She tossed his body to the side like a child throwing a tantrum.

I had my sword in front of me. Ready. "Here goes everything," I said under my breath. Her feet were heavy on the ground. They took dirt every time she moved.

"I want to repay the favor," she sneered.

Our swords smashed together. "It was an accident." I tried to explain. She brought the sword to the right. I barely blocked it.

"Accident, really?" She pushed harder.

My strength was depleted. "Yes, I didn't realize what I was doing?" I shouted over metal hitting metal.

"Maybe, but you are not winning this fight," she grunted.

"That's where you are wrong." Derek was right behind her, his sword to her back. She paused to the touch of metal.

"Go ahead. There is only one way to win this game." She was edgy, ready to die. Derek didn't move.

"What are you waiting for?" I asked.

He calmly stated, "Nothing." Then he drove the sword into her, and her body broke into a million pieces and dispersed.

"Congratulations. You have successfully passed level 1," the woman voice returned. The room turned green, then black. Loud clapping came from the other end of the room.

"Well done. You guys show promise." Ash was standing by the entrance of the room. We stepped from the box.

"You call that level 1?" Annora exhaled.

"That's easy," Brees said.

"You should try level 10. Now that is a doozy," replied Cormac.

"Are we good?" I was staring at Lois. There was no point in keeping anger.

"I think we're good," she said.

"Good," I replied, the bitterness in my voice dissipated.

That was the end of it. She crossed over to me and stuck her hand out. Then she crossed it over her chest. I remember the salute from the party. I returned the gesture. "Now that we got that out of the way, let's begin level 2," Ash said.

Ash and the other members stepped away from the entrance. We entered the box to fight another unknown enemy.

"Good job, everyone. That was something," Derek said.

I could see his smile from the purple glow decorating the box.

"Smart idea, Jewels, making us separate," Octavion said.

"But let's stick together for this next one, please," Annora chimed in.

"Sure," I said.

The voice said, "Your next challenge will require trust and understanding of one's weaknesses. Please get ready."

Her voice was gone. The purple glow halted, and the room went dark. I closed my eyes. I inhaled the air and exhaled. My mind drifted. I saw the same figure again. It was closer to me but still so far away. Like the previous times, I couldn't hear what it was saying.

I can tell that it's frustrated with me or its current situation. Then it was gone. I opened my eyes, and we were at a party. Everyone was dressed up, including the Crypto-Hept. It was a black-tie event. The boys were in tuxedos with bow ties. I looked at Gwen, who was in a one-strap black satin gown. The dress gathered at the bottom, making a bell-shaped form. She had diamond earrings and a diamond necklace to match.

Annora's gown was long-sleeved. The arms were sheer black, and the back was open. The texture of the dress was of bombazine fabric. Flair's dress was strapless and heart-shaped at the top with silk. Her waistline, tucked in. The bottom of the dress flowed to the ground.

I looked down at my gown. It was a black turtleneck gown. The neck and arm were made of satin, and the sheathed part of the dress was made from leather.

We looked at one another, amazed. "How are they doing this?" Quint asked. His hair was parted to the right side.

"I don't know, but I like it." Flair's hair was in a slick ponytail to the side. She had red jewels attached to the front of her hair and a red ruby holding the ponytail together.

"What's our task?" Annora asked. She was rocking a braided bun.

"Maybe there is a clue in the house," Gwen said as she pointed to the mansion in front of us. Her straightened hair bounced to every movement she made. The estate was being filled with eager participants.

"Well, there's only one way to find out," Derek stated as he walked toward the steps leading to the front door.

"How are you going to get in?" We all paused at the sound of the voice. It didn't come from someone out in the open, but in our heads. That's when we noticed the small clear earpieces in our ears.

"Who's this?" Octavion asked.

"It's your instructor. Now listen carefully."

We all stayed silent as the mysterious voice gave us instructions. "The only way you can get into that party is if you have an invitation."

I asked, "Are you going to take over their computer and add us to the guest list?"

The voice answered, dripping with sarcasm, "This isn't a James Bond movie, sweetheart. All the invitations were sent out in the mail, no technology. You are going to steal someone's."

Annora answered, annoyed, "All of us can't go in if we steal only one invitation," shaking her head.

"Exactly! The invitation is only good for one person and a guest. You must choose who goes in and who stays out. There is a task for those who go in and for those who stay out. Please choose wisely. I'll wait."

The earpiece clicked. He was gone.

"So much for staying together," Annora scoffed.

"This looks like a job for me," Octavion said seriously.

"What if we need you outside?" Derek countered.

"You will have Gwen, she's tough," he threw back.

"Thanks for the faith, but I think I should go inside," Gwen said.

"If I could add something? I think Flair and I should go in. The instructor never said it had to be a female and male. Also, Flair is great under pressure. She could also distract the crowd, allowing me to do whatever the instructor needed."

"That's a good point. But what if we had to fight?" added Derek.

"Jewels could just knock them out. She can manipulate air, remember?" She had faith in me, which was nice. I think we could actually understand one another. The others nodded in unison. Flair was satisfied, "I think we are set."

"Someone call him back," said Octavion.

"How are we going to do that?" Annora asked.

"Have you made your decision?" The instructor's voice came from nowhere.

"Yes, we have decided that Flair and Jewels will go inside." Derek spoke for the group.

"Excellent choice. You will find a man by a tree, in a black tuxedo with a blue flower in his front jacket pocket. He has your ticket. Go." Then the voice was gone again.

"I guess this is it. Good luck," Derek said.

"Thanks." Flair walked away from the group. I trotted after her.

"Smart choice," she said, turning to face me.

I grinned. "Really? Thanks. I figured if we had to make a daring escape, fire and oxygen would be great to have."

Flair smiled. "Indeed."

The man we were looking for was leaning against a Western Cottonwood tree. "Hello, ladies." The man sang his words. "I heard from a little birdie that you needed an invitation."

Flair asked impatiently, "Yeah, do you have it?"

He answered calmly, "Yes." Then the six-foot man with black hair reached into his pocket and pulled out a cream piece of paper with a black border. Flair took it from him and inspected it. The paper read:

You have been invited to Mr. James Harrison's
Company 30th Anniversary Party.
Thursday August Nineteenth, Two Thousand and Eighteen
2212 Ronda Road, CA 5600

I noticed the logo *Borton* at the bottom. At the very bottom, Flair's name magically appeared with her job title. She was an equipment analysis.

"Tell me you saw that," I said.

"Yes," she said shortly. Why wasn't anyone surprised at certain things? The sky could fall and they wouldn't blink.

"We are at an oil company's party," Flair simply added.

"How do you know?" I wasn't skeptical; I just couldn't figure out how she knew.

"I read a lot, especially about oil companies. They claim to help but, they have more secrets than you know." I decided to leave it at that. She added, "Let's go in."

We left the man standing by the tree. Mr. Harrison's home was elegant. The outside looked like a Roman temple, just expanded. The front had four ten feet columns that supported the thick creamed roof. Then there were the eighteen windows displayed in the front. The bottom windows were rounded at the top. The top-level windows were squared. The house had many edges sketched into it. When you walked beneath the canopy, there was an outdoor chandelier. "Wow," I breathed. "Amazing. I can't wait to see the inside."

Flair handed one of the guards our invitation. He looked it over and then looked at her.

"Enjoy the party," he said and handed her the invitation back.

We walked through the grand entrance. The inside was more impressive than the outside. The floor was hickory hand-scraped canyon crest, a very dark and elegant color. The hallway was long and spacious. There were several rooms before you made it to the living room. Many people occupied the entire space. Everyone dressed in black.

"I wonder what we are going to have to do." Flair was looking around.

"Me too," I said.

"Can you hear me?" The instructor was back.

Flair and I walked to a corner, away from the dancing bodies.

"Yes. What are we supposed to do?" Flair asked.

The voice responded, "You have to get into Mr. Harrison's office and get his secret documents. He's planning on expanding his company."

"How is that bad?" I asked.

"The construction is too close to wildlife. We need the public to stand in the way."

Flair stared at me. "I told you they were bad. Where is his office?"

The voice again responded, "It's on the second floor, down the hall to your right."

"Okay, we can do that," I said.

"Where are the stairs?"

Flair looked through the crowd at the other end of the room. As the only thing, there was a large glass window that took up the whole wall, we didn't know where to go. On the outside were more people and two pools.

"Go to your right," the instructor said.

"Are you here?" I asked.

"Not physically," he replied.

"Let's go." Flair carefully maneuvered down the hall, away from any prying eyes. Sure enough, there were the stairs we needed to take.

"Excuse me, can I help you?"

We stopped in our tracks. I was the first to turn around. It was a guard.

"Yes, we were looking for the bathroom."

"There is one over there."

He was pointing in the opposite direction. I looked over his shoulder to see if anyone was around. It was clear.

"Flair, cover your nose."

She immediately did as I asked. I focused, careful not to spread the CO too far. The man was about to call for backup on his walkie before he staggered back. He hit the wall. I ran to him, trying to muffle the sound before he fell to the floor.

I returned the air to a breathable state. "We're good."

Flair took her hand from her nose. "Nice job, where are we going to hide him?"

"In there." I pointed to a closet.

The man was heavy and sweaty, but we got him in the closet. Next, we quietly walked up the steps. "Take off your shoes, they are making too much noise." Flair said to me as she was taking off hers. I followed suit. We made it to the last step and walked down the hall. Flair was the first to turn right. She stopped and came back. "That was close. There are two guards. They just came out of a room. They are headed this way."

I breathed. "What do you want to do?" I asked.

"Do the CO thing again." She motioned with her hands. I shook my head. "I don't want to push it." I didn't want to try that a second time. The visions were recurring at an alarming rate, and I couldn't risk an episode. Not when Flair was so close to me.

"You don't...okay then. We fight." She inhaled and placed her heels on the floor. The first guard stepped around the corner. Flair grabbed his arm and stuck her foot out. The guard flipped forward then landed on his back. The other guard grabbed his walkie talkie. I jumped out of my hiding spot and knocked it out of his hand.

He looked at me, surprised, and then punched at my face. I sidestepped then punched at his open body. He staggered to the ground. While he was down, I kicked the back of his head, and he was out. I turned to find Flair next to an unconscious guard. "That wasn't bad." She let out a deep breath. "Come on. The others could be waiting." We quickly hid their bodies in a nearby closet. "Night, night." She smiled as she shut the door.

We ran to the office door. "Wait." Flair put her head to the door. "I don't hear anything." She pushed the door open. Once I was through, she closed it behind me.

"Hello, are you there?" I was trying to reach the instructor.

The voice mercifully responded, "Yes, nice job. Now the fun can begin. Flair, your hairpiece is a flash drive. Plug it into the computer."

"What if she didn't come inside the house?" I asked.

The voice said with certainty, "I knew you would make the right decision. Now hurry."

He didn't answer my question, which was slightly frustrating. We walked deeper into the office, and around the corner stood the host's desk and his computer. "It's over there." Flair ran to the computer, her heels in her hand. "Okay, now what?"

The voice instructed, "Put in your hairpin. It will break his password and cancel any firewalls that he has."

Flair placed the red jeweled flash drive into the computer. I stayed in the hall, watching her and the door. "Jewels, look at this." I ran over to find the screen turning blue and black with yellow words across the screen. Then the windows screen appeared.

"We're in."

"Now go into his folders and save them onto the flash drive."

Flair said, "Okay."

I said, smiling to myself, "This reminds me of every spy movie ever made."

She was just as excited. "I know what you mean. I just hope it doesn't take that long to download."

I assured her, "It shouldn't. That's added fluff to make the film better." We watched the computer as it downloaded each file onto the flash drive. We had one file to go.

"I think we spoke too soon," Flair said.

She was right. The file was stuck at 80 percent.

"You have to be kidding me. I'll watch the door." I ran back to the door.

Flair was no longer in my sight. I heard footsteps. "We have company," I whispered to her.

"Man, okay. It's almost done." The door handle moved back and forth. I ran back to Flair.

"We're out of time," I whispered.

"Hang on. We are almost done." It was at 97 percent.

Then suddenly, "Your party is a success, like always." It was a woman's voice.

"Thank you. Would you like to see the balcony?" Now it was a man's voice, probably Mr. Harrison's.

"Yes, I would," she giggled.

Flair and I exchanged looks. We both wanted to gag.

"Done," Flair said as she took the flash drive out.

The computer returned to normal. We tucked under his Jacobean arched desk and waited.

"What a lovely sight." Her voice was so cold and fake.

"It is." His voice was deep. Then their conversation trailed off as they shut the balcony door.

"Let's go." Flair pulled me by the arm.

We quietly ran past the balcony and out the door. "Now we need to leave." She was right.

"I think we got that handled." It was Derek's voice.

I was surprised to hear his voice. "How are you communicating with us?"

He said, "The instructor put me through."

"Okay, so what's the plan?"

Derek answered, "You are going to leave through the back."

I asked him, "Why not the front?" That would be less conspicuous.

"Where's the fun in that?" Derek asked.

Flair said, "Okay. We are heading there now."

"You there, stop!" It was Mr. Harrison. We both slowly turned around.

"What are you two doing up here?" His deep voice matched his stature. He was a thick-boned Mediterranean man with a staggering height. He was wearing a white tuxedo with a black tie, breaking his own rules.

The lady attached to his arm was wearing a revealing black dress. Her left leg was exposed from a slit. The top of the dress was a heart-shaped bust, with the waistline hugging tight. Her sharp nose stared down at the two of us.

"We...were looking for the powder room." Flair stepped forward.

"Is that so? Do you know who owns these?" Mr. Harrison lifted Flair's heels.

"Shoot!" she hissed.

"Ah, so you do know whose these are?" He was looking at her feet.

"We wanted to stay in a quiet space. My friend here is claustrophobic—she had an attack when several of your guests danced around her," Flair clarified.

He frowned. "Do you work for my company?"

I quickly jumped in. "No, we are guests. Our boyfriends, Mike and Daniel, work here."

"I know those two. They are hard workers." He walked over to us and handed Flair her heels back. "Please stay downstairs." Then they walked back into the room.

"I can't breathe." Flair was bent over. She placed her heels back on.

"Do you need air? I can share." She looked at me, and we both laughed.

"How did you know those names?"

"Simple, they are among the most common names in America."

"Nice. Let's get out of here before he realizes we are lying."

We ran down the steps then through the hall. I opened the closet we threw the guard into.

"He's not there."

"Okay, let's go out the back. Keep your head down," she cautioned.

Flair moved swiftly through the crowd of dancers. We casually walked through the glass door. Two guards were directly on the other side. They didn't give us a second thought. We got halfway down the path before a guard shouted. "You there, freeze." He couldn't be serious. Like we would ever stop.

"Sorry, we can't." Flair dashed for the end of the yard. I followed her. The guards were close.

"Flair, fire!" I shouted as we ran.

She looked over to where I was pointing. Along the path were braziers in the shape of large birdbaths. The flames danced in the night at a low volume. Flair gathered the flames, making them stronger. I conducted a strong gust of wind blowing the fire straight toward the guards chasing us. They dodged out of the way, trying to escape the raging flames.

Flair laughed to herself. "Almost there."

Derek's voice rang in our ears once again. "Okay, hop over the hedge."

I said, "It's kind of tall."

"No problem." Flair picked me up and threw me over the hedge. My body flapped in the air as I lost control over it. I landed in someone's arms.

"Hey." It was Gwen.

"Hey," I repeated back. My body was shaking from the adrenaline and from the unexpected lift Flair gave me. Flair followed after me; she bounced over the hedge with ease.

"Move out." Derek ran to the neighbor's house. We followed.

"What do we have to do now?" Flair asked.

"The instructor wants us to drop the flash drive off at a location he gave us. He left a car for us," Derek said.

"Where?" I finally stopped shaking.

"The car is parked in front of the neighbor's house."

"So it's not our car?" I asked.

"Well, not exactly," Derek admitted.

"Great," Flair remarked with sarcasm.

We ran to the waiting car. It was a navy-blue SUV.

"I'm driving," Derek decided.

"You don't have a license," I said.

"Does it matter?" he asked.

"Not if you want to get caught." I went around to the driver's side. Derek leaped into the passenger seat. "Where am I supposed to go?"

"He gave me an address. I'll put it into the GPS." Derek proceeded to do just that.

"Starting route to Wild Oak Café 3111 E Chevy Chase Drive, Glendale, CA 91206." The computer's voice boomed.

I asked, "We're meeting him at a café?"

Quint responded, "Yup."

I put the car into drive and pulled out of the parking spot. We left Mr. Harrison's house in a dash. The GPS took us on the highway. I slowed down whenever I saw patrol officers and then gassed the car. "We should be there soon," I said. "Keep a lookout for the café." Derek and the others peered out of the windows.

"There it is." Derek pointed to my left.

Trees surrounded Wild Oak Café. We were the only ones parked. Across from the building was a neighborhood. Other than that, there was no sign of life.

"Now what?" I asked.

"He said to wait." Derek opened the car door.

The others also exited the vehicle. "This is ridiculous. If you have someone steal something, you should be here on time!" Annora huffed.

"I agree." Flair stretched her legs and took a lap around the car, checking our surroundings.

"Guys, there's a car coming." Quint was facing the north side of the street.

Three SUVs pulled into the parking lot, coming to a screeching halt. They were tented black Suburban, secret service style.

We all gathered next to our car and waited for the instructor to get out. A few seconds went by before there was movement. Then the door opened.

"Thank you so much. I must say it was easy for you guys to steal my work." The voice was familiar. Mr. Harrison came around the car.

"You have to be joking." Flair exhaled.

"You knew the entire time who we were?" I asked.

"Not until Flair left her shoes," Mr. Harrison said.

"Who was talking to us?" Derek demanded with a stern body language.

"My assistant, you wouldn't know him." Mr. Harrison's voice was sneaky.

"Why did you want us to steal from you?" Octavion leaned against the car.

"I wanted to see how vulnerable my system was. I also need new bodyguards." This was insane! Something was off. But I couldn't place my finger on it.

"You sure do." Flair scoffed at Mr. Harrison. "Are you moving your oil company into wildlife territory?"

He answered patiently, "No. Borton specializes in creating trenchless technology that protects the environment during mining."

"Is that your slogan? You might want to change it." Flair laughed at her successful snap.

He ignored her remark. "Well, you guys have passed the test. Now if you could hand me the flash drive."

"Wait," I called. "Where is the location of your next mining site?" I remember seeing Mr. Harrison's future plans for his mining expedition. If this guy was really who he said he was, then he should be able to answer this simple question. Instead, he looked stumped. Then his fake smile returned.

"Why, the south of Wyoming, of course."

"Wrong." The word escaped my cold lips. "He's not Mr. Harrison. We just collected information for the enemy."

Mr. Harrison walked back to his Suburban. "Get the flash drive."

His SUV burnt rubber and left the way it came. His guards advanced toward us.

"I think it's time we use those combating skills," Octavion bellowed. He was excited to punch something with his bare hands.

"Let's go," Derek shouted.

We all ran toward the guards, colliding into one another. The fight didn't last long as we had the upper hand. We knew how to fight in close proximity, without weapons.

Then the room darkened, and the purple light greeted us in the large box.

"Well done. You have passed level 2. You all have proved trust is within your Crypto-Hept. Please exit the cube." The woman's voice quieted afterward.

The door opened, allowing us to exit. Ash and the others were waiting for us on the other side.

"That was fun." Annora was grinning.

"Yeah, Jewels, you did a great job." Derek gave me a nod.

"Thanks," I said warmly, feeling vindicated.

"Go, Fire Breather!" Octavion shouted. I smirked and slipped through his bear hug.

"You all have done well for today. The lesson of trust and seeing through the hidden veil has been complete. We will pick up tomorrow. You all may go to lunch then meet Beetly in your dorm Hallway," Ash said before him, and his team left the room.

"You guys, I think we can actually do this." Gwen had walked back to the ring.

"I think we can too." Annora stood next to Gwen. They high-fived each other.

"I believe in us too, but I also believe in food. And right now, I want lunch." Octavion walked back to the entrance.

"All right, let's go eat." Derek wrestled with Octavion.

The Long Haul

We all gathered in the hallway. The large door opened, and Beetly came gliding in. "Well done, Crypto-Hept. You are becoming very strong. As stated earlier, today's lessons are about trust. Your challenge this afternoon will be to save each other under tremendous pressure. Let's start, shall we?"

The room was submerged in Beetly's purple smoke. We were no longer in the hallway of our dorms. We were inside the dome once again. "Now I want Annora to go first," Beetly said, as he slowly disappeared.

"Okay, what do I have to do?" Annora asked.

"Save them," he said as his voice fainted away.

Everyone except Annora was submerged underwater in a metal box. Water slowly filled it. "This should be easy for her," Derek said. "Everyone stay calm."

"Easy for you to say. You're not claustrophobic," Gwen yelled.

"Since when?" he asked.

"Since birth," she threw back.

"We just have to wait," I said.

"The water is rising." Quint spoke.

"Thanks, Captain Obvious," Flair snarled.

"Woah, everyone, chill. Annora can do this." Octavion's calm voice shushed us all.

The box was filling up fast. We had about six inches of air left. "Guys, I just want you all to know that...the stench you are about to smell did not come from me." Octavion was far away from us as possible.

"Are you serious?" Flair covered her noise. My laugh filled the tiny box. I couldn't stop. We were about to die, and Octavion had to fart. The others stopped staring and joined in the fun. At least our last moments would be with a smile.

Then the scenery changed, and our clothes were dry. I looked around, and Flair was gone.

"Where is Flair?" Derek searched around us.

"She's doing her challenge," Annora said from across the room.

"Annora, how was it? What did you have to do?" Derek asked as he ran over to her.

"I had to face my biggest fear," Annora said as she slowly approached us.

"What was it?" Gwen asked.

"I'd rather not say. It's stupid now that I faced it."

"It can't be. What was it?" Gwen pushed.

Annora sucked her teeth and gave in. "I had to face a challenge by myself. It's the fear of failing when people are counting on me." Annora looked away from us.

"This place is not creepy at all." She changed the subject. Annora was right, though. The area was dark and wet. The surrounding walls had streams of water falling down into their individual pools. There was an orange glow, allowing us to see the cave.

"It smells," Annora said as she wrinkled her nose.

"That's leftover fart, courtesy of Octavion." Derek said.

"Wow, okay." Annora squinted her face.

"What was your challenge specifically?" I questioned.

Annora adverted the conversation long enough.

"Yeah, I'm sure you saw us in the box of water," Quint added, a little more eager than I was.

"I was kidnapped. Then I had to find my way out of a box-like yours. The whole time I could see you guys. You were on a projector or something similar, but I was unable to hear you. You all freaked me out for a while, then I saw you guys laughing. That helped me to refocus and find my way out. As I escaped, you guys were simultaneously freed."

"That's amazing. I'm glad we could help."

Gwen walked over to Annora and gave her a hug.

"Now I wonder what Flair has to do." Gwen exhaled.

Then the dim orange glow was brighter and hotter. The room filled with fire. "This is insane! They can't burn us alive." Annora moved away from the glowing flames. We were surrounded from all angles.

"Jewels, can you breathe fire again?" she asked.

"Yeah, Fire Breather!" Octavion cheered.

Now it was up to me. I have to do this. "I'll try." I focused all my thoughts on the fire. Nothing happened. I used my hands. Again, nothing happened. "I don't think we can use our powers. It's like our other challenge."

Derek moaned, "That's just great."

Annora sounded confident, saying, "Don't worry. Flair will figure it out, I did." Her voice was energetic once again; she was back to her usual self.

"I guess we wait," Gwen said as she circled our small group. She was careful not to touch the fire. With every breath, the fire expanded and moved closer to its target. Us. The heat was overwhelming. I stepped away from the group and singed the hair off my arm from the heat.

"Guys, if we don't make it..." Octavion said.

"Do not fart!" Gwen and Derek yelled simultaneously.

Octavion took a step back and placed his hands up in defense. "I was just going to tell you all that I love you, but never mind." Octavion's feelings were actually bruised.

"Sorry, man, love you too." Derek gave Octavion a bro hug, which consisted of a rushed grab of the hand and one pat on the back.

"It's all good," Octavion responded with a high-pitched voice as if fake crying. Gwen and I exchanged looks. Then we cracked under pressure and laughed.

"The fire is closer," Quint broke the awkward moment. Our reality came crashing back to us. Flair was running out of time. Then snap, it happened. We weren't in the cave anymore. We weren't anywhere, really. The room was dark and cold. I couldn't find my bearings or the other members.

"Guys," I yelled. Nothing. "Guys," I tried again. I couldn't hear my own voice! I screamed. The same figure appeared next to me. It was shaking its head and covering its face. It looked hurt. "Hello?"

The figure turned toward me. Its mouth opened wide. Why couldn't I hear what it was saying? I was scared, afraid for it, and for me. I didn't understand why I felt so responsible for the figure. "What's wrong?" I wanted to ask, but the figure was gone, and suddenly I could see.

I was confined to a large rock, about six feet wide and eight feet tall. My legs and arms were wrapped with vines. I looked left and right. I found the others attached to their rocks as well. We were deep in the forest. Monkeys and birds were looking straight at us.

"This is really something. What is Derek afraid of?" Flair asked.

We understood the challenge now. Whoever was taken, their gift was our fate. It's up to them to conquer their fear if they want to save us.

"I don't know, but these vines are hurting me." Gwen tried to wiggle. The vines moved with every struggle.

"Stop moving! It's making them tighter!" Quint yelled over to Gwen.

"Beetly knows I'm claustrophobic," Gwen yelled.

"Can we skip Gwen's challenge?" Octavion whined over Gwen's yelling.

"She's going to have to go whether you like it or not." Flair hushed both Gwen and Octavion. Flair also caught Annora's attention.

"Flair, tell us what happened." Annora was closest to her.

"I don't want to," Flair shot back.

"No? Why not?" Octavion smirked. "Was it bad?"

Flair stared straight ahead. "No. I just don't want to tell. Simple as that." She rolled her eyes. "I don't see what you could possibly get out of this."

Their exchange was curt, and they taunted each other.

"Nothing, we just want to help." Gwen was distracting herself from her fears with Flairs.

"Help? If anything, that challenge woke me up," Flair snapped.

"To what, Flair?" Annora's eyes pulled at Flair. This whole time, I had never seen any of them cry. Flair's eyes teared, but not a single drop fell.

"We need to get out of here. He needs to hurry up," Flair exhaled.

"It will be over in a second," I said. "Flair, remember when we had to download the files?" I looked at her.

She peered at me. "Yes."

I tried to jog her memory. "We were in a rush and made a comment about it being a movie." I wanted her to remember.

"Oh, yeah." She was smiling. "I couldn't believe it." Her laugh was loud. She abruptly stopped. "Thanks."

That was that. We were quiet. The only sound came from the vines moving up our bodies. "Anytime now," Annora said.

We were out. But not out. We were locked in a cave with rocks crushing down. "You jinxed us." Flair hit Octavion on the shoulder.

"I don't believe in that stuff." Annora crossed over toward the wall. The rocks caved us in and were now filling up the little space we did have.

"She had to go sometime soon," Quint said.

"It's freezing." I grabbed at my shoulders. Rubbing my arms up and down, trying to make friction.

"I'm not cold," Flair said.

"Neither am I." Annora walked over to me. "Let me have a look at you."

I made a full turn. Annora gasped, "This can't be part of the challenge." I looked at my side. I had a large gash. The loss of blood was making me cold and nauseous. "Sh...we call Beetly?" I asked, my words becoming slurred. The realization of having a two-inch-deep cut drained my adrenaline. The pain was horrible.

"We can try." Annora walked me over to the side of the cave. She slowly helped me sit down. "Beetly, you there?" Annora's soft voice called for him.

"Yes." I didn't expect him to appear. But here he was. Not fazed at all.

"She's hurt." Annora looked at me and back at Beetly.

"I see. That is a part of Gwen's challenge. Jewels will be fine if Gwen succeeds." Then he was gone.

"That was helpful," Flair scoffed.

"Don't worry, Jewels. Gwen will find her way out of any box," Annora soothed. I stayed as still as possible, trying to avoid the pain. A lot of time went by. We all sat against the cave wall as rocks crushed us in. There was little room to move around now. I slipped in and out as the pain was too much for me. Annora occasionally slapped me awake.

"Not so hard," I squinted.

"Sorry." Annora grabbed me closer to her.

"It's getting harder to breathe," I said, blood coming from my mouth.

"Hang in there. Gwen's almost finished—I can feel it." Annora looked down at me.

"Derek, what was your challenge?" Annora stared at him. I was curious too.

"I… I had to fight myself," he said. We all paused.

"So, you are afraid of yourself?" Quint shifted away from the fallen rocks.

"I'm afraid of failing. I put a lot of pressure on myself. I had to learn to accept the things I can't change," Derek said solemnly.

"Woah, and how did you do that?" Octavion questioned.

"I let myself fail." Derek turned from us.

"I'm glad you figured it out." Annora grabbed his shoulder.

"What did he figure out?" I coughed.

"That he can depend on us," Annora smiled.

I closed my eyes. The darkness felt warm. I looked at my body as it slipped away. "Wake up." Someone was smacking my face. I opened my eyes and found Gwen over me.

"That hurt." I rubbed my cheek.

"Get up," she shouted.

"I can't. I have a cut." I touched the area to show her.

"You must have lost a lot of blood. You're fine now." She sat me up.

I examined the cut that was no longer there. "You did it!" I yelled. She smiled.

"I did. Beetly is giving us a break. He said we will start first thing in the morning."

"After breakfast, of course." I looked over and found Octavion leaning against the wall. The rest of the Crypto-Hept were here too. All were watching me on the floor.

"How did you do it?" I asked Gwen.

"I don't like small spaces, but that is not my biggest fear. My fear is doing what I know has to be done," Gwen said nonchalantly.

"Is this about killing humans?" I asked.

"Yes." She helped me to my feet. "I had to do what was necessary."

"What we all have to do." Flair walked over to her room. "See you, guys." She was gone.

"Yeah, it's late." Derek left.

Soon, Gwen and I were the only ones left. "Do you think Flair will tell us what happened?"

Gwen shook her head. "She won't tell *us*, but she will confide in Annora."

"I hope she's okay."

"I know she is. She's just stubborn."

REFLECT AND ACCEPT

Every time practice ends and a new day begins, I rise sore. Even though the practices were fabricated, they felt real. They left a lasting pressure in my flesh. One that could not merely be erased with sleep.

My door suddenly rushed opened, and in sprinted Sarah. "Hey," I said as I sat up.

"What's up? How was practice?" she asked as she hopped on my bed.

"You mean, how was Ash?" I said.

"No!" she yelled. "I heard you almost killed Lois."

"Oh, that, well, she started it. I just finished it. And I didn't try to kill her. I promise… I was only fake choking her." I grinned.

"You and air don't mix, hon." Sarah laughed.

"I know," I said as I laid back in my bed and pulled the covers over my head.

"Besides that, how was practice?" Sarah pulled the covers off me.

"It was fine—I got to fight against a samurai. Well, Zappa," I told her.

"Neat. Zappa is cool. He's odd but cool."

"I agree." We exchanged looks and burst into uncontrollable laughter.

"When do you have to go to practice?" Sarah brought me back to reality.

"Beetly said first thing in the morning." I grabbed the closest pillow and covered my face.

"I will have none of that." Sarah took the pillow from me. "I want to show you something before you go. Come on." Sarah hopped out of my bed and ran out of the room. I waited for a second. Maybe this was a prank.

"Sarah, are you there?" I yelled out to her.

"Come out," she yelled back. I jumped out of bed and picked up my new pair of white clothes. With one arm in my shirt, I ran out of my room. "Follow me."

Sarah was running down the hall. She pulled the door back. I tried to keep up with her, but my legs were stiff. "Slow down," I called after her.

"Catch up," she laughed over her shoulder.

Sarah took me through three hallways, up two flights of stairs, and through five redwood doors. "Are we there yet? I can't be late for practice," I told her.

"We're here." She stopped. I looked around, there was nothing. Only a dark room that was an endless void of space.

"I don't see anything." I didn't like this at all.

"Look closer." I searched for something. Anything. Out of nowhere, a dancing figure greeted me. She was sparkled blue. Her dress and body were the same color. She came toward me then stopped. "Hi," I said.

Another figure popped into view. She was purple. The sparkle blue fairy greeted the purple fairy. They danced in the air beautifully. Their synchronized movements intrigued me.

I looked at Sarah. "This is amazing."

She smiled at me. "It's not over."

I looked back at the ceiling. Four other sparkled dancers came from nowhere and everywhere. They were yellow, green, red, and orange. "This is so cool." They danced for a while. Splashes of color bounced off the walls as they passed. All at once, their color changed to one. They were white. They sparkled like diamonds. Then they disappeared. Warm red lights came on, and I saw ALICE.

"That was you?" I ran over to her.

"What did you think?" She was beaming.

"I loved it. You should do that at the next party we have." I gave her a hug. It felt good to be away from work.

"I'm glad you liked it. I knew you could use some pick me up entertainment." She hugged me back.

"Thank you, I really did." We smiled.

"Don't forget about me." Sarah joined in the hug.

I spoke, "I should get back. They might be waiting for me." I didn't want to be late.

"Okay, I'll take you back. Are you coming, ALICE?" Sarah and I looked at her.

"You know it." ALICE was between Sarah and I. Sarah took us back through the five doors, two flights of stairs, and three hallways. We finally made it to my hall. "Thanks again," I said.

"No problem." Sarah smiled.

"It was nothing," ALICE smirked.

"See you later." I opened my hall door and walked through. The others were waiting by their doors. "How long?" I asked.

"Five minutes, no biggie." Gwen came next to me.

"Where were you?"

I paused then said, "Sarah and ALICE showed me the coolest thing. "It's hard to describe," I said.

"Maybe they can show us later then." She smiled back.

"Octavion, you will be first." We turned to find Beetly by the entrance.

"Way to sneak up on us," Flair said. We snickered in response. Now that we knew his gift, he liked to overuse it.

"Get ready," he instructed as he ignored us altogether.

We were dropped into a landscape that was filled with neutral colors. The grass was like hay in color. "I know where we are," I said as I focused on Flair.

"Me too." My eyes moved to Gwen as she spoke.

"It's the African savannah," Quint answered.

"My guess is that we will be chased by lions or cheetahs," Flair scoffed.

"Don't forget the hyenas," Quint chimed in, trying to make light of it.

Flair glared at him. "Thanks."

"Guys, focus. We need to get out of the open." Derek resumed his role.

"Sure thing, boss man," Annora said as she walked over to a shaded area.

The more we progressed toward the trees, the more detail I could detect. "Annora, stop right there," Derek whispered sternly. Derek clearly saw what I saw. It was a family of cheetahs resting in the tree. They were sleeping. "Everyone back up slowly, *now!*" His emergent voice radiated chills through my body.

After getting a few feet away from the large cats, we sprinted. We made it to a nearby watering hole. "That was close," I said as I tried to catch my breath.

"We need to move from this area too. There could be…" Derek was cut short from the sound of zebras entering the area of the watering hole.

Their distinct call sounded surreal as they calmly walked toward us. We watched in silence as they filed in and filled the watering hole in massive numbers.

Their similar black and white coats were bouncing off the neutral savannah. "They're so close," Annora said in awe as she walked up to one of the wild animals. She stretched her hand toward it. The zebra didn't move, inviting her to come closer. Their eyes stayed locked with each other. Annora caressed the zebra's neck. A foal soon approached the two. The rest of us stayed away from the wild animals.

Annora bent down and gave it some attention. "Hi there." She was grooming the foal.

"Can I come over?" I asked.

"Yeah." I walked over to her and the two zebras. I stretched out my hand slowly. Annora grabbed my wrists. "Don't be scared." Then she thrust my hand forward. My hand connected with the zebra's coat. It felt soft and warm. I was touching a zebra the size of a miniature horse or a large donkey; either one worked.

"Oh. My. Gosh." I tried keeping my composure.

"Women fall for the smallest of things," Derek yawned.

"Hey!" I turned in his direction with disgust. Gwen hit him on the shoulder.

"Thanks, Gwen. If I were over there, I would do it myself," Annora said through her giggle.

"We should get moving." Derek stepped closer to Annora. She stood and smacked him on the shoulder, harder than Gwen.

"There." She laughed.

"Now can we go?" He asked.

Quint answered. "Actually, we are safer here. Zebras' coats confuse predators. The more that are in a group, the less likely we are to get attacked." Quint stepped next to the mother and patted her back.

"I'm staying here. Besides, Octavion is probably halfway done," Flair said as she sat on the ground next to the foal. The baby placed her legs over Flair and sat down.

"Okay then, that just happened." Flair tried to hide her enjoyment.

"For a simulation, they are lifelike," I said as I grinned and played with another foal that wanted attention. Gwen played with the same foal as me. We stayed like this for a few minutes. Then the animals were gone. Our scenery changed, and we were in the darkness.

Not this again. I didn't want to see the figure. I couldn't help it. I didn't know what it wanted. "Hello?" I yelled.

"You don't have to scream," Flair stated.

"Oh, sorry," I shot back. At least I was not with the figure. "Where's everyone?" I asked.

"Right here." I recognized Gwen's voice, but I couldn't see her.

"I know who is missing," Annora stated as she laughed.

"What gave it away?" Derek sarcastically asked.

"We're in the dark." Annora happily answered.

"What's his fear?" Octavion asked.

"What was yours?" Derek asked.

"I'm a goof. I know it, you know it, but I have potential. I just needed to believe. You know?"

Derek's tone was sincere. "Yeah, I do."

"So what's the danger here?" Annora asked.

"I don't know. I'm sure it will reveal itself." Flair's voice was closer to me. I reached out and grabbed something. Flesh.

"Hey." It was Octavion.

"Sorry. I'm trying to find my footing." I whispered so the others couldn't hear, "Was it scary? The challenge, I mean."

There was a pause. "A little. You're essentially facing yourself. It's intense. The others are downplaying it, but I'm telling you the truth."

"Thanks. I think?" He made me concerned. I was next, and I wasn't ready for it.

"I don't want to scare you," he added. I couldn't tell if he was using his animal abilities to hear what I was thinking, or he just knew I was anxious.

"You didn't. I'm fine." Liar. I couldn't even fool myself.

"I found Jewels." Annora was grabbing my arm.

"Hey, Annora." I touched her hand. Grateful for the distraction.

"What's up?" I could feel her smile through her tone.

"Woah, who touched me?" Flair snarled.

"I didn't," I immediately answered.

"I sure didn't," Derek uttered.

"Well, something touched me," Flair insisted.

"Watch it," Octavion snapped.

"That wasn't me," I said.

"There is something in here," Annora repeated.

"Guys, what is it?" I asked.

"I don't know," Derek's muffled voice rang, indicating that he was far from me.

"I don't want to find out. Quint needs to hurry." Gwen was holding my other hand.

"Pay close attention the next time it touches you," Octavion instructed.

"Ah, it's soft," Flair yelled.

"Eww, it touched me," Gwen said.

"What did you feel?" Octavion requested.

"It's soft and small," Gwen repeated. We all waited.

"It can't be evil when it's soft and small, right?" Annora asked.

The lights returned at that moment. Beneath our feet were a bunch of rabbits. They hopped all over the place. Small, large, black, brown, gold, and white. We all laughed at the irony.

"We freaked out over this." Flair was toppled over. I stared at them as they played with the rabbits. The cold, hard truth came crashing toward me. If we could see each other, then Quint finished his challenge. I was next.

My vision was stripped away from me. I felt my eyes were opened, but I could not see a thing. My heart pounded to the buzzing noise in my ear. I wanted to get my challenge over with.

My sight returned. I was on a cloud, alone. Everything was hazy. The colors were dull. I looked around. I was surrounded by blue and white. There was no sound. I walked around, hopping cloud to cloud, trying to find a clue. Nothing.

In the distance, I saw a figure. I ran over to it. It was Kaura. She was on the ground gasping for air. "What happened?" I screamed, but she couldn't answer me. Her breath was gone. To my right, another figure appeared. I was looking at Sarah. She was walking toward me, her arms stretched out. I ran over to her. Her demeanor changed. She looked scared. "Sarah, wait," I yelled.

She stopped dead center. "Turn around," I said. Then she turned. It hit me—I was controlling her. "I'm sorry." I tried letting her go. It wasn't working. I had no control. One by one, the Crypto-Hept surfaced. They looked at me with disgust. "I'm sorry," I kept repeating. Their faces didn't change. I was angry. How dare they? "Stop it," I shouted.

The wind increased in speed, but I couldn't hear the wind pass by. All noise fell silent. The others started to fall to the ground. They had no air. I didn't stop. One by one, they fell unconscious. I realized in that moment that they were the problem. They were always looking down on me. As if I were the issue. If they trusted me, maybe I could have control. I was not the problem. I felt warm liquid on my hand. I looked down and saw blood running from my nose. My sight was gone once again. I blacked out.

"Dad, what's that noise?" I reached for my alarm clock. I felt cold, hard cement. My eyes snapped open. The light in the room was bright white. I couldn't tell where the room started or ended. My head was pounding. I tried sitting up but failed. The pain made me still. "Hello?" I called. "Is someone there?" I waited.

A soft click came from the far wall. The wall opened, and a lady came through. She was wearing all white. Her head seemed to float in the air from all the white. "Hello. Where am I?" My voice was hoarse.

"I'm here to help you. You caused quite a stir during practice." The woman walked over to me. "May I?" She pointed to the bed I was laying on.

"Sure." I sat up to give her space to sit next to me.

"Hi, my name is Dr. Maz. I'm here to see if you are feeling better." I quickly understood exactly what she was here for. She was a shrink, and she was trying to figure out if I had a mental break.

"Where am I? What happened? I was in practice and..." I couldn't speak anymore; my throat was raw.

"Yes. Well, you were in practice and didn't pass your challenge. Consequently, we had to evacuate the rest of the Crypto-Hept."

I finally faced her. She understood the look on my face and provided me with settling information. "They are fine. It's you I'm worried about. You wouldn't stop bleeding from your nose. We also couldn't get close to you without losing consciousness."

"How *did* you reach me?" Every word came with tremendous pain.

"They wore gas masks and gave you a sedative. You screamed the whole time." She reached out to touch me. I pulled my hand away. "Sorry, do you have more questions?" Of course, I had questions.

"Where am I?" I winced at the pain.

"You are in the west wing. It's dedicated to helping members of the Crypto-Hept find balance with their gift."

"Nátàl Mater said she would send me here." I winced again.

"Oh dear, let me get Vivienne." She stood and briskly walked back to the wall. Its mouth opened for her. I tried to stand, but the door opened once again. I fell back down. In walked Vivienne and the shrink. "Hey, how are you feeling?" Vivienne walked over to me.

"My throat hurts. My whole body hurts." I couldn't hold my head up anymore; I lay in the bed.

"I'm going to help you." She moved her hands over my throat. I could feel the healing. Vivienne moved her hands from my head to my toes. "You are deeply injured. I wish I'd known. I could have saved you a lot of pain."

When she was finished, I could feel myself again. There was no pain. I was me. "Thank you, Vivienne." She smiled at me. I sat up in the bed. "Am I getting out of here?"

Her smiled disappeared. "Not now. You need to rest."

I wasn't staying here. "I can rest in my room," I snapped. They can't keep me prisoner here.

"It's for your safety," the doctor said. I rolled my eyes.

"There you guys go. It's for *your* safety. Not mine." I reminded them. "You can leave."

Vivienne tried to explain, "Jewels, I'm only trying to help."

I wouldn't listen. "Leave."

Vivienne rose. "I'll let Sarah and ALICE visit later." I laid back in my bed and had my back facing her. I knew she left when I heard the soft hum from the door opening. I dozed off to sleep.

The Next Day

"Jewels, wake up." I rolled over and found Sarah sitting at the edge of my bed.

"Sarah!" I quickly sat up. "I'm glad you're here." I hugged her.

"Me, too. You scared me, you know?" I peered into her eyes and saw the truth. She wasn't afraid of my powers; she was worried that she might lose me to them.

"I'm sorry. I don't mean to be this way. I try and try, but something always happens. It's like I'm unfinished somehow." I felt my eyes tearing up. I blinked in rapid succession, not allowing them the chance to fall.

"Don't worry about it. I just want you to know you are not alone. I'm right here when you need me." She came closer to me. I reached out to her hand.

"You're the best, you know that?" I beamed at her face. She was smiling.

"What about me?" I glared over to the sudden intrusion. It was ALICE. She looked adorable in her red pleated dress with red and pink polka-dotted socks.

"You already know you got it going on." I stretched my arms out wide. ALICE ran over and received the hug.

"When do you get to ditch the loony bin?" She was smiling, which meant she was joking. She was always joking. I squeezed her tighter. "Ouch." She wiggled her way free.

Sarah erupted with laughter. "I hope you get out soon."

"Me too." I groaned. "There's nothing to do here. I just watch the walls."

"You could practice your powers. That's what this place is for," stated ALICE.

"Are you crazy? *Not* with you guys in here. I'm tired of hurting people." I meant it.

"If you want to get better and leave, you must practice." Although I didn't want to acknowledge it, I knew Sarah was right.

"I do," I admitted.

"So practice," Sarah said as she hugged my neck tight and walked toward the wall. ALICE followed, and they were gone. *Now what? What should I practice? I was already good at taking people's breath away. What was one thing I knew wouldn't cause a huge commotion? I could try flying?* I jumped out of my bed and walked to the center of the room. All right, let's do this. I placed my hands by my side and pushed the ground down with imaginary force. I shot into the sky, hitting the ceiling. I fell down like a bullet, fast and hard without any warning. I laid flat on my back. Pain pierced through my body.

"Why was it easier inside of the challenge?"

"Maybe you believed."

"Someone is snappy."

I realized I was conversing with myself. I refocused. Let's try this again. "Here we go." Instead of physically trying to lift off, I thought of what I wanted to do. I saw myself in the air. I was perfect. I went around the room, past my bed, the bathroom, and the secret door. I was free. I opened my eyes and found myself just below the ceiling. I did it. Well, now for the hard part. I had to start moving. I pictured myself, with my eyes open, moving from the left wall to the right. I was going too fast. "Stop." I covered my face from the impact, that was about to happen. My eyes burst open, and I was inches away from the corner wall. I did it again. This isn't bad at all. "Maybe I can do this?"

"I know you can. I have faith." I knew that voice. I faced the voice and found Nátàl Mater grinning at me from down below. "Can you come down?" She asked me.

I laughed to myself. "I haven't practiced that part yet." I made it to the bottom, but it wasn't smooth. I landed on my butt. "Ouch." I stood and faced Nátàl. I wanted to rub my butt, but I was in the presence of royalty. I withheld the urge and stared at her eagerly.

"Now I need you to go back to practice and try that challenge again. You've only been in here for a day, but I have faith in you."

I was excited. "I get to leave the loony bin?"

She was stunned. "Huh? Yes. Saraphine is outside. She will return you to the team."

I smiled. "Thank you." I was out of the room before Nátàl could turn around. "Hey, Saraphine." I was happy to see her. She was bright as ever in her sensible sheer orange outfit with goddess sandals.

"Dearie, how are you? I'm sorry I didn't come earlier. I was so busy. We have a lot going on around here." I could see she regretted saying the last part.

"Really? What happened?" I was curious. If something was wrong with Refashion, I wanted to know.

"Come now, you're already late." She briskly walked away. I had a chance to look around as we walked. The west wing was modern compared to the rest of Refashion. There were lights and plastered walls. Lovely painted walls and comfortable cushions. "Why don't you update the rest of Refashion?" I finally caught up with her.

"Why do people build new buildings and refuse to fix the old ones?" She answered my question with a question.

"I don't know…maybe they like new things but want to keep history?"

She glanced at me. "You do know. Come now, dearie."

The west wing was farther away from the main building. We walked what seemed like fifteen minutes before we made it to the

Great Hall. "Why are we meeting here? When I left, they were in the dorm hall."

She explained, "They have been practicing shooting while you were away. Don't worry, they saved the good stuff for you."

I opened the door then stopped short. "I'll figure this out." I knew it.

"Dearie, you don't need to keep apologizing. Every Crypto-Hept season has its late bloomer. But trust me when I say they always turn out on top. Especially with the help of others. Go in." She shooed me away.

I opened the door wider and found the others standing around. "Don't wait on my account," I said. Gwen greeted me first.

"Jewels, you're back! Boy, did I miss you. How are you feeling?" I was happy to see her too.

"Much better, thanks." The truth this time.

I looked at the others. They seemed happy to see me too. "So what's today's practice?" I questioned.

"I think we are doing some more combat," Derek answered.

I was confused. "Shouldn't we be in the Jar Room?"

"But first, I want you to finish what you started. I thought the space might help." Beetly was standing by the door.

"Okay, I'm ready." I believed it this time.

"Good, you start now." Beetly disappeared.

My eyesight was gone, but I kept sight of my confidence. I didn't panic. As I stood in the darkness with no sound and no light, I waited patiently for it to return. My heart was beating fast, but I ignored the pounding pressure in my chest. Even the queasiness in my stomach. Finally, my eyesight returned in an instant. I could see the foggy and eeriness of this world, the gray color of the sky, the exceptional fluffiness in the clouds. I walked straight. I knew what was coming—the glares, the hate, the distrust. I was ready.

I found Kaura on the floor. She was gasping for air, and it was my fault. I didn't focus on that too much. I decided to give my best friend air. She inhaled. Kaura stood before me and smiled. "Thank you. I knew you could do it." Then her body disappeared like a cloud. She shifted away from me. I knew what came next. I found Sarah.

She was running toward me with her hands outstretched. I walked over to her. I touched her on the shoulder and looked in her eyes. "Peace," I commanded! Then she was still. She smiled and walked away from me. Sarah disappeared in the clouds.

Now for the final step, the Crypto-Hept. Their six figures were visible once they were distant from the clouds. "I know what you think of me. It's okay, I'm not fully ready yet. But somehow, together, we can make it. I just need you to trust me as I learn to trust you." There was no indication that they heard me. We stared at each other for a while. Just as the silence was unbearable, in an instant, one by one, they disappeared. "Is it over? Did I pass?" I asked as I watched Gwen fade off last. "Congrats. You passed."

I was now starring at Beetly in front of me. We remained alone inside my deepest fear—placing trust in myself and trust in others. "I acknowledge that you have passed this level, but like the others, you too have to let go of some issues. However, for now, you can proceed."

I couldn't believe it! "I would have to do this again?"

Beetly said, "Something like it."

I shook my head. "When?"

"Not for a while. You passed. That's what counts."

My eyesight was taken from me. This time I could hear distant chatter. "Welcome back," Octavion said as he yawned. I opened my eyes. I was in the Great Hall.

I asked, "Are you guys okay?"

Octavion shrugged. "We're fine. It was nothing."

I had to be sure. "Where did you guys go?" I asked.

Flair answered, "Like the other challenges, we were trapped in the missing person's power. So we were trapped in the air, in a continuous fall."

I asked with disbelief. "Wow, really?" That sounded intense. Falling for so long, never knowing when the bottom was coming.

"Of course, the first round didn't work out so well." Flair slyly jabbed.

I winced. "Yeah, I am so sorry about that. I lost myself."

Flair didn't let up. "You can say that again." Flair was glaring at me. Not a deliberate glare; it was literally her face.

"What now?" Quint turned his attention to Beetly, who patiently waited for our greeting to end.

"You will go to the Jar Room. Ash has something planned for you." Beetly walked out of the room. I guess he was tired of using his powers for no reason.

"All right, sounds like fun." Octavion was the first to walk toward the door. "Come on, guys." We staggered after him. The walk to the Jar Room was quiet. I was trying to figure out what the others were thinking based on their body language. I had no clue. Except Flair, it was obvious she had a problem with me.

Returning to the Jar Room after my previous two incidents made me feel weak. For some reason, I didn't feel whole. Like I was off-balance somehow. I couldn't place what was missing or what was wrong with me?

"Welcome back." Ash was smiling. At all of us. I would have expected my incident to make him anxious around me. "I want you to meet a couple more of my friends." On cue, more members of the Guard came rushing in. They were all in their black leather and red rubber uniforms. "I thought you guys could use some more practice. You guys were successful taking down a few samurai, but how about the most experienced fighters in the world? I thought we could have a battle. You against us." He paused for effect. "What do you say?"

"I think we are going to kick your butt," Octavion roared. He and Derek gave each other a high five.

"You think? It's twenty against seven. The odds are not in your favor." Ash was laughing. He knew we couldn't beat them, not yet.

"I think we can handle that." Annora returned Ash's soft tone with confidence.

"Well, let me tell you the rules." He glanced at each of us. "First: You cannot use your powers. We don't have any, neither should you. Secondly, you may defeat us anyway necessary. We will do the same. Third: The last one standing is the winning team. Fourth: There are only thirty minutes in the game. If we run out of time, the team with the most members at the end wins. Simple, right? Finally, when you lose, don't cry." His entourage erupted with laughter.

"So funny," I commented. They stopped laughing. Out of shock or fear, I am not sure.

"Let's get this started." Flair broke the awkward silence.

"Suit up," Ash instructed. He pointed to the same garage door that had the knives, swords, nun chucks, and machetes in them. I grabbed the same sword as before. "Ready?" Heather asked.

"Always," Derek answered. Then we started fighting.

The Games Begin

We were submerged in an old-time fighting scene. They were at one end of the field, and we were on the other side. Thick, bushy green hills between us. The ground dipped at the center of the battlefield, creating an unescapable bowl.

The Guard was in black and red armor slick metal that covered themselves head to toe. Their symbol attached to the breastplate. We were in a blue and black armor similar to theirs. A black helmet covered our ears and head. Our faces exposed to greet our opponent with a grin.

"Quickly, guys, we need a plan." Annora brought us out of the trance.

"She's right. Anyone have ideas?" Derek gathered us into a huddle. In the distance, I could hear the other team laughing.

"I want to wipe their smiles off their faces." Flair was excited.

"I say aim low, go dirty. They aren't going to take it easy on us."

Quint was glancing over us. "They're getting restless." He bent down, back into our huddle.

"Okay, let's go." Derek was in the center. With three on each side, we charged. The twenty of them came toward us. In slow motion, we clashed. Twenty against seven wasn't fair. But we would make it work. While seven fought us, the other thirteen stayed back. My opponent was a tall, dark-skinned teenager. Her curly black hair moved with every step.

"I'm Rivera." She was smiling, which took me off guard.

"Hi, I'm Jewels."

She laughed. "You sure that's your name? You sound uncertain."

I didn't think she was funny. "No, that's my name. I just didn't see you introducing yourself."

She suddenly stopped laughing. "Well, how else am I going to make a new friend?" I stared back at her.

"Good point. Are we going to start?"

Her stare turned into a mock. "Sure, whenever you're ready." I showed no fear. I took a deep breath and released it. "I'm ready," I confirmed.

"Good." She lunged toward me with her metal spiked nun chucks. I dodged out of the way. I wasn't fast enough. The spikes grabbed at my arm. I grunted, trying to take a breath. "You all right?" She paused, looking me over.

"I'm fine," I said through clenched teeth.

"Okay, then." She came again. I was ready. I sidestepped and missed the nun chucks. I then slashed at her left side with my sword. Her reflexes were sharper than mines. She moved out of the way in one fluid motion. "You have to try harder." Rivera liked to talk.

I was the first to attack. I went as fast as I could, throwing my sword at her, left and right. Each attempt failed with me getting cuts on my arms and legs. I decided to switch things up. I motioned for her to come toward me. She let out a sharp cackle. "If you say so." When she was close enough, I stepped from her thrust and brought my sword down. Of course, she blocked it, but she wasn't paying close attention to my fist. I knocked her to the ground with enough force to the face. She glanced at me from below. "Now we're talking." She hopped to her feet.

"Come on." She taunted. I thought she was mad, but it had the opposite effect; she was enjoying this. I came at her again. I stepped forward. Yet I was careful not to go too close.

"Watch your foot placement," a voice suddenly said. In all my efforts to beat Rivera, I forgot about the onlooking crowd.

Gwen finished fighting. She was shouting commands at me. "Go for her left side."

I found that useful. I followed through. I placed all my efforts into her left side. She could block me but not as well. At the last second, I attacked her right side. She wasn't ready. My blade connected with her armor and took a piece from it. I stabbed at her again. She grabbed my blade, her hand armor ripping. Blood flowed from her hands. She showed no signs of pain. Rivera took the sword from me and placed it under my neck. *This was it. I was going to die. I knew it.*

I woke up to reality. I couldn't give up so easily. I swung my arms up, catching her off guard. The blade slipped from her grasp. She looked up to get it. I stared straight at her. I placed my arms around her neck and brought her face down. My knee pushed into her chest. This was my signature move. I threw her to the ground and walked over and picked up my sword. She was still on the ground when I turned around. I ran over to her and placed the blade through her armor. Her body broke into a million pieces. I successfully killed another Guard. "That wasn't bad." I walked over to Gwen.

"You did great. You took too long, but you did great." She snarled. A large grin splattered across her face.

I smiled. "I'll be faster next time."

"Well done, Crypto-Hept. But it's not over." Ash was happy for a guy who just lost seven members of his team. "Get ready." He yelled over the increase in wind. The green hills danced as the grass moved with the wind. The clouds grew darker and covered the sun. The land was dark. When the sun returned, the arena had changed. We were in a large warehouse. Crates stacked all down the aisles. There were three levels. Each of them overlooked the other. Allowing no blind spots. The rusted warehouse croaked from the sound of heavy footsteps trying to find a hiding space.

"Guys, we look awesome." Quint was right. We were decked out in SWAT gear, vests, and black uniforms. To top it off, we each had a helmet with night vision and a Berretta 92FS, 9mm. "Turn on your night vision," Derek commanded. "Can you see anything?" Derek asked Annora.

She glanced around the corner. "I don't see anyone." None of us could see anyone.

"We need to get to the top level," Derek instructed. "Let's move."

We turned the corner and were immediately fired upon. The red and orange sparks obstructed our vision. We ran back to our hiding spot. "I thought you said there wasn't anyone in there?" Derek yelled over the gunfire.

"They weren't there when I looked." Annora answered with no emotion, "Flair, are you a good shot?"

Flair shrugged. "I've been practicing." The gunfire stopped. They were waiting for movement. Flair took the opportunity to step out. She raised her 9mm and shot twice. After a while, she came back to us. "That's two down."

"Nice. Let's move." Derek was the first to go around the corner. We looked left and right to find potential threats. "This has to be the coolest challenge yet." Octavion was talking to us through our radio.

"I agree," Quint answered back. The repeated sound of a click and white noise from our com was the only indication that we were not alone in the fight.

"Focus." Derek turned.

"Yes, sir." Octavion couldn't stop joking. Derek raised his fist. We stopped. With his free left hand. He motioned for us to turn left. The corner was a tight squeeze. One Guard walked past us. Derek waited till he passed, then stepped out. "Hey," Derek called. I heard the other guy's shoes shuffle. He must have faced Derek. There was a commotion then nothing. "Come out." The guy was knocked out on the ground.

"Did you kill him?" I asked.

"I had to. It's how we get to the next level." Derek answered me. "Put him in that corner."

Octavion and Quint picked up the body and tossed him in the corner. "Three." Flair was keeping count. We made it to the stairway. Our boots sounded like thunder as they hit each step. Derek counted off Octavion as he waited to open the door. "Three, two, one." Octavion opened the door, and Annora went through first. She checked left and right. "Clear." No one moved. She turned around. "I'm positive." We moved out. We went straight down. I could see someone moving below. I turned my gun toward them and shot.

He went down, but I gave up our location. "Nice going!" Flair snapped. She was hunkered behind a metal barrel. Bullets flying in complete disorder.

"Jewels, look around. See if you can find a specific location." I ignored Flair and tried to focus on the task Derek gave me. The loudest popping sound came from my left. I peeked around my barrel and found a spark of light. It was across the aisle on the second level.

"Derek, top left of you." He leaned on his barrel and aimed. The body fell over the railing and shattered into a million pieces.

"Four," Flair chirped.

"Jewels!" Derek shouted. I glanced again. I found two sparks third level. "Derek and Gwen, two top right." They both aimed. The bodies shattered.

"Six." She counted.

"Again!" Derek demanded politely.

"Same level, look to the left of you." He aimed down the hall, and she burst into pieces. "Seven."

We took off our helmets. The warehouse lights came on. "That's what I'm talking about," Octavion shouted and moved toward the railing. "That's all you got?" He taunted the other team. Ash looked at us from the first floor. I had a chance to see who was left. Ash, Beckett, Zappa, Lois, Brees, and Cormac.

"We'll get you out first, Octavion!" Ash said with a grin.

"Sure, you will." Octavion tormented them.

The room changed. Ash and the others were no longer below us. The floor ripped, and the crates fell through. Suddenly the warehouse walls fell and disappeared into the bright light. One by one, I watched my teammates fade into nothing. I was next.

On the other side, I was alone, alone in a sea of hedges, a maze. *I must assume the others are alone, including the Guard.* At least I had regained my sword. My outfit changed. I wore a sheer white shirt with white bellbottom pants. A black belt held my sword. I was comfortable.

I ran straight. At the end of the walkway, I had the choice of going left or right. I took a right. I barreled straight again until I had the option of going straight or left. I kept straight. I was almost at the end. I stopped.

Beckett was staring at me. She was wearing a black outfit like mines. "Look what we have here." Her grin stretched from cheek to cheek. Her eyes were lit with a raging fire. If I could, I would have been afraid of her. But not today. "I was hoping to fight you," she said.

I looked her square in the eye. "Why is that?" Lois was obviously her best friend. "Lois and I no longer have a quarrel."

She scoffed, "That's not why I want to fight."

I again asked her, "Why?" Every time she talked, she came closer to me.

"I want to fight you because you pose a real threat." This was nonsense. "Me, really? Have you not seen me fight?"

Beckett threw back her head and laughed, "Exactly, you don't overthink. From what I can tell. You also leave yourself exposed. Others see that as an opportunity to attack. They're wrong."

I paused. "So you want a challenge?"

Her glare was just so hateful. "Bingo."

I refused to fear her. "Flair is amazing with the sword. So is Annora. You should have picked them."

Beckett chuckled. "They're okay." I couldn't believe what I was hearing. She saw me as a threat.

"Does this have to do with my powers?"

She placed her hands on her hip and sucked her teeth.

"Not in the least. You have extraordinary power but lack the skills to use them."

I said with sarcasm, "Thanks. I think we should start now."

Beckett mocked, "Are you asking or telling me?"

I challenged her, "Telling you!" I took my sword off and tossed it to the ground. She followed suit.

She came toward me with a blinding force. The hedge next to her waved slightly from the breeze she made. I didn't have a chance to raise my guard before she attacked. Her fist connected with my soft and freshly healed face. I stumbled back and raised my hands.

I charged. My left fist jabbed her chin. She smiled; her teeth were red. She spit blood and continued. With her left fist, she came for my right side. I ducked and swung my body to my right. I stood straight and punched at her open body. She quickly turned and caught my fist. She took me by the throat and tossed me. I flew back past two hedges before I stopped on my back. I sat upright and saw Beckett coming through the hedges after me. I quickly stood to my feet. I raised my guard. She jabbed first. I stepped to the side and watched her fist hit the air. I used her momentum to swing her body. She flipped in the air and landed on her back. I stood over her and punched.

She grabbed my neck with her left hand and pushed it down. I fell to the side. We both stood up, ready. "You can do better." She wiped her mouth. I was breathing heavily. She wanted a challenge? Be careful what you wish for. I rushed her, my right fist ready. She did the amazing. She went down into a split and kicked my leg from under me. I was falling face first. I placed my hand beneath me and caught myself. I rolled over away from her kick.

"I just want to say, that was cool," I complimented. She smiled for a second. *Focus*, I told myself as I went back into the moment. I watched her steps. Eye to eye, she kicked at me. I dropped her leg by pushing it down with my palms. I thrust my left fist toward her sharp chin. She held on to it. I side-kicked her. Beckett was still holding on to my arm. I kicked again. She let go of my arm.

"Come on. You're going too easy," she taunted.

"Really?" I yelled. My white outfit was green and brown. I had rips and blood marks. "I think we are going hard." I hated how sure of herself she seemed.

"You can do better," she snapped.

"Okay, then." I ran through the holes. I heard her follow me. I saw my sword to the left. I ran toward it. I was knocked off my feet. She was on top of me. I was faced down. She was pushing my face into the ground, choking me. I tried to wiggle my way free. But her grip tightened. Finally, I stopped struggling. I could feel her hesitation. Then she released my body and stood over me. She sucked her teeth, "What a shame. I really wanted this to be great." She was still over me, but her guard was down. I saw my chance and kicked my leg to the left. She fell on her back. I stood up and ran for my sword. She was on my tail. I grabbed it and turned around. She ran right into my black steel sword. "Well done." Beckett smiled and turned into a million pieces. I seized my sword. I exhaled and examined the damages. I think I may have a broken rib.

I ran down the path and made a left. For a while, I turned left or right. I didn't run into anyone. Everything looked the same. The only difference was the sun. Sometimes it was on my left. Other times, it was on my right. I made a right. I collided with Quint. "Ouch, my rib," I yelled and grabbed my left side. "Dang. That hurt."

Quint stood first. "Are you okay?" He reached his hand out. "Not really. I think my rib is broken." I mumbled as I reached for his open hand. Quint carefully brought me to my feet. "Have you had a battle yet?" He looked me over. This was no time for him to be funny!

"Was that supposed to be a joke, Quint? I don't find you humorous at this moment."

Quint smiled; his teeth caught the light. "Yeah, I was trying to distract you."

"So have you seen anyone?" I said, holding onto my throbbing chest.

"Nope, you are the first person I've seen. Who did you fight?" he asked as he placed his arm around my waist and helped me to the ground.

"Thanks." I was quiet for a second. Quint looked down the path. There was no one there. "I fought Beckett," I said through every wince.

"How was it?" He was pushing for information. I wanted to tell him, but I was having trouble catching my breath. I kept quiet, hoping he would catch my drift. "So?"

But no, he didn't.

"It was fine. I can't talk much." I looked up at him.

Our eyes met, and he nodded. "Ooh, sorry. We should keep moving." He gave me his hand. I took it. We were going at a slow pace. "Maybe the others are almost done."

I gave him a side glance. "Maybe." It was a slim chance. This place was enormous. In all this time, Quint hasn't seen anyone. One thing was certain. There were only five Guard members left.

"Well, I am amazed." We turned around. It was Ash. "I was not expecting to see you two." He looked rough. His black suit had tears in them.

"Who did you fight?" Quint ignored his rude comment. It was still nagging at me. I stood straight, even though it hurt.

"Octavion. He did give me a fight. We tussled for a while. He made his mistake when he went for his weapon. I easily stabbed him in the back." He smiled at us. Evil.

"We won't be that easy," I snarled.

"Oh, look at you. Who did that to you?" He smirked.

"Beckett." I glared at him.

"Wow, what a job. How did you kill her?" Ash glared back.

"She ran into my sword," I simply answered.

"Well, I can assure you, I won't do that." He snarled. I exhaled a sharp laugh. I didn't let him see my pain. "We'll see." I ran toward him. With my sword at my side, I got close enough and pulled my weapon out. I cut his right shoulder. His sleeve fell to the ground. Ash raised his sword to block my next move. We danced back and forth, heavy metal clashing together, making high-pitched music.

I stepped to the left. I finally got his back to be toward Quint. I swung my sword toward Ash. He stepped out of the way. Quint was closing in on Ash. Ash still had a smile on his face. Quint was about to thrust his sword forward, but Ash saw it coming and turned to face him. Ash blocked his attempt and kicked him in the stomach. Quint went back. Ash walked toward him. I ran behind Ash, and he turned toward me.

"I told you I wouldn't be easy!" His face took on the look of a jackal.

I braced myself. "I am going to wipe that smirk off your face." He tilted his head. "I believe Flair said that, right before Zappa killed her."

I stopped dead center. "What? Flair is dead too?"

Ash's laugh sounded louder than usual. "She sure is. Zappa and I decided to split up. We wanted this game to be over. Now I'm with you." He added as an afterthought, "And him." He pointed to Quint, who was back on his feet. "I didn't want to discourage you." He placed his sword on the ground.

"You didn't. If anything, you helped," I said as I dropped my sword.

He came for me. I was ready. I watched him. He favored his right side. He was weak on his left. With his right hand, he punched.

I easily blocked his efforts. I swung my left arm. It connected with his side ribs. Ash held on to me. I was being kicked in the stomach. I felt other ribs crack from the pressure. Quint came from behind and pulled Ash away from me. I fell to the ground. I watched as Quint and Ash fought. Quint was faster than me. He blocked and threw successful punches. Ash had to keep up with him.

Ash made contact with Quint's face. He stumbled back. Ash hit him again and then another time and another. Quint's face was bleeding and swollen. "Stop!" my voice commanded as I tried to get up. Ash was standing over Quint. He punched him again. I got up and stumbled over to them.

I jumped on Ash's back. I grabbed his throat and squeezed. Ash's focus was on me now. Quint was coughing up blood. Ash ran toward a hedged wall and turned his back. I went through it first, and he fell on me. I lost air and let go of him. He got up. He picked me up by the throat. He squeezed. The area around me was dismal and dark. Through the disarray, I saw a blurry figure come toward us. Ash spit in my face. He let go of my throat and dropped to the floor. I landed on my knees and wiped my face. It was his blood. Ash broke into pieces. "Thanks," I said to Quint as I barely could stand.

He looked far worse than I did. "No problem. Thanks too."

I gave my best smile through the pain. "You're welcome."

The sunset and the area were dark. I couldn't see a thing. "Quint?" I called.

"Here," he answered and touched my shoulder.

"Is it over?" I asked. He helped me to my feet.

"I'm not sure."

Bright lights appeared down the walkway. I looked at him or what I assumed to be him. "I guess we go through," I offered.

Quint shrugged. "I guess." We walked forward, clapping and cheering came from the other side.

"You did it!" Flair and Octavion said at the same time.

"Where are the others?" I asked. Octavion pointed. "Behind you."

Quint and I turned around and found Annora, Gwen, and Derek walking toward us. "We beat them," I said.

Gwen was the first to react. "I knew we could do it." The door we walked through closed with a soft hum.

Annora looked at Quint. "You look horrible."

Quint looked down at himself. "Really? I thought this look was working."

She chuckled. "Not really." He shrugged. "I'm sure Martin can fix me."

Flair and Octavion came closer to us. "I want to know who fought whom." Octavion was smiling.

"I fought Beckett and Ash. Quint helped me fight Ash too." I announced.

Octavion hit me on the back. "Ouch," I yelled.

He winced. "Sorry, didn't know."

I tried to smile, but it came out shaky. "It's okay. Derek, whom did you fight?"

He told us, "Zappa, and he was a tricky person. He flipped here and there. I finally stabbed him in the leg. Then in the stomach."

I frowned. "Gruesome." He nodded.

"Annora and I fought Brees and Cormac. Talk about messed up," Gwen snapped.

"I agree, they would fight separately but end up together. But when they were together—"

Gwen finished Annora's sentence. "They had practiced fighting combos. They switched on us, going back and forth."

I was fascinated. "How did you beat them?" I asked.

"Annora jumped on Cormac's back and choked him. I stabbed Brees," Gwen said. I remembered my fight with Ash. Being choked or the one choked was an intimate act that took a toll on both parties involved.

"Well, I think we deserve a break." Quint was holding his face.

"Well, never have the Crypto-Hept beat us on the first try." We turned to face Ash. He and his team were standing guard, all twenty of them. I found Rivera in the crowd. She was grinning at me. I couldn't help but smile back.

"I think we all need a visit to the infirmary. Don't you?" Ash insisted.

"Yes, please," I said.

"Sorry about the ribs. I heard them when I kicked." Beckett was staring at me.

"It's okay. I messed you up too," I said. She smirked. An approval from her.

"That's all I have for you today." Ash and the others turned and left out of the back door. We went out of the front.

I lay in my bed, reflecting on the day's challenges. Not just today's challenges but also the struggles I've come in contact with since I arrived here—below the earth. I failed many times. With every mistake, I gained knowledge about myself. Information that allowed me to grow and succeed in the best way possible. Next time, I would be ready. Somehow, I would find peace with the underlying force that tried to hold me back. For now I would be going to bed. Vivienne healed me once again, but the effects were somehow still deep within my bones, muscles, and soul. I breathed, rolled over, and fell asleep.

Check and Mate

The next morning found me full of energy. I felt a lot better than yesterday. The high from yesterday's win and my revelation that I was the maker of my own doing set a raging fire through my soul. Even my aches were dulling to the point I could crawl out of my comfortable bed without groaning in sheer agony.

At an even and jolly pace, I scampered to the couch where my new outfit laid, ready for me to wear and start the day. I was given flowing silk white pants and a silk tank top that hugged me. I took my time in the shower. The warm water loosened any last kinks my body had. After quickly lathering myself in lotion, I slipped into the soft and warm material that hugged me. I hoped they discovered my size, but it seemed they are still not sure and have taken it upon themselves to create a smaller than needed one of a kind outfit. Nonetheless, it wasn't too terrible and unwearable.

After placing my hair finally in a perfect bun, I walked out of the room. I set eyes on Gwen, Annora, and Flair chatting in the middle of the hall. They each dawned a unique silk wardrobe. Flair was in a red romper that covered her long legs. Annora was in perfect fitted oversized shorts and a short-sleeved top. Gwen was wearing a silk jogger's outfit. The pants had elastic around the ankles, giving her outfit a swank look.

"Good morning," I called to them.

Flair responded, "Hey. The boys are saving us a table."

I grinned. "Good. I'm starving." I believe I skipped a couple of meals in the last few days. Between being locked away and fighting, the thought of eating was last on my mind.

"How'd you sleep?" Gwen was looking at me from the corner of her eye. She was smiling, solace written on her from head to toe.

"Like a baby," I told her. For once, this was the utter truth. The day could only go up from here. We descended to the Great Hall. No matter how many times I walked through these halls, I never eluded the constant reminder that I was different from the rest. Not because of how I looked, although that was a factor, but because of what I possessed. I and the other six obtain a heavy job, one that seemed overwhelming, but these people had faith in us. We were picked for a reason. I was chosen for a reason.

Gwen brought me from my haze with her honey vocals. "Me, too. Vivienne is a miracle worker."

Annora agreed, "Yup." She too looked different. Free.

We were almost at the Great Hall. "I can smell the food from here." I sniffed the air. "I smell biscuit." The girls looked at me, astonished, and snickered.

"Well, I guess you are starving," Gwen said and gave me a look. One full of jokes.

The boys sat at our usual table by the water fountain. Sarah and ALICE were among the group as well.

"Good morning, ladies." Octavion was smiling. It seems everyone felt better after yesterday's rush of events.

"Good morning," we said all at once.

"I still can't believe yesterday's challenge," Octavion spoke as we sat down.

"Believe it, because it happened." Flair commented after the waiter came and took her order.

"I wonder how they're going to surpass that challenge," Derek said. He then told the waiter what he wanted.

"I don't know, but it should be exciting," Quint said as he sipped some of his water. Our waiter left to retrieve our food.

"I heard about it. You guys did awesome," Sarah complimented as she took a drink.

"Thank you." Octavion smiled at her. His demeanor claimed all of the praise, as if the rest of us were not sitting right beside him.

"She was talking to all of us," Flair laughed.

"I know." He shrugged his broad shoulders.

Our waiter reentered with our food. We ate in silence for a while. I enjoyed every bit of it. Silence wasn't the worst thing. It gave me time to think. We were practicing so much that I never gave the outside world a thought. I nearly forgot about my father. I wondered how he was doing. I wondered where he could be? Who was he with? Why didn't he tell me he wouldn't be back? It did not make sense. Nothing made sense. The more I stayed, the more I felt like I was home, but I also felt like I knew nothing.

"Jewels, are you here?" Quint asked me.

I balked but only for a second. "Yeah." I smiled at him. Everyone finished eating. I still had food on my plate. I guess I wasn't as hungry as I initially thought.

"We are going to leave soon," Sarah said, looking at me. They all were. I needed to say something. Too many times had they caught me in a state of disarray.

"I was thinking about the next challenge."

Gwen sounded skeptical. "Yeah, okay, right."

"Really. Maybe…they will have us fight zombies." I don't know why zombies came to mind. Possibly from the lasting impression television's idea of what an apocalypse should feel and look like. No one moved or said a word. They all gawked at me. Then like a bullet, they erupted with uncontrollable laughter that bounced off the walls and caught the attention of others around us. Instead of sulking at their laughter, I joined. We laughed until we could no more. Then a wave of actuality crashed. We were quiet again.

"I doubt that." Gwen couldn't stop smiling.

"Let's get to work." Derek shook his head, holding back another outburst. If I couldn't be the girl that had everything together, at least I was the one to put smiles on others faces.

Our waiter came by and collected our plates. We left out of the Great Hall. Other members of Refashion followed us out with their eyes. We tried to ignore their stares, but it was too apparent.

Sarah and ALICE left us to conduct more experiments with ALICE's system. As for the Crypto-Hept, we were instructed to go to the Jar Room. Inside, Ash and his mini crew were waiting for us.

"Had a good breakfast?" Ash spoke.

"Sure did." Octavion was snickering. The rest of us joined in at the thought of fighting zombies.

"What's funny?" Beckett asked with a serious face.

"Nothing important." Octavion was able to get out.

"Okay." She shrugged it off.

Calmly, Ash spoke. "Today, you guys are going to go into another simulation. You will fight…zombies."

"Shut up!" Flair yelled. My jaw dropped. The whole room seemed to have lost air.

"You have to be kidding me." Derek looked at me and I back at him. I was right? My face was still shocked.

I looked at the others and back at Ash, asking, "Are you for real?"

Ash straight face turned into a sneer. "Of course not." The air came rushing back in. "We were in the Great Hall too."

"Yeah, Octavion repeatedly said zombies. We knew we had to get you all." Beckett was enjoying our heartbreak. This was the second time I've seen her fully smile with actual emotion. The first time was when she and I had faced each other in the maze.

"Nice try, Jewels," Zappa gave me an empathetic look.

"Shall we move on?" Ash looked us over.

"Sure," Derek said after a beat.

"Today, you will be doing target practice," Ash announced.

"That's all?" Octavion was disappointed. We all were.

"Not just any kind," Axel spoke to us for the first time ever.

"He's right. Beckett." Ash looked at her, and they understood each other.

"Follow me." She motioned. She took us to the garage and opened J5. "You'll find attire in there." We walked into the room. Inside were black vest with red flashing lights. I think I had an idea of what to expect. "Guys, I know what we are doing next." They all gave me their attention, wanting to know more. "What?" Their eyes called with hunger.

I shouted, "Laser tag." I was excited. I've only played it like all the time. I got this. I realized my outfit made me a sitting target. White was a horrible color for a laser tag fight.

"I need to change," I said.

"Why?" Gwen asked.

"I'm wearing white. Bright colors in a game like this make you a sitting target."

"Oh. We can't change, though." She was right. Our colors were our uniforms. Gwen walked over to the closest vest hanging and slipped into it.

"And you're not the only one that is going to glow." Quint rubbed the back of his neck and snorted ever so slightly.

"I think it's safe to say we will all glow," Octavion said. Quint was playing around with his gun. He accidentally hit Octavion's vest—lighting the darkroom with a red light.

"Dude," Octavion bellowed. He was smiling, a sign that he wasn't angry with Quint, just that he caught him off guard.

"Laser tag sounds fun." Annora laughed as she placed her vest over her head.

"I've heard about it, never played." Flair was stuck in the corner. She already had her vest secured. I looked at them.

I looked at the five members that have never left the safety of the underground. "That's right, all of you've been inside here."

Annora agreed with me. "Yes, that's true. But we can make this time a memorable one."

I smiled. "Potest non prohibere nobis," I said as I placed my hand out. They repeated our phrase and placed their hands in, one at a time. "Let's go," I said. Our hands skyrocketed in the air, and then we dropped them. We walked out of the room tall.

"Follow me." Beckett brought us to J18. The others were waiting for us. Ash handed Beckett her vest. Theirs glowed green. They too looked ready, but my team had something they didn't. A true hunger to shut up Ash's big fat mouth.

"May the best team win." Ash looked at us.

"Oh, we will." Flair shot back. The room glowed red. A loud siren blared throughout the room, sounding the countdown till we could enter the room. Then the door opened, and we ran through. Loud, intense techno music played overhead, my heart pounding to the beat, and the excitement of playing one of the best games ever created.

Immediately, I ran upstairs. Getting to higher ground was the best way to win. I shouted for the others to follow me. They trailed behind, deeming me the leader for this challenge.

From the top, I scored a full view of the area. The walls were splattered with different colored neon paint. Our side was a castle. We had a bridge leading to the top. If someone dared to cross, we would know. The end of our castle was a walkway for snipers. From any angle, they could take out anyone they pleased.

Below were several boxes made from wood and plaster, painted black with stripes of neon paint on them. Three large holes were cut in each of them, large enough to hide a body. In several places, mirrors were strategically placed. Mirrors allowed the player to bend their laser's light tagging their opponent.

Right beneath us was a secondary entrance. This was our secret exit if the ends of our castle were overwhelmed. "Keep an eye out," I told the team. I was taking this challenge seriously. I always win. "Derek, two o'clock," I shouted. He turned and found Lois sneaking around. He shot his laser at her, and her vest flashed. She raised her hands and ran to a hiding spot.

Derek was laughing. "I got her." Then his vest flashed and beeped.

We all ducked out of view. I looked through a tiny hole at the front of the castle to see if anyone was around. Zappa was crouched low by the base of the bridge. He had a clear shot of Derek. *He couldn't see me, though.* I raised my gun and fired. His armor flashed green. He ran to another hiding spot.

"I'm loving this." Flair was grinning.

"Gwen watch out," I screamed. I pointed to Ash, who was coming through the secret doorway. She shot him, his chest glowing green. Instead of leaving, he stayed there.

I said, "He's a distraction."

It was too late. All our suits started beeping. I reshot Ash after my suit stopped. While he was going out the secret door, he gave an evil laugh.

"This is a minor setback," I said.

"You are taking this seriously," Gwen said as she approached me.

"I never lose!" I searched the surroundings. I saw Brees. I aimed and shot him. Next to us, Derek was shooting Lois. Flair was busy shooting Beckett. "Some of us need to move, and take them by surprise," I yelled.

"We can't go down the bridge," Gwen stated.

"You're right. That's why we are going down the secret path. You, me, and Quint should be enough," I shouted.

"Sounds good." She ran over to the others and told them my plan.

I watched for intruders from above. Gwen was the first to go down the ladder. "Jewels…" Gwen was whispering. She checked the area and then told us to come down.

"How are we going to get across without being seen?" Quint asked.

"Watch and learn," I answered as I glanced out, careful not to show my vest. I saw Lois inside one of the boxes. I aimed for her shoulder and fired. Her vest glowed. She grunted then ran from her hiding spot. Her efforts attracted all eyes. I noticed Brees and Cormac to the left, closest to the door. They were hunched behind double blocks. I shot them. Their lights blinking green. They retreated into hiding. Up from above, Ash and Beckett were hit. "Thank you, Derek," I mouthed. Heather and Axel were located beneath the sniper section. I shot their vest. While everyone was waiting for their vests to recharge, I ran to Lois's spot. Gwen and Quint followed.

"Nice job." Quint was impressed. "What now?"

I looked at Quint and Gwen with a devious smile. "We attack."

Gwen understood my strategy. "Because we know all their locations. They don't know we left."

I was beaming. "Exactly! They handed us the game, and now we wait for our opportunity." We each took a hole to cover. I had to take care of Lois, Heather, and Zappa. Quint took care of Ash, Axel, and Beckett. Gwen took care of the twins.

We watched and waited for any sign of Ash's team. I spotted Heather. I aimed my laser gun and let the beam hit its target. Heather's vest blinked green. Gwen took a stab at Cormac. His vest blinked. Quint's vest beeped.

"I think they found me."

I thought quickly. "Leave this area. They will think that you were the only one here. We could still have the upper hand."

Quint agreed with my reasoning. "I'll go back to our group," he said as he left the box. His vest was still blinking.

"I can see Brees," Gwen whispered, looking out of her side of the box.

"Hold steady. They are watching this area."

"So should we leave too?"

No, I knew that was a bad idea. We just had to wait one more second. "No, the others will start firing soon."

I guessed right. Up from above, our team hit the other team. Quint must have told them where they were located. Vests were going off all around the room. There was nonstop beeping. "Five minutes." The woman's voice from earlier broke through the speakers.

"Do you think we are beating them?" Gwen asked.

"By a long shot. They haven't hit us a lot." I believed.

"True. But you never know." Gwen shrugged.

"Game over." Her voice blared through the speakers. We slithered from our hiding spots and walked to the exit. Inside the box, the woman's voice came back. "I will now announce the winner." Her voice went silent for effect. "Winning with 1256 points, the green team!" We were stunned.

"What!" My voice echoed in the small metal cube. "That can't be right. What was our score?"

She answered, "A losing score of 1250."

"Six points! Six?" I barked. I never lose.

"I said, don't cry when you lose," Ash laughed.

I glared at him and shouted, "I want a rematch."

His laugh bellowed louder than my yell. "In time. Right now, you have a meeting with Beetly."

"Unbelievable," I was speechless. All of my training and I lose to these guys. "Fine!" I snapped as I walked to the cube entrance, and the door opened.

"We'll get them next time." Gwen ran next to me.

"Yeah, we will." I was looking forward.

"You don't have to take it so seriously." I finally looked at her.

"You're right." I loosened; a small grin replaced my glare.

She gave me a sideways smile. "I wonder what we could be doing with Beetly today."

Octavion jogged to meet us, "I feel as though we practiced all we can. I want some action."

Gwen warned, "Be careful..."

Octavion chose this time to mock Gwen's voice. "What you wish for." He sounded like a teenage drama queen, nothing like Gwen at all. She smacked him on the arm. A loud snap came from his bicep. He yelled, "Jeez. Can you lay off?" Gwen smirked and walked ahead of Octavion. I looked at Octavion with pity. Gwen's slap sounded like it hurt...a lot. I ran to catch up with Gwen.

"Nice one. He probably will be sore."

She laughed. "I'm counting on it. He can be a piece of work sometimes."

"Do I sense something blooming?" I grinned at Gwen.

Her face was pure shock. "What? No!" she yelled. "Why would you say that?" Her face was red now. She hid her face from me.

We heard Derek's voice from behind us. "Guys, wait." We stopped while the others caught up with us. Gwen was still hiding her face.

"Annora thinks we are going to practice pushing our powers further," Derek announced to the group.

"That makes sense." Gwen pulled herself together.

We had to do some amazing things. How we were going to top it, I was not sure. I was ready for the challenge. "There's only one way to find out."

We entered the usual meeting place, the Great Hall. Beetle hadn't arrived yet. The room was completely empty. "I'm taking a seat," Octavian said as he walked to one of the tables and sat down.

"How are you holding up?" I didn't notice Quint next to me.

"Fine, thanks," I told him.

"No problem." Silence.

"Um, have you thought of your mom?" I realized it was the wrong thing to ask.

His face was sullen. "Yes. She's always on my mind. What about your dad?" Touché.

"Sometimes, I think of him. Other times, I'm trying not to kill you guys." Quint's low chuckle bounced off the walls. I looked at him, cross-eyed. "I'm serious. I'm dangerous."

Quint stopped laughing. "Nah, you're you, nothing more, nothing less."

My face squinted. "Was that from a fortune cookie?"

"Maybe." He was facing forward with a smile. "I could just be good with words."

"Hmm, okay," I joked. He laughed again. Not at me, with me.

"Where is Beetly?" Flair took a seat and placed her feet on the table. "This is not like him." Annora walked to the main door and opened it. She left the room. We lost sight of her for a second. Then she was back.

"He's not out there," She shut the door behind her. The loud clank vibrated the room.

"Maybe Ash was wrong?" Octavion said.

"I doubt that. He usually gets things right," Gwen countered.

"We will wait." Derek let go of his intake of breath. He sat across from Flair. I walked over to the fountain and sat down. The continuous water flow was peaceful. I watched as the different species of fish moved around the large enclosure. Some of them were in each other's way, but they never collided.

It had been a while, and still there was no sign of Beetly. "If he's not here in five minutes, I'm going to take a nap." Flair slapped her legs to the ground.

"You can't leave," Derek hollered from across the table.

"Watch me," she scoffed.

"There will be no need for that," Beetly said. We all stood at the sight of him. He was standing at the side entrance door, looking concerned.

"What happened?" Gwen asked him with respect.

"Yeah, where were you?" Flair questioned.

"I'm sorry for the delay. I had to take care of something," Beetly responded.

"Saraphine said the same thing to me earlier. What's going on?" I asked as I walked closer to the group.

Beetly stared at me. "Nothing you have to worry yourselves with." He clapped his hands. The sound was too loud for the quiet room. "Shall we begin your next challenge?" He looked at each of us. It was clear that he was not going to explain his absence.

"Sure," I said. I looked at the others. Their curiosity was printed on their faces as well.

"First, I will explain the rules. Then you will begin." Beetly spoke to us, yet his mind wasn't on us at all. He kept looking behind us.

"Beetly?" Gwen called his name.

So he resumed. "Rule number one, to win, you will need the most points. You don't necessarily have to kill each other."

"Excuse me?" Annora uttered in shock. We were all confused.

"Yes, it's an inner challenge. You guys will fight each other."

"Impossible—we're uneven." Flair placed her weight on one leg and tilted to the side with her hand on her side.

"Yes, one team will have more. The other team must handle it. Life isn't always fair." He glared at the door again. "You earn points by using interesting ways to defeat your opponent. The more combinations you use, the better. Second rule…" Beetly's voice trailed off. He had a confused look on his face.

We turned around to find Nátàl Mater walking toward us. She had five armed men trailing her. We never met any of them before. They must not be a part of the Guard. "I'm sorry to interrupt your lesson, but your services are needed elsewhere." She tried to hide her concerns, but I could tell it was eating her.

"What happened?" We all asked at once.

"Follow me, please." She turned and went straight through her protection detail as they split apart and then swallowed her. We gave one another confused and troubling look as we stumbled after her.

What You Wish For

After taking us several different ways down hallways and stairs, she stopped in front of two large redwood doors. "Inside, you will find the Scourger you met earlier this week. I need you to contain him. It also helped to aid Ray's escape," Nátàl Mater explained.

"Wait, he's out? I knew having him here was a bad idea," Derek grunted.

"Maybe, but his DNA is vital to us. Everyone is on full lockdown. Please get it done," Nátàl demanded.

I was up for the challenge. "We will, Nátàl Mater. Leave it to us. Potest non prohibere nobis, right guys?"

Gwen squeaked, "Yeah."

Derek snapped, "Whatever." He obviously was too upset.

The guards opened the door, and I was half expecting to see the creature there and half wishing he escaped somehow. But nothing was there. There was only darkness. We stepped through and found the reason. The Scourger or Ray had knocked out all the lights.

"Quint, you want to help us out?" Derek asked.

"Sure."

He raised his hands, and bright yellow light erupted from his hands. The room was immediately visible, and we could see that the Scourger was no longer in the facility. Instead, he had broken a hole through the wall, and there was black acid surrounding the corners of the broken clay wall.

"He's out in the open. We need to tell the others so Nátàl Mater can get to safety," Flair said.

Gwen spoke up. "I'll run back."

Derek refused. "No, we stay together."

Flair did not like being ordered to do anything, "We split up before."

Derek explained, "Yes, but this time. The danger is all too real."

Octavion was the voice of reason. "Either way, we can't protect and find the creature."

"Octavion is right, Derek. We need to split up," Gwen added.

"We can do this, Derek." I made sure I sounded confident even though the idea of fighting a real Scourger was overwhelming.

"Okay then, Gwen and Octavion, you go guard the Queen. The rest of us will search for the creatures," Derek declared.

"Sounds good." Octavion and Gwen ran back to the entrance. You could hear small sharp movements before there was silence.

"Okay, they are on the move. Now we should do the same," Derek ordered.

We went through the large hole that the Scourger made one by one. On the other side was a hallway. There were only two ways out of the hall, and it looked like the creature chose one of the doors.

"Should we split up again?" I asked.

"Yeah, I'll take Annora and Flair. Jewels, you go with Quint." Derek whispered.

"Okay." I turned, and Quint was already walking to the other end of the hall; I had to run to catch up. "Would it be mean if I said I hope the Scourger is through the other door." I probably should've just kept the thought to myself.

Quint abruptly stopped and turned to face me. "Yes, it would." Then he turned around and kept on walking. Over his shoulder, he added, "I was thinking the same thing. But we both know the monster went this way."

I gave a strained laugh and shook my head. "Yes, the creature is over here."

He stopped once again at the door and placed his hand on my shoulder. "Don't worry. Nothing can stop us, right?"

I nodded. "Right!"

He pushed open the doors, and I closed my eyes. The open door let in a rush of wind, and I found comfort in that. What I didn't find comfort in was the smell. It was a pungent order that wouldn't go away, no matter how much you covered your nose. I couldn't even open my mouth to talk, afraid of sucking in some type of venom.

Quint had the same idea because he motioned with his hand to follow him.

One thing that was clear about the smell was that it confirmed that the Scourger passed through here. Meaning I would be fighting one more time. At least I wasn't alone. After following the odor for several hallways, it suddenly stopped. The air was now fresh. I gave Quint a look, one he understood to mean danger.

"Keep quiet," he instructed. He had crouched down low-ready for an attack.

On the other side of the door was the library. If the Scourger and Ray were hiding in here, it would take hours to find them. This library holds all the books ever written. "I am not splitting up," I said.

"Good. Because neither am I," Quint responded.

I let out a sharp laugh, which I immediately regretted because then there was a growl. It was a deep growl that radiated throughout the room. Books rattled in their spot, and the ground beneath our feet shook.

"Sorry." I winced.

He gave a small sigh. "Get ready."

Shortly after, the Scourger appeared from one of the bookshelves. Only it didn't seem much like a Scourger. For the simple fact, that it was Ray.

He carried a smug look on his face. One, I didn't think he had the right to carry, mainly because we were going to kick his butt. Now I sounded like a cliché.

"Well, look what we have here. I see a couple of wannabe saviors." The other Scourger came up next to Ray, like a loyal dog.

"Wow, did you steal that out of a movie or something?"

Ray stuttered at my comment. "What? No, I didn't."

Quint told him, "Doesn't matter because we are taking you in."

"I don't mean to sound judgmental, but that also sounds like it came from a movie, maybe *The Avengers*?" I joked.

"Can you focus for a second?" Quint gave me a look.

"For real, this is a very serious moment," yelled Ray. His dog growled.

Smiling at them both, I simply stated, "I know. I was just trying to be the diversion."

Quint asked, "The what?"

Right then, Gwen stormed in and hit Ray with two large marble stones. He flew against one of the bookshelves, toppling it over and the one next to it. Derek had gathered some vines and rapped Ray several times, sending him into the air. Ray radiated white sparks, and the vines caught fire and burned off. Ray dropped to the floor. He stood up and emitted white sparks from his hands. "You shouldn't have done that."

"Oh yeah? That was nothing, try this." Flair gave it her best shot and made a tornado of fire around Ray. The tornado was bright red and yellow. Heat suddenly consumed the room along with the smoke. We all coughed, including Ray.

I decided to do my part and make the smoke disperse. Focusing on my task, I carefully went into my trance. My space was free of pain, doubt, remorse, anger, and sadness. The only thing I felt was happiness. I imagined the smoke disappearing from the room. It flowed perfectly into thin air and then nothing. When I felt like my work was done, I imagined myself waking up from a dream. I visualized myself walking up to my friends and being in their presence again. Before I could, the same figure from earlier was blocking my view. Its outstretched hand was coming toward me. I took a step closer. In the back of my mind, I remembered I was fighting. I had to get back to the others. Who knows what I've done?

When my eyes opened, Ray was on the ground, coughing for air and sweating from the heat. Barely able to stand, he regained his position, and his hands were glowing with white sparks once more. Before Ray could do anything with his energy, Annora splashed him with a ton of water, and he went out like a light switch. His body flew into the bookshelves, breaking the case and knocking the books in a pull of water.

Annora gathered all the water, standing ready for another attack. We found Ray unconscious with a *Dummies* guidebook on his chest, with the title *How to Be a Better Person*.

"Now that is ironic," commented Flair.

The Scourger charged, we had messed with its master long enough.

"Gwen," Derek warned.

"I'm on it." Gwen grabbed one of the bookshelves and knocked it into the creature. It went out like a light. "That was easy."

Quint and Octavion each grabbed one of Ray's arms while Derek made sure the vines around him stayed secure. They did the same to the Scourger.

"How did you guys know we were in here?" I asked.

Derek said, "We followed the stench."

I said, "Well, thanks. That's how we found them too. We make a pretty good team."

"Yeah, I guess we do," Derek admitted.

Octavion urged, "Let's get these guys back before they wake up."

"Here, I can help with that," Gwen took one of the large marbled stones she hit Ray with and pointed to the boys. They dropped the two of them onto the floating rock, and Derek added vines to them and the rock. Now Ray and the Scourger looked like a sushi roll. "Nice job," Octavion said.

Realizing that he instructed Octavion and Gwen to protect Nátàl, Derek asked, "Weren't the two of you suppose to guard the Queen?"

"Yes, but Nátàl Mater told us to leave, once we got to the bunker. No offense, but we follow her orders over yours," Gwen explained.

"No, I get it." Derek walked ahead of the group. His shoulders were tight from the stress.

Making it back to Ray's cage seemed to take forever. We only took six turns, but I expected him to wake up, and we would have another mini battle right here in a crowded hallway. We finally made it back to the lab room.

Gwen placed Ray back in his cage. His cage was different from the Scourger's cell. There was no thick glass; it was metal. Derek took off the restraints, and Gwen took the stone from the cage. A scientist came by and locked the cage with a code. The scientist then took the Scourger into a back room. Beyond the door were more cages and test tube equipment. Then we were left in the room alone with Ray. A soft clap broke the silence. "Well done, Crypto-Hept." It was Nàtàl Mater, who stood before us with five guards, Ash, Lois, Brees, Cormac, and Beckett. Beetly, Vivienne, and Saraphine were there also along with ALICE.

Nàtàl continued, "Of course far as everyone knows, we were conducting a safety test. There was no Scourger breakout."

I had to make sure of what she was saying. "Excuse me."

"Yes, Jewels."

"Why lie about it?"

Nàtàl answered me with a straight face, "I don't believe in instilling fear, remember? It is safer if they do not know."

Okay, that would have to do, so I said, "Yes, I remember." After a short pause, I added, "Ray *is* dangerous. We met him a few days back."

"We?" Gwen implied.

"Yes, Sarah and I. Ray ambushed us. He caused her to lose control of her mind. It wasn't safe," I patiently said to her.

"See, that is exactly why we need to kill him," Derek snapped.

"Derek, we cannot kill the only sources we have to the cure. Not when we are so close." Nàtàl patiently measured her words.

"But he got out once. Trust me, he will find another way, and this time, he will be ready for us," he warned.

Nàtàl Mater muttered, "Maybe, but he is the only thing closest to their ruler." Nàtàl Mater seemed to regret her last statement and tried to change the subject. "Remember, you are not to speak of this." She gave each one of us a look.

Suddenly, the sanctuary's alarms sounded. The sound was deafening, like a foghorn. We all exchanged questioning looks. *What was happening?*

Zappa came through the corridor. "My lady, we have been breached. Please come with us. We need to get you somewhere safe."

Nàtàl Mater stared in disbelief. "By whom?"

Zappa was impatient. "There are at least two dozen of them. They are climbing down our passageway as we speak."

Nátàl asked hurriedly, "What measures are you taking to secure the people?"

Zappa spoke with urgency. "The Guard has already started transferring people into the bunkers. We need to get you and the Crypto-Hept there as well." My heart pumped blood faster as he spoke. I could feel the excitement from the others. Everyone was on their heels, feeling the need to do something. We wanted to help.

"No, we have to help you fight," I shouted over the foghorn.

"Not likely, you guys are only half ready," Zappa shot back.

"We can handle this," Flair said.

"Yeah, we did capture two Scourgers," Gwen added to our defense.

"Gwen's right. They did take down two real Scourgers," Beckett defended us.

Nátàl ordered, "Ash, prepare a small team. You and the Crypto-Hept will leave for battle."

Ash shook his head. "Mater, with all due respect."

Nátàl Mater was not to be reckoned with. "It would be wise of you not to finish that sentence and do as I say." Ash and his team left the room.

She then faced the Crypto-Hept. "Your ALICEs will be with you constantly. You all will be leaving the sanctuary soon."

"When?" Gwen asked.

"You all will leave first thing. There is no time to waste. We have found their location, and you will be sent to Germany. That is where the virus is most prevalent. It is also where our spies have spotted movement in the night."

Annora's voice shook. "Finally, seeing the outside world would be exciting under different circumstances, seeing how we have to face the most vicious villain ever in human history."

Saraphine added, "Yeah, which is a problem, isn't it?"

I was concerned. "What about you, guys?" If we left, how would they manage?

Saraphine was most confident. "We will be fine. We have the best fighters in the world," she assured the group.

Beetly stepped up, giving us an order. "Go now, ready your things." None of us moved. We all had questions. Questions that would sear our brains on the way to Germany if we didn't get answers now.

"Well, go on then. Move those feet." It was Saraphine. She had come up next to me and gave me a jolting push. The others soon followed Saraphine and me out of the room.

"What just happened?" I asked her.

"You all are about to go to war, dearie!" I didn't want to admit fear. I just breathed.

"I didn't think it would come so soon. I thought we would have more time to…" Quint cut himself short.

"The world is dying, dearie. You all have a part to play."

"Is it that bad out there?" I questioned.

Saraphine said, "Yes, the virus has spread to all continents. It is a full-blown pandemic."

"Why weren't we told earlier?" I demanded. My friends! Oh gosh.

"You couldn't have done much, dearie. You guys were still in training, and the cure wasn't complete."

"Is it ready now?" Annora asked, hopefully.

"Yes, when the creature escaped, we were close to a cure. We just needed to take more blood. That thing hurt two of our scientists while trying to escape. That's where you came in. Now we have the cure, and all we need is to defeat the Scourgers."

Flair stated under her breath, "Oh yeah, no big thing."

Saraphine let out a growl of laughter. "Yes, you have a journey ahead, but I believe in you all."

Annora was smiling. "Thank you."

Saraphine told us, "Now then, you all need to go and pack for the journey ahead." They gave Saraphine reassuring smiles and nods then ran back to their dorms.

I stopped right in front of Saraphine, and when she turned around, she didn't seem startled like a normal person would be. "Can I help you, dearie?"

I shook my head violently. "Yes, yes, you can." I paused because I already knew what the answer would be, "Can you come with me… I mean, us?"

She growled with laughter. "I wish, but I would be no use to you." She grabbed me into a hug. "Remember what I told you about what will happen when you win?" I was in distress. *If we won, everyone would lose their powers. If we won, my life would not be the same. If we won, my dad might not let me stay in Refashion.* I was scared for myself, for the others, as well as for my father. I just wanted all of this to be over. The reality of what I had to do was taking my breath away. "Dearie, are you all right? You look pale, and your skin is sweaty."

"I'm fine. I will be fine." To take her mind and mine off my current situation, I added, "What am I supposed to remember exactly?"

Saraphine took the bait and showed her pearly white teeth with a large smile. "You and I will share a dance when you win." Oh that.

"Ah, yes. I remember." I returned her smile.

"Good. Now, let's get you back to your room." She held my arm.

"Okay, but…" My voice faltered as I felt the nausea. The tips of my fingers went numb. The weight of my body seemed too heavy for me to keep up. I looked at Saraphine because I knew what was coming next. The room swirled around me, and my legs fell from underneath me. I could no longer hear the siren. It was quiet. Before I blacked out, I felt warm arms wrap around my body.

A figure approached me from afar. Its mouth was moving, but I couldn't hear anything. My voice was mute, as I tried to yell at the figure. I wanted to know what it wanted. Why couldn't I hear it? Then the figure was gone, and my area was dark.

Sometime After Blackout

I woke up to the sound of a soft hum. My hands spread across the bed, and it felt like silk with a vanilla scent. The pillow I was laying on felt fluffy just like a cloud, enough so that my head disappeared within all the feathers. For that short moment, I was at peace. I couldn't remember anything the night before. A knock on the door took me from the quiet hum of the room. It was then that I realized I was no longer in my dorm but a small-sized room with the lights off. There were two circular windows, and the light coming from them was enough to light the room. Immediately, I thought of Quint and the others, which made me think of everything else. The notion of them made me feel mentally tired.

"Come in." I sat up in the bed, and ALICE poked her head around the door.

"Hey, you can come in." She opened the door wide enough to scoot through.

"Good afternoon."

"It's that late?" I asked. Where did the day go?

"Yes. You know you black out a lot. I think you should get that checked out." I rolled my eyes and ignored her smart comment.

"Where are we?"

She simply replied, "In the *Challenger* again." I rolled the covers off me and hung my feet over the bed.

"Where are we exactly?"

She answered, "Somewhere over the Pacific."

"Are you all right, ALICE?"

She said, "Yes. Why do you ask?"

I told her, "You seem off."

Her response was swift. "Well, actually I'm on. How else will I be able to talk with you?"

I jumped out of bed. "See, that's what I mean. You're acting smart."

The android snapped, "I beg your pardon."

I knew then something was wrong, "You're not ALICE, are you?"

"Yes, I am. I'm just not *your* ALICE. She's being rebooted at the moment."

Rebooted? "Why? What happened to her?" I wanted my own ALICE, not this rude mouth.

"Nothing significant. She just needed an update. Now please get ready. They want to go over the plan with you." She gave me a strained smile then walked out of the room. For someone who was programmed to be nice to the gifted, she sure was callous. I never knew a computer could have a personality. Oh wait, I almost forgot about Siri.

We no longer had to wear our specific colors anymore. This was the real world, and blending in meant more than anything. I found my bag of clothes sitting on the edge of the bed. I picked through them and noticed that the material was not as soft as the clothes at Refashion. The stiff cotton felt foreign and itchy on my skin. I decided to go with a red "I Love New York" tank top and dark-blue jeans. I opened the door to my room and briskly walked to the front of the plane. It always seemed like I was late…and out of place. When we found my dad, he would have a lot of explaining to do.

"Good afternoon," Gwen popped up from her seat and gave me an enormous warm hug.

"It's nice to see you too." I hugged her back.

"How are you feeling?"

I wasn't doing too hot. Lying was more manageable. "Better, thanks."

The sight in front of me was astounding. This was the challenger but bigger. More the size of a US army plane, but with a decked out interior. Each of the Crypto-Hept was guarded by their very own ALICE. The same face was printed seven times. It looked freaky and yet very cool. Ash's most trusted members were also on the plane. Beckett and Lois, Heather, and Axel occupied the turning chairs. Brees and Cormac were on the couch. Zappa and Ash were seated on the adjacent couch. Everyone stared at me as I stood without an ALICE. "Where is ALICE?" I added, "My ALICE." I realized there were six more.

Vivienne spoke up. "She's rebooting in the room." Her gaze was to the room from where she stood.

I wasn't satisfied. "Okay, is she all right?"

Vivienne assured me, "Yes, of course. We were uploading new combat moves and safety measures. She should be ready soon."

I pressed on, realizing she was all right. "So you guys have a plan?"

Vivienne stood and walked to the middle of the seats. "As a matter of fact, we do." She then motioned for Gwen and me to sit down.

Vivienne elaborated, "The Scourgers are located somewhere west in the Gobi Desert." Confusion instantly flooded my thoughts. If I could remember correctly, we were supposed to be heading to Germany. That's where the disease had broken out.

She continued, "I know what you are thinking. Why did we tell you we were going to Germany? The truth is, we did not want"—she paused—"Ray to know that we were on the right track. Ever since he came, we've had more attacks on Refashion. We didn't tell you about these attacks because we wanted you all to focus on your task of getting a better handle on your powers. But once we had an official break-in, there was no choice. We had to take the opportunity to attack."

She took a short pause. "Now that we have the cure and their location, it's time to save the world." A few claps and hollers, then she continued, "The Scourgers are located west of the Gobi Desert. We will drop you as close as we can without your location being compromised. It will take us some time to get to the Gobi Desert. So relax and enjoy the flight. She left us sitting and went to one of the separate rooms. I hope it was to check on my ALICE.

"I don't know about you guys, but I'm starving," I gasped.

Gwen joked, "Well, you were knocked out for a while." We all laughed.

"Yeah, that's true." I had to admit.

There was a call button next to my seat. I pushed it, and a few seconds later, a lady in a light-blue suit and white button-up shirt came walking in. She turned the button off and bent over. "Hello, my name is Amanda. How may I help you?" I realized she was the flight attendant Vivienne told me about on my earlier flight.

"Uh…can you tell me what's for lunch?" I said, staring at her.

"Yes, we have garden salad, Caesar salad, and veggie burger with fries. You may have any choice of drink. You can also have sides of mash potatoes, corn on a cob, and string beans." She was still smiling, but she had an otherwise blank look on her face.

"Okay, thank you. Can I have the veggie burger with fries and honey mustard sauce? For my drink, can I have a glass of water with lemon?" I told her.

"Sure, it will be right out." She responded. She asked everyone else what they would like, and then she went into the room where Vivienne was in. When she came out a few minutes later, she gave us a last smile and left to the front of the plane. "Now we wait," I said while tapping my fingers on the arm of my seat.

"Any of you got cards?" Octavion asked.

CONCENTRATION IS KEY

Amanda arrived with our food and set our plates down. She then stood in the middle of our seats and said "Enjoy" and walked out.

"I can't believe we get to leave!" Annora exhaled after she took a bite of her plain salad.

"I know, this is going to be great," Gwen said between bites of her veggie burger.

"It would besides the fact that we are going to one of the hottest places on earth. Also, we have to fight"—Quint was cut short by the rest of us—"scourgers." We all gave a hardy laugh. The atmosphere was full of light.

"All right, you guys. Very funny." Quint grabbed his neck and rubbed it.

"Hey, man, we all know what's at stake," said Octavion.

Flair walked over to me. "Hey, can we have a minute to talk?"

I looked up at her for two reasons. One, I was shocked she came over to me, and two, I wasn't finished eating. "Sure," was all I said, though. She didn't wait for me. She was halfway to the back before I could get up from my seat. I finally caught up to her, and she was seated on the edge of the twin-sized bed.

I didn't say anything. I wanted her to speak first. "So..." she trailed off. I continued to keep my silence. She got the drift and continued, "I wanted to apologize to you. I know I haven't been the nicest person to you, and that hasn't been fair. Since you're going to be a part of the family now, I have to learn to accept you." She paused for what seemed like minutes. "I want you to know I don't hate you necessarily. It's just the fact that you seem to question us and our capabilities. You have no trust in yourself or others, and I cannot trust someone in battle who cannot trust themselves."

I sounded more sarcastic than I intended to. "Oh, is that all?"

She snapped, "You can take it any way you like. I'm just trying to tell you the truth. The truth hurts more than a lie."

"It does." I wanted to explain myself, but talking to her was like talking to a wall. I took a deep breath and exhaled. I'll try it anyway. "It's just that I feel out of place. You all seem to fit in this particular situation better."

She also took a deep breath then exhaled slowly. "We all feel out of place. The trick is not to show it. It's ironic, really. I never felt important, and now I'm one of the most important people ever to walk this earth."

I looked at her and asked, "That's how you really feel?" I was shocked. It seemed like she had it all.

"Of course, none of us are ready to fight this battle. But we must. Just like the Crypto-Hept before us, we must succeed."

I smiled. "Who knew you were so inspirational?"

She gave a small laugh and rolled her eyes. "Very funny."

I just kept smiling at her, "So…are we okay? Well, as long as I believe in myself, that is."

Flair didn't smile as she said, "Yes, we are." She got up from the bed and walked to the door. "Let's join the others."

"Okay." My smile was gone.

The middle of the plane was loud. Octavion was turning into different animals. Derek kept egging him on. He was telling him that he couldn't turn into a horse or a kangaroo. It wasn't until Vivienne walked into the room that they stopped. "You two better get a grip," she scolded.

"Yes, Mom," they said in unison.

I laughed louder than I meant to. I do a lot of things that I don't mean. She glared at me. "I wasn't necessarily laughing at you, Vivienne. I was thinking of Sarah and how she called you mom too." I told her. Vivienne didn't say anything. She gave us a look then turned to head toward the room. "Oh, Vivienne, how far is ALICE?"

Vivienne stopped short. "She should be done in a couple of minutes."

I was delighted. "Okay, thanks."

"Well, if you wanted the air to leave the room, that's one way," Octavion commented.

"What's the other way?" Annora smirked.

He gave a large smile that spread from cheek to cheek. "Just ask Jewels to do it."

Everyone went wide-eyed. I could tell they didn't know whether to laugh or not. I found the joke to be hilarious and the sight of everyone's faces made it ten times funnier. I couldn't resist the urge to laugh, so I laughed uncontrollably. I couldn't stop, and the plane was filled with my voice alone. My laugh was contagious enough to make the others smile and laugh. I caught a glimpse of the Guard smirking. Even the other ALICEs were smiling.

Through the stomach pain, I said, "That was a good one, Octavion."

He seemed pleased with his joke.

"Jewels, if you wanted to, you could carry the plane." Everyone stopped laughing. Gwen broke the air with her comment.

"Are you suggesting I should control the plane?" I froze.

With confidence, she said, "That's exactly what I'm suggesting. What better way to get over your fear than to control a plane with your friends in it?"

I said, trying to disguise my nervous voice, "That logic makes no sense."

Finally, Derek spoke, "I'm with Jewels. That is not a good idea, Gwen." Derek stood from his seat. He walked over to Gwen and whispered, "We don't want to die. She barely stopped—"

"Hello, I'm right here. I don't want to do it either. I can't." Flair cleared her throat and gave me an I-told-you-so look. I frowned and straightened up.

"On second thought, I will do it."

Ash intervened. "You will not."

Gwen smiled at me while the others looked concerned. Flair, on the other hand, looked indifferent. She was trying to push me to prove her wrong, and I would. I closed my eyes like I usually do; I focused on the wind beneath and around the plane. I imagined how it moved, what speed I wanted it to go. The plane jolted for a few seconds. Everyone in the room stumbled. I could feel Derek staring at me with daggers. I tried to focus one more time and felt the weight of the plane in my hands. The aircraft stopped shaking and flew straight.

The speaker came on, and the pilot spoke. "Sorry, folks, looks like we hit some turbulence." Everyone stared at one another.

"You guys, I'm still holding the plane," I said proudly.

"I know you're doing great," Gwen said.

Vivienne's voice broke my concentration "You are doing what?" Her voice was filled with anger and fear. She walked over to me. "You stop this right now, I mean it."

I tried to explain, "I was trying to show—"

Vivienne shouted over me, "I don't care. But you will not take us down."

I wasn't trying to do that. "You don't understand. You never understand. How am I supposed to control what I have unless I practice?" I snapped back.

"That's just it. You can't truly practice unless you're under the guidance of an adult that understands. There is a difference between trying to master and showing off," Vivienne said, scolding me still.

I stepped back from her with a look of disgust. "I was not showing off. I just wanted to control one thing in my life. Ever since you came into my life, there has been nothing but chaos. I've lost so much. Now you tell me I can't practice because of an adult? Beetly isn't here. You're just scared."

She stared into my eyes. Her intimidation was tense, and her voice was sharp. "Jewels, this is not a conversation to be had. Wrong is wrong. You already hurt a teacher and your friend. I will not tolerate you hurting anyone else." I was heated. I could feel my blood boil. I wanted to punch Vivienne so bad. She made me sound like a child having a tantrum. How could she expose my personal information?

I glared at her while I spoke. "I wasn't doing that on purpose. I'm sure when the others first got their powers, they did something out of the norm. You can't penalize me for something unintentional."

"Jewels!" Someone was yelling at me. I think it was Beckett.

"What?" I shouted in no direction.

"You have to stop!" It was a different voice this time. Gwen? My mind wouldn't let me focus.

"Stop what?" I yelled.

"The plane, that's what. Slow it down," someone else shouted. A guy's voice. I finally noticed that the speed of the plane was out of control. The others were pressed against the walls trying to stay put. I was dead center, my feet glued to the floor. The pilot was on the intercom system, yelling, telling us to put on our seatbelt. The problem was that none of us could reach our seats. "I'm sorry," I said. The plane then slowed down and conducted a regular flying pattern.

"Don't apologize. Just refrain from doing something so reckless," said Vivienne. I felt horrible. Maybe Flair was right; perhaps I was not cut out for this, and the universe messed up with the selecting process.

"I don't understand? I need to use my powers more so I can have better control over them."

Gwen walked over to me after being pinned to the plane's wall. "We will help you. Right, Vivienne?" She looked at Vivienne, giving her a questioning look. Gwen never strayed from Vivienne's eyes. She held her ground, and Vivienne softened under her gaze.

"Of course, I will help her. But we need to take baby steps. No more controlling other things, yes?" I gave a shameful nod in reply. "Okay then, I will go check on ALICE." She walked from the main room. I couldn't bring myself to face the others. I almost killed them again. I could only imagine the kind of look I would be getting from Flair. I imagined a look between disgust and "I told you so." The flight attendee rushed into the room. Her hair was a mess, and her outfit was in a jumble. "Is everyone all right?" She looked around, realizing why we were staring; she straightened herself. "I would have come sooner, but I got stuck behind the food cart."

"We are fine, thank you. How are you feeling?" Gwen stepped forward, carrying her sweet smile.

"I'm all right. Just have a small headache. Can I get you guys anything? Aspirin? Water?" Amanda was still the flight attendant.

"No, that won't be necessary. You can take a break if you would like."

Amanda smiled. "Well, all right then. I think I will take that break." Then she was out of the room. I noticed that she was favoring her left side. It was my entire fault, and I did feel bad about it. She didn't ask to get thrown around a plane. After she was out of the room, I finally looked at the others. They were staring at me. I felt the same way I did at the Crypto-Hept party. All eyes were on me, exposed and alone.

"I'm sorry, guys. I don't know what happened." I looked down.

"Well, I for one wasn't worried at all," Gwen chirped.

"I don't know? She had me there. I could have sworn she wasn't even in the room." Octavion added with a displacing look.

"Yeah," Annora spoke up. "Jewels?" I turned to look at Annora. She wasn't mad, but she didn't try to hide her concern about what just took place. "You never are here when you use your powers. It's like air if you think about it. The only notion that we have of air is when the wind blows and breathing. But we can't feel it in our lungs. However, we can feel the lack of it." She turned to look at the rest of the group. "Jewels just needs to harness the presence of it. Visualize it moving with her eyes open. Don't drift off into the unknown… into air."

"I've never done it with my eyes open."

Annora simply stood from her seat without any effort. She didn't show the effect of her injuries bruising on her forearms. She was fluid in her walk. "Make up a color. Add the shape of it. Is it curvy or straight? Does it move fast or slow? Imagine your gift leaving your body and spreading into the area. How will it affect the others around you? Daydream." She paused and stared at me. "Well, are you thinking about these things? Or am I just wasting time?"

I hurriedly answered, "Oh…yes, I am." I closed my eyes.

Annora wanted more. "Well, what do you see?"

I stammered, "Uh, I see a wave, a slow-moving wave that vibrates around the objects in its way."

She pressed me for more details. "Go on. What color is it?"

I breathed, "It doesn't have a color. It's more like a fog but not completely cloudy."

"Good. Now decide how it comes from your body."

I knew I had that. "That's easy. It comes from my mind."

"Well done. When the time comes, you should be able to handle it better." I opened my eyes and found Annora smiling at me. They all were.

Octavion sat back in the cream-cushioned chair. "Wow. Who knew Annora was such a good teacher?"

Derek projected, "Yeah, Nora. You really know your stuff."

She tilted her head and shrugged her shoulders. "It's nothing. I just taught her something I had to teach myself."

"I appreciate it. I think I can understand better." I was trying to sound confident in front of them. I wasn't sure if I could truly master it. This was harder than I thought it would be. "Does anyone know how many hours we have left?" I asked. I was done focusing on me.

"We have six more hours to go," Ash answered me. He grunted as he sat down on the couch.

"That's not bad at all," Flair's sarcastic voice chirped. I took this time to glance at her to see if she gave me a thought. She wasn't even looking at me. Her face was fixed on the window, looking at the fluffy clouds. "I'm going to take a nap. I've been up too long on a plane with you all. It's starting to mess with me." She stood from her chair and whipped right past me.

"Have nice dreams, Flair," Gwen chimed.

"Thanks, Gwen. I will imagine molten lava crashing over Pompeii," Flair said.

Quint gasped, and a short laugh escaped. "That's dark."

Flair deviously laughed. "Haven't you heard? Fire doesn't have pity."

Octavion snapped, "Oh, you definitely need a nap."

Annora's chuckle was contagious, which started an uproar of laughter from the rest of them. The only ones not laughing was Flair and me. Before leaving, she gave me a half glance.

"What's her deal?" Gwen asked.

"I don't know, but she's a hothead." Octavion rolled his eyes.

"Really? Okay, the first one was funny. Now it's just too much," Lois snapped.

"I know, but I'm on fire." Octavion snarled with laughter, in which Gwen replied with a roll of the eyes.

"Seriously, though." Derek slumped in the chair.

Octavion put his hands up in surrender. "I know, I know. But you have to admit my jokes were…smoking."

Derek's sharp voice broke the air. "Enough already, we all could use some rest. In six hours, we will be landing in China."

Octavion spread his large body on the couch and turned his back to us. "All right, you all heard the man."

Gwen gave me a questioning look. "I guess he has the couch?" She then walked into the same backroom that Flair went in and shut the door. Annora walked off after Gwen. When the door opened, I could hear Flair's voice. "Why can't you share a bed with Gwen?" she was already half asleep, so her voice was groggy.

"I can't because Jewels is sharing one with Gwen," Annora replied.

"Fine," was Flair's grouchy response. Then the door closed; there was silence.

Derek walked to the back of the plane too. "I'm going in the room next to theirs."

Ash stood. "I'm going to the other room up front."

Brees and Cormac replied at the same time, "Sounds good." The three of them went to the front. The curtain swooshed as they passed.

"Don't worry, Jewels, you will get the hang of it," Lois said then walked past us behind the curtain.

"She's right," Zappa remarked then left too. The only ones left in the room were Quint, Octavion, Beckett, me, and the ALICEs. Beckett decided to sleep in the chair by the window. The six ALICEs all simultaneously stood and walked over to one of the corners and turned themselves off. Funny enough, that's not the creepiest thing I've seen. Even so, it was still strange.

"Now that was weird," I said to no one in particular.

Quint smiled to himself and said, "Yeah. If I'm honest, I don't really like mine. She snaps too much."

I shook my head in agreeance, "I know what you mean. I had the pleasure of meeting her."

"It's insane, I think you have the best one."

My smile reached from cheek to cheek. "That's what ALICE said to me."

"I believe it." His voice was a soft song. Quint then tilted his head. "Are you going to stand the whole time?"

I walked over to the couch opposite him. "I didn't notice I was standing."

"Ah." He asked me, "How are you feeling?"

"Better, thanks. I didn't mean to scare you."

He crossed over to where I was. "You didn't."

I didn't believe him. "Are you sure, because I scared myself?"

Leaning back on the couch, he let out a loud yawn. "Nope, you didn't. I knew you could do it."

I gave him a long look. "Why were you so sure?"

"Because you're like me in some ways." I was surprised by his answer.

I squinted my eyes. "I doubt that."

"No? Okay, try this on for size. One of your parents is no longer with you. You are half Refashion. You don't understand why you were picked for the task of saving humanity. You also have issues with your powers."

I thought about what Quint was saying. The one thing that nagged at me was the fact that he thought he was not in control of his powers. If I remember correctly, he was blinding Scourgers left and right during practice. I never noticed his insecurities. "You don't seem to have a problem," I told him.

He let out a tired laugh. "No, I don't. That's the key. You know that saying, 'Fake it till you make it'? Well, that's what I'm doing. I try to believe that I can. I also think about what the others before me would do."

"I guess it's working for you."

He laughed. "It is, and I'm sure combining what Annora and I said will make you unstoppable."

I had to smile at him. "Thanks."

He grinned back. "No problem." Quint yawned and sheepishly smiled afterward. "Why is it that after eating, the human body wants to sleep? If you ask me, that's a real bad habit. You should want to run it off—instead, you are sleeping like a hibernating bear."

I laughed. I thought he was going to say sleeping like a baby, but of course not. Quint had to switch things up; he was unique.

"You can go to sleep, you know. You don't have to keep me company," I told him.

He looked at me sideways once again. "I wasn't staying up for you."

Slyly, I said, "Oh, no?" His head bopped up and down to an imaginary beat.

"No. I just don't feel like going to sleep."

Okay, right. "Is that so? You know it's okay to admit defeat."

Quint toyed with me. "Hmm. Why would I do that?"

I refused to take the bait. "I don't know but, you should. Women are always right. Unless they are wrong, in which case they are still right."

He let out a half yawn, half-laugh. "I don't think that's right?"

I shook my finger in his face while making a tut-tut noise. "What did I just say? Women are always right." Quint shook his head once again to an imaginary beat. He then stood up and stretched his limbs and asked, "You know how you said the others might have had a bad experience when they first got their powers?" Then he sat back down, closer to me this time.

I admitted, "Yes, I remember. What about it?"

He faced me. My heart pounded. I just knew he was about to tell me a secret. "Well, I did have a first bad experience. I was driving with my mom, and she was yelling at me about my school grades. Which were not that bad, by the way. Anyways, she was yelling, and I wasn't listening. After making a couple of turns, we were on a bridge. I don't remember what I said, but it caused her to turn her head. I just remember the look she gave me. Then she turned back, but it was too late—our car was careening over the bridge. Next thing I know, the car was consumed with water. The scary part, it seemed we were all alone. Drowning. The only thing I could think about was how sorry I was. I wanted to tell my mom that but, I had to get us out of there." He took a short break, finally looking at my face.

I tried keeping a straight face because I didn't want him to see how shocked I was.

He continued, "I thought about a signal I could send. Next thing I knew, the car and the water around us brightened. Then I heard muffled voices. I blacked out."

I pressed to know more. "What happened? Well, I mean, I know you're okay, but how is your mom?"

Quint's eyes saddened. "She...she's okay, I think."

Astounded, I asked him, "What do you mean, you think?"

His eyes filled with tears, but he didn't let them fall. "Well, this purple smoke called, Miesgyn, came to our house and swallowed her up."

I felt he must be joking, but he didn't look as if he was. "Are you kidding me?"

He was offended. "Quite the opposite."

I waved him off. "No, it's just that a friend of mine was taken by the smoke too."

He sighed, "Well, would you look at that? I told you we were similar."

I agreed, "You did. What's your mom's name?"

He said proudly, "Lillian Goodwin. What's your dad's name?"

I said, equally as proud, "Warren Stellar."

Quint hummed, "Jewels Stellar. It fits, sort of."

Octavion suddenly groaned, "I hate to break up this touching moment. But *I* would like to go to sleep."

"Of course." Quint sounded concerned, but then he added, "You know there is another bed in the back room?"

"I see how it is." Octavion slowly stood from the couch, looking at us with tired eyes, and slowly walked to the back room.

I said, "You know we could have gone to the front of the plane. There are seats there."

He shrugged. "I know, but I did him a favor." Quint showed his teeth. "Look, when we leave, the six ALICEs might wake up, and he would be surrounded by them. Do you know what a scary sight that would be?" My eyes widened at the thought of the same six faces and twelve eyes looking at me while I slept. My body was overcome with a quick freeze, which caused me to shudder. "Exactly!" Quint smirked.

I decided to change the subject. "Did the others tell you how they found out about their powers?"

Quint seemed to welcome the change. "The boys did. Derek was in an environmental class, and they were looking at types of plants. He touched one of them, and the root sprouted over his arm, covering most of his upper body. It's funny because he freaked out and caused a scene."

I couldn't imagine that. "Derek. Freak out, never."

Quint insisted, "Oh, but yes. He regained himself, and then the plant recoiled back to normal."

My burst of laughter was loud, and I tried to rein it in. "Sorry. I just wish I was there to see it."

His laugh was light; he was trying not to show how tired he was. "Me too. I've tried to imagine it, but I'm sure my visual just doesn't do it the same justice."

"What about Octavion?" I asked. Quint's body language seemed to wake up. He pushed more to the edge of the couch and placed his elbows on his knees.

"Octavion was wrestling with a wrestler named Vido. He was winning until Vido made an unexpected move. It was a move that caught Octavion off guard." Quint stopped to laugh, a loud laugh. The sight made me smile because his laugh was so contagious. He watched me through squinted eyes. "Then…then Octavion transformed into a—oh this is good—he transformed into a mouse." Quint found this funnier than me. I didn't see what the big deal was. Quint stopped to a halt after he realized I wasn't joining in with him. "Oh, you thought the story was done?" He gave me a reassuring smile. "In fact, Vido is known to hate small crawling creatures, especially a mouse." I started to understand, and I mouthed OMG in response. "There you go, Vido screamed so loud, more like a screech. The rest of the bystanders burst with laughter. Vido was more embarrassed then Octavion, who turned into a mouse."

I giggled. "What a way to shine."

Quint cackled too. "No, kidding."

I looked at the clock on the desk next to the couch, and the time read 3:30 p.m. I couldn't believe we had been talking for an hour. It never feels like time passes with him. Quint noticed me staring at the clock and stated what I was thinking, "Wow, I can't believe the time. On the bright side, we have five more hours until we land in the land of the dead."

"What?"

"Well, nothing really grows in the Gobi Desert, hence the name."

I looked at him. "Oh, I thought you were referencing to all the dying people?"

Quint rolled his eyes. "Of course not. I'm not that morbid." He stood one last time from the couch. "Well, I better get some rest."

I stood as well. "All right. I'm going to the front to see how Amanda is feeling." He gave me one last smile before turning to leave.

Know the Plan

The room suddenly felt dark. The only thing to keep me company was the hum of the plane, Beckett, and the six sleeping ALICEs. There was a faint beeping noise coming from them as they charged. I decided to walk to the front to find Amanda. Maybe she could keep me company till everyone woke from their slumbers. I passed the rooms where the Guards were knocked out. One of them could snore. I heard the sound from outside the room. I passed another curtain and found Amanda. She was seated on one of the seats placed in front of the window. When she heard me whip back the curtain, she turned toward me. "Do you need anything, Jewels?" She smiled at me. Her smile was warm and welcoming, just like the other Refashions.

"No, I'm all right. Thanks." I came closer and picked a chair across from hers. "I just wanted to say I was sorry about everything. I know you are in pain."

She waved her hand and smiled. "Nonsense, I'm all right. I'm all healed." I looked at her, and she was right. There was no bruising anywhere. She didn't even favor her left side.

"Are you a Gyniatric?" I asked her. She seemed pleased that I knew what she was.

"Why, yes. Besides Vivienne and I, there are only two others."

I asked her another question. "How do you guys get these gifts?"

She welcomed the conversation. "Well, we are close to the Queen's guard. She bestows gifts to those who deserve it. Also, who the creator deems fit."

Now that statement seemed odd. "Creator?"

She just looked at me and asked, "You didn't think she made the earth, did you?"

I wasn't sure of anything anymore. "Well, actually…" I trailed off because I sounded ridiculous.

Amanda looked out the window to the sky. "He created the world. She just helps keep balance."

Oh, I got it or I pretended to and said, "That's wonderful."

She turned to face me. "It is."

"Amanda, can I ask you a question?"

"Besides that one? Sure."

I scooted to the edge of my seat and leaned in. Almost like I was sharing a secret with her. "How old are you?"

Her laugh was long, hard, and loud. It was more like a croak. "I'm twenty-four," she said while wiping a tear from her eye. "I suppose you want to know how long I've been twenty-four?" I shook my head up and down. "I've been twenty-four for..." She trailed off, trying to think. Her head tilted to the sky, and she moved her hand in the air marking the sky with invisible numbers. She picked back up, "I've been twenty-four for fifty years now." Overcome with shock, I looked at her like she was crazy. She let out the same croak and broken laugh. "Fifty-years isn't that bad. Others are seventy to a hundred years. I don't even want to mention the Queen."

"I'm sorry, it's just that I don't know anyone who looks like you and is supposed to be seventy-four years old." Her head moved up and down.

"I guess not. Where did you live before here?"

I told her, "In Colorado. I don't suppose you heard of it?"

She pretended to be hurt by my judgmental comment. "Contrary to what you assume, we do learn about the outside world."

I wanted to crawl into a shell, and my gesture relayed as much. "No worries. I'm surprised that I have heard of Colorado, seeing that nothing goes on there." She gave a crooked smile and a small grunt to her joke. I received her stab as a way of getting even.

"I don't do much. But there are a lot of attractions." I remembered the long list I gave Quint.

"Oh, how nice. Do you have siblings?" Amanda pried.

"No. Well, not if you count my best friend, Kaura." For so long, I haven't thought of her. I wondered how she was doing, if she was even alive, if the others were okay too.

Amanda sensed my sadness. "I didn't mean to make you sad." I forgot Amanda was in the room, she was so quiet.

"It's all right. Do you think my friends are okay?" I asked, I hoped. Amanda waved her hand once again and gave me the famous warm smile. "Of course, they are. You don't have to worry about them."

I missed everyone so much. I said, "I wish they were here."

She moved closer to the edge of her seat. "If they were, they would want you to focus on dispersing the cure and defeating the Scourgers." I could tell she was trying to distract me with a different subject, but it only made things worse. Now I was thinking about the battle ahead. Could I do it? Could I help save humanity? As if on cue, Amanda spoke up. "You can do anything."

I appreciated her kindness. "Thanks. You know, all of you are so nice. I couldn't expect a more welcoming place." I felt at home for once.

"Well, we are your home," she said with an ecstatic smile.

I said happily, "You're right. I do belong here."

Amanda agreed, "Of course, everything happens for a reason. Right?"

I nodded, "Right." She stood up from the chair, "Good. I better check with our pilots. See how things are going."

I looked up into her blue eyes and said, "When you do, can you tell them I'm sorry?"

She gave me one last smile. "Of course."

Then she was gone. I felt alone once more.

I decided to go back into the room and found Vivienne and ALICE sitting on one of the couches. ALICE jumped up from the couch. "Hey, Jewels, how's it going?"

I was glad to see her. "I'm doing okay. How are you? Are you updated?"

ALICE answered right away, "Sure am. I heard you fainted yet again."

I admitted, "I did."

ALICE shook and bowed. "You are easily scared, my friend."

I had to laugh at this. It sounded like something the other ALICEs would say. Yet when it came from her, it was nicer.

"Glad to see that you still have your humor." ALICE's cheeks formed like chipmunks after she smiled. I looked over at Vivienne, who was writing something down on a small piece of paper. "Vivienne?" I called out to her. She didn't move at first. I tried again. "Vivienne?" Then her pen stopped moving, and she slowly pulled her concentration from the paper.

"Y-e-s," she said, stretching out the sound of each letter. I tried to speak, but I was caught up on the fact that I wasn't the only one who needed to say sorry. Half of me believed she would apologize, but the other half argued she wouldn't.

I made the first gesture. "I want to apologize for using my powers. I could have caused a lot of harm."

She raised one eyebrow. "Okay." I knew it. She was stubborn and would never apologize. What a waste. "I'm also sorry." I was caught off guard. I couldn't believe it.

"What did you say? I didn't catch that."

She rolled her eyes and gritted through her teeth, "I'm sorry."

I smiled and teased, "Oh, I thought that's what you said." ALICE chuckled. Vivienne turned to look at her. ALICE's laugh quickly turned mute.

"It's all right, Vivienne we have to do it sometime," I replied.

She moved in her seat. "Yeah, well, I don't like it." Vivienne turned her attention back to the paper on the desk.

"What are you working on?" I asked to break the tension in the room.

ALICE jumped in. "It's a plan."

"Plan?"

It was Vivienne's turn. "Yes, we can't waltz in their home."

I let out a loud huff. "I know that."

Vivienne shifted another time in her seat. "From the words of our spies, they have an underground layout as well. We will need Gwen…" She seemed to think about what she was going to say. "Can you wake up the others? I do not want to repeat myself twice."

I thought about it. I didn't like waking people up. They always yelled at you and made it your fault. At least that was what I did when I was having a good slumber.

"Can the other ALICEs do it?"

Vivienne took a deep breath in and let it out slowly. "Fine. ALICE, please wake up." At once, they all opened their eyes.

"Yes," they said simultaneously. *Creepy.*

"Can you please wake up the others? We need to go over the plan before we land," Vivienne said with little care at the sight of them.

Four of them walked away. One went into the boys' room, and the other went into the girls' room. The other two went past the curtain. After a few seconds, you could hear Flair. "What are you doing?"

This was followed by Gwen's voice. "You don't have to be mean."

ALICE walked from their room with a straight face. "They will be here soon."

I turned to ALICE. "Why are they so weird?"

She smiled at me. "I told you I was the best one. They are like that because they are clones of me."

"Clones? I thought you all were made separately?"

"Nope, they come directly from me. Which explains the different personalities. If I wanted, I could make them disappear."

"Wow, who would have guessed?"

She started to laugh. "Well, everyone. You're just late."

"So if I turn you off, will they disappear too?" ALICE's face straightened. She understood what I meant. Shut up. I turned to find the rest coming from the bedrooms. They all looked refreshed and ready.

"So what's the plan?" Derek asked, ready to resume his role.

"Let's start with the location. It's underground," Vivienne informed us.

Octavion interrupted Vivienne, "Oh, that should be easy for Gwen."

Vivienne glared but continued, "Exactly. Gwen, you will have to make us a hole. But quietly please."

Gwen sat down on one of the comfortable chairs. "No problem."

Vivienne continued with the plan. "Once we are in, Octavion, you will turn into a small animal, insect, or whatever you like. You will have to locate the Scourgers in our path. Once located, Quint will quietly get rid of them."

Quint shook his head. "There's no sunlight underground."

"You don't need the sun to make sunlight. That's the whole point of your powers," Becket imputed.

"All right then." Quint's voice was polite, with a hint of force attached.

Vivienne continued once more, "We probably should keep doing this until we find the right door to their ruler's layer."

"It's a shame we don't know his name." Octavion sighed.

"Yeah, a real shame." Vivienne snapped with sarcasm. She was tired of his interruptions and the long flight. We were all tired…of the long flight.

She continued, "Once we find the right door, I'm sure he will be guarded by Scourgers. That's where everyone comes in. We stick together. We stay strong. We conquer."

Octavion was the first to respond, "Simple plan. I like it."

Gwen shouted, "Potest non prohibere nobis." The rest followed, and we chanted the saying over and over. Getting louder every time we sang it.

Amanda came into the back and joined in the chanting. I genuinely believed we could pull this off. We *were* stronger together. The pilot interrupted our chanting, "We will be landing in Mongolia earlier than expected. Please prepare yourselves for the landing." A soft click came after.

"Everyone, please buckle up," Amanda commanded nicely.

Each of us found a seat, and soon the plane descended. Which also happened to be the worst part of the plane ride. It was a total of fifteen minutes before we landed. How did I know? I was looking at the clock. It seemed to want to move fast only when I didn't. The plane had a bumpy landing. It swerved and then straightened. Our bodies hit the sides of our seats as we braced for impact. I wonder what happened on the tarmac to cause the plane to swerve. When the flight ended, Amanda stood. "You are now free to move about the cabin."

Octavion was the first of us to jump at the opportunity. "Let's do this."

"Hold your horses." Ash stopped him from leaving the plane.

"Yes, we need to figure out where we are going to stay for the night," Vivienne said.

"Why can't we stay on the plane?" Gwen asked.

"It's not safe. With all the destruction, the plane might get hijacked. The pilots need to leave." Vivienne moved back and forth. Then she took out her phone and made a call. She was on there for several minutes before she hung up.

"So we are on our own, then?" Gwen grilled.

"Yes. But don't worry. We will be back in no time. I got us a place to stay," Vivienne said after she returned to our huddle.

"Let's go," shouted Octavion.

"The woman said to wait. So we wait. Got it?" Annora said, rolling her eyes.

"Whatever," Octavion was defeated.

"Before we go outside, you should know the sight might not be pleasant. The world as we knew it ended. There are scared, innocent people. You are not to interact with them under any circumstance. Do you understand?" Vivienne asked.

Simultaneously, we said, "Yes!"

She continued in the same displaced voice. "We are going to stay with a comrade that lives here. He will be able to provide us with the tools needed to accomplish our task. His name is Lazaro. He lives in the south of Mongolia, close to the Gobi Desert."

Octavion just couldn't be quiet. "That's all?"

Vivienne stared at him sternly. Then she relaxed, ordering, "Yes. Let's go."

"Now we're talking." He clapped his hands and rubbed them, as if he were cold.

The sight outside was disheartening. The area was broken and deserted. It looked like a scene from an apocalyptic movie. The buildings had burned marks from previous fires, and others were crumpled, exposing the inside. I looked back on the tarmac to find out why our pilot had to swerve. I found a large piece of a building and a broken plane lying on the ground in shambles.

"This is insane," Annora said as she did a 360, taking in the devastating surroundings. "I can't imagine what the rest of this place looks like."

Unlike before, there was no one to pick us up. We moved through the airport, trying to find a vehicle. The Guard had their guns out. They were on alert, as they created a barrier for us. We found plenty of abandoned cars. The problem was there weren't ones big enough to carry all of us. "This is going to take forever." Flair stopped in the middle of the aisle of cars, placing her arm on her hip.

"She's right. We need a better idea," ALICE said while still looking through the aisles.

"All right, what do you suggest?" Ash said.

Octavion moved through us to the front of the pack. He turned around and gave us a smirk.

"I got this." Then he turned himself into a hawk and soared high in the sky. To show off, he did several flips in the air before leveling out. Five minutes later, he signaled us that he found a car by circling over it. We jogged to the car, and I must say he did a great job. It was a black-tinted Chevy City Express van. The inside was a gray and black interior with leather and cloth.

"Nice job, Octavion," Derek complimented as he walked up to the front door on the right and opened it.

"There isn't enough space for twelve people. We need another car," I said.

We all searched the surrounding area for another van.

"Found another one." Lois was standing next to another black Chevy City Express van.

"Okay, Guard, you travel in the van behind us. I'll lead us to Lazaro," Vivienne said anxiously. She didn't want to be out here all night, and neither did we.

"Guard, with me," Ash said as he led the others to the van.

"Well, I'm not sharing." Flair spoke up first, setting the tone of the situation.

"What has gotten into you?" Annora asked. She stepped up to Flair and looked into her eyes. "You have to think of others."

Flair fawned innocence. "There is nothing wrong with me."

Annora had enough of Flair's attitude. She snapped, "Are you sure because ever since we left, you've been a pain in the butt."

Flair seethed with anger. "You—"

ALICE interrupted their argument. "We will all have enough room." She went to the side of the van. "All I have to do is retract the other ALICE's. Then you all will be able to stretch out."

I breathed. "See, there was no need for that."

Vivienne came in front of the group and looked down at ALICE. "We will get through this together, yes?"

Quint, Octavion, and Derek jumped in the back seats. But they then decided to change because Octavion needed more space. He moved to the passenger seat in the front. After they were seated, Gwen and Flair hopped in the next row. Flair had grabbed Gwen; she didn't want to sit next to Annora and, of course, not next to me. Before I stepped into the van, ALICE started to combine the rest of the ALICEs. One by one, they faded and then moved into her body. With everyone she added, her body seemed fuller and more complete. She even had a slight glow to her.

"ALICE, put on this jacket," Vivienne commanded.

"But it's hot," ALICE whined.

"You can't feel anything," Vivienne explained.

"How do you know?" ALICE jokingly challenged.

"ALICE, get in the van." Her patience was running out.

ALICE plopped next to me. "Can you believe her?" ALICE questioned. I gave her a small nod to answer. Of course, I could believe that. Vivienne didn't want to attract attention with ALICE's glowing body.

"Now that we are all settled in, let's get going." Vivienne put the car in drive, and we were off, driving down the road closer to our destiny.

Dress to Impress

The drive to Lazaro's hideout wasn't as long as expected. He wasn't located in a populated area, and after the outbreak, it wasn't safe for him to be near people. Vivienne told us that he lived just outside of Ömnögovi. It's located near the Gobi. The plane dropped us off at Khanbumbat Airport. That was located southeast of the Gobi Desert, almost in China. All we needed to do was go west.

Mongolia was a crowded place with buildings packed close together. Some of them were colored with bright pinks, greens, and yellows. Others were burnt from fire and destroyed. We barely saw people out in the open. They were cautious. But when we did see travelers, it was a sad sight. The virus was clearly in their systems. Their eyes were red from stress and oozed yellow liquid. Their noses were running, and their skin was dark from the infection. Their veins were visible from the disease.

There was one group that tried to get a ride from us. They didn't have the virus, but Vivienne would not stop. She said we didn't have time to help. Gwen's conscience tugged at her. She wanted to help but knew Vivienne was right. We could save them all later when the Scourgers were defeated. After two and a half hours of driving, we were finally able to get out of the van. "Ughh." Octavion stretched loudly. "So where is he?"

Octavion had a point. Where Vivienne stopped, there was no sign of life, just a lot of dirt and sand. Vivienne looked past the vans over the hill and pointed. "There." We all followed her hand, and sure enough, an older guy was standing on top of the hill. He was wearing a long black overcoat with brown leather boots. Attire I didn't find appropriate for this weather. The black coat had a green hood that covered most of his face. He walked toward us. His walk was fluid, barely leaving prints in the sand beneath him. This was proof that he was Refashion.

Up close, I could see he was wearing dark black sunglasses and three claw scars on his face. "How was the journey?" he asked in a low voice.

"Well," said Vivienne.

Lazaro then turned to look at us. "So these are the new Crypto-Hept? They are much smaller than the last ones." He started to chuckle. His laugh was similar to Vivienne's hiccup, just thicker. I guess he could sense our lack of appreciation for his humor. So he tried to clean it up. "Well, don't get your panties in a bunch. I'm just playing. Follow me, please." Did he just say *panties*?

"What about the vans?" They were too noticeable to leave them.

"We have to take them with us," Vivienne instructed.

We returned to our earlier spots in the vans; only this time, Lazaro was with us. He smelled like dirt but with honey mixed in. I don't know where he found honey.

Lazaro was giving Vivienne direction to his hideout. She went straight for several miles before she had to make a sharp turn. After going straight for a mile, we hit a bump in the road. Lazaro put his hand up. She stopped the van, and he got out. I could see Lazaro step in certain spots. Once he stood still, the ground shook, and the land dropped.

The van shook for several seconds before everything was steady, and we could see an opening to a tunnel. Lazaro waved to Vivienne. She drove up to him, and he jumped back into his seat. She went down the dark tunnel for what seemed like miles. The van drove over rock and dirt. No one said anything.

At the end, there was a bright orange light. With more focus, the one light turned into several small lamps. The van then came to the end of the road. Lazaro opened the door once more and did the same steps from earlier. After a second wait, the wall moved to the side. Vivienne drove through without Lazaro this time.

She put the van in park and turned back to us. "Everyone out," she ordered.

Lazaro closed the door and turned to us. "Follow me, please." He took us up several steps. It was very dark and hard to see past my hands. I tripped on several steps on the way up. "My apologies. Let me turn on the lights." He grabbed a match from his coat pocket and struck it against the wall. Then he placed it on the wire hanging against the wall. It caught fire and turned several lamps on, making the room brighter. I could see my feet and the wooden steps they were on. I also could see the rest of the room. It was an underground cave, large and dingy. The ceiling had several rocks that cascaded from it. Some of them were on their last legs. "Follow me." Lazaro went up another flight of steps before stopping in front of a door, saying, "Please enter." Vivienne was the first one through. We heard her gasp. We all piled in, trying to see why Vivienne gasped.

It was wonderful. There was a whole room dedicated to armor. Not just any armor, the kind that we would need to defeat the Scourger. I walked over to one section that was filled with all types of knives and swords. The different shapes that could be made were astonishing. The one that caught my eye was a charcoal black steel hand knife. The handle had an engraved symbol of three swirls inter-twining together. The blade was shaped in a sharp curve. "You have a good eye," Lazaro said.

"Can I?" I asked. He motioned with his hand. I picked up the knife and instantly felt something resonate within me. "Wow," I exclaimed.

Lazaro said as he stood at the entrance, "What you are feeling is the others before you, their strength. This knife was meant for you and only you," Lazaro turned throughout the room "All of you have certain items that belong to you. It's been passed down through gen-erations of Crypto-Hept."

Octavion never knew what to say. Or he did but not at the right moments. "These are hand-me-downs?" he asked with slight disappointment.

Lazaro leaned against the door frame and laughed. "Something like that, young man. They will conform to your fit."

"So how will we know which ones ours are?" asked Derek, step-ping in front of the night gear section.

"Well, there is a symbol on each outfit. It represents your gift. This young lady...uh, what's your name?" Lazaro asked.

"Jewels, sir."

He smiled at me. "Jewels has found hers. Look around, see if you can feel the presence of yours." I found the rest of my gear easily. My outfit was a steel gray armor top with my symbol carved in the front. The pants were the same. It was light yet sturdy. The under-shirt for my armor was thick black leather. Along the arms were two white lines that reached from the shoulder to the wrist. I placed the thick leather over my shirt, and it felt perfect. It looked heavy but felt light on my body. I never felt like this in clothes before. The rush of energy that flowed through my body was amazing.

I found my belt, which had several holsters. I placed my sword and knife in their place. I turned around, and the others looked sim-ilar to me. The only difference was the colors of their lines and what symbol they represented. Derek's sign was located on his chest and side amour. His sword and knife had the same symbol carved into it. The curve of the blade was unique. It moved in and out like a plant looking for the sun. The stripes on his leather undergarment were green.

Annora's symbol was also located in the same positions. Her blade had three holes in them. It was like the water bending to its surroundings. Her sword, however, was smooth and calm. Blue strips covered her leather. I looked over at Flair; the color red glowed bright all over her armor. Her knife was straight until it got to the very end, where it curved ever so slightly.

Octavion's and Gwen's were not as expected. Octavion's leather undergarment had orange stripes. His blade was thick and sturdy. The handle reached far from the blade, giving a robust appearance. Gwen's sword had a skinny handle that curved to the left. At the top of the handle was only one wing to place the hand. The blade itself was thin and lightweight. One side of the blade spread away from the other toward the middle until it closed at an angle, connecting the blade. Creating a gaping hole at the bottom. Her knife was built the same way, just on a smaller scale.

I finally looked over at Quint, who was peering down at his new ware. The chest of his armor was covered with the sun. Quint's sword handle was ordinary. But the blade was unique. The blade went two inches before it opened to a large circle that then closed and finished the rest of the blade. On the blade was a curved swirl extending from the top of the circle to the tip of the blade.

"You all look amazing," said Vivienne.

"I'm sure they do," said Lazaro.

"Oh, now, hush. You know it's no use talking like that. It's not good for your health."

He abruptly laughed. "Huh, my health," he said, turning his attention to us. "Do you hear that, children? My daughter is worried about my health. I haven't seen or heard from her in five—no, for seven years—and she is worried about my health."

Vivienne scolded, "That is pure nonsense. How am I supposed to get ahold of you if you don't have a phone? I had to reach you just now through a connection line." We were all stunned!

"Wait a second, your daughter?" Derek said what we all thought.

Lazaro ignored Vivienne's comment. "Yes. I suppose she didn't tell you. Nor did she tell you that I was blind."

Now that was a shocker. "I would have never guessed. You walk around here totally normal," I said. I figured that's why he never had any lights on.

"Well, I hope I'm good at it by now. I've lived here for eighty years." Lazaro laughed.

"Really? How old does that make you?" I asked him.

"You must be the newcomer, Jewels, is that right?" He looked at me with fascination. I felt sheepish. I knew I probably should stop asking about everyone's ages, but it was just too fascinating. He found the chair that was seated by the door. "Let me think. I've lived in Refashion for twenty years. Then after I was cast as the Crypto-Hept, I moved. I've lived here for eighty years. That makes me one hundred or so. I lost count. Who knows, I could be only ninety."

"I don't mean to sound rude, but I thought you all stopped aging at a certain age?"

Lazaro was patient with me. "Ah, no. What we do is age slowly. Some of us age slower than others. I assume I look around thirty, correct?" He did. But he didn't look like a tired thirty-year-old who has had two jobs and an apartment they couldn't afford.

"Yes."

Lazaro smiled. "Well, that's lovely. Are you all hungry?" I was. "Starving," Octavion boasted.

"Mhm, well then, follow me. Oh, but first, take off your attire. You don't want to get it dirty."

We shuffled out of our newly fitted uniform and followed him down the path. "Is no one going to address the fact that he said he was a Crypto-Hept?" asked Flair. She finally spoke since the car ride here.

Lazaro chuckled. "You have a good ear. Yes, I was a part of the Crypto-Hept. I controlled air. It was wonderful. I could make it do whatever I wanted. I could start a storm and fly. I could even make people fall to sleep by putting more CO in the air."

I laughed. "That's me. But I'm having trouble."

Lazaro's deep hiccup laugh echoed throughout the cave. "I'm not surprised that you are the one to receive this gift. You are full of everything that makes a Refashion or human. You feel as though your gift is more of a burden. Am I right?"

I nodded then remembered he couldn't see me, so I answered, "Yes. I just don't want to hurt the others."

He smiled. "I understand. It took me a while to master the gift. But don't worry, you will in time." He stopped in front of another door. "Please go through."

After everyone went through, he lit another candle, and it opened the room. There was an old walnut table sitting in the center with only four chairs. They were mismatched. The surrounding area had tons of books lying around. A closer inspection and I could see there were Braille books. "Please excuse the mess. Sit. Please. I will be back soon." Lazaro left out of the same door and turned right.

"Why didn't you tell us we were meeting your dad?" Flair demanded.

"I don't know. I haven't seen him in forever," Vivienne said as she walked through the room, trying to find a clean space to sit.

"Were you around when he fought?" Quint asked.

"No, that was about twenty-five years before I was born."

"My parents fought with him, though. They said he could command the air like no other," Zappa said.

He looked away from us as he spoke. Zappa opened a dusty book and then coughed after. The entire room was dirty.

"Your parents were on the Guard?" I asked.

"They were one of the best." Ash jumped in. Zappa gave Ash a sympathetic look.

"How did he lose his eyesight?" Quint asked.

"I lost my eyesight during the battle." Lazaro came back into the room, holding a tray full of food. He placed it on the table along with plates. It was carrots with mashed potatoes, gravy, and green beans.

"Father, how did you get all this food?" Vivienne asked.

"I have a neighbor who is kind enough to bring me things," Lazaro answered.

"A neighbor out here?" Vivienne continued to push.

"Yes, dear, there are still good people," her father answered.

Vivienne probed further, "Is he the one I spoke to earlier?"

Lazaro confirmed, "Indeed. I don't like having a phone, but it's necessary sometimes."

He turned to us. "Now eat. I will tell you the story." Lazaro paused for effect. "It was the influenza of 1918. Never had I seen so many lives lost. The numbers were never concrete; it was between twenty million and fifty million humans. But it affected five hundred million people. Our task was to find the leader and kill him for good. But somehow, he always eluded our reach. We've searched for years, trying to find him all the while people were dying." His head moved throughout the room. He smiled when he heard us munching. "Is it good?" he asked.

"Delicious, thank you." insisted Gwen.

"Wonderful. Now where was I? Oh yes, we thought we had him in London. Our spies saw men going in and out of a factory for days. We soon figured out they were spreading the disease from there. Then the day came when we attacked. It was heroic, really, we charged in with our matching gear. We were ready. Or so we thought." Lazaro grabbed the closest lamp and placed it beneath his chin. The response was our laughing voices. He actually thought that would freak us out. "The Scourgers attacked and attacked. It was a never-ending battle. When we finally secured the virus, we were tired and beaten. We checked the whole factory, but he wasn't there. Our lives were crushed. You see, we never felt like we did our job. But the humans got their vaccine, and we lost our powers." I suddenly felt a wave of sadness.

"Woah," Octavion said after finishing his last bite of mash potatoes. "But how did you lose your eyesight?"

Lazaro answered, "Oh, yes. Well, Ren controlled light, and he made the room very bright, trying to get rid of Scourgers. It also blocked me from seeing a Scourger that crept up on me. It scratched my face with its three claws. I didn't lose my eyesight at first—it was just blurry for a while. Shortly afterward, it went altogether." There was a moment of silence.

"Excuse me for asking, but why didn't a Gyniatric heal you?" Flair said.

"They didn't have Gyniatrics back in my day. I also left Refashion before I received word that there was such a thing. I didn't know my daughter received the honor either," Lazaro stated solemnly.

"Can it still be healed?" I asked.

"It's a part of me now. If I got my eyesight back, I'm not sure I would like what the world has become. I hear some of the music, and I really do question it." I had to agree with him.

"I think we all do," Quint said while taking a sip of water.

"You just left your daughter?" Flair asked the tough questions. He ignored her.

"I'm sure you all are tired. Let me show you to your sleeping chambers." Lazaro stood from his seat. "Don't worry about the plates, I will handle them later."

"I'm sure ALICE will be delighted to help you," Vivienne said while giving ALICE an I-dare-you-to-say-something look.

"I would love to help," ALICE said too enthusiastically.

"Wonderful! Thank you, ALICE. The kitchen is to the right. The rest of us will go left." Lazaro spoke. I looked at ALICE and gave her a look of pity.

"It's all right. I should be used to being used as a servant. After all, that's why I was built. I'll just extend an invite to the other

ALICEs to help," she said and then under her breath to me, "Now you go before you get lost." I smiled then hurriedly caught up to the rest of the group.

Lazaro brought us to a large room that had several beds. Unlike the dining area, it was clean. The beds even matched. "You never know when you will have company staying over," Lazaro simply stated. I found that statement ironic, seeing that his dining room was a mess. We walked in further, and the room smelled of honey, I couldn't find one trace of dirt smell anywhere.

"Thank you. This will do just fine," Vivienne spoke without turning to her father.

"I hope so because I have no other place to put you all," he laughed at his joke. I could tell he was happy to be talking to someone. It must be very lonely, living alone in the dark. He left the room, and each of us took a bed.

"Your dad is interesting." Derek placed his head on the pillow and dozed off.

"Yes, he is," Vivienne whispered. Those were the last words I heard before I fell asleep.

Date with Destiny

"Wake up, Jewels. Vivienne wants us back in the dining room." Gwen was shaking me softly and whispering in my ear.

"Can I have five more minutes?" I looked at Gwen through one opened eye. She was staring at me with a smile.

"No. You have to get up now." Before I knew it, she had picked me up out of bed and placed me on my feet. "Much better," she said then walked out of the room.

I looked around and noticed that I was the only one there. Everyone, as always, was probably waiting for me. One day, I would be there before them all. I put on a new pair of jeans and T-shirt that I brought with me from the plane. Then I rushed to the door, turning right. Inside of the dining hall, everyone was seated, eating breakfast. The smell of pancakes filled the air. "Come in. Sit down and eat." Lazaro somehow knew I came into the room. I found my place next to ALICE.

"Hey. Do you know the plan for today?" I asked.

"Nope, Vivienne is going to share intelligence with us now," ALICE said, then stood up and placed her hand out. She was emitting a 3D image. It was of the Gobi Desert. Beneath the Gobi Desert was a detailed outline of the structure. Like ants, many twists and tunnels were leading to different sections. The only problem was that it didn't show where the Scourgers were.

Vivienne stated, "What you are looking at is the 3D image our spies worked hard to retrieve. The outside is not guarded, as not to draw any attention. We can sneak in through here." Vivienne was pointing to the left of the image. It was three hills made of sand.

"I'm not looking forward to finding sand in places I don't want them in," said Octavion. Derek chuckled slightly but regained his posture.

Vivienne continued as if nothing was said. "That's where Gwen will come in. You will make a path for us to this section bypassing the first three layers, which I am sure will be heavily guarded." She pointed to the left side on the fourth level.

Octavion raised his hand. "Are you sure that's right? I thought the more you go down, the more guards there are." Again, Vivienne ignored him, although her face showed that she heard him.

"Once we bypass several top levels, we should be able to locate their ruler easily. You locate by the smell. The stronger the smell, the closer you are to finding him." Vivienne paused then looked at us. "You all are so brave to take on a burden of such magnitude. You are facing dangers that require your all. Like my father, he has given up something close to him. I just want you all to remember that no matter what happens, you are all greatly appreciated. Now I want you to go out there and kick some Scourger a…butt." Vivienne received laughter and hollers from us.

"We appreciate you too, Vivienne," said Annora through white teeth.

"Thank you." She sat down. "Finish your meal and pack your belongings, and then we head out."

The others left out of the room. Lazaro sat in his rocking chair across from my seat at the table. I stared at him, trying to figure out how to start the conversation. "So…" and I had nothing to say.

"I suppose you want some tips?" Lazaro offered. I felt relieved as he spoke. "I will tell you, out of all the seven gifts, yours is the hardest to master. You can slip into nothing for long periods."

I was eager to share with him. "I do that all the time. I also see a figure." I didn't mean to intrude on his speech. But this was my only time to get tips from the person who controlled the air.

"You see a figure? I never experienced that. What does it look like?" Lazaro seemed eager too.

So I shared further. "There's nothing to look at. The figure is pure black. Sometimes it looks like it's trying to talk, but I can't hear it."

Lazaro bobbed his head. "That is very interesting. I am sorry, I can't be of any help on that matter, but I can tell you the secret of your gift."

My body language perked. "Please tell me." He paused before continuing.

"Okay, the secret to your gift is to believe in your team. Believe that they trust you. Believe in yourself." He didn't speak after that. Was that all? I sunk back in my chair. Out of nowhere, Lazaro laughed like his daughter, just thicker. "I'm messing with you. That is important but not the secret. Do you want to know?"

I breathed, "Yes!" I could tell he was a jokester.

"Well then, you must picture your every move. Command the air to do what *you* want. This gift does not control you. You control it. Remember that, and you will be fine."

Okay, that seemed easy enough. "It's that simple?" Annora was truly onto something.

Lazaro nodded. "Yes. If a reckless guy like me can do it, then you can too. Also, you are not fighting alone. You have six other members, who fear the same thing—losing. If you guys come together as one, then absolutely nothing can stop you. You guys become the strong hand in the battle."

Um, "strong hand" has a nice ring to it. "Thank you for the help." I stood up from my chair. I had to get ready.

Lazaro bowed. "It's my pleasure." I grinned then realized he couldn't see. I was almost at the door when he grabbed my arm. "Be careful of your dreams. They have a way to move mountains or crush you." I stood in the middle of the door frame. My face fixated on the man in the chair.

"Excuse me?"

Lazaro smiled then turned his head to the right. "ALICE is coming, so you better get a move on."

"Come on. You are going to make us late!" ALICE said as she burst into the room just as Lazaro predicted. Her force knocked me two steps back into the room. "Sorry, Jewels. I didn't realize you were right there." Then she turned to Lazaro. "Vivienne wanted me to tell you thank you for the hospitality." No response came from him but a crooked smile. That smile was meant for me.

"Let's go ALICE," I ordered.

After a few minutes, we were back in the chamber, packing our bags. "This is it, guys. We are officially on the job." Derek was fixing his chest armor.

"I'm just glad it's with you guys. I may seem like I don't care, but I really do. That's my problem, I think. I care too much," Flair said, leaning against the wall, already packed and armor ready.

"We know. It's okay, though. We love you too," Gwen taunted Flair.

"Oh, stop it," Flair said hastily and distantly, but she was smiling.

"Is everyone ready?" ALICE stood planted in the doorway.

"No, but let's go," I said. ALICE gave me a look of awe as she realized we had this conversation back at my house. The thought seemed so long ago. I wondered if the house was still standing. Had someone raided it? Did someone live in it now? Was my dad's car still there? I couldn't think about that right now. The only thing that mattered was the task ahead. I needed to focus. I could not and would not mess up. I certainly couldn't mess up while using my gift.

"Come on, Jewels, we are heading to the van." ALICE was pulling at my arm. The others were out of the room; I hadn't noticed that they left. She gave me a look of concern that I tried to ignore. I wanted to tell her what Lazaro said but thought otherwise. What if my visions were something horrible and would cause me to lose my trust with the others?

"Ready, kiddo?" I looked down at her, trying to give her my best smile. My dad used to call me that.

She turned her face from mine. "Actually? Yes, yes, I am," she said.

We were back in the van. This time, ALICE took the front formation, a second protection. Apparently, she could deflect items from the car on top of being a lightsaber and video projector. I mean, who would have guessed? We only had to drive for forty minutes before we had to ditch our vehicle and walk from there. The sun was relentless. I couldn't see one cloud in the sky. Even though the armor was never meant to be dense, it wasn't refreshing either. "Jewels, can you do something about the heat?" Gwen whined.

"Like what? There are no clouds in the sky. I can't make shade," I snapped. The exhaust was clouding my people skills.

"No, I guess not, but what you can do is make wind," Zappa smirked.

"Yeah, you can do that, Jewels." Gwen grabbed my arm, more pleading than believing.

"I'll try. Just stay put, please." I walked away from them as not to hurt anyone. I found a spot covered by a hill. They were out of my sight, and most importantly, I was out of theirs. I took a deep breath and exhaled slowly. I remembered what Annora and Lazaro told me. I saw my gift moving from me in waves. It was foggy but not too cloudy. I imagined it doing what I wanted. I saw the wind appear and cooling the area down. I imagined feeling the air against my skin. How refreshing it was. I opened my eyes. Suddenly I felt the wind on my face. The relief was all too real; I finally did something right. I didn't have to be woken up. *I can do this.*

"Awesome job." Annora snuck up on me. I never heard her coming.

I scolded her, "Thank you. You know you are going to have to walk just a tad bit louder."

Annora smirked. "It's one of my best qualities. I can catch anyone doing anything."

"I'm going to have to remember that for next time." I didn't like anyone sneaking up on me.

"How much further is it, Vivienne?" Flair asked as she reached the hill.

"Not much further, we should hit it in a mile or so," Vivienne confirmed.

"Only a mile?" Flair's sarcastic tone came back with no surprise.

"Come on, you've done worse," said Ash. The thought brought me back to our training days.

After climbing the steep hill of sand, Vivienne spoke. "Just a bit further." She let gravity take over as she came down the mound. The wind was still blowing in our direction. I didn't have to think about it too much. Vivienne was right. We didn't have to walk but a mile before we hit their hideout. The only difference, Scourgers, were outside. It looked like a dozen of them. They were unloading and loading a truck with boxes. They probably held the virus.

"I thought you said they wouldn't be on the surface?" I said, confused.

"I don't understand." Vivienne was in more shock than the rest of us.

"How are we going to get in? Better yet, what's different about the inside?" Vivienne looked at each of us. None of us were coming up with answers. Then I had a thought, a crazy idea. One that might not work, but we should try.

"What if I sneak into one of those boxes? Then they will take me inside, and I could knock them out. Then you guys can come in when the coast is clear." No one said a word for a while. I took that as a good sign. Maybe they were really thinking about it.

"Are you insane?" Vivienne muttered. I spoke too soon.

"Vivienne, this could work," I voiced.

"How?" She asked. I was stumped but only for a second.

"All we have to do is get me over there without being seen."

"Yeah, that's a piece of cake." Flair moved closer to us, so she didn't have to yell.

"It really can." I stood my ground. We were wasting time, we didn't have.

"There has to be another way. We can't risk it," Quint said. A part of me liked that he cared for my safety, but the other part said "Shut up."

I looked over the hill and saw that the truck was not occupied, "Look, here's our chance. Once you see that the outside Scourgers are knocked out, it's safe for you to come in. I'll stay hidden till you come."

"It's too dang—" Before Vivienne could finish her sentence, I hopped over the hill and ran as fast as I could to the front of the truck. I looked around to make sure no one was coming. When I thought it was safe to, I ran to the rear of the truck. I placed my arm over my nose; the stench was overwhelming. I quickly opened one of the heavy metal boxes and set myself in it. The only thing I didn't realize was that the box was empty. If I was in it, that meant there was weight, and they might check it. Hopefully, I get a stupid Scourger to lift the box. A loud clang was heard above me. Did one of them just lock me in here? I felt the box lift from the ground, and I stayed still. My breathing, however, could be heard through the box, I was sure. If the weight didn't give me up, then my breathing would. There was no light. Just deep breathing coming from the Scourger caring me. I could tell we made it inside, because the stench was unbearable. There were multiple sounds of growls and muffled voices. I was in the den.

After a few minutes, I was placed down. The creature grunted loudly, and then there was silence. I needed to focus. I was supposed to knock out all the Scourgers on this floor. I should have them knocked out in no time. I tried to keep my eyes open while picturing them losing consciousness, one by one dropping to the floor in a deep sleep. I imagined the oxygen depleting from the area. As if on cue, I heard loud crashes that echoed through the hall. I think I successfully put all of them to sleep.

Now, I had to wait till the others came in. Waiting was the worst part. I was sure it had only been a minute since I dropped the Scourgers, but the others should be here by now. I was starting to freak out. No, don't do that. Man, if someone told me eleven days ago that I would be trapped in a coffin size metal box with no way out, I would say that they were insane. But here I was, locked away and forgotten. *I just needed to stay focused and breathe...breathe, it was all right. They would get me o*ut soon.

I pushed on the top of the box to try and make it move but with little results. The panic set in, and I realized I was in more trouble than I could handle. I came to the conclusion that no one would get to me in time. Those creatures would find me in here and gouge me before I even had a chance to fight back.

Okay, breathe. Just breathe. I could not think like that. They would find me, and I would make it. Just take deep breaths. Okay, breathe... breathe...bre—Just then, I thought to myself, *What was I doing? I was the one in control here. I could do this. I could get out*

I took a deep breath and exhaled, decreasing my heart rate. I thought about what Annora said and focused on my gift. The color of it and the way it moved through space. Like the air in the lungs.

I placed my hands on the sides of the crate and applied pressure. I envisioned the air forcefully, leaving my hands and breaking the box. Suddenly, the crate shook violently, and the hinges were undone. I added more pressure, and the whole box exploded from the stress. I closed my eyes to avoid the flying wood chips. My body fell to the ground with a thud.

I opened my eyes and focused on the figure standing above me, who, to my surprise and happiness, was Gwen. "Nice party trick!" She outstretched her hand.

I grabbed her arm, and she pulled me up. "Thanks."

"No problem." Gwen asked me, "Are you okay? We left you in there for a while."

"I'm great," I said, which was the truth.

"Come on, girls, we need to get a move on," Ash quietly demanded.

Vivienne was leading the way. ALICE was next to her, showing the detailed 3D model of the area. "Can we trust that?" Derek asked.

"We have no choice." Vivienne then turned left at the split hallway. "We need a tad bit more light."

"I'm on it." Quint brought his hands together and made a ball of sunlight. The light immediately opened the hallway, and we could see clearly. The walls were much like Refashion in that they were made of dirt. However, it wasn't neatly compacted; theirs had rocks and cracks coming from the wall. There were no emeralds or rubies, just disease. The smell was horrible too.

"We must be going the right way because the smell is getting worse," said Ash. It was a foul smell, more pungent than a decaying body and spoiled cheese.

"Hold on, guys," I said. The others stopped in their tracks. I moved the air, trying to clean the area around us. I created a giant bubble that only I could see. It pushed the odor from us. The oxygen was breathable again. I watched them as they took a deep breath in. "It smells so much better," said Annora.

"How are we going to track them now?" Flair asked. "The smell is gone."

I stood my ground. "We can still follow all of the acid." That's when they noticed the walls were covered with their discharge.

"Well, then." That's all she could say. I smiled to myself.

"Let's continue," Ash instructed.

Vivienne pushed on. She turned a corner and then pushed us back against the wall. "There are three of them." Immediately, the Guard took point. They guarded us like royalty.

"Can you get a closer look?" Vivienne asked.

Lois barely pulled her head over the corner. For a few seconds, she was motionless. Her body seemed to perk up. "Quint, can you make that ball of light brighter?"

"How much?"

She smiled. "A whole lot brighter." Quint realized what kind of Scourgers were around the corner. He stepped into the hallway in front of the three Mists.

"Hey," Quint called to the Mists.

The misty black ghosts turned toward him and charged. He waited for a second, and my anxiety grew. Why didn't he blast them already? I wanted to scream but knew that would distract him. Quint slowly—I do mean slowly—raised his arms. Still holding the light, he expanded it. The Scourgers were still coming for him, not realizing they were sealing their fate. When they were about five feet in front of him, he let go of the light. It took over the hallway, nothing could be seen beyond it. I covered my eyes. When I felt the sun off my face, I opened them. Quint had walked back to us, no Scourger insight. "Way to go, Quint!" Octavion boasted and slapped Quint on the back. In response, Quint grabbed his shoulder from the pain. "Thanks."

"Let's go," Ash asserted. Instead of Vivienne and ALICE leading the way, the Guard took point. We bypassed several doors. No Scourger insight. Then ALICE stopped. "I'm picking up human heat signatures." I could not believe the gear on her.

"Where?" Vivienne acted like this was an everyday occurrence.

"To your left."

In front of Vivienne was an exceedingly large double door. It was wooden with several rusted bolts outlining the doors. "How many do you have?" ALICE checked one more time. "Only two." No, it couldn't be.

I asked, "Do you think it's my friend?"

Quint interjected, "It could be my mom too."

"Only one way to find out," said Gwen as she approached the door.

Vivienne pointed to the door, and Gwen pushed on it. Without any struggle, the bolts broke, and the doors were opened. It was dark but not for long. Quint stepped forward with his ball of light and moved through the room. It was a small prison. There were six cells, but only two were filled. "I see someone at the end." Quint walked fast to the end of the hall. When I caught up to him, I was filled with disbelief. My dad was sitting in the cell. How it was possible, I didn't know. Either way, I was happy to see him alive! He was scrawny and dirty, but he was alive. Tears fell onto my cheeks. "Hey, Dad."

"Hey, kiddo." He smiled, tears falling from his eyes.

ALICE walked over and pulled at the lock. It broke with ease. I ran to him and gave him the longest hug I could.

"I've missed you, Dad."

He squeezed me back. "I've missed you too."

ALICE walked over to the cell next to the one that once held my dad. The cell next to his had a woman in it. She called out, "Quint, is that you? Oh, how I missed you. Come here, let me have a look at you." ALICE pulled at the lock, and Quint's mom collapsed in her son's arms. Quint was immediately covered with her love.

"Mom, I miss you too. But I'm working." His mother didn't care about that at all.

"Oh, hush," she said and kissed him on the forehead. "Now introduce me to your friends."

Always the leader, Derek asked, "First things first, did you see what the Scourger's leader looked like?"

Gwen spoke with kindness, trying to cover Derek's impulsiveness. "That would be Derek, and I'm Gwen."

Quint's mother did not seem to mind. "Nice to meet you both. But I'm afraid I haven't seen the leader. We were put here as soon as that purple fog took us. We only saw people when they gave us our food." She looked sad.

"People? You didn't see Scourgers?" Derek insisted.

"Oh, heavens, no. We—" Ms. Goodwin was cut off by Vivienne's urgent voice.

"Sorry to interrupt, but we should be on our way." Vivienne stood in the center of us. We left out of the small prison and turned left.

"Dad, stay close."

He beamed at me. "Look at you, I'm so proud."

I smiled, but it was soon replaced by concern. "Dad, how are you here?"

He was stunned. "Well... I...what do you mean?"

"No, don't get me wrong! I'm happy to see you, but Vivienne said you disappeared. I never thought they took you?"

My dad regained his composure. Whatever I said seemed to haunt him. "I was taken by those creatures."

"How? Why?"

"To tell you the truth, I don't know. I woke up in there." He pointed to where we came from.

He was vague on purpose. "I'm not little anymore. I can handle it."

"I'm telling you the truth, kiddo. I felt something hit me on the back of the head, and then I was here. Promise." He paused then smiled. "You have grown. I'm proud."

"Thanks." I was happy that he could be proud of me, but I knew he kept something from me. "Hey, Dad...when this is over, we have to talk about Mom."

He stopped in his tracks. I tried to pull him forward, but he wouldn't move. "So you know?" That's all he said.

"I know some. I need you to tell me more," I flatly responded.

My dad picked up his stride and walked in front of me. "After you win, I will."

"Fine, you can't avoid it forever." I surpassed my dad and caught up with Quint. "How's your mom?" I asked.

Quint smiled but kept his face forward. "She's great. She's very interested in ALICE." I looked to the front and found ALICE explaining her 3D model to Quint's mom.

I laughed. "That's something."

He said as he finally faced me, "How's your dad?"

I heaved a puff of air. "Fine. He won't answer my questions about my mom, though. In fact, he won't answer anything truthfully."

Quint understood. "My mom's avoiding my questions too. But what can you do? They've been doing it since we were born, avoiding our questions."

"Yeah, but it still hurts. What do you think their king looks like?" I asked, trying to distract my thoughts.

"I'm not sure, but I imagine him to be really ugly and big. Like a giant beast with spikes coming from his body and his blackened skin, tough as leather."

"I see you gave this some thought," I teased.

"Only a little," he said while laughing.

"Come on, you guys!" a voice shouted to us. I didn't realize that we fell behind. Gwen was waiting by the corner.

"We need light, Quint," Beckett shouted as we came down the hall. We caught up to the rest of them, and he went to the front to lead. Vivienne stopped another time. From her expression, there were more than just three Scourgers. "Everyone, get ready. Mr. Stellar and Ms. Goodwin, please stay back."

We turned the corner, and the sight was horrifying. There were dozens upon dozens of Scourgers. They were all staring at us. Flair fired, and seven of them were turned into dust. The rest of us geared into action. Gwen, Quint, Beckett, and Ash took the left side. Derek, Lois, Brees, and I took the middle. Flair, Annora, Cormac, and Octavion took the right side. Zappa stayed back with the others. It was amazing watching all our gifts at work. All the colors—red, blue, yellow, green, brown, and white, all working together. The walls were lit with color. Scourgers were being tossed from wall to wall. Their screeching voices filled the hall and echoed through my ears.

I picked up three Malfises, tossing them in the air. Gwen took rocks from the wall and crushed the Malfises together. I glanced at Gwen and gave her a side smile, which she returned. Octavion had turned into a vulture. But it wasn't just any vulture. He was the king of vultures. His body was white with a black tail and wing-tips. His eyes were piercing gold. With his large multicolored head, he scanned his surroundings. His wings were no less than five feet, casting a large shadow on the wall. He picked his prey and grabbed a four-legged beast. Octavion took the screeching beast into the air, ready to drop it. At the same time, Flair just finished burning a dent in the Scourger's numbers. She saw Octavion in the sky and cascaded her fire upward toward him. It was like a hose of fire going against gravity.

She burned the screaming Malfise into nothing. In response to Flair's help, Octavion gave her three high-pitched squawks while circling over her head. "You're welcome, just don't crap on me." Octavion came down to land. Instead of turning back into a human, he turned into a lion. Having a predator so close to you and not being afraid was empowering. He charged at the oncoming Malfise and Treed and pounced. He had one Malfise in his jaws and crushed its throat. The other remaining Scourgers surrounded the lion. Annora came to the rescue and pushed two Treed away with a thrust of water. Derek also helped by grabbing the rest with vines and wrapping them tightly. They were crushed under pressure.

I had just finished tossing Scourgers to Flair when I saw Gwen about to crush one with a rock. It immediately turned back into a human, a small girl, crying. It was an Impostor, and it was pleading with Gwen, "Please don't, kill me, I'm only a child. Please." For that instant, I watched Gwen as she froze. The heavy rock slowly came down. I knew Gwen would never be able to harm that thing even if it was a Scourger. So I saved her. I pushed the Scourger out of the way and held it against the wall. The others were busy, and Gwen wasn't focused. "Zappa, get Gwen!" He had stayed back to protect our parents along with ALICE and Vivienne.

"Okay." He quickly ran over to Gwen and grabbed her arm. Once they were at a safe distance, I took the oxygen from the small girl's location. She gagged, unable to speak. I almost felt bad. Well, almost. Then she was knocked out. But I kept going, making sure she wouldn't wake up ever again. I dropped her body once I was satisfied. Flair came next to me and burned her body. "Nice save." She told me. Flair ran back to help Derek, who had several pinned against the wall. I ran over to Gwen, who looked dazed. When she realized I was standing there, she spoke quietly.

"I'm sorry. I know it wasn't a girl, but I still couldn't..." she trailed off, staring at me with pleading eyes.

"I know. It's all right." I gave her a quick hug. "Come on, we have some butt to kick."

She brightened up, and her honey smile was back. "Yes, we do."

There were no more Scourgers in sight. It was safe to let the rest come out. "Nice hustle, everyone." Vivienne was smiling.

"I don't know about you guys, but I'm tired," Octavion said.

"Try not to change into large animals so much. It takes most of your energy," Vivienne said. There was no force behind her statement; she was trying to be helpful.

"Let's go." Derek took a deep breath in. We turned to find four rows of Scourgers. It was Mist, Malfise, Imposter, and Treed, all standing in our way.

"You have to be kidding me," complained Annora.

I stared at Annora and remembered something. "Hey, I have an idea." I took her by the arm. "Make a wall."

She was confused. "How is that going to help?"

We didn't have time for this. "Trust me," I insisted.

"All right," She raised her arms and focused on creating the same wall she did at the Great Hall. The wall of water came out of nowhere. It covered the middle of the room from top to bottom.

"Push it forward," I said.

So she stretched her arms out, palms facing flat. The wall moved toward the Scourgers. She grabbed them in and held them in place. I then pictured what I wanted the air to do. The room chilled, and the water froze in place.

"Hey, Flair?" I yelled in her direction.

"Yeah?" Flair answered with curiosity.

I smirked. "Have you ever boiled Scourgers before?"

She smiled. "You know I never had the chance to. Why don't I try?" Flair smiled brightly.

"Be my guest. Annora, I'm letting go." I informed them both.

Annora shook her head. "I have them."

Immediately the water was back to normal, but they were still unable to move. Flair looked at the water with anger. The water evaporated into steam. Then it was boiling. The Scourger's voices were muffled but still audible. Their screeching didn't stop until one by one, they turned into black goo in the water. Annora's wall of water was mud now.

"Gross," Ms. Goodwin said.

Everyone turned to her because it was weird hearing an unfamiliar voice in our midst.

"Annora," I signaled. "You can bring the wall down now." She calmly moved her arms from left to right, and the black water dispersed.

"Quint and Ash, check the next hall," Vivienne instructed.

Quint and Ash each took a side of the hall to inspect. When they finished, they returned.

"The coast is clear," Ash yelled.

"Good, let's move out," Vivienne ordered. Halfway down the hall, I noticed my dad wasn't with us. "Did anyone see my dad?" Confused faces looked back at me.

"I haven't seen him since you called me over," Zappa answered me.

"ALICE, you didn't see him?" I asked.

"No, I'm sorry. We were all watching you with that girl." ALICE was furious with herself. I felt terrible.

"What, girl?" Annora asked.

"Long story," ALICE left it at that.

"It's okay. I'm going back." I turned to leave. Quint grabbed my arm. "I'll go with you."

"No, it's fine. I think I got a handle on it. Besides, the team needs you. I will be fine."

Derek offered, "She's right. I'll go with her instead."

Then Lois offered, "Me too. You never know."

"Thanks." I took the extra hands because they wouldn't let me leave on my own. If I said no to Derek and Lois, then Gwen would offer.

"All right, we're turning left then right and down the tunnel. We will see you soon. Be careful." Vivienne said then disappeared around the corner.

Annora looked at Derek. "Be careful."

Derek smirked. "Always am. Let's go, Fire Breather."

"Why that name?" Lois asked as we went back the way we came, trying to find any sign of my dad.

"I tried to stop a fire by taking in the oxygen. Instead, I breathed in the fire." Lois looked impressed but said nothing.

"Is it me, or does any of this not look familiar?"

"I know what you mean. It's like the landscape changed," Derek said while scanning the area for any threats.

"I wish we could carry Quint's light," I commented.

"Wouldn't that be great?" Derek was tense. "I don't see him anywhere. Maybe we passed him." How? We just made two rights and kept straight. There was nowhere for him to hide.

"Or maybe he went into there." Lois was pointing at an open door. There was a bloody handprint at the bottom of the door frame.

"I think he is in here." Derek gave me a concerned look. Lois went in first, holding out her sword. Derek followed with his sword in hand. I forgot we had those.

"Can't you just use your powers?" I asked Derek.

"Sometimes you can't. It might require extra strength," Lois said.

I tried to walk deeper into the room, but Derek put his hand out, stopping me in my tracks. "What is it? What do you see?"

"A Scourger at twelve o'clock," Derek whispered. Sure enough, there was one pretending to be human. It was bleeding. Red blood oozed from its gut. "You and Lois go left, and I'll go right. We will trap it."

We crept toward it, surrounding it, preventing any escape. Derek was closer to it than Lois or I was. However, something seemed familiar about it. The closer I ventured to it, the more I realized who it was. Derek was about to strike it with his sword. I tried to stop him, but my voice was mute. The only thing I could think of was to push this person out of the way. Yet I wouldn't make it in time. So I stood in front of Derek's sword, inches from my face.

Derek was heated. "What are you doing?" He stepped forward to kill.

"No, don't. This is my friend, Keith."

Keith was frightened. He looked worse than my dad and Ms. Goodwin combined. I bent down next to Keith, who clearly couldn't believe it was me. "What happened to you?" I asked. His stomach and legs were gashed. Dark red, almost black, blood poured from his body.

"I-I was attacked by a monster. I escaped some time ago and was trying to leave. I kept turning into the wrong places." Keith was barely able to speak. He lost his breath after finishing. Derek caught Keith as he fell back.

"We need to go," Lois said as she was keeping an eye out by the door.

Derek picked Keith up from the ground with little effort. Keith groaned from the pain.

"Can you hold him?" I asked.

"Yes, it's nothing, really. Let's go and find your dad."

Suddenly, Keith said in a panic, "No, no. Don't...he attacked me. We can't..." Keith grabbed my arm. "Jewels, you can't." Keith stopped talking because Derek knocked him out.

I hit Derek on the shoulder. "Now why would you do that?"

Derek simply shrugged. "He was screaming—it would have attracted attention."

"He was saying something important, though." I realized Derek wasn't listening to my reasoning, so I changed the objective. "We need to go find my dad."

Derek hesitated. "You heard what he said. Your dad is a Scourger."

"No, he isn't."

Derek shook his head. "What I mean is that a Scourger is pretending to be him. We could take the wrong one." I didn't care. I had to take the chance to save my dad.

"Not likely, I would know the difference."

But Derek didn't agree with me. "That's what you think."

I was frustrated with Derek. "You have no right." I walked off, leaving Derek behind. Of course, he caught up to me, though. Even caring Keith, a large man, he could catch up. Lois was guarding our back. She occasionally seemed interested in our conversation.

"I'm sorry." Derek was staring genuinely at me.

I softened. "It's okay, I know you're just trying to be careful."

Derek nodded. "I'm glad you understand."

"So what if we do find him? How will we interrogate him?"

Lois offered, "Casually, you should mention certain things that only your dad will know right now. What did you say to him when you saw him? Try that sort of stuff."

I agreed, "Oh, okay, that shouldn't be hard."

I turned from her to Derek, who stated, "Don't worry, we will cross that bridge when we get to it."

We were halfway back to the group, and things started to look familiar again. The scene where we fought four rows of Scourgers was quiet and empty. It was as if we never battled in their space. For one, I never understood their system. If someone came into my home uninvited, the whole neighborhood would have heard about it. But I should be glad we don't have to fight so many. *I wondered how Refashion was doing? Had they defeated the Scourgers? Was Nàtàl Mater okay?*

After turning the corner, the area was no longer marked with Scourgers. The surrounding area looked healthy. "I think we made a wrong turn?" I said. I remembered during practice how the Scourgers left a mark behind every time they encountered something. But the area was clean.

"Why do you say that?" Derek stopped in his tracks. Keith was still knocked out, slumped over his shoulders. Lois paused, still three feet away from us.

"Well, the area is clean. Scourgers leave death where ever they go," I explained.

"Good point. Can you take your shield down so we can smell the area? Try to find our way back." Lois asked. I realized that I forgot to put it back up. I was focused on finding my dad that I didn't think about the smell.

"I don't have it up."

Derek placed Keith on the ground and folded his arms. "I guess we are lost then. No worries, let's go back." He stretched his arms. He tried to relax them. Then he grabbed Keith and placed him over his shoulder again.

"Don't you find this whole thing a little odd? Even if we made a wrong turn, we should still be able to smell them." I tried to keep up with their long strides.

"It is strange. Maybe they left this level, and that's why the air is clean," Lois said.

"That could be. I just have a bad feeling about this," I said to them both.

"Come on. We can find our way out of this," Derek huffed. The weight of Keith affected him.

"I know you are trying to be positive... I think? But this has *ambush* written all over it," I added.

"Maybe, but we can't stay in one place. They will find us that way," Lois said.

I sniffed the air to find any sign of the Scourgers. There was nothing. We made the same turn previously. Only the hallway where we fought the Scourgers was not there. It was a larger double door. There was blood coming from the bottom, pouring toward our feet. However, the blood wasn't red; it was thick black goo.

"I think we found trouble." I groaned.

"Yup." Derek stepped back. His head moved from side to side, searching.

"What are you looking for?" I asked him.

"We need a place to hide him. I can't keep him safe and fight them at the same time."

I also looked around, trying to find any sign of a good hiding spot. Everything was in the open. "What if you cover him with vines and hang him on the ceiling?"

Derek burst with laughter, "That is an insane idea. But it might work."

He placed Keith down. Vines and leaves unraveled from his arms and palms. They quickly made their way down to Keith. The vines started at his feet then moved swiftly to his shines, then thighs and waist. When they made their way to his chin, I thought they wouldn't stop. Suffocating him. They stopped just in time, leaving his face exposed for air. "Cutting it a little close, are we?" I commented, to which Derek had no reply.

Derek then moved his arms in an upward motion. The vines crawled and walked Keith's body along the wall, making their way to the ceiling. They then spread away from Keith's body. Suddenly, there was a spider web made of vines that caught a large boy. Derek took it a step further. The leaves disappeared. No, camouflage into the background.

"How?" I asked.

"It's simple, really. All leaves and plants have pigmentation. I just manipulate them. The leaves are still there, just a different color, so it looks like they are invisible," Derek explained.

"That's pretty neat."

"Thanks." Derek walked over to the door. I was impressed. The others kept discovering new skills from their gift. "Okay, now we can go in." He grabbed one handle. I took the other. Lois was in the center. She would go first. "One, two, three." We pulled at the door handles, and they slowly opened.

THE LAST BATTLE

I still couldn't believe what I was seeing. A giant Scourger was lying on the floor with his head under a rock. His body was already going through the decaying process. His blood was melting through the ground. The smell was revolting.

"This looks like handiwork from Gwen." Derek didn't seem shocked at all.

"Do you not see this?" I pushed my arms in the direction of the giant.

He was confused. "Yes…you fought one of these."

"Not one of this size. The other one I fought was a baby compared to this."

Derek said, "That I can agree on." He searched the area. "I don't see them." I didn't like what was happening here. We had no control over anything it seemed.

"Maybe we should get Keith. This place is shifting around. We probably won't be able to find him again." I suggested.

"Jewels—" I didn't get to hear the rest of Lois's sentence because a loud bang followed by an echoing roar covered the sound of her voice. We turned our attention in the direction of the sound. Across the room was a crushed double door. The ceiling surrounding the door was missing a few pieces, courtesy of the giant. Orange and yellow lights broke through. They carried a rhythm to them, orange then yellow. Orange then yellow.

"I think we should go help them," Derek commented.

"On the bright side, the smell is back." Both stared at me. I shrunk in my armor. I thought the news would be good, seeing that we were lost. They left me standing next to the door and gradually sprinted toward the other end of the large room. I followed them, going around the decaying giant body that was swallowing at the floor.

"They sound like they need our help," Lois shouted over the beast's screams.

"You got that right." Derek rushed through the broken double doors, sword raised. I was right behind them. The first thing I noticed was how bright it was in the room. The marble color of yellow and orange illuminated the space. I found Quint off to the side where the light was brightest. He protected himself with his light and sword. Any Scourger that could withstand the light only got closer to face certain death. He stabbed them, and they crumbled beneath his feet. Gwen also had her sword out, cutting and crushing into the flesh of the rotten, vile creatures.

I ran to Annora, who was the closest to me. "Annora, why does everyone have their swords out?" She had just finished stabbing a Malfise with spikes and a rotting mouth. Its red eyes turned to black as it died under her blade.

"For some reason, the Scourgers are stronger. It takes more than just our power to kill them. It takes both." A loud screeching sound came from behind us. Then I felt heat. I turned around to find Flair trying to kill a Treed. Only, this one didn't die; it was sauntering through her fire. It was headed straight for us. Annora quickly brought her sword in the air and cut the Treed's throat. The head rolled on to the floor, its long yellow tongue sticking out of a hideous mouth.

"Woah, nice save, Flair," I said.

She finally looked at me. "No problem. Get your sword out, you are going to need it."

I pulled my sword from its holster and raised it in the air, examining the beauty of it.

"Okay, Arthur, let's get back to it, yeah?" Gwen grabbed my arm.

"Sorry. It's unreal." I smiled.

"Yes, the sword is beautiful, shall we?" Flair motioned for us to move on.

Octavion came down from the sky, landing in his human form. "You're getting the hang of it," I said.

"I try. So what's the plan?" Octavion asked.

He was killing Scourgers that ventured too close to us. His bulky sword sliced through their skin with little effort.

"If they are guarding this area so heavily, then their king must be beyond those doors," Flair said after kicking a very small Scourger that had the appearance of a gremlin-sized Malfise in the face. The creature flew backward with a pitiful yell. "Did anyone else find that funny?" She was smiling.

"Kind of," Annora admitted.

"We are going to need a diversion," Quint stealthily came next to our huddled group.

"Yeah, well, who is going to be the fall guy?" Derek trotted over to us.

Gwen followed behind him. "I'll do it." Of course, Gwen wanted too. She wanted to do something big for the group.

"Are you sure?" Derek said with real concern.

"Oh, yeah. I got this." She jumped up and down and shook her arms like a boxer getting ready for a fight.

"Well, go at it." Derek finally gave her permission to do something.

Gwen wasted no time. She reached the other side of the room and called all the Scourgers to her attention. We hid behind a large boulder that fell from the ceiling. Gwen's work, but of course. "Here, ugly ducklings. Come to momma." They all turned in her direction. Thick, Scrawny, Mist, Treed, short, stout, and ugly. All of them headed straight for her. Gwen didn't seem intimidated at all. She grinned at the Scourgers' presence. They moved with broken steps toward her. She kept her stance. However, when I glanced at her a second time, her smile was gone. She looked aggravated and serious. All of the fallen rocks shook the ground beneath our feet. Several lifted into the air, surrounding Gwen. Then they closed around her. Large boulders moved swiftly toward her.

They stopped just in time. I could see what Gwen was doing. She was making a rock robot (I would need to work on the name). It was amazing to watch! The Rock Robot even had a face. A deafening roar escaped the large, heavy clump. I didn't think rocks could do such a thing. The roar was intense, creating a strong wind that blew away the rocks hiding us. The Scourgers stood still for half a second as they tried to keep from falling. Once Rock Robot decided to stop yelling, the Scourgers regained their stalking. We waited patiently for Gwen to give us a sign. The first Scourger attacked Rock Robot, and with no hesitation, he swatted him like a fly. The Scourger lay flat against the wall with blackened blood coming from its body. The rest charged straight for Gwen. She was ready. Gwen crouched low and waited like a tiger, patiently for the right moment to strike.

They came closer and closer to her. My heart pounded from the excitement and anticipation. I edged forward, trying to get a better look from behind the rock.

"Stay down." Quint grabbed my arm.

"Sorry." I was absentminded.

I wanted to see what Gwen would have Rock Robot do. The moment seemed to take forever. Everything slowed, and I was left waiting with my heart out of my chest. I breathed heavily. The lack of oxygen to my head made me feel dizzy and sleepy. I shook my head. I had to stay awake.

Most importantly, I couldn't harm the others. I stared at Rock Robot with Gwen inside. Then it happened.

They came close enough to her that she expanded her arms and raised her knees, jumping to the ceiling. It was at least ten feet. She came down hard, and the ground made a ripple effect. Then the dust and wind came crashing. The majority of the Scourgers laid flat against the wall. The only ones left were the ones that could not be killed by her. They couldn't be killed by any of us, except Quint. The giant rock spoke. "You can do your thing now." We were hesitant to move. I thought I imagined the rock speaking to us. But it did.

Quint was the first one to move. Coming around the large boulder, he raised his arms. Light emitted from his hand and radiated over his entire body. I had never witnessed him glow before. It reminded me of the time ALICE saved us at the gas station. This time, Quint was the one protecting us. He was also brighter than ALICE was. His eyes had no iris or pupil. It was swallowed up by bright yellow light. He then opened his mouth, light oozing from it. Soon the light reached the Mists. They tried to escape, some going through the ceiling where holes were. It was no use. Quint stretched his arms out in surrender, and the brightest of light came through. It was bright white and blinded us all from its presence.

The Mists screamed louder than I ever heard them before. The white light burned them. It was pure light and never seen by man. The last of the Scourgers were now gone. Gwen dropped her Rock Robot, its body slamming to the floor. She descended on the arm of Rock Robot. Quint stopped emitting pure light. The rest of the Crypto-Hept, the Guard, Ms. Goodwin, and I all ran over to Quint and Gwen.

"Wow, Quint… I have never seen anything like it before. How did you do it?" Vivienne asked with curiosity in her voice.

"I-I don't know. It was like I wasn't there. I was outside my body." Quint was holding up his head. "Now I have a major headache."

"Sorry to hear that. But it was awesome." Annora came closer to Quint and patted him.

"I can fix that." Vivienne stretched out her arm and touched Quint on the forehead.

"Thanks, I feel much better."

I walked over to Gwen and gave her a quick hug, "Gwen, you did an amazing job too. How did you make it talk?" I asked.

She smiled. "I was talking. It just came out deep because of the barrier." I was proud of them both.

"Neat." Octavion was messing with the arm of Rock Robot.

"I think it's time we finished this. Don't you?" ALICE moved toward the double doors that now were free from Scourgers.

"I do," Derek said as he moved closer to the door as well.

"This is it. Everyone, give your all," Vivienne directed. I could tell she was concerned. She didn't want to lose us. I looked around at the others. In this group, I'd made friends and enemies. But somehow, we all came together and turned into a family. I watched as they came together with swords raised, ready for our last battle.

I stretched my sword in front of my body. "Potest non prohibere nobis." The others stared at one another then smiled.

"Potest non prohibere nobis!" they shouted while laying down their swords on top of mine. Vivienne, ALICE, and Ms. Goodwin placed their hands on our swords and repeated the phrase. This moment was my hope. Hope that we would finally defeat him.

Defeat all diseases. After today, my world would be different. Derek pushed open the door, and we went through.

The place was dark. Quint quickly used his hands and brightened the room. Unfortunately, his light was back to yellow. It was still bright; it just didn't seem as bright as the white light.

The room did not feel nor look like the other rooms we'd been to. The room looked more like a king's court. There was no sign of dirt anywhere. Concrete was placed along the floor and the walls. It was cold and musty. Thick fifteen-foot red ribbons were dropping from each column, some draped along the wall. There were curtains placed around the room but no windows. The floor had a thick red carpet with gold trim that went from wall to wall. The king's chair was bulky and made from concrete. His throne was leveled above four large steps. Cracks were destroying the chair.

One thing I did notice was that the room was empty. There were no Scourgers or any smell of them. Their king was not present either. Shock took over my body. I didn't want to believe that he was not here. He was just hiding, that's all. He feared us.

"Check around," I said, more demanding than I meant.

"Jewels, I don't think—" I walked away from Gwen as she tried to grab my arm.

"He's in here. Look, over there. There's another door." I ran over to it. The others tried to keep up with me. I opened it, expecting a Scourger to jump out. But there was none. It was just a closet with nothing inside. My heart sank. The reality of the situation came over me, and I couldn't hold my body up.

I fell to my knees and closed my eyes, trying to hold on to what hope I had left. If he wasn't here, then where was he? It was our job to find him. It was our job to defeat him. It was our job to save the world. We failed. We failed, and the world would go on the same. But no, not the same.

I am not the same. My friends, they are not the same. My new family, they worked so hard and without any results.

"We lost him," I softly said as my hope diminished.

"Don't worry, Jewels. We will find him," Gwen said, kneeling next to me on the floor.

ABOUT THE AUTHOR

Photography by:
Tiffany Love Film

Rolynn grew up reading and writing fantastical adventure stories. The story of *Breathless* came to her in a dream seven years ago while still in high school. Because of her love for writing, she pursued a career in screenwriting, receiving a Bachelor of Science in Film and Digital Media. She has written and directed shorts and a feature that were official selections in various film and screenwriting festivals. When she is not writing or reading, she is watching movies or on set making them.

CPSIA information can be obtained
at www.ICGtesting.com
Printed in the USA
BVHW072144160222
629290BV00001B/23